THE TESTAMENT OF THEOPHILUS

Also by Leonard Wibberley

Mrs. Searwood's Secret Weapon
Stranger at Killnock
The Quest of Excalibur
Take Me to Your President
McGillicuddy McGotham
Beware of the Mouse
The Mouse That Roared
The Mouse on the Moon
The Mouse on Wall Street
A Feast of Freedom
The Island of the Angels
The Hands of Cormac Joyce
The Road from Toomi
Adventures of an Elephant Boy
The Centurion
Meeting with a Great Beast

NONFICTION

The Shannon Sailors
Voyage by Bus
Ah Julian!
Yesterday's Land
Towards a Distant Land
No Garlic in the Soup
The Land That Isn't There

JUVENILES (FICTION)

Deadmen's Cave
Kevin O'Connor and the Light Brigade
The Wound of Peter Wayne
John Treegate's Musket
Peter Treegate's War
Sea Captain from Salem
Treegate's Raiders
Leopard's Prey
Flint's Island

JUVENILES (NONFICTION)

Wes Powell—Conqueror of the Colorado
The Life of Winston Churchill
John Barry—Father of the Navy
The Epics of Everest
Man of Liberty—the Life of Thomas Jefferson
Young Man from the Piedmont
A Dawn in the Trees
The Gales of Spring
Time of the Harvest

THE TESTAMENT OF
THEOPHILUS

A Novel of
Christ and Caesar

by
Leonard Wibberley

WILLIAM MORROW & COMPANY, INC.
New York   1973

Printed in the United States of America.

Library of Congress Cataloging in Publication Data

Wibberley, Leonard Patrick O'Connor, (date)
  The testament of Theophilus.

  1. Jesus Christ—Fiction. 2. Rome—History—
Tiberius, 14-37—Fiction. 3. Rome—History—
Caligula, 37-41—Fiction. I. Title.
PZ4.W632Te [PS3573.I2]   813'.5'4   72-14252
ISBN 0-688-00149-1

Dedicated to
Charles (Chuck) Donlon
Teacher, Redondo Union High School
1952–1970

About *The Testament of Theophilus*

FEW BOOKS TURN OUT as the author intended them to and this book is no exception. Originally I had planned a novel which would take the whole of the Christian experience from the time of the Crucifixion (with which I ended my previous book on this theme, *The Centurion*) to the death of Peter and of Paul. I did my research with that in mind, but when I got down to the writing, I found that I had so much material (a great deal of it imaginary, of course) that I could bring the narrative only to the reign of Caligula and not even to the end of that.

When a writer tries to conjure up ancient times he is wise if, like the geologist, he reflects that what happened long ago is happening also in his own time. This provides him with a model and saves him from the error of deciding that people who lived two thousand years ago were a different sort of human being from those in the world today. My model for ancient Rome will not astonish the thoughtful reader. It is modern America, though it could be, for that matter, modern England or modern France or any other modern nation of the first rank with the exception, perhaps, of the Soviet Union. (I except the Soviet Union because I do not know the Soviet Union and assume that life there—and thus morality—is rather closely regulated.) In Rome of the time of the emperors, the old religion was falling into tatters, and a people whose armies had spread throughout the world were embracing new worships, openly or secretly, looking for answers to questions of life and death. Religions and philosophies were being imported from Egypt, from Greece, from Persia, from Britain—from everywhere that Roman influence reached. Judaism had a strong hold in Rome. The cult of Mithras had particularly permeated the Army, and astrologers were in great demand. Side by side with this was a growing demand for entertainment among the leisured masses of Rome itself and the other cities of the Roman world. These leisured masses were not necessarily wealthy. They were often unemployed and unemployable and lived off a dole. Baths were thrown open to them to provide one kind of entertainment—a place to wash in and idle and gossip. And gradually there was an increase in chariot racing and wild animal hunts in the arena and, finally, massive gladiatorial games—all staged to entertain the idle and keep them out of mischief.

Turn now to the United States—or Britain or France if that hurts. The old religion—Christianity—has become greatly discredited among the young. They turn to new worships. Some worship science. Some worship psychology and some worship Buddha. Young Americans walk about with their heads shaven, wearing saffron robes, rejecting the old religion and following some Eastern cult. Astrology is perhaps as important in men's affairs as it was in the time of the Babylonian empire. In the city nearest me, Los Angeles, some people practice devil worship, and the leisured masses and their children attend the gladiatorial games every night, by which I mean they watch television. There they can get pleasure out of seeing men shooting men and beating each other, and women as well. Like the Romans, they watch these things while drinking or eating —beer and popcorn in the American case; wine mixed with water, pasta and something akin to *burritos* in the case of the Romans. No need to say, "How *could the Romans* take their children to see men cut down in the arena?" We do the same with our children each night, and it is not a defense to say that ours are only pretended killings—the movie camera shows us the soldier cut in half by machine-gun fire with far more detail than the poor Roman, sitting so far away in the arena, could see the gladiator fall. The soldier's death in Vietnam is real, though, like that of the gladiator, it *does* take on the appearance of entertainment after a while.

Do not misunderstand me. I am not preaching against this. I am only showing you where a writer (myself in this instance) gets his material about ancient times. He gets it from modern times. Rome was not all brutal. Nor is the United States. The same forces were at work in both civilizations—leisure, wealth, the collapse of the old beliefs and disciplines, the search for pleasure, hedonism, the insistence on the right (even the duty) to "do your own thing," the resistance to military service, the concept of patriotism as a kind of intellectual evil. All these were present in Rome; all are present in America. Side by side with them (becoming in Rome less and less politically powerful) were kindly, fair-minded, self-disciplined citizens whose waning influence could not save the Republic or the Empire from the rule of the Army and emperors who owed their authority to the Army. How far is the Roman pattern to be followed in America—or Britain or France? One must decide for himself.

As to the question most often put to an author, a question which leaves most of us bewildered, Why did you write this book? I have in this one instance only an answer. I have many times read the Christian Testaments, the Acts of the Apostles, and much of the Epistles of Paul. I find them inspiring, consoling, convincing—and lacking. What they lack in my view is explanations of the circumstances in which Christ preached and died, and Peter and Paul also. *The Testament of Theophilus*, then, is an attempt to fill this lack—to place all this divinity among the affairs of men and to view the Christians as a pagan would have viewed them. The figure of Theophilus I took from the opening verse of the Acts of the Apostles, attributed to Luke, the verse which begins (Jerusalem translation), "In my earlier

[xi]

work, Theophilus, I dealt with everything Jesus . . ." I very well know that there may never have been a Theophilus as a person; that the word translates roughly into "Lover of God." I have taken the liberty, however, of assuming that there was a real Theophilus and of re-creating a part of his story.

My history comes from sources available to all—Suetonius, Tacitus, Josephus, the Christian writings, various histories of the Jewish people by modern writers, and Philo Judaeus. If you should find in this novel some contradiction of statements made in these sources, reflect, I beg you, that *this* book is written by Theophilus. He was capable of error, as Tacitus was capable of bias, and Suetonius overpartial to gossip. Reflect also how much you have remembered incorrectly regarding public affairs of your own lifetime, and be merciful to Theophilus.

LEONARD WIBBERLEY

BOOK I

BOOK I

I

CIRCA A.D. 70. It is I, Theophilus, who write. You will be sure of this when you see my handwriting. What I have put down is true and may be relied upon. I have seen and heard these things which I record myself, or I have received them from others who themselves were witnesses and whom I know from long acquaintance to be trustworthy. If there are some who object and say that that which we have heard from others is not to be believed, then no nation has any history, for there is no man alive who has lived through all the generations of men to be an eyewitness to their story.

Who is to say in the face of such objections how great Caesar fell? Is Cinna who struck him down still alive? Is Cassius among us yet? Is there anyone still on earth who saw that look of anger and of pain that crossed the face of Caesar when the Egyptian priests at Alexandria gave him the head of Pompey in a jar? No. All those who saw these things are dead. We have them only at second and third hand. So it is with those events which I am about to record. Some I have seen myself. Some I obtained from those who themselves saw them or heard them. I have put nothing down that is mere gossip, for if I did then this testament of mine would be ten times as long. You may rely on what is written here. It is the truth.

It is possible that there are some now who do not know me. To be known throughout the world belongs only to Caesars. I will not hide my identity. I am that Theophilus whose *theta* is still to be found on the lip of amphorae distributed throughout the known world. All came from the clay pits and the factories which I owned in Egypt, in Italy, and in Turkey where there is a white clay, readily glazed, which will hold the most volatile perfumes with little loss.

I am that Theophilus whose fleets of ships carried the grain of Egypt, the hides of Spain, the sweet-smelling timber of Cyprus, as well as its ores, to every port of the Great Sea. To say more of myself would be to boast, which is never done without the spites taking their vengeance.

I will add only that I am that Theophilus who was once a slave. No one will be surprised that a slave, freed, should rise to such wealth and fame as mine. It is a common enough matter. Pallas, formerly a slave, became, as everyone knows, the friend of the Emperor Claudius and the lover of his wife Agrippina, while his brother Felix, who had likewise been a slave, became governor of Judaea. Narcissus, too, who was responsible for the downfall and murder of Messalina (the wife of the Emperor Claudius whom Agrippina replaced), was a slave also. I knew him well. No man was ever more treacherous than Narcissus. It was only just that, having been the cause of an Empress's murder, he himself should have been murdered on the orders of Agrippina, whom he helped become the wife of Claudius. (I am well aware that Narcissus committed suicide, but he did so only after being arrested and tortured at the instigation of Agrippina and knowing that the executioner's noose awaited him.) I could go on with the list of slaves who rose to great heights but this would be without profit. Let it suffice to say that they were many and their number greatest, I think, in the reigns of Caligula, Claudius, and Nero. If subsequent generations should wish a reason it is easily supplied. He who owns a slave and looks only to his own ease and pleasure soon becomes the slave of his slave, for the slave is constantly working and thinks all the time what can be used to his own advantage. The idle, in short, can never compete with the industrious. Who forgets this loses his freedom.

I am now an old man. You will find some digressions in my story and these you may attribute to my age, for old men have this in common with children that they will not go directly to any place, but must stop and wander here and there, looking at the moving clouds, the whirls of dust in the road, and the different colors of grass, which on one side is often silvery and on the other deep green. So now I look at the sea below me, which is pale green in places and in others deep purple. The wind lays a frosting of waves over the water, and in the gusts flattens out the ocean as the face of a cat is flattened with anger. I know the sea well, its appearance in every weather and that sulphurous smell which precedes its storms. It was the sea which was my mother and my dearest friend and the sea which showed me the way to freedom.

It was on the sea that Cephas, called Peter, first earned his living. I think of him now with tears.

II

CIRCA A.D. 30. Although there are many who think that it is not necessary for a wealthy man to work but only to give orders concerning his business, this is by no means the case. Others will never take care of your interests as well as you yourself, so the only work which may be entrusted to others is that of lesser importance. Consequently in the eighteenth year of Tiberius, having sent the necessary presents ahead and made every arrangement, I went to Caesarea to see Pontius Pilate, the Procurator at that time of Judaea, concerning an aqueduct which he planned to bring water to that city so that in the event of a revolt the legions stationed there could not be forced to surrender through thirst. This aqueduct was a favorite project of Pilate's. It was in connection with the financing of this project that I had arranged for an audience with him.

Despite my careful arrangements, however, I did not arrive at an auspicious time. Delayed in my voyage, I found on reaching Caesarea that Pilate had gone to Jerusalem, where he had taken temporary residence in the Antonia fortress overlooking the Temple. This was because the Feast of the Passover, commemorating the Jews' liberation from slavery in Egypt, was approaching. On this feast, Jews from all over the world come to Jerusalem; and the city, which is normally overcrowded, becomes at this time a seething mass of fanatics, easily roused to a state of frenzy and murder if the slightest insult to their religion is offered.

To control them, cohorts are brought in from every part of Judaea and even from Syria, and legionnaires in great numbers are stationed at various points through the city and on the walls surrounding the Temple. But the whole place is like tinder awaiting only a spark to burst into flames. It is no time for conducting business with a Procurator.

Before I arrived several people had been beaten to death in the streets by the mob, and no soldiers could get to them in time to save them. One soldier had caused a dangerous riot by lifting up his skirts and breaking wind from the top of the Temple wall on the Jews assembled below. That riot, which might have resulted in scores being killed in an attack on the Antonia, was only brought under control when the soldier responsible was flogged to death by his commanding officer and his flayed body displayed (outside the Temple, of course) to the Jews.

"These Jews are driven mad by their god," said Pilate

when he had greeted me. "Their god denies them all the normal pleasure of man. Their god, if he exists, is mad himself. What kind of a god is it who decrees that fornication is to be punished by death? I tell you anyone who killed the god of the Jews, and so set them free to live happily in the world, would do them all a great service."

"No man may kill a god," I said.

"Come, Theophilus," said Pilate. "If men make gods, may they not also destroy them?"

"Men make gods?" I said, for it does not do, whatever one's private opinion, to assent publicly to blasphemy.

"Caesar is a god, is he not?" said Pilate. "Yet I seem to have heard that he fell at the hands of men. And Augustus is now divine, though I recall seeing him, an old and trembling man, with urine down the front of his toga where he had wet himself. And surely you are aware that Pompey, ignoring the terrible fate promised for such a sacrilege, looked into the Holy of Holies of the Jews, where their god lives and saw—nothing. He wasn't destroyed on the moment either."

I tell you this so you may see immediately that Pilate was a man devoid of religious feeling. But he was not devoid of all feeling. He had his moments of tenderness and of affection. Also he was devoted to his wife Procula, who was fat and freckled and had wiry red hair. It was her relation to the Claudian family which had secured for Pilate the post of Procurator, for he himself was but of equestrian rank. Many men resent wives who have more influence than they, but Pilate loved Procula and it was a great sorrow to him that she was barren. She, like a dutiful wife, brought many women into her household in the hope that one of them would give her husband the son he longed for. Yet, though the world will not believe this, I do not believe that he slept with any of them. Nor did he use any of the many opportunities for pleasure offered him by the young men who attended on him—slave, freeman, or Roman. His love of children I know to be sincere. Once he turned to me, viewing a crowd of the Jews among whom were many children, and, pointing, said bitterly, "If I picked one of them up, they would kill me."

Pilate, like many others of the equestrian rank, had some of the virtues of the older times. He was a just man and would take no bribe where justice was concerned, though it is only natural that he should enrich himself in other areas. He hated the Jews, however, and was always planning some way of putting the High Priests and their followers (whom he looked upon as challenging the Roman authority) at a disadvantage.

Procula, as is often the case with childless women, loved small animals and had a marmoset (privately called by Pilate 'The Divine Augustus) which was always with her, in her lap if seated, on her shoulder, or playing at her feet. It was a very destructive animal and scarcely housebroken; and although Procula was in most things neat and considerate of others, yet she so doted on this animal that she did not see these faults. She put great faith in soothsayers and astrologers and had her own horoscope and that of her husband cast for every hour of the day. The practice of astrology had been forbidden in Rome for many years (some say from the time that the soothsayer had warned the divine Julius against the Ides of March) and some had been put to death for attempting to cast the horoscope of Tiberius. But Judaea is a long way from Rome and Procula had a magician from Persia to foretell the future for herself and Pilate. His name was Xerithes—a tall man, robed in saffron, with a face the color of ashes and watchful eyes of which the white part was inordinately large. The marmoset disliked him and once bit him on the hand. But that proved fortunate for him, for one of the household slaves who had likewise been bitten by that nasty creature lost her hand, so poisonous is the bite of these animals. But Xerithes' hand healed rapidly, testifying to his powers.

Having arrived at so inauspicious a time, I paid my respects to the Procurator and asked that he excuse me from attending on him, the fortress being overrun with soldiers and their officers. "I will withdraw to Caesarea, for here I can only add to your troubles," I said.

"Stay," he commanded. "I may need you." It was Pilate's habit when faced with a problem to ask the advice of outsiders, thinking they might be less prejudiced than his own court. So I assumed that in the difficult days of the Pasch, he wanted me, an outsider, to be available for advice or at least distraction.

The following day he summoned me to attend him. It was scarcely dawn when I was disturbed with the summons to the balcony outside the Praetorium. I had time only for a sop of bread and olive oil for breakfast and when I arrived Pilate was shivering in a chair on the balcony with a brazier of charcoal nearby to keep at least one side of him warm.

Standing at the foot of the balcony, with half-a-dozen Temple guards about him, his hands chained to a guard on either side, was a tall, young-looking Jew. Caiaphas the High Priest was there with Annas, his father-in-law, and perhaps a score of others, all standing back a little so that the man and the soldiers stood alone in an empty space. The man's cheek was swollen so I could see he had already been questioned. The blow is father to the truth, as all men know.

"Listen to this and bear me impartial witness, Theophilus," said Pilate when I arrived. Then he turned to Caiaphas and, plainly repeating a question already put, asked, "What charge do you bring against this man? Speak plainly. Let me know what it is that you have against him."

"Pilate," said Caiaphas, "we would not have brought him here to you on the very eve of our Great Pasch if he were not a notorious criminal. He has offended against our Law and our God and he deserves death."

"Your law and your god have nothing to do with Rome,"

said Pilate. "Am I a Jew? Am I one of the priests of your church? Take him yourselves and judge him yourselves. Rome does not interfere in these religious matters."

They were taken aback by this rebuff, consulting among themselves—the priests, scribes, and others—and then Annas spoke up. He was a man of about sixty years, and it was to his daughter that Caiaphas was married. He was a swarthy man, very big, and whenever he spoke, he moved his hands not in the gestures of a practiced orator, but in little pleading and servile movements.

"Your excellency," he said in a soft voice very much at odds with his size, "you say that Rome does not interfere with religious matters, but this matter concerns Rome. This man says he is the King of the Jews, and he goes about the country stirring up people against Caesar."

"The King of the Jews," said Pilate. "Now you bring out something with which I can deal. I will question him on that charge. But I am freezing out here and I will question him inside the Praetorium. I have deferred to your religion by shivering in the cold long enough. Now perhaps you will defer to your ruler and come into the Praetorium while I question this man."

Of course they could not come in, for to enter the Praetorium would be to render themselves unclean and unable to partake in the coming Pasch. This was but Pilate's method of taunting the Jews and also insuring that he could question the man alone.

"Do you come, Caiaphas?" Pilate asked on leaving. Caiaphas covered his face with his sleeve in horror at the suggestion. "You see," said Pilate, "they refuse to be present while I question this man. Everything must be done their way. They will not bend to anybody else."

We did not go into the Praetorium itself but into one of the chambers in which lawyers consult with their clients. These rooms are nicknamed "Argentium" because it is here that the client gives money to his lawyer and it is here too that the lawyer gives money to the judge if, in desperation, he must resort to additional bribery, though most judicial bribery is of course arranged well beforehand.

A brazier was already alight in this room, and Pilate went straight to it and held his robes over it to drive out the chill of the morning. The accused Jew stood by the door, with the guards of the High Priest about him, and these were now replaced by Syrian legionnaires under a centurion. The soldiers of Rome disliked the Temple guards, in the pay of the High Priest, who earned more than they. When he had warmed himself, Pilate sat in a chair and beckoned the guards to bring the prisoner to him.

"Answer me straightly," he said. "Do you claim to be King of the Jews?" It was easy to see that the accused man was from the country, for his garments were handwoven on one of those large country looms, so that there was no seam in them, and his sandals were of heavy leather and closed over the toes to protect his feet from thorns. His hair was bronze in shade and his neck strong and thick. Beard and hair, which were of the same shade, formed a mat across his chest. He stood before Pilate without fear and replying in Greek dared to ask Pilate a question.

"Do you ask me whether I am King of the Jews because you think I am, or do you ask me because others have told you that I say I am?" he said.

Now, the Jews are always waiting for their king, whom they call the Messiah, to come, and Pilate immediately caught the inference of that question. "Do you take me for a Jew?" he demanded. "I ask you because that is the charge which is brought against you by the High Priest and those others out there."

"I am indeed a king," said the Jew. "But my kingdom is not of this world. If my kingdom were of this world, my own followers would have fought to prevent my being handed over to the High Priest. You would have a rebellion to put down as those who ruled before you had rebellions to put down. But where are my followers? Where are my soldiers? As you see, I am alone. I have no followers; no soldiers. One of those who followed me did indeed draw his sword and strike off the ear of one of the men sent to arrest me. But I bid him put his sword up and I undid the harm that was done. Tell me, Pilate, of all the kingdoms established by the sword, how many do you think will last? Where is Alexander's kingdom? The kingdom of the pharaohs?"

To speak truly, up to this point I was not greatly interested, but now I paid more attention to the Jew, and Pilate too changed his attitude.

"You are a philosopher," he said.

"The philosopher loves wisdom," said the Jew, making a play on the Greek. "Wisdom loves truth. Truth is my kingdom. It is a kingdom which has not yet come but will come, and will endure forever. I came into this world to establish the Kingdom of Truth and all those who seek truth are of my kingdom and I am of them."

"Truth?" said Pilate. "What is truth? Truth is the lie that everyone believes for his own profit. If you are the king of truth you are the king of nothing. You are guilty of no offense but dreaming."

He rose angrily and went out to the balcony where the accusers awaited him. "I have questioned this man, but I find no guilt in him," he said.

"It is not your law but ours he has broken," they shouted back. "You have to uphold the Laws of the Jews as well as those of Rome."

"Under our Law he is guilty of death," cried Caiaphas. "We demand his death." A tumult broke out immediately, all crying out for the death of the Jew.

"I know your law well," said Pilate when he had quietened them down. "To show you how I respect your law I will remind you of a custom which you have forgotten. Do you know Barabbas?"

This, of course, was purely a rhetorical question. Barabbas was not merely a brigand but a fiend. He mutilated those he robbed, blinding some and cutting the nose off others as his pleasure suggested. He was so notorious that it was a joke among the Jews, meeting a man who had lost a hand or an ear, to say, "So you know Barabbas?" Nobody then replied to Pilate's piece of rhetoric, but they remained quiet to hear what he had to say further.

"It is your custom—please note how well I observe your customs—to have released to you at this time one man who is condemned to death. Now in keeping with this custom I give you a choice. Whom will you set free—this man here or Barabbas? State your preference."

Pilate was astounded by the reply. He confidently expected that they would choose to release the Jew whose name was Jesus. But instead they clamored to have Barabbas set free, and Pilate turned amazed to the Jew and said, "What have you done that they hate you so?"

(I hope you will not find it tedious in me that I describe all these things so minutely. Certainly many men have been condemned to death. None of us are strangers to such cases and that one country Jew should be so condemned is scarcely worth a moment's consideration. It is what followed that gave this particular case so much interest.)

The trial had now become absurd. The judge could find no guilt in the prisoner but the accusers were determined that the prisoner must die. It was the centurion who suggested a compromise which might satisfy both sides. It was one of his men who had been flogged to death to satisfy the Jews, and the whole legion to which he belonged seethed for vengeance.

"Excellency," said the centurion, "give this Jew to my soldiers. We have a score to settle. Maybe when we are through with him, these others will be satisfied."

"Take him," said Pilate. "But bring him back alive and

within the hour." The Jew was then taken away and he went without a murmur or a plea for clemency, which surprised me.

Pilate was now merciful enough to invite me to breakfast, for, as I have said, I had had but a mouthful since rising. It was a good meal—fine bread, fish, honey, wine (the grapes of Judaea are excellent for wine making) and the inner meats of mountain sheep served in a brain sauce. But fat, freckled Procula, who shared the meal with us, was nervous and full of forebodings. She had dreamed of the Jew, she said, and had been warned that he was a just man and begged Pilate to set him free. If he did not do so, some great misfortune would overtake them.

"The priests hate this man and if I do not deliver him to them, they will plot against me in Rome, where they have a great deal of influence," said Pilate, helping himself to some wild honeycomb. "As much as I can, I will do for him. But I am not going to endanger myself for him. Why do they hate him so? That is what surprises me. I have scarcely heard of the man before."

"My women tell me he has performed many miracles," said Procula. "He has cured the blind and lepers and even raised the dead."

"If he has that kind of power," said Pilate, "he will return from his flogging without a bruise. Women believe anything."

Procula continued to plead and eventually Pilate became angry and ordered her away and she left in tears.

What a meal it was. I had no pleasure in it though the food was good. And when it was over, the flogging of the Jew was to no avail. Pilate took him out on the balcony again and ripping the cloak off him showed how the legionnaires had avenged their comrade. The whip marks showed like sword wounds crisscrossed on the man's body. The soldiers had allowed the lash to strike his face too. The nose was almost torn in half and his beard was full of blood like a sponge with water.

[14]

But the crowd, far from being moved to pity, only shouted, "Crucify him. Crucify him," in a kind of frenzy. Pilate made a last effort. He took him into the Praetorium again and said, "Why don't you say something in your own defense? Don't you realize that I have the power to set you free or the power to crucify you?"

"You have no power over me unless God gives it to you," he said. "It is the will of God, not your own office, which gives you power over me now. But do not be so fearful, Pilate. He who handed me to you is more guilty than you." It was very strange that this man facing death should be comforting Pilate, who had been shaken by Procula's warnings.

I felt sorry for the man. How many flogged slaves have I seen in my time, trembling and dumb, wishing only for death? He reminded me of them. I found a cup of wine and without consulting Pilate gave it to him. He refused it saying, "It is not from the cup of comfort that I must drink now." Then looking me full in the eyes, his face painted red with blood, the lips split and the nose half off, he said steadily and gently, "I will be your friend, Theophilus. I will never leave you. Remember that."

Pilate made one more effort. He took the man out again before the crowd and on his behalf announced his verdict. "This man is innocent," he said. But all shouted that he must be crucified and either Annas or Caiaphas cried out above the tumult, "He says he is our king. If you set him free, you are no friend of Tiberius." The very mention of the name was enough for Pilate. He went to the Judgment Seat, which is of stone and erected on the pavement below the balcony. He called for a ewer of water and washed his hands and dried them. He said, "I call on you to witness that I am guiltless of the blood of this man, who is without fault."

"We'll take the guilt," they shouted. "Let his death be on us."

Pilate had made his last effort on behalf of the man.

"Take him then and crucify him," he said. "It is your will, not mine. And put over him public notice of his crime. The words to be used are 'King of the Jews.' "

That was a blow at them and they were aware of it immediately. "The notice should read *He says* he is King of the Jews,' " said Caiaphas. But Pilate wrote the notice out in his own hand—King of the Jews—and gave it to the centurion.

"What I have written I have written," he said. " 'King of the Jews' it shall be."

They took the Jew away to crucify him, that being the death of those who plot against Rome who are quite rightly treated as the worst of felons. (Roman citizens, of course, cannot be crucified, and had the Jew been a citizen either by purchase of citizenship or service in the army or by birth in a Roman city such as Caesarea or Tarsus, he would have been merely beheaded. However, Pilate established that he had been born in Bethlehem close to Jerusalem in the reign of the divine Augustus, and so was an alien.)

There were two other events of note that day. About the middle of the afternoon, when I had retired to my quarters for the afternoon sleep, the sun was darkened, and there was an earthquake. I was awakened by the earthquake, which set the whole Antonia rolling like a ship at sea and was accompanied by a deep growl. I have experienced several earthquakes but never got used to them. The first tremor was only slight—just enough to awaken me. The next was worse. The third was like a wave passing under the building. Plaster fell from the walls and my chamber was filled with dust. Caballus, my German bodyguard (I will tell you about him later), was in a panic. He lay on the floor, banging his head on the tiles and roaring like a bull. He had blacked his eyes and raised a great lump on his forehead, the fool, before it was all over.

For myself I just lay there promising sacrifices to different gods to be spared. I offered a bullock to Mars and then two black ones to Vulcan, and a statue to Janus in his temple at Rome (he is often neglected) and a thousand gold pieces (well, I want to be truthful—it was really five hundred and a shipload of corn—to Jupiter the Thunderer). The darkness and the stupid screaming of Caballus made it all the more frightening. I would have got up myself and lit a lamp but the room shook so much all the lamps had fallen on the floor and spilled oil about.

Then the earthquake subsided at last and I got out of bed and gave Caballus a good kick for frightening me so. The light also returned and I went out to see what damage had been done. People in the Antonia were entirely distracted. Even the soldiers had lost their nerve and were clutching and kissing the amulets which they, all of them, carry for their safety. The courtyard was full of people who had rushed to the Temple to pray at the first sign of darkness. The Jews pray by rocking backwards and forwards and repeating formulas which they all know by heart but they were now in such a state of hysteria that even the soldiers were afraid of them. Some had covered their heads with dirt. Others were beating themselves on the chest and on the head with their clenched fists. Some shrieked above the responses as if possessed. It was both unnerving and disgusting and I wished that someone would make an ordinary and sensible remark which would calm everybody. Procula was no help. I sought out Pilate and she came rushing in on him in the midst of all the confusion, for he of course had to deal with all the damage done and see that his soldiers were safe and there was no looting or rioting.

"It is the Jew," she cried. "It is because you crucified the Jew."

"What Jew?" demanded Pilate angrily, for in the turmoil he had momentarily forgotten the man.

So, I confess, had I. His full name was Jesus ben Joseph of Nazareth.

III

THERE IS A TIME when a business project should be pushed with energy and another time when it should be abandoned and no reference made to it until matters have changed. Regarding my own project for financing Pilate's plan for an aqueduct to Caesarea, as I have mentioned, I realized that, circumstances being as they were, I could only damage my scheme by pushing it at that moment. My proposal was a simple one. I would find the money for the plan and advance it at interest which would give Pilate an opportunity of making an ample profit on spending it; or I would provide the materials and the subsistence for the men required (wages would not be needed since soldier and slave labor would largely be used) which would provide me with an opportunity of gaining a profit from caterers and material supplies in case Pilate wanted to keep his reputation entirely clean in this matter. In return for the latter service, Pilate would award me the contract for collecting the olive tax, which is an assessment against the olive harvest—the principal harvest of Judaea, for I think that without the olive tree the Jews would perish, so great is their dependence on it. The collection of taxes carries with it the right to assess up to 20 percent of tax for the tax collector, so I could be sure of recouping whatever money I laid out for Pilate's aqueduct.

But that evening, when we were at dinner, Pilate informed me that he had another plan. He would seize the money in the Temple treasury and use it on his aqueduct.

"No friend of Caesar," he said, recalling how that afternoon the High Priest had accused him of being no friend of Caesar's. "No friend of Caesar surely would refuse the use of these funds for the purpose of insuring the safety of Caesar's legions at Caesarea." Pilate's policy was always thus tinged with malice against the Jews, for which I could not really blame him, for they are a proud, stiff-necked people holding themselves superior to all on earth as the chosen people of their mad god, who has no regard, it seems, for anybody else but them and is not the same as Mars or Jupiter, whose existence they deny. Really I found the Jews in those days intolerable with their god. For instance, if anyone not a Jew wished to gain the favor of their god and become one of them he had to cut off his foreskin as an offering. Now surely that is a strange gift for a god, yet I must remind you that the worshipers of Cybele castrate themselves and offer their testicles to the divinity, so perhaps in this the Jews are not so stupid as they appear, after all.

Now when Pilate told me of his plan, I saw that it would bring down on him the enmity of the Jews. In business it is not possible to have friends, yet I had no desire to see Pilate ruin himself, for I had some influence with him. Were he deposed, I would lose this influence in a powerful place, so I cautioned him against his proposal. "Excellency," I said, "I hope you will not needlessly anger the Jews. It would grieve me to see you lose your power as a result of their enmity, for I would then lose many opportunities of profiting from your position, and might not have so close a relationship with your successor."

Pilate liked such frankness and replied without rancor. "The Jews cannot touch me," he said. "I will have them begging me for clemency. They must learn that Rome rules and all they have they have at the grant of Rome, generous to friends, implacable to enemies. Tiberius has ordered them out of Rome. They have no power there."

This was true, but Tiberius, unlike the Jews, would not live forever. The only real profit I had had from my long journey to Jerusalem was the sharp warning that Pilate would undoubtedly one day be displaced because of the malice of the Jews and that it would be wise for me to try to discover whom the Jews favored as his successor. To use sea terms (for it was through the sea that I, a former slave, gained my freedom) any fool can trim sail for the present wind, but the wise sailor trims sail for the wind to come. Who would succeed Pilate, and when, would not be easy to discover. The gloomy Tiberius took no one into his confidence. Yet slaves, like damp in winter, penetrate everywhere and, with a wide acquaintance in the world of slaves, I was confident I would get early news when news was available.

We dined late that day because of the earthquake and the eclipse. Half the staff had fled and not returned to the kitchens, so our main dish was of lentils supplied from the soldiers' kitchen. These had been flavored with sour wine instead of honey and tasted poor. But hunger has its own sauce and I ate well. The wine was good, not resinous like Greek wine or sour like that of Gaul, but fruity and warming, and I drank toasts with everyone and was soon half-drunk and happy. Pilate became a kindly and friendly man and even Procula cheered up, having been assured by her magician that the stars favored her and Pilate, or some such rubbish.

I wished, however, that I was in the palace of Herod, whose wife Herodias was not prudish about new adventures, nor Herod himself overprotective of her. You see, I do not hold anything back. Let that itself be a witness for the truth of my testament. Beware of the historian like Livy who pretends to a greater nobility than the people of whom he writes. His mouth is full of lies, as the Persians say.

Warmed by wine and my thoughts turning to pleasant lechery, I took the opportunity to examine the women about, seeking a bedmate for the night. I had two in prospect and was debating which choice would make me the fewest enemies when I began to feel the effect of the soldiers' lentils of which I had eaten so heartily. The call of Cloachina is not to be denied, so I answered her and she called so often thereafter that my plans for the night were utterly disrupted and I had to beg leave of Pilate and go to my apartment. There, I being still in great distress, Pilate sent his physician, an Egyptian. Judaea lying adjacent to Egypt, there were many of these quacks about, some of whom obtained high places, and this one had risen in Pilate's favor because he claimed to be a diviner and Procula could never resist anyone who possessed occult powers.

He mixed me a drink so bitter that, suspecting poison, I made him drink half of it himself. It numbed my mouth and only increased the pains in my bowels, so I sent him away. He was replaced by a Greek. He, having inquired what I had eaten, kneaded my stomach with his fists, then poured a little water into a bowl and, going to the brazier with which the room was warmed, picked up in the tongs a glowing coal and dropped it in the water.

"Drink this," he said when the hissing had subsided. "And take as much of the ashes of the coal as you can."

I obeyed him—the sick obey everybody—swallowing several gritty pieces of coal, and he sat on a stool by the side of my bed quietly and waited. The effect was wonderful. In a few moments the pains had ceased, and the constant demands of my bowels were appeased. I felt so comfortable that I thought again of the women I had been planning to enjoy and mentioned my desires to the Greek. But he advised against any strenuous exercise that night and said it would be better if I spent the night in sleep.

"What is your name and where do you come from?" I asked, closing my eyes.

"My name is Luke and I am a Greek from Antioch," he replied.

[21]

IV

I REMAINED SEVERAL DAYS in Jerusalem and had with me
my little staff, who always accompanied me on journeys,
to attend to my needs. My secretary Philip was a Macedonian, highly educated, whose feet had been broken by
his mother in babyhood. She had done this for the very
sensible reason that a boy with broken feet cannot be
used as a slave in mines or galleys and so (the state of
their affairs being such that slavery was inevitable) he
might be employed in a household at light work.

I found him when he was a boy at a slave market in
Ostia. He was no longer handsome and was being sold by
his master, and I bought him for his knowledge of Greek
—my own being imperfect. When he found that I did not
wish to use him for pleasure, his gratitude was touching.
Not only was he always available at my command, but
he did not steal anything from me, which was a great
relief, for the price of a slave is not just the initial cost,
but also the amount which he or she steals or breaks or
destroys, so that what seems to be a good bargain on the
rostrum turns out to be a disaster later on.

Also Philip was healthy despite his broken feet and
so cost nothing in doctor's fees. The problem of what
to do with sick slaves is a big one, for they often cannot
be cured, they refuse freedom since there is no one to
feed them, they cannot be put to death because of the
effect on other slaves, and so they become an intolerable
expense. I digress, yet these are points people ought to
consider fully in purchasing slaves. Philip, who had to
get about on crutches, had a scholar's mind (perhaps the

result of being limited in getting about), and learned Persian and German from his fellow slaves and was interested in philosophy and history—two quite worthless studies, for there is not a penny to be derived from either of them. He was a very good listener and a great reader and often amused me with little tales out of history or with philosophical points of view when I was not able to sleep at night.

The others of my staff when traveling were Cestus, my cook and butler, and Caballus, whom I have already mentioned. Caballus, you will guess from his name, was not only my bodyguard, but also arranged my land transport, hiring post chaise, horse, litter, mule, or whatever was required for me. He had cost me a great deal of money, for I bought him out of the gladiators' school at Pisa after my Thracian bodyguard had beaten me when he was drunk and robbed me. (The man was arrested by the police—this happened in Rome—and brought to me expecting death. But I knew there was no malice in him and I find it quite impossible to kill a fellow slave. Also he had cost me forty denarii, so I sold him to the gladiators' school at Ostia for fifteen denarii and then had to buy Caballus for sixty.) The Thracian kissed my feet with tears in his eyes when he discovered I was not going to have him crucified and promised me to make sacrifices on my behalf regularly to Jupiter the Merciful. His name was Minades. The rest of my slaves were angry with me that I had not killed him. He had often bullied them and they would have enjoyed seeing him die of torture.

But to return to Caballus. Everybody knows the Germans are the best bodyguards. They are stupid and loyal and quite without fear. As treachery is bred into the Greeks through learning, so loyalty is bred into the Germans through ignorance, and they believe that they can go to their heaven (which they call Valhalla) only if they die in battle. If they desert their chief or master, they certainly will never reach that happy place.

Of course Germans do not make perfect slaves because they cannot learn to have a slave's mind. In short they tend to think of themselves as persons rather than as just a class and they get stubborn, and not all the beating in the world will subdue them.

But they are loyal, and Caballus, as big almost as the horses after whom he was named, was as loyal to me as a dog. This wasn't because I bought him out of the gladiators' school. Loving fighting, he was angry about that and sulked for days. It was because I took the iron ring off his neck and bought for him a German girl, Erithus, who was an excellent pastry cook and quite as good a brawler as he. I took the iron ring off his neck because it produced a sore which was costing me doctor's fees. I could never get it into his thick head that he was still a slave. He insisted that in removing the iron ring I had taken away a disgrace to his manhood and set him free. The main thing was that he was an excellent bodyguard, entirely loyal. That is what I was buying and that is what I got, and I well knew that you cannot buy a slave's mind. Those who are the most submissive are those who will betray you the quickest.

Among Caballus' faults was the habit of relieving himself wherever he wished. In Rome of course the side of any building or any gutter is good enough and people are not so narrow as to deny their fellows this simple easing of their need, though there are many excellent lavatories with running water. However, many do not take this easy view, and I cautioned Caballus solemnly against this habit before reaching Judaea. Among the Jews public urination against the wall of a building defiles it, particularly if the offender is a Gentile. So all the time I was in Jerusalem I was anxious lest Caballus forget himself, which would certainly cause a riot and perhaps result in his death, despite his huge strength. But you are already aware of the thousands of worries resulting from the possession of slaves.

This then was the little staff I had about me in Jerusalem, my little family, and I found the dispatch service was excellent in the Jewish capital, so hardly a day went by that I did not receive some news sent to me by my agents by land or by sea. It was while I was in Jerusalem that I got confirmation of the rumored deaths of Nero Caesar and his brother, Drusus Caesar, the sons of Germanicus, who was himself the adopted son of Tiberius.

The secretive Tiberius, of whom Augustus is said to have remarked that he would devour Rome in his slow-moving jaws, disliked to take any direct or open action against those he conceived to be his enemies, and he had ordered the two boys imprisoned—Nero on the island of Pontia and Drusus in a cellar of the palace—and then had them starved to death. Drusus Caesar, who was but eight years of age at the the time, had not only been starved, I learned from my correspondents, but had been beaten by his guards and slaves, who broke his arms and his legs. When he was dead his body was cut into a score of pieces, so that no recognizable corpse remained. The boy in his desire to live had eaten the stuffing of his mattress, but to no avail.

His mother, wife of Germanicus, had also been exiled and had died of starvation, though in her case the death was suicide. She must have known that as soon as Germanicus had been poisoned, her own life was in danger as well as that of her sons. But she was a proud and unbending woman who, instead of currying favor with Tiberius to protect her sons, had dangerously accepted public sympathy and laid the death of her husband at the door of the Emperor. Her own end was as miserable as that of her two sons. Exiled to the island of Pandataria she was, at the order of Tiberius, stripped and flogged by a centurion, who laid the whip on with such zeal that he destroyed one of her eyes. She then starved herself to death, and such was her determination to die that, although her jaws were prized open with levers and food stuffed in, she would swallow none and so succumbed.

Thus ended the family of Germanicus except for one or two inconsiderable members. One was Gaius Caesar, who was known as Caligula because, brought up among the soldiers of his father's legions, who took him as a sort of mascot, he loved to carry a small sword and shield and wear a tiny pair of soldier's boots which are of course known by that name. This boy was adopted by Tiberius, and he soon learned to embrace vice in favor of safety. Nor is he to be blamed, for he knew his father had been poisoned, his two brothers and his mother starved to death. He had three sisters, Agrippina, Drusilla, and Livilla, and these also learned that vice was safer than virtue in the palace of Tiberius. But I will say no more about him and his sisters until later.

Having, however, now received full details of the manner of death of Agrippina and her two sons, I discussed this with Pilate, filling in details of which he was not aware. Pilate emphasized that the sure source of Germanicus' downfall and the destruction of his family was not purely his military success in Germany. No. Germanicus had been unsubtle enough to avenge the overwhelming defeat of Publius Quintilius Varus at the hands of the German tribes under Arminius. That was his mistake.

Everybody knows the story of that defeat. It will surely be remembered to the end of time. Varus, with three legions, had encamped in the depth of the Teutobergian Woods, and had been warned by Segestes (one of the German chieftains friendly to Rome) that Arminius, though pretending friendship, planned treachery.

Varus was a fool. Ignoring this warning he gave a big feast for all the German chieftains and while this feast was in progress the encampment was attacked. There has surely never been such a slaughter of Roman arms. Hardly a man escaped. Even worse—a disgrace without precedent in Roman history—the eagles of the three legions fell into the hands of the Germans under Arminius. The disgrace hastened the death of Augustus, who was himself a great general. The story is told that a secretary found Augustus in the last year of his life, sleepless and pounding his fist on the wall of his bedchamber and crying, "Varus! Varus! Give me back my legions."

Well then, it was Germanicus who gave them back, for he penetrated into the Teutobergian Woods and discovered the very site of the battle. He found the rotted bodies of men and horses, lying about in great mounds, the broken weapons, the bone-strewn altars of the Germans at which majors and colonels and other officers had been sacrificed to their gods after the battle. The skeletons lay heaped about the altars still wearing military insignia to mark their rank. Several hundred skulls were found nailed to trees, and the place where Varus himself had committed suicide was also discovered. All these things Germanicus found. He decently buried the Roman bones in mounds and then, meeting with Arminius, defeated him sharply and recaptured the lost eagles, which he sent to Rome, in particular the eagle of the Twenty-ninth legion—a legion specially dear to the Romans.

Having recaptured the eagles and buried the dead, what was more natural than that Germanicus should become the darling of the whole army? Certainly he stood far higher in its affection than Tiberius; and even old legionnaires, still in the service though toothless and crippled by their wounds, men then who had no reason to love generals, would run to Germanicus and seize his hand and kiss it, tears pouring down their faces because he had got the eagles back for them. Could such a deed be tolerated by Tiberius? Not at all. And so Tiberius ordered Germanicus (his son by adoption) to return to Rome and receive his well-earned triumph. "Do not delay in Germany, but leave a little glory there for others," he wrote. Germanicus was a simple and honorable man who did not know that in completely capturing the love of the army, he had destroyed himself and his family. He was in short an honest man, a plain soldier who suspected nothing. He had his triumph and was sent off to the East to straighten out matters in Syria, and there Gneius Piso, on the orders of Tiberius, murdered him by witchcraft and poison.

It was all natural enough, viewed from the point of view of Tiberius. Was it not the army after all that made Julius Caesar emperor? And Augustus? And Tiberius? Can an emperor afford to have another man more popular with the army than he himself? Certainly not. As for the wife of Germanicus, Agrippina, she was, as I have said, too virtuous and too trusting in the loyalty of others to survive. The first step towards ruin, in any critical situation, is to believe that the gods will avenge the innocent. She believed they would and she trusted to the loyalty of the officers of her husband. But the gods did not stir themselves, and those officers who loved Germanicus and had sworn to protect his family were dispersed to Spain and to Britain when Tiberius noted how soldiers hailed the widow of Germanicus when they met her in the Forum or elsewhere about Rome. She might have saved herself by indulging his lechery, but there are some so foolish that they cannot preserve their own lives if they must go against what they call their nature to do so. I have heard that Tiberius sent for her several times at night but she would not answer the Emperor's summons. Well she died, as I have said, and so did her children and such is the reward of virtue. Her starving son, eating the flocking of his mattress, paid for his father's courage and his mother's chastity. It is not a fair price, but it is the price the world exacts.

Varus, Pilate reminded me, had close ties with Judaea. He had been legate in Syria when the revolt of Judas the Galilean broke out and Sabinus, who was Procurator in Syria, had appealed to Varus for help in putting down the revolt. Varus was far more effective against the Jews than he had been against the Germans, to whom he had lost his eagles. He had not only put down the revolt very swiftly but he had crucified two thousand Jews, the crosses stretching all the way from Jerusalem on the main road to Jericho. As a reward for his firmness on this occasion, Varus had been given command in Germany and the Jews, of course, rejoiced at the disaster which had overtaken him there and said that this was but the justice of their god for the crucifixion of two thousand.

"As for myself," said Pilate with a smile, "I doubt I have crucified a score of them. And they all deserved it—except one or two maybe. Like that fine fellow the other day who said he was King of Truth. He was quite innocent, I am sure, but it has struck me as apt that I have had to crucify the King of Truth to satisfy the High Priest of the Temple, who is certainly the King of Lies. What was that Jew's name—the Galilean?"

He addressed the question to his secretary but it was his wife Procula who answered. "It was Jesus," she said. "Jesus of Nazareth. He has risen from the dead."

"Of course he has," said Pilate. "They all do. He was to rise on the third day, I believe. Caiaphas told me so. The Jew had said that he would rise on the third day and Caiaphas begged me for a guard to put on the tomb since plainly his followers would steal his body and then, pointing to an empty tomb, announce the resurrection. Right in the middle of that earthquake, with people screaming in the streets, buildings on fire, and looters busy, that fool Caiaphas was here tearing at his beard and asking for soldiers to guard the tomb. I told him to use his own—I had none to spare. Of course he couldn't trust his own, which is why he wanted our soldiers. But he used his own soldiers and I presume they were bribed and the body stolen. Now they will have more trouble from the man dead than they had when he was alive, and serve them right.

"I love to see the Jews divided, Theophilus," Pilate continued. " 'Divide and Rule' was always an excellent maxim. They have the Pharisees and the Sadducees and the Samaritans and the Essenes and the Zealots and the New Convenanters and I hope they will soon have a group who believe this Jesus was their Messiah. It will certainly be my policy to credit stories that Jesus has been raised from the dead. It will discredit the Temple and it will divide them all further."

"But he *did* rise from the dead," said Procula. "He has been seen by many people at one time."

"It is all very well for the Jews to believe that," said Pilate a little testily, "but it is unpardonable in Romans. Raised from the dead, indeed. Well, let him come before me. Then I will believe it."

"You must believe it," said Procula. "It is true."

Must was not a word to use to Pilate. I saw his neck begin to flush red with anger. To divert the Procurator I said I had heard in recent gazettes from Alexandria of another resurrection, this time not of a man but of a bird.

"That magical bird called the phoenix," I said, "has been seen in Egypt, according to my correspondents in Alexandria. Many, they say, have seen it at one time. As you know, it is supposed to have a life span of about fourteen hundred years. When nearing death it collects a quantity of myrrh, builds a nest of stones and sets itself afire using the rays of the sun. As soon as it is consumed, a new phoenix arises from the ashes."

I thought I might relieve the tension by relating this story, solemnly detailed to me by my correspondents in Alexandria. But Procula, when I had finished, looked at me almost in terror and dashed from the room to consult with her astrologer.

"I must separate her from that damned Persian," said

Pilate, looking after her. "Let us see how well he can cast his own horoscope," and he beckoned to one of his guards.

V

BEFORE LEAVING JERUSALEM I had, of course, to pay my respects to Herod Antipas and to the High Priests Annas and Caiaphas. Pilate and Herod, who had long been unfriendly, were now on cordial terms, for Pilate had acknowledged Herod's authority by sending the Jew Jesus (who was a Galilean) to him. He had also hoped that Herod would handle the whole problem, thus relieving him of the necessity, but the Herods of the Hasmonaean line are not so readily trapped. Pilate, a mere Roman, could not out-Herod Herod, and so he got the Jew back again. Still the two were now on good terms and so I could wait on Herod without incurring the enmity of Pilate.

Herod did not live in the palace which his father Herod the Great had built on the summit of the hill just within the city walls and overlooking the Temple. He lived in a second palace, lower down, closer to the Temple and to the Antonia fortress. It was a splendid building of the same stone from which the Temple was built, laid out with its main axis running east and west. Thus the balconies, loggias, rooms, and meeting places in the front of the palace all faced south, getting the fullest benefit of the sun whatever the season. The stone had a golden tinge, the terraces were paved with black and white marble, the columns were in the graceful Ionic style, the finest carpets of Turkey and of Persia hung from the walls, and the bedrooms were carpeted with sheepskins so that one could get out of bed without first summoning a slave to put on his slippers. Herod hated to be cold. If a Roman hates to be cold, he insures that he is cold some of the time to strengthen his character. That is, an old Roman, but Augustus set the fashion of wearing a chest protector in winter and also putting woolen gaiters over his thin legs. Caesar wore much the same clothing winter or summer.

But Herod was a Jew and, hating to be cold, he did his best to remain warm at all times. Braziers glowed in every room, giving out a sweet fragrance, and of course the floors of the larger rooms were heated. It was very pleasant on a sharp day to come into Herod's palace and stand over one of the gratings in the floor and allow the hot air to rise up inside your clothing.

Herod Antipas was one of the sons of Herod the Great who escaped being strangled at the orders of his father. His mother was Malthake, Herod's third wife, and he had a brother Archelaus. Malthake was a Samaritan, and Herod had married her not only because she was desirable but to form a strong alliance with the Samaritans to offset the power of the priests of the Temple, for the Samaritans, though Jews, refuse to worship in the Temple, which they jeer at as the "divine countinghouse." You must know that the politics of Judaea are the politics of religion, which is another form of the Jewish madness. Men struggle against each other not for land or mines or forests or rivers but for religious doctrines. The Samaritans, occupying the vast fertile area to the south of Judaea, and refusing to worship in the Temple or send tribute there, were Herod's natural allies against the Temple party—itself divided between Pharisee and Sadducee. Herod's alliance by marriage with the Samaritans saved the life of his son Herod Antipas and his brother Archelaus.

There was much about Herod Antipas to be admired.

He had made an art of deceit, which is a great tribute to his agility of mind. Lacking subtlety, I myself have found frankness and honesty in all matters my best policy, but this does not prevent me admiring those who, possessing a finer intellect, can use deceit and deviousness of purpose with great skill.

A man could no more pin Herod Antipas down than he could catch the wind in a net. Yet he had a weakness and the weakness lay in women. For political reasons he had early married a daughter of King Aretas IV of Arabia. But he divorced her and seduced Herodias, wife of his half-brother Philip, whom he met in Rome, and married her. The woman caused him trouble from the moment she entered his palace and yet he could not get rid of her. He was so infatuated by Herodias that no one dared advise him to poison her or have her drowned as by accident—matters which are very easy to arrange. He would not divorce her either, though she was shamelessly promiscuous. Herod was nominally a Jew and, although none of these highly placed Jews follow their religion closely, they could do nothing openly that violated its basic laws without causing hatred among their subjects. But Herod had violated the Jewish law by marrying his sister-in-law, for the Jews hold such a marriage incestuous and abominable, though if a married man dies without issue, then his brother must marry his widow (if he is not already married) so that she may not be barren all her life.

All the Jews then hated Herod for marrying Herodias and one, formerly of the sect called Essenes, called John the Baptist, was bold enough to denounce the marriage publicly. He was, of course, put immediately in prison. But Herod was afraid of this man John for he believed him to be a prophet and a miracle worker. Herodias, however, was determined that John should die. But whenever she stormed against him and demanded his death Herod refused out of superstitious fear.

She arranged then for her daughter Salome to dance

before Herod and his guests when he was drunk and feeling lecherous, and he was so stirred by her dancing that he promised Salome to grant her any favor she would ask.

Salome, advised by her mother, asked for the head of the prophet, John the Baptist. Herod was then trapped. No one could trap him but this woman Herodias, who led him about, as people said, not by the nose but by the genitals. He regretted his promise to Salome. But he had made it before his guests and, as is the way with men when they are drunk, he thought his honor involved, though his honor mattered nothing to him when sober and in his right senses. He gave orders reluctantly for the beheading; and the head of John the Baptist was in a few moments presented to Salome on a dish, still hot and the eyes bright and open. I am told that Herodias closed the eyes herself with a smile of triumph, but later they were found to have opened again. But one cannot believe all these stories and one has to remember that, Herodias being hated by the Jews, every kind of evil tale was circulated concerning her.

I had no quarrel with her and was certainly more at ease in her company than in the company of Procula with her soothsayers and charms and astrologers. Herodias loved power and the pleasures of sex. Well, can any honest man condemn this? Power is a great pleasure and so is sexual indulgence and if the pursuit of pleasure is deemed wicked then the whole world stands condemned. No. I understood Herodias and she understood me. But Procula always made me feel nervous. As for Salome, I can truthfully say she had no appeal for me at all. The mature woman—that is the best companion. I have made it a rule never to drink new wine or seduce virgins.

Now, why should I be telling you all this? You will soon know. When I called on Herod to pay my respects I found him in a ridiculous state of depression and fear, and really, when I tell you the reason you will scarcely believe me. It was this. He had heard the rumors that the Jew Pilate had crucified had risen from the dead.

Now what will you say when I tell you that Herod not only believed that this crucified Jew, Jesus of Galilee, had risen from the dead but he believed also that he was none other than John the Baptist? You will say that Herod was mad. Yet that is exactly what Herod did believe and he told me in a great fright that this John the Baptist thus had twice risen from the dead. He had been beheaded and he had returned as Jesus of Nazareth. Then Jesus of Nazareth had been crucified, and he had returned, raised from the dead—as whom?

"They say the Messiah," said Herod in a whisper full of dread. "You know about the Messiah, Theophilus?"

"Majesty," I said (Herod loved that title), "certainly I know that some great and heroic deliverer has been promised the Jews by their prophets and that his advent has been expected for hundreds of years. The Procurator, with whom I have had an opportunity to discuss the matter and who sends you his warmest affections, tells me that twelve Messiahs to his knowledge have been executed among the Jews since Anthony's time. But you know that every nation has a story of a great deliverer whose coming is always expected when national fortunes are low. The Macedonians still look for the return of Alexander, or at least his father Philip. The Persians are convinced that Darius will come one day thundering out of the hills in his war chariot with his bowmen launching arrows of fire and behind him four lions, their manes dark with blood. Even the Germans look for the appearance of a great champion who will lead them to the conquest of the world, and you are well aware that all the rebellions among the Gallic tribes recently took place because they thought their own particular champion had returned. In short, deliverance by a divine champion is the common hope of mankind and you should not therefore take such tales seriously."

But Herod was now all Jew in his fears and had on him that god-madness which is the curse of that people. How comforting it is to be able to turn to Jupiter and

Mars and Neptune with a pinch of incense or the inner meats of a bullock as the occasion warrants, rather than serve that Jewish god who, as I have said, seems determined to drive all his worshipers mad. In Herod's case there was another influence to explain his ridiculous fear. His father, Herod the Great, uneasy on his throne, had had a terror of the coming of the Messiah. In fact, when three Persian astrologers told him about thirty years previously that the Messiah had been born in Bethlehem (a hamlet outside Jerusalem), so great was his fear that he had all male babies in the whole of Judaea slaughtered so as to be sure that the Messiah was killed. The slaughter was thorough indeed, for the soldiers of course did not tenderly inquire the age of every child before impaling it or slitting its throat. Not at all. They cut down every infant they could find, and as soldiers will, they made a great deal of money at the same time, taking bribes from parents to spare their babies and then decapitating or spearing them in any case.

Herod Antipas had inherited his father's terror of the Messiah's coming. I had proof of that before me. But his situation was worse, for it was not babies he was dealing with now but a man raised twice from the dead (as he believed) and therefore indestructible.

Now when a man such as I stands before a terrified prince, he will not be true to his nature if he does not consider what profit is to be derived from the situation. It seemed to me that if I could banish Herod's fears effectively, I would make a very powerful friend, whereas it would be no advantage to me at all to play on them, though by so doing I would certainly be serving Pilate's policy. Still I judged Herod the more powerful of the two. He had the firm friendship of Tiberius (or his marriage to Herodias would have been the end of him) whereas Pilate, if he continued his present policies of animosity to the Jews, must eventually be brought down. I decided then to serve Herod and said what soothing words I could. I told him not to believe the stories he had heard, however well attested, pointing out that it was to the advantage of many to insist that Jesus had risen from the dead, since this could discredit the Temple party under the High Priests, who were heartily hated outside Jerusalem.

"As powerful a prince as you, your Majesty," I concluded, "should have no difficulty in establishing the truth of this matter and putting your mind forever at ease."

"But who am I to trust?" demanded Herod. "This is a land of causes and of lies. There is no man in all Judaea whom I can believe on this vital question."

A fool would have spoken at that moment, so I remained silent and, having offered what further comfort I could, withdrew, begging him not to act upon rumor or to make fear his master. You will not be surprised, I am sure, to hear that the next day Herod sent me a large present of money and begged me, as a man unbiased in the matter and known to be honest and painstaking in his inquiries, with informers everywhere, to investigate the whole truth of the story of the resurrection of Jesus.

"Bring me proof that he is dead—that the grave was only robbed of his body—and you may command anything I possess," he said. In making this promise Herod was of course sober, so I knew his honor was not involved and the promise would not likely be kept. But I might, however, look for his favor and who is such a fool as to despise the favor of a Herod? Also the money present received had saved my journey to Jerusalem from being utterly unprofitable. It was a large sum and cause for reflection that, deprived of my profits on an aqueduct, I had nonetheless reaped some benefit from a burial. So I decided to investigate the resurrection story myself, and started with interviewing Caiaphas.

VI

Two weeks had now passed since the crucifixion of Jesus, who was *not* the first man of whom I had heard that he was raised from the dead. There had been a case in Turkey ten years before and another in Alexandria and everybody knows how the whole world trembled (some with joy and some with fear) when it was reported that Germanicus had been raised from the dead, and was on his way to Rome. Although the case in Alexandria proved to be true, the other two instances of resurrection turned out to be frauds, in which someone resembling the dead man had been guilty of imposture with the connivance of close friends. So you have always to look for frauds in cases of men rising from dead. I have never known a case of a woman being raised from the dead, that, I suppose, being because of the unimportance of women in world affairs.

Of course I was not deceived in the present case, knowing the resurrection to have been inspired by reasons of both religion and politics. But having taken Herod's money I interested myself in the story and went first to see Caiaphas the High Priest. (There were two at the time —Annas and Caiaphas—and they held office in alternate years. It was Pilate's idea.)

Caiaphas sensibly pooh-poohed the whole story, but with rather too much zeal. One could not of course blame him for wanting to discredit the whole thing. Yet I reflected as he talked that he must be hiding something from me about the Galilean; for if Jesus had been just another imposter or blasphemer, in a long line of imposters, why hadn't he been stoned to death in the normal way? The

Jews are allowed to stone people to death for blasphemy or adultery (believe me, as a young man, and without boasting, I would have been buried under enough stones to rebuild Rome if subject to their law on that score). The reason that Jews can stone people to death is that it is impossible to point to any one person as the killer, and so prosecution in such cases is impossible. But Caiaphas had insisted that Jesus be crucified at the orders of Pilate, which seemed to me odd. Pilate, as I knew myself, had had a hard time finding Jesus guilty of anything. Unlike Judas, the Galilean in the time of Varus, he hadn't led an army of zealots against Rome or advocated the withholding of Roman taxes as Judas had done. Someone told me (I think it was my secretary Philip) that Jesus had very neatly avoided the whole issue of taxes by telling people to give to Caesar what belonged to Caesar and to god what belonged to god.

Anyway there certainly did seem to be something special about this King of Truth called Jesus who had no organization, no army, no plan of campaign, no enmity to Rome, yet had been so dangerous to the High Priests that they had found it necessary to put him to death.

My interview with Caiaphas took place in the lovely lower garden of his palace, the earth fertilized by the huge quantity of animal blood that flowed from the Temple altars every day. Here plum, peach, orange, pomegranate, and Syrian apple produced a profusion of blossoms, it being full spring.

"Caiaphas," I said when we were together (great wealth allowed me such familiarity and frankness), "tell me honestly, recalling that I was present at his trial on that miserable morning—why did Jesus have to be sentenced by Pilate? Why wasn't he just stoned?"

"Why?" echoed Caiaphas. "Reflect a moment, Theophilus. Because of the mob, of course," and he gently moved a bowl of plump early cherries towards me (they were a little sour). "He was the hero of the mob, the champion of the slums. He had an immense following among the gutter people of our nation—publicans, prostitutes, pimps, thieves, tax collectors, ne'er-do-wells. All that is horrible in society supported him—people of no economic worth, people without the slightest reverence for the Torah and for tradition; lepers, beggars, the loveless, and the worthless. They were all his henchmen. To have stoned him would have brought on a riot. You recall the tension of the time? The only way he could be executed was for Rome to do it. The mob knows that Rome will not stand for riot."

That seemed very reasonable to me and increased my respect for the High Priests. There have been two occasions when mobs, inflamed by an utterly false report, burned down my warehouses at Ostia, which fortunately were almost empty at the time, though thought to be bursting with grain. Mobs are no more controllable than weather. "Excellent," I said. "I quite understand and sympathize with you. But tell me this: Why did he have to be executed at all?"

"He planned the overthrow of the Temple and the priests," said Caiaphas. (Really, in private conversation, he was quite a reasonable man.) " 'Beware of the scribes and the Pharisees,' he warned. 'I will destroy this Temple and rebuild it in three days.' Those are his actual words. Now, my dear Theophilus, while I know that you are not a Jew, think in your own terms, as a Gentile. How long do you think anyone would be tolerated in Rome who cried out in the Forum, 'Beware of the Vestal Virgins. Beware of the Priest of Jupiter. Beware of the College of Augurs. I will destroy the Altar of Mars and build it again in three days.' How long, Theophilus?"

"Not long," I said.

"Precisely," replied Caiaphas. "And if you Gentiles, following a false religion, will not tolerate disrespect for your priests and altars, how much less can we tolerate such a thing; we Jews who have a covenant with the true God and are his chosen people?"

There it was again—the Jewish madness. It angered me. Everybody else's god was false. Only theirs was the true god, and they were his chosen people—when any god in his senses, choosing a people for his special regard, would have chosen us Romans a hundred times before the sly, stiff-necked, corruptible Jews. Really, it was intolerable, but I restrained my irritation, contenting myself with refusing more of the cherries and saying they were sour. This had no effect on Caiaphas. Get a Jew on the subject of his religion (if he will stoop to talk to you about it at all) and you have lost half the day and all your self-respect.

"Heresy sprouts faster among our people than among others because they believe so passionately," said Caiaphas, settling down to a tirade. "We are the chosen people and we were promised a Messiah. So every man is looking for him and every glib hysteric who makes an impression on a country synagogue thinks he is the one. This leader of thieves and whores had convinced thousands that he was the Messiah. Now is it likely that the Messiah would come and that the High Priest of Israel would not know of it? It never occurs to these people that when the Messiah appears it will not be in some wild hill place like Galilee, where the fishermen still throw a stone in the water to frighten off devils before embarking in their boat and shepherds run to the synagogue with an offering when a flight of blackbirds passes over their sheep. Oh, those people. They sicken me. They have drenched this land with blood with their Messiahs. Putting this Jesus to death probably saved the lives of two or three thousand of his mob of filthy followers and now instead of being quiet, they're resurrecting him. Well, when they feel Rome's lash, they will have only themselves to blame.

"By next year there will be another Messiah and then another, and so on. The promise of a Messiah is a trap for fools and a sharp test of fidelity for the devout. One thing is certain. God will not keep the Messiah hidden. When he comes, the world will know of it."

It surprised me to realize that Caiaphas, like Herod, actually believed in the Messiah himself. But then, of course, he was a Jew, and in matters of religion the Jews are beyond all reason.

Herod having spoken of miracles said to have been performed by Jesus, I mentioned this aspect of his work to Caiaphas.

"Country wonders," he said with scorn. "None took place in the Temple or in Jerusalem, and those who have come to tell us of them have been mere bumpkins. Oh, we have had lepers come to say that they have been cured of their leprosy and blind men to testify that Jesus restored their sight. But we have had the same thing happen before the appearance of Jesus. Among such a people as we, there are many who drive themselves into madness from a sense of guilt and think themselves lepers or blind. A kind word, a touch of the hand, and they are restored to sanity. No. And then you know we priests must certify leprosy in the first instance—leprosy in people, clothing, houses, and so on. Sometimes we are wrong and what we think is leprosy is just a skin disease. I cannot say that I know of a single true cure achieved by this imposter Jesus.

"I went to Golgotha myself and stood before him and called out to him to perform the one miracle which would show beyond all doubt that he was the son of God as he claimed. I didn't believe for a moment that he was, but I wanted to demonstrate that he was a fraud. 'Come down from the cross,' I challenged, 'and I will fall on my knees and adore you. Save yourself,' I said. 'Surely if you have saved others, you can save yourself.'

"But he couldn't save himself. Not at all. He was powerless. He only groaned and cried out, 'I thirst.' 'I thirst.' Can you imagine it? A simple physical need. Did God send rain to quench his thirst? Do you know, Theophilus, that if it had even rained at that moment, I might have been a little shaken. But it didn't rain. God did not even send a drop to quench his thirst. It was a soldier, not God, who gave him a sponge on a stick. His crucifixion was the test of this imposter. God would surely have saved him if he was His son as he claimed. But he died miserably. By insisting upon his crucifixion, we priests showed him to be false, and gathered our flock back around the one and only true God. The impious, however, will no more be saved now than they would in the time of our father Abraham. God does not condemn men. They damn themselves.

> " 'My name is Yahweh,
>   I will not yield my glory to another.'

"So God spoke through the prophet Isaiah.
"And again:

> " 'I am the first and the last;
>   There is no other God beside me.
>   Who is like me? Let him stand and speak,
>   Let him show himself and argue it out before me.'

"Tell me. Does the son of God die the death of a criminal—the last drop of blood gone from him, and not one hand stirred to save him? If God saved Daniel in a pit of lions, would He leave His own son to die of torture?"

"Caiaphas," I said gently, "you do not have to convince me. I am not a Jew."

"Then go and convince Herod, for it was he who sent you," said Caiaphas. "Tell him that his fears are groundless and that in indulging them he is giving strength to a most dangerous rumor which can pull him down and the Temple as well. Tell him that if he digs deep enough he will find Pilate is behind this rumor. Yes, Pilate, whom Herod now thinks his friend. On the day the Jew was crucified Annas and I warned Pilate that there was a resurrection plot; that the followers of Jesus would steal his body and, pointing to the empty tomb, claim that he was raised from the dead and so the true Messiah and the son of God. We asked Pilate for Roman soldiers to guard the tomb, Theophilus, because the Temple soldiers are not to be trusted. The ones we could trust among them— the Jews—could not, of course, be put on duty on the Great Sabbath. That left us with Syrians, who have no real loyalty to the Temple, the High Priest, and to God. Everything happened as we expected. Pilate refused us a Roman guard. We used the Temple guard consisting entirely of Gentiles. They were bribed and the body was stolen.

"Theophilus, you are a man of affairs. So I do not have to ask you why Pilate refused us a Roman guard or where you think the money to bribe our guard came from. But I now realize that the worst thing I did in the whole matter was to go to Pilate and tell him of the resurrection plot, for I unwittingly presented him with an excellent opportunity of dividing our people further and shaking public faith in the High Priests and the Temple."

"My dear Caiaphas," I said, "with the offer of a few sour cherries, you cannot expect me to listen to unworthy innuendoes against my good friend Pontius Pilate. You Jews always make the same mistake. You think you are constantly foremost in the minds of everybody, and that is not so. I happen to know that when you came to Pilate to ask for a guard, he was very busy with an earthquake and the last thing that concerned him was your fears of a resurrection plot, as you call it. Be sensible, Caiaphas. Is a man, responsible for a whole city shaken by an eclipse, an earthquake, and teeming with panicky pilgrims, really going to spend his time plotting to make it appear that an obscure Galilean rabbi has risen from the dead?"

Caiaphas smiled and shrugged. "I am sorry the cherries are sour," he said.

"Concerning the earthquake and eclipse," I persisted, "wasn't that a sign of something special about this man—whom Pilate, I must remind you, found innocent. The gods protest injustice. That is known."

I made mention of the gods, of course, to annoy him by reminding him that other people have a religion too, it being a Jewish concept that other people have only superstitions. But it is unwise to argue religion with a Jew and Caiaphas soon had his revenge.

"At the moment before the commencement of the eclipse," he said, "I was on the street outside the Temple and saw a man whirl about and strike a little child who was begging. The child was quite innocent, but was knocked to the ground by the blow. Perhaps, my dear Theophilus, that was the reason for the eclipse and the earthquake sent by the gods, as you think. Also I have already heard that the greatest damage from the earthquake occurred in the cities of the Decapolis—Philadelphia, in particular—where several temples fell and many houses. If the wrong was done here, why did the people of Philadelphia (Gentiles like yourself) suffer so badly?"

"My dear Caiaphas," I said, "you are entirely right and I hope you will forgive my remark about the cherries. It seemed necessary to me to point out, in self-defense, that everything done by the Jews is not perfect."

"You have always been generous to us, Theophilus," said Caiaphas, "and we in the Temple know you are at heart a friend to the Jews. And the cherries *are* sour."

"We understand each other," I said.

Before we parted company, Caiaphas said something that impressed me. "Concerning this resurrection plot, what one individual believes does not matter, Theophilus. What does matter is that our nation should not be led astray. We must be faithful to God or we are lost. Without him our people are like dust before the wind—lost and gone for all time. We Jews have our identity only in God. He alone preserves us. Do you not see then why we must destroy imposters without mercy? As a man, I could have pitied this Jesus. As an imposter, I hated him and he filled me with fear and with loathing."

I came away from my interview greatly impressed with Caiaphas. He and those around him had been called (it was Pilate's phrase) "a hissing of vipers," and while Caiaphas' personal life was a scandal, yet his zeal in protecting his people from imposters was not to be put aside as mere show. In that zeal he had lied to me about Jesus, for it was by no means true that his following had consisted only of what is called the rabble. I knew, for instance, that he had been buried in the tomb of a wealthy Pharisee, Joseph from Arimathea, a substantial city not far from Jerusalem. Also another of the Pharisees (and they were not of the rabble, the Pharisees) who was actually a member of the Sanhedrin or governing council of the Temple —a man called Nicodemus—had been a secret follower of Jesus and had donated the very expensive ointments needed for the anointing of his body. No, Caiaphas had lied in his zeal and, thinking of this as I left his palace, I decided to go to the cemetery and talk to any of the gardeners I could find there.

The Jews, as the world knows, were at one time captives of the Egyptians, the greater part of the whole nation having been taken to Egypt as slaves. The Egyptians worship many fearful gods in the form of hawks and crocodiles and hyenas and, like the Jews, are ruled by their priests, who control the king or pharaoh. They are in love with death and spend fortunes insuring that their bodies will not decay, and I have profited by that by selling many shiploads of nitrates from Spain to Egyptian buyers who use this in preserving the dead. From the Egyptians, the Jews, when freed by their great leader Moses (a name which is Egyptian and not Jewish), brought back many beliefs and customs, among them this practice of preserving the bodies of the dead in preparation for a resurrection. Only the wealthy, of course, can afford it. Certainly no builder's son from Nazareth could pay for the needed oils and other preservatives, nor the many yards of purest linen required to swaddle the body. So it was no small gift that was given to the crucified Jew by the Pharisee Nicodemus.

The distance from the palace of Caiaphas to the burial ground was not far—less than a mile, though the road twisted and wound up hills and in places the streets were cut in steps for they would otherwise have been too steep for safety in the winter rains. Golgotha, the place of execution, was just beyond the city walls (no more than two hundred yards) and the sepulcher in which the body was laid only one hundred yards from that. So those who had buried him had not had far to carry him. The only disciple who had stayed with him was the one named John, but he and Nicodemus had carried the body the short distance, aided by the fact that it was already stiff in death —the gardener told me that.

"There the tomb is, sir," he said. "I helped to roll the stone in front of it." The stone was a huge wheel, which rolled in a groove across the face of a cave, the door of the cave being built out square so that when the stone was in front of it, the entrance was effectively closed.

It is the custom to make a seal between this stone and the door it covers, for Israel has its grave robbers just like Egypt and a broken seal means a grave has been robbed.

The stone before this sepulcher was massive, and it would take three or four men, I think, to move it.

"The body is not there now, I hear," I said.

"No."

"It was stolen?"

"Are you from the Temple?" he asked.

"No. I am making private inquiries."

"Some say it was stolen. Some say it wasn't. Look for yourself," the gardener replied. "I was not here. It was the Great Sabbath. Nobody was here but the guard."

I climbed up the little hill and unexpectedly came

across the stone for sealing the tomb, lying among the scrub, for the stone had not been just rolled back from the entrance, it had been flung out of the groove in which it rolled to some distance away. A huge force had flung that stone. I bent over to examine it more closely and then became aware, in the silence, which was interrupted only by a slight hollow noise made by the wind as it passed across the open mouth of the sepulcher, that someone was watching me. I looked up and there, standing on top of the cave, was the crucified Jew. There was no mistaking him. I would know that great neck and strong face anywhere.

There came immediately to my mind the words he had spoken, "I will not leave you, Theophilus." Then a mist formed around him, and around the tomb. And when it dissolved, he was gone.

VII

WHEN I RECOVERED MY WITS the gardener was gone. He had hurried off and so I could not ask him whether he too had seen the figure. While the man Jesus stood there, I was sure of a physical presence, but then reason returned and suggested that what I had seen was not flesh and bones but an apparition.

Such apparitions are common. It is everywhere accepted that when any great violence has been done to someone innocent the spirit lingers on earth to protest the injustice. So the ghost of Julius Caesar has often been seen at the place where he was struck down. Also at the pass of Thermopylae the ghosts of the betrayed Lacedaemonian soldiers have many times appeared, their hair freshly combed and curled, their faces clean shaven and gleaming in the moonlight, and their cloaks folded about them, the shield within the fold.

That the spirit of Jesus of Nazareth, crucified, though certainly innocent of any crime, should return to haunt the place where he had been killed, was not to be marveled at. Yet I was made uneasy and returned quickly to the bustle of the city with but one backward glance at that terribly empty tomb.

Herod that night was sullen and dined alone. The following morning a boy who had been flung out of a window of the palace was found in the courtyard. His head was shattered and there were whip marks on his body and several places where he had been burned, so it was assumed that Herod had been amusing himself. Like Tiberius, Herod knew no bounds to his search for sexual pleasure and natural intercourse no longer afforded him its previous delights. The boy had been happy enough to attract Herod's attention, and had thought his fortune made to have gained the favor of so powerful a prince. Herod mourned him for two days, staying in his own quarters.

I mention this trifle only because it brought me into a more intimate contact with Mnenaus, who was Herod's steward. Herod keeping himself private, I was invited to dine with Mnenaus, who greeted me warmly and inquired after my health with real interest. I expected a cunning man and perhaps he was cunning, but he had an openness that was surprising and told me many secrets of Herod's household of value to me. One boy, done to death by Herod or Vitellius or by Agapas of Bythnia or by any personage of note, was not of course a topic for two such men as he and I. Yet in loyalty to his master Mnenaus had to touch on the matter and dismiss it casually.

"The boy was a fool," he said. "Had he put up with a little suffering, he could now have had enough wealth to keep him and his parents for twenty years. You were a slave, Theophilus. You know how it is with powerful men. You must endure and please them. It is wise even for a freedman to do such things, and there are, as you know, wives of Senators who in their family interests have not quibbled about being agreeable to the Emperor. Yet the boy threw himself from Herod's window. He was a slave. Where did he get such concepts of self-respect? A slave is a slave and has no self to respect, as you know."

He spoke in Greek and in Greek the word for slave, *soma,* is the same as the word for corpse. This is but one example of the logic of the Greek language. Mnenaus prattled on like a good host. He inquired whether the women of the palace were being agreeable, whether I would prefer other company at night, said (which I already knew) that Herod had lost interest in Agrippina so she was lonelier than usual.

This gossip put aside, he then asked me whether I had anything to report about the Jew Jesus, and said that he knew I had already seen Caiaphas and had gone to the burial ground. "You know, of course, that I have had you watched," he said mildly. "Don't worry about what you do here in the palace. I have no plot against you by which I can profit. If you could, however, give me a little information about the Jew which I can pass on to Herod, it would be a help to me."

"You referred to my days as a slave. . . ." I said.

"I mean no offense, I assure you," said Mnenaus.

"I take no offense," I assured him. "But you were never a slave, and so you do not understand the mentality of a slave. We slaves have a love of facts. We find that we can profit only from facts. Dreams, beliefs, hopes—they are useless to us. I have no facts I can give you."

"But you suspect something?"

"Who followed me to the graveyard?" I asked.

Mnenaus did not want to mention a name and said, "Come. You may take vengeance on the informer."

"If vengeance were something that appealed to me," I

said, "there are many in the mines and the war galleys far more worthy of my notice than whoever followed me to the house of Caiaphas and then to the cemetery. Come. You are playing with me. Who was it?"

"Why do you want to know?" Mnenaus countered.

You will understand that I was anxious to find the person who had followed me to ask him if he also had seen the figure over the tomb. But I shrugged and said it was not a matter of importance, that I had nothing solid to pass to Herod beyond the fact that the stone before the tomb had been thrown a great distance.

"That is known," said Mnenaus. "And it is easily explained. The earth shook, as you know, during the afternoon and there were other tremors during the night which tumbled the stone from its groove. There were a lot of graves opened in the same way. It is said that the dead walked that night, you know. People saw them about the streets. And in Egypt the phoenix was seen." (He would have learned of that from Pilate's wife, Procula, I assumed. News travels always in circles.) "And that afternoon the sun was darkened. You know, Theophilus, it is not only Herod and Caiaphas who are disturbed about these things. If you have anything to say, do not keep it back. Tell me. I have a need to know."

"Why do you have a need to know?" I asked.

"All right. I will confess," said Mnenaus. "The boy whom Herod threw out of the window was the one who followed you. The burns and the whip marks were added later. Why did Herod throw him out of the window?"

I paused before replying. "Because he was fool enough to tell Herod that he saw the Jew standing over the top of his tomb," I answered.

"He lied?" asked Mnenaus.

I made no reply.

VIII

YOU WILL UNDERSTAND that it was necessary for me now to leave Jerusalem immediately lest the anger (really the fear) of Herod be turned against me. I told Caballus to have horses ready at the gates of the city on the afternoon of the following day, and I would meet him at the gate. He was to contrive to take Philip with him, on a mule, for the poor fellow had a hard time on the Jerusalem slopes with his crutches.

Caballus was sulky. He did not want to leave and he had never learned that the duty of a slave is to obey. As I have said, he hardly regarded himself as a slave since the removal of his iron collar. It seemed that he did not wish to leave because he had an assignation for that night with one of the women of the palace, and it was only some time later that I discovered that Herodias was to be the fortunate woman.

In his resentment at the many frustrations he had suffered while in Jerusalem, he allowed his horse to urinate close to the Temple wall instead of using his quirt to prevent this. There was an immediate outcry and he enjoyed himself beating off those who surrounded him screaming at the defilement. So my leaving the city was not by any means secret, but then Caballus had no use for subtlety.

Leaving late in the afternoon, I intended to travel for only two or three hours before taking a lodging for the night, going northward into Samaria and so to Caesarea, but avoiding Galilee, which was directly under the government of Herod.

To ease my departure I left letters for Herod saying how much I grieved for him in his loss, assuring him of my friendship, and saying I had to leave to look to business interests with which I did not wish to plague him. I left also a present of an excellent rare vase coming from China, with a picture below the glaze of a fat person who looked quite like Mnenaus. The gift was costly. I do not think there are three such vases to be found in the whole of the Roman world. Yet only a fool counts the cost of personal safety. At Caesarea I hoped to find one of my vessels, which would take me to my villa on Crete.

We made good progress and that night stopped at Emmaus, at the foot of the Jerusalem highlands, where Philip had gone ahead and found me accommodation at an inn and Cestus, my butler, had already started a good dinner for me of a leg of spring lamb, of which I am very fond. The sheep of the highlands of Judaea are, I think, the finest to be found in the world. The spring grass there, nourished by early rains, gives an excellent flavor to the meat, and who has not desired the comfort of a cloak made of the fine, silky wool of Judaea? I ate well, glad to be out of Jerusalem, which, I concluded, comforted by the excellent delicate flesh of the lamb, is a city of madness. It was nice to be in this old inn in the sensible world of Emmaus and to gossip with the landlord, who, himself a Jew, agreed that Jerusalem might be regarded as a concentration of lunatics.

"It is a city where sane men lose their wits," he said. "Decent fellows from around here, for instance, making their livings with vineyards or olive groves, or flocks, treating the stranger among them as a brother as the Torah bids them, go to Jerusalem and behave like savages. Of course you know, sir, that when a fellow is away from his wife and his home, he undergoes a certain change. That is natural, and I see plenty of it at the inn. A little ill-behavior is to be excused when abroad, after all, and sensible wives will ignore it. But rioting, fighting with fists and sticks, stoning what are called 'blasphemers,' insulting the Romans—that is nothing but the 'Jerusalem madness,' as we call it in these parts.

"Still, better that people behave that way there than here. We're peaceable folk at Emmaus, sir, minding our business, paying our taxes and getting on with our work."

Really I liked the fellow immensely, and when he spoke of his appreciation of Roman rule, he did so honestly. Certainly his admiration for Tiberius was boundless, for though it is true that in Rome the Senate and the order of Knights and even the priests groaned under his tyranny, the provinces benefited beyond measure from the rule of Tiberius. You see now why I myself live in Crete. Who wants to be neighbor to a lion? Yet to live in the territory of a lion without being close neighbor to the beast is to be freed from many marauders.

"The roads are clear of brigands now," my host said. "People aren't afraid to set out on a journey and that's all to my benefit, you may be sure, for my inn is seldom empty. Look at the great good that comes from such journeys—the increase of trade, new goods brought in to make us all happier, money flowing about, men getting to know each other and tolerate each other better. Now if we had some other ruler than Rome (I will go no further than that) half the profit from my business would go to buying protection from brigands, and travelers setting out would have to be accompanied by a troop of horse to be sure of getting alive from Jerusalem to Joppa. Why, here's yourself, sir, a man of great wealth, can ride here without having a private army to see that you are not kidnapped on the road and held for ransom. In my father's day you would likely have been taken as soon as you cleared the city of Jerusalem."

Is it strange that my heart swelled with pride to hear Rome so praised—I who had been a slave of Romans? Well, I have to confess that it did. With all her violence and cruelties and wickedness I love Rome. For there is in

Rome and nowhere else a desire for order and justice under the law, and the heroes of the Romans are men of honor and of loyalty. Philip tells me that this is not entirely true, that the stories of the heroes are false. Well, I am sorry to hear that Horatius did not save the city single-handed, but I do not see that it matters. What men admire decides their character as much as what they do. And the Romans admire courage, loyalty, and honor. And so the world admires them.

I invited the innkeeper to sit with me and have a bedtime cup before the fire. His inn was clean—no cockroaches glistened in the corners of the room, and although I could feel bedbugs biting through the cushion on which I sat, an innkeeper can scarcely be blamed for such infestations which are brought in daily by travelers. He questioned me about my knowledge of the country and served some of the delightful wine from Hebron, where the grapes are not picked for wine making until they are beginning to ferment on the vine, so the wine is full of tiny bubbles which prick the tongue to produce a very pleasant sensation.

"We have a blessed land here, sir," he said. "A little Egypt. The oranges of Bethany in Perea have no match anywhere in the world. I think it is a touch of salt in the soil that gives them their sweetness, for you know the old saying, 'The strongest light is neighbor to a shadow,' and again, 'The sea is the mother of the sweetest water.' Also the olives of Jericho are held the rival of those of Greece. No, you will travel far to find a better land, and if Jerusalem is full of madmen, then at least it can be said that we Jews have all our madmen in one place."

I was about to say, "As Rome has hers," but since this might involve him and me in a charge of disloyalty to Tiberius, I refrained. Instead I asked him how it was that he, a Jew, could sit at a table and drink wine with me, a Gentile.

"Why, as to that, sir," he replied, "didn't Moses sup at

Pharaoh's table many a time? To be sure he did. And how are we to treat the stranger as a brother as the Torah tells us, and yet call ourselves defiled if we share a glass of wine with him or a slice of lamb? That's just priestcraft, sir, and all this purifying ritual, as they call it, is a source of great profit for the Levites in the Temple. Keeps a whole stream of gifts going in—goats and sheep and doves —all of which the priests keep or at least turn to their profit.

"Oh, every now and again when my wife gets after me, I go up there myself and am purified with a pigeon or two or maybe a goat and then it's back to business as usual. But man can be ruined by this defilement business, you know, for the scribes will tell you that you can be defiled without even knowing it in a thousand ways. Defilement isn't a voluntary act at all. If we took the scribes seriously, we would be running to the Temple every day being cleansed. But that's all part of the Jerusalem madness, sir. And the cure is to stand out in the sun on a summer's day and look at the good grass and hear the baaing of the flocks in the fields around. There's more purification in that than you'll find in all the rites in the Temple."

Well, he was a fine fellow, my innkeeper, and the wine was good, so we had a cup or two more. Having learned that I had recently left the palace of Herod, he was astute enough to tell me that if he should hear a troop of horse coming down the road during the night, he would give me warning.

"I have watchmen posted on the road in both directions," he said. "In my business I like to be prepared for guests. Without wishing to pry into your affairs I would judge from the lateness of the hour of your arrival in Emmaus, you left Jerusalem unexpectedly."

I thanked him for his concern and he asked whether I was returning to Rome and said that the ships at Caesarea to the north were still crowded with Jews returning to their homes after coming to Jerusalem for the Great Pasch. "You might do well to go on to Haifa or to Tyre," he suggested. But that would mean a journey through Galilee, which I wished to avoid, so I decided instead to go to nearby Joppa.

Just before going to bed, we were both startled by a knock at the front door, but I sent Caballus, who was snoring in the corner, to see who might be there. He returned, having peered through the grill, to announce that those who knocked were not soldiers, so the landlord admitted them. There were three men and they wanted lodging for the night and food, for they said they had been all day walking from Jerusalem and had not eaten since noon. The landlord soon set before them the remains of the lamb and a jug of wine. I paid them no attention but went off to bed. Caballus was sleeping on the floor with his sword by his hand.

Wine is a great inducer of dreams and my sleep was troubled that night by visions of buildings falling, great waters bursting through the passes of mountain ranges to flood the plains beyond, and lastly a dream of myself being lowered into a hole in the ground at the bottom of which there was no air. I awoke stifling to be comforted by the sound of Caballus snoring. But I lay awake the rest of the night brooding over what may be the meaning of such dreams of disasters, for no dream is sent by the gods that is without meaning, and those who ignore these messages and warnings deserve whatever misfortune befalls them. I determined when day at last dawned to find a soothsayer as soon as possible and get an interpretation and advice, if disaster threatened, on how to avoid it.

The following morning I found two of the Jews who had arrived the night before waiting at the office to settle their bill. Philip had, of course, taken care of my affairs and Caballus was getting the horses and mules. An argument broke out between the Jews and the landlord. One of them said, "You have made a mistake in the bill, sir. There were three of us to supper last night, and you have only charged for two."

"My friend," said the landlord, "I am an honest man, and I served only two of you. Why do you say there were three?" This greatly surprised and interested me.

The two looked at each other in consternation, and one said, "We were indeed three, sir, and have no wish to cheat you."

"Nor I you," said the landlord. "There were two of you and no more, and you will not get me in trouble with the authorities by getting me to overcharge you. That trick has been tried before. Now," he continued, "bread, wine, and meat for two is an asse each, bed is two more apiece, and I will charge you one further for the use of the toilet, making a total of seven."

The men shrugged, paid, and went out. I was very puzzled. What was the object of the landlord in pretending that there had been but two of them when I knew there were three? These landlords are very sly and without a doubt he had a reason for entering in his accounts that he had served dinner to only two and insisting that no third man had been present.

What that reason was, of course, I could not guess, but I was glad that in the warmth of the wine and companionship the previous night, I had said nothing to him which could compromise me with Herod. If you wish to live long and prosper, trust no one—that is an excellent rule, of the truth of which I have had many reminders in my life.

When the horses had arrived and Caballus had put my moneybags safely before him, slung from his saddle, we set off. Having now some suspicion of the landlord, I was careful to take a very cordial good-bye of him, assuring him of my friendship and inviting him to visit me at my villa in Crete should fortune bring him that way.

"Why, sir," he said, "that is not impossible, for I have a brother Joseph, called Barnabas, in Crete, and my father and mother are still living there." And so we parted.

IX

IT IS A PLEASANT ROAD indeed that leads from Jerusalem to Joppa on the western shore of the Inland Sea, particularly when traveled in the spring. At that season a light wind, soft and warm as milk, flows from the sea over the land, bringing with it the scent of the wild flowers which abound in the fields around. Prominent among these, lying in swatches on the ground like drifts of snow, is that magical flower narcissus which displays in its center the initial of that god of the Greeks who fell into a pool and was drowned while lost in admiration of his own beauty. A few blood-red poppies were already opened here and there, and in the folds of the fields were sheets of lupine, both blue and yellow, of which the seeds, steeped in water to remove their bitterness, are the staple food of slaves.

Having eaten my fill of them in my time I cannot abide them or lentils either. Yet to see them growing wild in such profusion made me wonder whether a profit might not be derived from harvesting them to sell in Rome when corn is short, as is often the case. You have heard, I am sure, the saying that the Nile flows with the bread of Rome, for on the flooding of that river each spring depends the supply of Roman corn. When the flood is poor, Rome goes hungry.

I told Philip to make a note to inquire the lowest price at which lupine seeds, bought in bulk, could be obtained and whether they were efficiently harvested or merely picked as needed. It is the fool who says that money does not grow on trees—slaves and the very poor know different. A keen man will, as the saying goes, pick a coin out of a dunghill with his teeth.

We had hardly gone a mile through this very pleasant country, which even affected Caballus so that he started to sing an interminable German song of which each verse ended with the words *hoch, hoch hoch,* when we fell in with the two Jews from the inn. They were on foot, had staffs to help them walk, and were so busy with talking to each other that Caballus, riding ahead, nearly knocked them down in the road before they were aware of his presence and hastily darted aside. One in fact fell, his robe (hitched up above his knees for walking) falling and tripping him. His companion picked him up and they stood to the side, heads bowed, to let us pass.

Now I wanted to find out about the third among them, who had disappeared during the night and whom the landlord at the inn had pretended not to have seen. So I reined in my horse and offered them each a stirrup to help them on their way. They might have refused on the grounds of defilement (a shadow, let alone a touch, can defile among these lunatics) but they did not. One was a strapping fellow, light-haired and light-skinned, and I asked him whether he was not one of the Macedonian Greeks, like Philip.

"No, sir, I am from Galilee," he said. "There are many like me there." His name was Cleophas and his companion, rather smaller, with the birdlike lightness of an Arab, was Thaddeus. They spoke a rough Greek, which produced a few chuckles from Philip, saying for instance *strati* for *street,* which really means a ruler, and *salassa* for *sea.* The Jews generally have trouble pronouncing the *th* sound, and this was once a test among them, separating one group from another.

Having inquired where they were going and to what

purpose, and having received only vague replies, I asked who was their companion who had eaten with them the night before. They both looked up at me surprised.

"You saw him, sir?" asked the one called Cleophas.

"Of course I did," I replied. "I don't know what the landlord's game was pretending that there were only two of you, but there were three of you sitting at the table. The third was as big as Cleophas here. Who was he?"

"Sir," said Cleophas, "it is a marvel to us that you saw him also. We had thought the landlord saw him, but he did not."

I had about my neck a whistle which I could use to re-call Caballus if he got too far ahead of me. I blew on it, and he came back at full gallop, still singing that intermi-nable song of his with the *hoch hoch hoch* ending to each verse. I cut into the song before he got to the *hoch hoch hoch*.

"How many men were at the door of the inn last night?" I demanded.

"Two," said Caballus. "Those two."

"Think," I said. "Didn't you let in three—these two and one other?"

"Only two," said Caballus.

"But there were three," I protested. "I saw three."

"You drank too much wine," he replied. "There were only two."

"Three of them sat down to dinner," I insisted.

"Two," said Caballus. He said it again in Greek, and then in German and held up two fingers and pointed to the two Jews with me.

"Two, master," he concluded. "No more. But then you were only half drunk. If you had been fully drunk like a good German, you would have seen four," and delighted with his sally, he galloped off again.

"Who was the third man?" I asked when he had gone.

They were not at all willing to tell me, and I had to press them again and again before they finally answered me.

Then they said, "Jesus of Nazareth, who was crucified and who has now risen from the dead."

I could not believe it. Yet the men were entirely serious and certainly they had no reason for deceiving me.

"Tell me all you know about him," I said, hiding my surprise, and beckoned Philip to come closer so that he also could hear and record what he heard.

So they told me about him for the rest of the journey. While they spoke the sweet westerly wind flowed around us full of the fragrance of new grass and of flowers. The sun was warm on my shoulders and face and brought a great ease to my body. The shadow of my horse and myself made a pleasing pattern on the road, and even the sound of the hoofs had a soothing and consoling rhythm. Philip tells me it is disgraceful and contrary to all literary rules to record these things, since they have nothing to do with what was said. If I wish to achieve elegance in my writing, he insists, I should stay rigidly with the facts and firmly throw out all that does not concern them. Yet it seemed to me that the warm spring wind, the peaceful clopping of the horse's hooves on the road, the blue mist of lupine around and the gleaming mounds of cloud passing slowly over the sky had something to do with what was said. Do not the circumstances in which a story is told lend credibility to it? Stories of ghosts are certainly well told by the flicker of torchlight, and a pleasant countryside lends support to tales of wonders and well-meaning spirits such as that which followed. Here is the story Cleophas and Thaddeus told me about this Jesus.

"Sir, I would first of all explain that my brother and I are shepherds and in the wintertime we bring our flocks down from the heights where they have been eating the grass in the summer, to the lower hills, to escape the frosts and the winds and to find better forage in the valleys. This we do every year. Now in the time of Augustus when the census of all the world was taken at the orders of the Emperor, we had our flock in the hills around the Pools of Solomon near Jerusalem. The weather was very cold that year, sir, and the east wind stark and the sheep were huddled together in the field around us, for so it is with us shepherds of Israel who live with our flocks and do not drive our sheep but teach them to follow us and so can call many by name.

"My brother slept in our tent on this particular night, and I was on watch outside lest wolves should come, or wild dogs which are driven to attack the flocks in winter. Imagine my amazement when in the middle of the night the sky became as light as day and the sharp wind as warm as it is now, sir. All this happened in an instant. I was terrified, cried out, and fell to the ground. My brother, hearing my cry, rushed from the tent and was amazed by the light. The other shepherds with us—Ephraim, and Samuel the Small, and Judas of Hebron—these all also can testify to the sudden blinding light which aroused them too. Then a voice bade us raise our heads and we saw an angel of God standing before us, clad in shining garments and with a face as bright as the sun so that we had to put our arms before us so as not to be blinded by the light of this angel.

"The angel said, 'Do not be afraid. I bring you news of great joy, a joy to be shared by the whole people. Today in the town of David a savior has been born to you; he is the Messiah, the anointed of God foretold by the prophets. Here is a sign by which you will know him: you will find a baby wrapped in swaddling clothes and lying in a manger. That is he.' Immediately a host of angels filled the sky and they sang most beautifully, praising God and saying, 'Glory to God in the highest Heaven and peace to men who enjoy His favor.' The sound of that singing, sir, filled the whole world and echoed back from the hills. Then the song died and the angels departed and night was restored.

"We decided to go immediately to Bethlehem, which is the city of the Tribe of David, to find the Messiah. And indeed we found a woman in a cave which was used as a stable, who had just given birth to a child. The child had been wrapped in birth cloths and lay in a manger full of hay. There was really nothing special about the baby, but we knew it was the Messiah, and gave the mother sheepskins for a covering for it. Then three magicians arrived, and a star shone very bright in the sky over the cave. They said they had consulted their charts and from them had learned that the time had arrived for the birth of the one who was to be king over the Jews and the whole world. They would find him at that place where this star stood directly overhead. Then they gave the baby gifts of gold and incense and myrrh. The name of the mother was Mary and of the father, Joseph, a stonemason, as we learned, of Nazareth in Galilee.

"That child was the same Jesus of Nazareth who was crucified a little while ago and who has now risen from the dead."

"What else do you know of him?" I asked.

"Sir, for many years we knew nothing more of him," said Cleophas. "Our lives are spent among our sheep, away from cities, and we pay little attention to the world. We saw no more angels, sir, but about three years ago we began to hear stories of wonders and we knew that these were the work of the Messiah about whom the angels had told us and whom we had seen almost as soon as he was born. The first of these wonders was a small thing—the turning of water into wine at a wedding feast at Cana. Then we heard of lepers being cured and of the blind being healed and the lame and crippled being made whole. But although many people saw these miracles, most doubted them and there were stories that these were just tricks and not real wonders, or if they were real wonders they were performed not by God but by Satan. It was I, Cleophas, who was sent by the other shepherds to find this miracle worker and ask him whether he was the Messiah who was born in the stable in Bethlehem. This was two years ago.

"He was not hard to find, for the whole country knew

about him, and such crowds followed him that he had at times to escape from them, going up into Syria and at other times into the wilderness beyond the Dead Sea or again into the mountains. Most of the people came to see marvels, not to listen to him. I found him in the wilderness with a crowd of many thousands around him who had followed him there. Those people came from Tyre and from Sidon as well as Judaea. They pressed around trying to touch him, and his disciples had to struggle to prevent his being crushed to death. Even his touch cured demoniacs and the blind, and every kind of sickness.

"But in the hubbub and the struggle about Jesus I could not get close enough to ask him whether he was the Messiah who had been born in Bethlehem. At last he and his disciples got everyone to sit down, saying he had a message for them. We all believed that he was going to tell us openly that he was the Messiah and lead us with the hosts of Heaven at our backs to the conquest of the world.

"But what he told us was a great mystery which even now I do not understand. He told us to love our enemies instead of hating them. He told us to be glad if we were poor, for we would inherit Heaven. He told us to be happy if we were hungry, for we would be filled, and to be happy if we were full of sorrow, for we would soon be full of mirth. He said we were to bless those who cursed us, to pray for those who ill-treated us, and if we were struck on one side of the face, not to strike back but to turn the other cheek for another blow. If a man robbed us of a cloak, we were to give him our undergarment as well, and we were to give to anyone who asked us, and if we were robbed of goods we were not to ask for our property back or go to court to obtain justice.

"I did not understand what he said. He seemed to be raving. I did not understand why he allowed himself to be crucified. If angels were present at his birth, as we know they were, why was there nobody present at his death? That is a big mystery to my brother and me, sir. We thought perhaps he sinned, and so God his father deserted him. And yet, sir, could the Messiah sin? Is that possible?"

Cleophas had forgotten for the moment that I was a Gentile and he spoke to me for a moment as a Jew. Although I do not like the Jews I felt flattered.

"How did you meet him yesterday?" I asked.

"We fell in with him on the road," said Cleophas. "My brother and I are going to Joppa to talk to the merchants there who buy our wool. It will soon be time for the shearing, as perhaps you know. On the road yesterday, we were talking of the crucifixion of Jesus and met a man seated by the roadside who joined us, and asked us why we were looking so sad and talking so earnestly with each other.

"I said we were discussing the crucifixion, and he asked what crucifixion. We thought him the only man in Judaea who had not heard about it and asked him where he had been. So we told him all we knew and he showed a great knowledge of the prophets and their sayings concerning the Messiah.

"At this time, sir, we did not know who he was. He was only a stranger, met on the road. At Emmaus we asked him to join us at supper and you saw the three of us admitted to the inn. At supper he blessed the bread and the wine and gave them to us and said, 'Whenever you eat this bread or drink this wine, do it in memory of me.' His face glowed as bright as an angel's, but he told us to say nothing to rouse the others at the inn; to do our business in Joppa and return to Jerusalem and meet with his followers there, when everything that was mysterious would be made clear to us."

"It was an apparition then, a spirit?"

Cleophas shook his head. "Sir, a spirit cannot eat bread and drink wine," he said. "Does a chair creak under a spirit when it sits down? No, sir. He was no spirit but flesh, bone, and blood as are you and I. And, sir, when he took the bread and wine and blessed them, the marks of the nails were on his hands and blood was streaming from them."

They told me many more things about Jesus which I will tell at another time. Together we stopped to eat at a little shack set up at the side of the road and Cleophas gave me bread and wine and said, "Let us eat this bread and drink this wine in memory of him."

Since I needed a charm against the disasters which my terrible dreams seemed to forecast, I did so. Then I inquired at what price they intended to sell their wool and what quantity would be available, for marvels should not so occupy a man's mind that he neglects profit. That way lies ruin.

X

JOPPA IS A PILGRIM PORT and was before the time of Tiberius a notorious haunt of pirates. A hundred of these sea robbers were crucified on the walls of the city and many hundreds more sent to work in the copper mines of Cyprus and in the galleys of Rome before the piracy abated, though it was never subdued. Those sent to the galleys were first blinded, since a galley slave has no need of sight. Blinded men need not be heavily chained and so the burden of the galleys is lessened and they are swifter under oars or sail. It is held an act of kindness to a slave to relieve him of chains by blinding him, but those who say so have not been slaves.

It was at Joppa that Andromeda, having offended Neptune, was chained to a rock and constantly torn and bitten by a sea monster slain by Perseus, who married her. The place where the goddess was chained is still to be seen, and those who doubt this story are reminded that Scaurus, Pompey's captain, coming to Joppa, stole the carcass of the monster and transported it to Rome, where it was seen by multitudes of people before it deteriorated in the wet weather. It is said to have been a serpent fifty feet in length, though a piece was broken off towards the tail. The head was like that of a bull. The sword cuts of Perseus were to be seen plainly on the neck and head and the eyes in the enormous head were no bigger than hazelnuts.

At Joppa I parted from Cleophas and his companion. We came to an agreement concerning the wool crop, and when that was done, I made them a present of money and begged them to offer a sacrifice for me, for I was still troubled by the dream I had had in the inn at Emmaus. That dream became all the more grave in my view when I learned at Joppa the terrible news that Sejanus, advisor to Tiberius, had fallenly suddenly from the Emperor's favor and been killed.

Now I thought I saw clearly the evil meaning of my dream, in one part of which waters bursting from beyond a mountain barrier were flooding a fertile plain and in another I was being lowered to the bottom of a deep well where I suffocated for lack of air. Lucius Aelius Sejanus was for me the mountain which had held back the floodwaters. His father was Seius Strabo, who had been prefect of the Praetorians and had been adopted into the powerful family of the Aelis. When the worthy father became governor of Egypt, his son Sejanus became prefect of the Praetorians, and finding them with no established headquarters but scattered about the city in rented quarters, he concentrated them in a camp on the Viminal Hill, improving their lodging, their discipline, and their importance in the city.

The Praetorians might indeed trace their rise to eminence in political affairs to Sejanus, who with so powerful a force at his back was soon the biggest figure in Rome, second only to the Emperor. And the Emperor, it must not be forgotten, had retired from Rome (at the suggestion of Sejanus, it must be admitted) going first to the village on the Ligurian coast and then to Capri.

It is impossible for a man in my position to deal successfully with emperors or kings. These hold so exalted a position that they have no need to bargain. A word from Tiberius, for example, has many times brought down the most powerful men of commerce and even members of the Senate of honorable lineage. All that is needed is for an officer to be sent with the message, "The Emperor requires your death," and the man is destroyed. If he does not honorably open his veins and, sitting in a warm bath, die easily from loss of blood, then the officer will cut him down, for that is his duty. No, one cannot deal with emperors. But with the ministers of emperors, who cannot say "Live" or "Die" with final authority, and who hold their position by making all things appear favorable, it is possible to do business.

I had done much business with Sejanus. Everybody but Tiberius knew that he dreamed of being emperor himself, and so he was believed the instigator of the death of Drusus, the brother of Tiberius who was poisoned, and also of the two sons of Germanicus, whose deaths, together with that of their mother Agrippina, I had discussed with Pontius Pilate when we received confirmation and details of them.

When Rome was short of corn (and this was often the case, for it no longer paid Italian farmers to grow corn faced with the floods of Egypt) it was to me that Sejanus turned to relieve the shortage and save him from the ire of Tiberius. I will not weary you with details of such transactions which drew me deeper and deeper into the Egyptian corn trade, but you may be sure that, whatever my profit, I passed on a generous share to Sejanus.

The profit from the sale of the corn itself was low and indeed it was possible at times to so arrange matters that on the books at least it could be shown that the corn had been sold at a loss—a necessary precaution since the anger

of Tiberius would certainly be stirred by charges of prof-
iteering out of a Roman famine. It was in the requisition-
ing of ships, the hiring of granaries, the sale of amphorae
that the real profits came to me. But to those who have a
mind for business, these matters are already known and to
those who have not, they are entirely without interest, so
I will not dally with them beyond saying that I had already
concluded that he who owned the Egyptian grain fleets
must soon be the richest man in the world.

It seemed, according to the story reaching Joppa by the
ship *Argos* just arrived from Ostia, that Sejanus in his ambition had at last overreached himself. He had planned to
marry into the family of Tiberius—that is to say, into the
Claudian family—and had been bold enough to approach
Tiberius with this suggestion. Tiberius turned the matter
down, saying that while he himself had some such marriage
in mind, yet he would wait awhile to consider it. Then a
letter was sent to Tiberius, put between the pages of a
book written by Claudius, the idiot grandson of the noble
Livia, wife of the divine Augustus, purporting to show
that Sejanus plotted to assassinate Tiberius and become
emperor.

I do not for a moment believe that this letter was au-
thentic. After all, Tiberius at the time was over seventy
years of age and it was no secret that he was gradually failing in health. Of course, he tried to prove his strength by
staying up all night at banquets drinking a gallon or so
of wine and making repeated visits to the vomitorium,
where a cup of pitch water quickly vented his belly and
enabled him to continue his debauch. Still this was not the
old Tiberius, who in his army days had been called "Bi-
berius Caldius Mero," that is to say, "Drinker of wine with
no water added." Then, Tiberius could drink not only all
day and all night but for a whole week and he ate as heartily
as he drank and loved to be served at table by naked slaves—
male and female.

So there was no need for Sejanus to plot to assassinate

Tiberius. He had only to wait and, with the Praetorians at his back, seize power when Tiberius died. No. It was plain that there was a plot against Sejanus, instigated by the friends of the dead Germanicus and of his sons, of whom the only survivor was Caligula—Little Boots.

So perhaps it was Caligula who was behind the plot, though he was still young and certainly not bold by nature. Whatever the facts, Sejanus, expecting to be announced Protector of the People before the Senate, was instead denounced by Tiberius, deserted by the Praetorians who had quietly come under the command of another, Macro by name, and put to death within a day or so of Tiberius' letter of denunciation.

"He was paraded through the streets and the mob threw dead cats and old eggs and horse droppings at him," said Nestor, who was the captain of the *Argos*. "When he tried to cover his face with his cloak the mob shouted to him to uncover or they would kill him there and then.

"Everybody in Rome hated him, sir. You know that. The Romans loved Germanicus, who had given Rome back its lost eagles, particularly the eagle of the Twenty-ninth legion. Well, right or wrong, they blamed the death of Germanicus on Sejanus and then when news came of the murder of Agrippina, his widow, and her two sons—all said to be the doing of Sejanus—why, there was no end to the fury of the crowd.

"He was taken to jail and put in a cell under the Emperor's residence. The Senate sentenced him to death, but he wasn't allowed to go out decent, cutting his veins. He was hacked to pieces by his own men—the Praetorians. He was stabbed in the groin and in the throat and in the belly and an ear cut off. I know what I'm talking about here because I saw the body.

"It was flung down the Stairs of Mourning, as is the custom with criminals, and it lay there on the steps three days while everybody kicked at it or beat it with clubs or thrust swords into it. There was one fellow used to put on quite

[71]

a show. He used to bring a basket of stray starving cats and let them loose to tear at the meat, and you should have heard the people laugh to see Sejanus reduced to cat food. This witty fellow even had a little ditty he used to recite that went:

> "Hey Sejanus, what are you at?
> You first starved Rome; now feed a cat.
> Noble lord, you've lost your wit
> And will soon reappear as cat shit.

"You should have heard them laugh over that, sir. It was as good as any comedy turn you've ever heard. As good as Calipedes—remember how he used to imitate a long-distance runner and never move one inch from where he stood on the stage?"

Nestor rubbed the tears of mirth from the corner of his eyes with his hands. He was a good-natured fellow, red-faced from drinking Greek wine, which contains too much resin, but with hair entirely white. I had met him once or twice before and found him honest, for he rarely broke into his cargoes for his own profit, though on every voyage one expects a 10 percent "sea loss."

I talked with Nestor in the cabin of his ship where we could be private (into every wall is built an ear) and had only Philip with me. Caballus stood on deck (a trifle nervous, for he disliked ships as do all Germans though they are said to come from seafaring stock) lest he be needed. "This fall is very sudden," I said. "So great a man as Sejanus cannot be brought down in a week or a month or even a year. Have you nothing more to say about it privately?"

"Sir," said Nestor, "I have only this to say. When I cleared Ostia the wind blew strong from the southeast, though at this time of the year, as you know, I would have expected a northerly."

Philip was mystified by this remark but its meaning was clear to me—and frightening. Capri lies southeast of Ostia and hard by Naples. Nestor meant that it was the rage of

Tiberius alone, and not any plot by others, that had brought down Sejanus so quickly.

Why this sudden rage? I knew something of the mind of Tiberius. Mind you, I had never met him, but who knows a man's slaves knows the man and I had my informants among his household and in every household of importance in Rome. How else was I to survive? No one had told me of any enmity or quarrels or even coldness between Sejanus and Tiberius. Yet I knew that Tiberius never acted suddenly and an action that appeared to others spontaneous was actually the result of long deliberation and equally slow decision.

For a long time then, Tiberius must have planned the end of Sejanus. I wished I had Pilate to talk to or, better still, Herod, for they both had agile minds in such matters and could readily find the deep and hidden meanings in the actions of others.

Alone, with only Philip as a confidant, I concluded that Tiberius had been aware of the ambition of Sejanus for some time, revealed by the proposal that Sejanus should marry into the imperial household. He had decided then to destroy Sejanus, but delayed doing so until Sejanus had first himself destroyed the family of Germanicus. That done, Tiberius could kill Sejanus and let the people think he had done so because of the death of the widow of Germanicus and her two sons.

I admit that this was not a very subtle explanation of the Emperor's actions and any schoolboy could think of something deeper. Indeed, I now think that Caligula, who had been summoned to Capri, had had some hand in the matter. He was a vicious youth and like Tiberius loved cruelty and lust. It is said that Caligula was the instigator of the famous "minnows" of Tiberius—young boys who went swimming with the Emperor and, diving below the water, nibbled at his testicles and penis to excite him. Yes, that was one of the pleasures of Tiberius at Capri and he had many others, having sent to Egypt for the book called *Ele-*

phant, which is said to be the largest and most detailed description of sexual pleasures ever compiled. The title does not refer to the great beast, elephant, but to its smooth tusk of ivory and so you may make your own deduction as to what it implied.

Tiberius had no imagination and so had to have suggestions from others regarding new kinds of sexual pleasure. Caligula, who was rumored to have had intercourse with his own sister Drusilla while still a boy, had an extraordinary imagination in this area. So the two suited each other, Caligula feeding the lust of Tiberius in return for safety. It was Caligula who suggested to the Emperor the use of flies, stripped of their wings, for stimulation, but I have good authority for believing that Tiberius himself devised the amusement of chaining young girls and throwing them into the clear waters off Capri so that he might watch them drown—his desire greatly increased by their convulsions and writhings. He found these writhings, followed by the stillness of death, a perfect parallel of the sexual act.

It certainly seemed to me on reflection that Caligula was behind the fall of Sejanus, but at the time I heard the news from the sea captain Nestor I could think only as far as Tiberius. I immediately wrote to both Pilate and Herod giving them all the details I could of the fall of Sejanus, and assuring them of my friendship and care for them, for often to preserve oneself you must first serve others, and when a storm threatens, no port is hostile to a seaman.

When that was done, I sought a certain man, Indarius, a Syrian, who owned a pytheness who was a great diviner. This woman walked around the streets of Joppa, sometimes in the day and sometimes at night, afflicted by her python and calling out strange words and phrases, most of which nobody could understand at all, for the spirits spoke to her in forgotten tongues or tongues unknown in the Roman world. She had a great reputation for the interpreting of dreams and I called on Indarius, and having agreed with him on the price, was admitted to the pythoness in her own room.

She was dressed in the most outlandish fashion and I was even afraid to be alone with her. On the other hand Caballus refused to come anywhere near her; and when I commanded him to accompany me, he handed me his sword, bared his belly and bid me plunge it in, for he would sooner die than be in the same room with the pythoness. So I had to be with her alone, and I can tell you I sweated with fear and carried in my hand a bone phallus as protection, having been assured that no female spirit could harm anyone who carried this object.

It is no small thing to be alone in the presence of an oracle or a pythoness. Indarius had cautioned me not to glance at her eyes for one moment, but keep my gaze on the floor. Several have been driven mad by the experience, for if the spirits are angry they deprive men of their wits. I had therefore inquired of Indarius what gift I could take the pythoness which would please the spirit that possessed her, and he said I might give her a pot of honey, which I indeed brought with me. The seer, clad in a robe made of the downy skins of bats with the dried carcasses of small snakes and lizards pinned here and there on it, stood in one corner of a room with a lamp at her feet which, flickering, cast an enormous shadow of herself about the walls and ceiling.

She did not speak in any one voice but in many—sometimes the voice of a child and sometimes a very deep voice and then a simpering voice like that of a male prostitute and then again a warm woman's voice, according to which of the spirits who possessed her elected to answer my questions.

It was the child who spoke first and said in tiny tones, somewhat singsong and with all the wrong emphasis on words, "You are the jar man. Why have you come here? Did you bring honey? You had better have brought some honey or I'll eat your brains."

Going on my hands and knees I put the jar of honey at the feet of the pythoness and she stooped and picked it up while the child spirit in her squealed with delight and did not stop until the pythoness had scooped a big glob of honey into her mouth with her fingers. "Jar man," said the simpering voice, "go away. I don't like you. You smell. You smell of something I can't stand. Look at my eyes. Look at my eyes. I have lovely eyes. Why don't you look at my eyes?"

This simpering voice had the attraction and at the same time the repulsion of a serpent. Who is there who does not feel the desire both to run from and at the same time reach out and touch a glittering snake? So I felt about the simpering voice, but resolutely kept my eyes at the feet of the pythoness, the sweat meanwhile beginning to gather on my face and neck.

"Be quiet," said the woman's voice. "Let us hear what he has to say for himself. Speak, jar man. But be careful you do not tell any lies."

So I told the spirits of my dream and asked what was its significance for me. But I had hardly finished speaking before the little child started crying out, "He's lying. He's lying. He's lying. That isn't why he's here at all. He's holding it all back. He's lying."

Then the simpering voice said, "That's why he smells horribly. Make him look at my eyes. Jar man, look at my eyes; you must look at my eyes."

"Yes, jar man," said the woman's voice. "Look up. Look at the eyes. You will see delightful things. Wouldn't you like to suck my tits? Come. Put out your big spittle-covered tongue and start sucking." I can assure you that the desire to obey such entreaties was very strong, and all the stronger when I saw the bat dress fall around the feet of the pythoness, so I was like a young man who first sees a woman put out the tip of her pink tongue at him as a gesture of assent. But I kept my eyes to the ground and then the graver voice of a man which I had not heard before spoke, in Ionic Greek reciting in a monotone, like the chorus at a play:

> "From the southeast the old wind blows
> In the life of the locust the old wind goes.
> The pigmy warrior brings pains and ills
> Seek the red door in the seven hills.
> Through the red door you must go
> Beyond lies all you wish to know."

But the child's voice cried out, "He's lying. He's lying. He's still lying. Make him come and lick honey and turn him into a dog."

A violent quarrel arose between the child and the simpering voice, the child screaming that I was telling lies and the simpering voice telling it to shut up because it didn't want to hear anything else I had to say. But the woman silenced the two of them. She was the real python and they were only guest spirits whom she could send away and had taken in only for her own amusement.

"It is true that you smell, jar man," she said. "You have a horrible smell. Every now and again I get a whiff of it and it nauseates me. Put aside the bone phallus and put your own tool into my honey jar. It is all ready for you—not a stitch of clothing to be removed in your anxiety. You will find it warm and soft and the greatest pleasure. Not many are invited. Come. I begin to writhe with desire."

But although the sweat was now breaking out on me heavily and I wanted to seize and ravish her, for her voice was even more inviting than the words she uttered, yet I remembered the warning of Indarius and did not move. Then the man's voice spoke again—the voice like the Greek chorus, but this time not in rhyme, but in the dialect of Naples. I will give you a sample, though Philip frowns at such vulgarity.

"Whoi don't 'e tell us abaht it? E's seen some fink wot makes 'im smell. What did you see, jar man?"

The simpering voice started screaming that it did not

want to hear and the child insisted that I should stop telling lies and only then it occurred to me what it was they
thought I was holding back.

"You mean about the Jew, Jesus of Nazareth?" I asked
and immediately they were all quiet. "I did not mean to
hold that back from you at all. He was crucified."

"Stop! Stop! Stop! Shithead! Corpse fucker! . . . Shut
up! . . . Shut up!" said the simperer.

"Quiet," said the woman's voice, which was that of the
real python. "Let him speak."

"Look at my eyes. Look at my eyes," said the simpering
voice. "I have something for you to suck. . . ."

"Quiet," said the python again. "Speak, jar man. What
happened to him after he was crucified?"

"He rose from the dead," I said. "He lives again—in the
flesh."

Immediately there was a terrible scream and a string of
abuse fouler even than that of the latrine slaves in Antioch.
A dozen arms lifted me up and hurled me across the room,
against the wall. My back and buttocks hit the wall but
I was thrown so high my head hit the ceiling and I fell to
the floor like a sack—the breath knocked out of me. A
whirlwind of stifling hot air rushed about the room, which
was filled with the smell of a cesspool. Tiny hands like a
child's started gouging at my eyes to pluck them out, and
the lamp at the feet of the pythoness was extinguished. I
could hear her moaning and threshing on the floor in a
fit. Then everything became still. Indarius rushed in and
clapped his hands over his nose because of the appalling
stench in the room. The pythoness stopped moaning and
writhing and, getting to her feet looked about her, bewildered. She discovered that she was naked and, seeing
the bat dress on the floor, reached for it, but finding of
what material it was made, flung it from her in horror.
Then she tried to cover her breasts with her hands and
retreated in shame to a dark corner of the room.

She was not a diviner any longer but just a thin rather

ugly girl; terrified at being naked in the presence of men. She started crying and although my back was stiff and my head ringing from being hurled across the room by the spirits that had possessed her, I gave her my cloak for cover. I had seen girls like her crying naked in the slave market many times, and I find these sights hard to bear. The four spirits—perhaps even more—that had inhabited her had gone, and she wasn't a pythoness anymore.

Indarius, when it was plain that the girl had lost her powers, became angry and threatened to sue me, and in the end I had to give him five thousand sesterces in damages to settle the matter, for he had had a good living from the girl and would now have to search for another possessed woman to replace her.

"How did you drive the spirits out of her?" he asked. "The exorcists at the Temple could not do it, for her own mother and father took her to them when she became possessed."

"I did not do it," I said. "They left when they learned that Jesus of Nazareth who was crucified had risen from the dead."

Indarius, of course, wanted to know all about Jesus of Nazareth and, hoping to reduce the price I would have to pay him in damages, I gave him what information I could. I told him he should look for Cleophas, who was still in Joppa, to learn more.

"What a fortune could be made if I could strike a bargain with such a magician or learn some of his secrets from him," he said. So it was that I was able to argue him down to five thousand sesterces' compensation for the loss of the pythoness—which had started with a demand for twelve.

When I prepared to leave, the girl followed me, which was natural since I had bought her. But I did not want her (she was not in the slightest attractive without the spirit in her) and I told her to go to her home, that I would give her a writ of manumission and set her free.

"Master," she said, "I have no home." Then she fell on the ground and kissed my feet and I could feel her warm tears falling on them.

So I was obliged to take her with me, and was put immediately to the expense of providing her with clothes. Slaves do not come free by any means. However, later I recalled the bat dress which had belonged to her and, sending for it, sold it at auction for three hundred sesterces, so not all was loss.

The girl's name was Tabitha. She went to Rome with me. Of course I now had to go to Rome instead of to my villa on Crete, to look to my interests following the death of Sejanus. Also the red door in the seven hills certainly had to be in Rome. That much of the spirit's message to me was clear. The sooner I found the red door and walked through it, the better. As for the rest of the message, I could understand that the old wind from the southeast was Tiberius but I was puzzled about the words "In the life of the locust the old wind goes."

"Perhaps it means that there is to be a plague of locusts and then a certain person will die," said Philip, whom I consulted as always.

"What is the life of a locust but eating everything that is in sight?" I said. "Perhaps there will be a famine. Or the Parthians will march against Rome and destroy the land."

That is the trouble with diviners. You need a diviner to divine what the diviner says. But it was certainly clear that I should go to Rome, both because of the oracle and to seek the favor of Macro, successor to Sejanus, now that Sejanus was dead.

BOOK II

XI

ALTHOUGH, HAVING HEARD of the death of Sejanus, it was necessary for me to go to Rome to attend to my affairs, it was dangerous for me to go as well. I might be identified in the mind of Tiberius as a friend of Sejanus (did I mention that the children of Sejanus were also slain when he fell and their bodies beaten and kicked by the Roman mob on the Stairs of Mourning? There were two or three of them, I think, and Sejanus had been very fond of them).

If Tiberius did decide to turn his anger on me, then my own body might decorate those terrible stairs shortly after my arrival. Yet I had no alternative, and to buoy up my hopes there was the prophecy of the pythoness that I would know all I wished to know by going through the red door in the seven hills. Certainly the seven hills could be no place but Rome, and I would not despite my apprehensions delay a day in going there. I had this also in my favor. I had become the most important factor in the shipment of corn from Egypt to Rome. If I were destroyed on the moment because of friendship with Sejanus, Rome might face a corn shortage in the autumn of the year because I alone knew how to organize the thousands of details involved in the supply from Egypt. But in going to Rome I missed my chance of witnessing many remarkable events concerning Jesus, for whose truth I have to rely on the account written for me by the physician Luke. Yes Luke, who you remember treated me when I became ill as a guest of Pilate, had himself become interested in the story of Jesus of Nazareth. It was natural enough that a doctor should be curious about one raised from the dead. It was to Luke then that Cleophas, whom I had met on the road to Joppa, turned for the account of the life of Jesus for which I asked him, and Luke wrote me an account of the life of the Nazarene based on his own inquiries and also an account of the doings of the followers of Jesus after Jesus had been crucified.

These Apostles, as they came to be called, met Jesus, according to Luke, many times after his resurrection from the dead. Luke says he was with them for forty days after his resurrection, settling their doubts, which were quite as strong as mine, and instructing them in the parts of the Jewish law or Torah which applied to Jesus as the Messiah. I am not going to bother you with all that he said about the Torah, for that is really just something for the Jews, and we Romans have plenty of equally important prophecies which have been fulfilled. When Jesus was with them, Luke wrote me, the Apostles were full of faith and constantly asked him when he was going to restore the kingdom of Israel. They thought of him as a Roman would think of Alexander, or a Briton would think of Vortigern; that is, as a leader with divine powers who would reestablish their nation and make it the greatest nation on earth, since they were (in their own view) the chosen people of God.

Jesus gave them only evasive replies to such questions though Luke isn't very clear in his account on this point. Jesus spoke to his Apostles not of the kingdom of Israel, but of the kingdom of God. Of course to the Jews that could mean the same thing. I think it did, for if (as they thought) they were the chosen people of God, then was not their country the kingdom of God? I myself like things plainly put, and I don't think that Jesus, raised from the dead, was entirely straightforward in answering the questions of his Apostles. You cannot blame them for being puzzled after they had not had the benefit of being present (as I was) when Pilate questioned Jesus, for he had said then quite plainly that he was indeed a king but his kingdom was not of this world, but his was the Kingdom of Truth. I remember distinctly the grave assurance with which he had said that. Also I remembered Pilate's sarcastic question, "What is truth?" and the look almost of pity which had come over the face of Jesus, knowing what pain the loss of truth had cost Pilate. (Pilate had said to me once, "Silence is beautiful, Theophilus, for in silence one does not have to consider what lie is being told and for what reason.")

Not even John of Zebedee, his closest friend, had been there when Jesus had plainly told Pilate that his kingdom was the Kingdom of Truth and not of this world. It certainly seems strange to me that he couldn't have plainly said to his own Apostles what he said without reserve to Pilate. Luke explained this, saying that the minds of the Apostles, fixed on a military deliverer, were not ready to receive such a denial of their expectations. To Pilate, after all, it meant little. But to Peter, John, James, and the other Jews it meant a complete reversal of the meaning of their scripture.

Well, perhaps I make too much of this whole point. Jesus did tell his Apostles something that might have consoled Herod, who thought him John the Baptist twice returned from the dead. He said that John the Baptist baptized with water, but that they would be baptized with the Holy Spirit. In that mysterious statement I think there is at least an oblique assertion that he and John the Baptist were not one. That might have allayed mad Herod's fears.

After Jesus had been forty days with the Apostles, during which time he frequently ate white food with them, and on one occasion let one of them put his fingers in the wounds made by the nails in his hands and the

[85]

spear in his body, he took them out to a little hill quite close to the place where he had been crucified and which is called the Mount of Olives, although there are only a few very old olive trees on it. There, he told them again that the "spirit" would soon descend on them and they were to return to Jerusalem. When the "spirit" had come to them, they would preach his doctrine throughout Judaea and Samaria and in fact in every nation on the face of the earth. When he had said that, he was lifted up off the ground and gradually enveloped in a cloud. The Apostles stood there staring at the sky, in which he had disappeared. Then two men, dressed in white, suddenly appeared among them and asked them what they were staring at the sky for. Jesus, they said, had been taken into Heaven and he would come back again in the same way—that is, out of a cloud and descending to earth—to walk among the people again.

All this, I warn you again, is from Luke's account, and you must certainly be aware that the Greeks are an imaginative people and love myths and wonders. However, Peter, and John have also assured me of the truth of Luke's statements, and it was from them that he got his story.

To go on, ten days after Jesus disappeared all the Apostles were together in the same room which had become their headquarters in Jerusalem and the rent of which I have heard was paid by the same Joseph of Arimathea who had given him his tomb for the burial. It was now the Feast of Pentecost, which is really a harvest festival of the Jews which falls on the fiftieth lunar day after the second day of their Passover. (The Jews have very involved methods of marking their feast days.) This day was, of course, the fiftieth day also since the resurrection of Jesus from the dead. Pentecost is a big feast for the Jews; and Peter, the chief of the Apostles and the others, being Jews, were gathered together to celebrate it. Mary, the mother of Jesus, was with them and Miriam of Magdala and Joanna and others. The city itself was packed with Jews from many parts of the world come to celebrate the harvest festival, and, as you may imagine, every civilized tongue on earth could be heard in the streets, for the Jews have converts to their religion in lands as far away as the Kush and Afghanistan.

Suddenly quite early in the morning (about nine o'clock our time) a violent wind struck the building in which the Apostles were gathered, which staggered under the blow though other buildings nearby were untouched. The timbers and walls creaked, the curtains dividing one room from the other were blown about like flags, tables and benches were hurled about, the dishes were sent tumbling to the floor, and all those present shrieked, thinking their end had come. As suddenly as it had come, the wind was gone, but a sheet of flame appeared in its place, hovering in the air. It hung there for several seconds near the ceiling and then separated into what seemed like tongues of fire, one of which came to rest on the head of each person present. Immediately all their fears left them. I will quote Luke's words on what followed.

"They [the Apostles] were all filled with the Holy Spirit and began to speak in foreign languages as the spirit gave them the gift of speech. Now there were devout men living in Jerusalem from every nation under heaven, and at this sound they all assembled, each one bewildered to hear these men speaking his own language. They were amazed and astonished. 'Surely,' they said, 'all these men speaking are Galileans. How does it happen that each of us hears them in his own native language? Parthians, Medes and Elamites, people from Mesopotamia, Judaea and Cappadocia, Pontus and Asia, Phrygia and Pamphylia, Egypt and the parts of Libya round Cyrene; as well as visitors from Rome—Jews and proselytes alike— Cretans and Arabs; we hear them preaching in their own language about the marvels of God.' Everyone was amazed and unable to explain it. They asked one another what it all meant. Some, however, laughed it off. 'They have been drinking too much new wine,' they said."

This being a harvest festival, the first of the new wine was being sold about the streets and in new wineskins, for there is an old saying that one does not put new wine in an old wineskin which will certainly burst.

Those who thought the Apostles of Jesus were drunk were not so foolish as to think that a man could speak several languages by drinking wine. Nothing is more common among drunken men than that they start singing and then they will amuse themselves by shouting out snatches of foreign phrases to show how clever they are—particularly in a place like Jerusalem, where every tongue under the sun is to be heard in the streets.

Peter, the chief of the Apostles, however, got up to a balcony overlooking the street, where he could be heard by a great number and the others stopped talking. Peter had a very strong voice and one that did not readily tire for, as I can assure you myself, a man who has been to sea even as a fisherman has to be able to shout down the wind.

He told the crowd plainly that he and his companions were not drunk and pointed out that it was only nine o'clock in the morning, so how could so many people be drunk at such an early hour? Then he said that the fact that he and his companions could now speak in a number of languages of which they knew nothing fulfilled the prophecy of the prophet Joel, who had said that the day would come when the spirit of their god would fill the people and they would be able to prophesy and see visions. Then he referred to David, who was one of the kings of the Jews and who was also a prophet. He wrote a song in which he said:

> My heart was glad
> And my tongue cried out with joy;
> My body too will rest in the hope

That you will not abandon my soul to Hades
Nor allow your Holy One to experience corruption.

This passage, quoted for me by Luke, was quite as mysterious to me as the saying given to me by one of the spirits who possessed the pythoness and it had been the subject of vigorous discussion by learned men among the Jews for many centuries. The fisherman Peter, who was quite without learning but filled with the "Holy Spirit," undertook to interpret it for them. He told the crowd who listened to him that the Holy One referred to had not been David himself, for his body was quite corrupted away and they all knew that, since David's tomb was a well-known shrine among them and those who had entered it knew that it contained only the dust of a few moldering bones. The Holy One referred to was none other than Jesus of Nazareth, who had been crucified by the Romans (this annoyed me, for the crucifixion had certainly been forced on Pilate), according to a preconceived plan of god, and had been raised from the dead. While he was on earth and before his crucifixion Jesus had worked many cures among them and preached to them. But few had believed him to be the Messiah.

Now he had worked the supreme miracle. He had been put publicly to death so that there wasn't the slightest doubt that he was dead. And he had raised himself from the dead and every one of them could testify that it was no spirit who had returned but the man-god Jesus himself. The Apostles had seen Jesus raised into Heaven themselves from the Mount of Olives, just outside of the city, and Jesus had told them to stay in Jerusalem when they would be visited by the Holy Spirit. That is what had happened to them that morning and that was why they could talk in any language to any man. They themselves were witnesses to the prophecy of Jesus, he said.

This address of Peter's made an impression on his listeners. The fact is that only a very small number of the Jews had anything at all to do with the crucifixion;

these, led by Annas and Caiaphas, had, I think, really been anxious to protect the people from being led astray by another false Messiah, encouraged into revolt against Rome, and thousands slaughtered as had been the case in the days of Varus.

Well, as I say, many of those who heard Peter and saw and heard the others talking in every conceivable language, decided that a very great wrong had been done and they asked what they could do to undo the injustice.

Peter told them they had only to repent it and to be baptized in the name of Jesus Christ when they would be saved from punishment and they would also be able to receive the Holy Spirit and talk in every language.

Luke says Peter spoke to them for a long time, using many arguments out of their law and quoting from the prophets with whole sayings with which he, Peter, was suddenly familiar. Certainly something very extraordinary had happened to Peter of which the great wind and the appearance of the tongues of flames over his head and the heads of his companions were only outward signs.

I myself can testify that when Jesus was brought before Pilate, Peter was nowhere to be seen. He was hiding. He had also denied, as I have said, that he ever knew Jesus, and acted in every way like a man in desperate fear. Now, however, he was bold to the point of recklessness and he even referred to that segment of the Pharisees (let me say again it was a small one, yet from its own point of view quite rightly motivated) who had asked for the death of Jesus as a perverse generation—that is to say, people opposed to the will of god—which is an even more terrible accusation than saying to a Roman that he is opposed to the will of the Emperor and the policy of the Senate.

I very much wish, as I said at the start, that I had been there to hear and see these things, but I was not. However, when I questioned Peter about speaking different languages he said he wasn't really aware of talking in Hamitic and Coptic and Persian and Greek.

"It seemed to me that I was talking in Aramaic, which is the language we always use among ourselves, and the language Jesus used when he spoke with us, but everybody understood us. But, Theophilus, the word of God is not to be imprisoned and held back by mere language. When God speaks everybody can understand for God is not bound by words."

Peter was a likable man, rather slow in thought, and often uncertain about decisions. Once I saw him off by himself, looking up at the sky with the tears streaming down his face. I could not tell whether he was waiting for Jesus to come again or remembering how he had betrayed him. Certainly he often confessed that betrayal of his, and it was no comfort to tell him that men have a right to protect their lives, and no man then need repent about saving his life by deserting a friend whom he could not save anyway. But that kind of good, sensible, Roman thinking was wasted on Peter and the Jews generally, who are inclined to hysteria more than any other people on earth.

XII

PERHAPS, AFTER ALL, I would have done better to dictate the facts of this testament to Philip and let him put them in good literary form. He has read what I have written so far and, having been asked to be quite truthful about it, he says it is poorly presented and does the exact opposite of what good writing should do. He says

[91]

my account puzzles the reader more than it informs him, and raises a great many questions which it does not answer. I was angry, of course, and it certainly seemed to me that I ought to beat him or at least deprive him of something by way of punishment for his disloyalty to me.

So seeking a more balanced critic, I sent my manuscript to Seneca, who had handled some business pleas for me and had a growing reputation as a writer and philosopher. I sent with the manuscript a handsome gift of wine, Greek raisins, and pickled herring of which he is very fond. He kept the manuscript for a very long time and then returned it to me with the following note:

"My dear Theophilus: Why do you concern yourself with madmen and idle superstitions? Are you not ashamed to have reached your age and be still dazzled by the miracles and wonders that keep the uneducated in subjection? I would not go across the street to see a man who had risen from the dead, but I would walk a thousand miles to talk with a man who had, by the powers of his mind, discovered some part of the significance of human life and could advise on the best way in which it should be spent. Of what use is it to rise from the dead (supposing there is any truth to this absurdity) time and time again, unless one has discovered a real purpose and significance to living? Would you really wish yourself resurrected to a repetition of your present follies? Enjoy your life, Theophilus. Harm no man. Learn to endure both happiness and pain with dignity and do not waste your time on childish miracles. I assure you that there is no magic without ignorance, and as ignorance is reduced, so magic evaporates.

"Your Jesus of Nazareth is but one of thousands of Jews who have been crucified, and the Jewish people, who have not learned to endure misfortune with dignity, have seized upon him as the miraculous healer of all their sufferings. They are a people steeped in magic and devoid of reason. Do not trust them. Of the gods we know nothing and can know nothing. Whether they exist or do not exist it is beyond the power of man to affirm or deny. Let man concern himself then with man and not waste his life on vain fancies concerning divinity. You waste your time with such stuff as you write now."

That was all he wrote. Not a word about the wine, the Greek raisins, or the pickled herring. That is the way with philosophers and lawyers. They pretend to be so interested in things of the mind, and principles, that mere bodily pleasures are below their notice. I don't think Seneca even read my manuscript. That is another thing about philosophers and literary critics generally. Give them something that runs contrary to their views and they dismiss it as nonsense and will not even look at it.

I was so angry with Seneca's letter that I threw it in the fire, but Philip saved it and pointed out that Seneca and Jesus of Nazareth had certain things in common. "They both say we should not harm our fellowmen," said Philip. "But Jesus of Nazareth goes further, for he says that if a man harms us, we should not take revenge but offer him an opportunity of doing us further harm."

"There is certainly madness," I said.

"Master," said Philip, "so it would seem. And yet possibly it is very sane."

"Show me the sanity of it," I demanded, still very angry with Seneca and hoping in my anger to expose Philip as a fool. For when you cannot strike one person, it sometimes affords relief to strike another.

"If a man is struck a blow and strikes back, this can only lead to further blows and which ever one of them wins the fight, the other will hate him and seek revenge," said Philip.

"And quite rightly, too," I said.

"However, if a man is struck a blow and does not strike back but instead offers himself for another blow and that also is struck and perhaps a third, then whoever strikes him will finally desist and wonder why no retaliation was attempted and then wonder whether he was justified in striking in the first instance. In the end such a man will come to be ashamed of striking one who does not resist and next time he will not be so ready to strike. If this were universally practiced, master, there would soon be no enmity between men, and no blows struck, for enemies would disappear. Certainly a man who does not strike back at you cannot be reckoned an enemy."

That took the wind out of my sails for a moment. But I soon saw the flaw in the matter. "Why," I said, "if such a policy were adopted among nations, what would mighty Rome be now? Nothing more than a smelly city on a smelly river infinitely inferior in power to any petty kingdom of Gaul. And would not the world then be deprived of all the benefits of Roman rule and Roman example and the Roman arts and Roman culture? Would you say then that that would be of benefit to the world? No, my dear Philip, the whole Roman experience shows how beneficial are blows even to those who endure them."

To this Philip could not make a reply, for the only reply possible was that Roman rule and Roman arts and Roman culture were not benefits to other nations, and such a view would not only be impious but nonsense. Peace will undoubtedly come to the world when Roman arms dominate the whole earth. Yet, reflecting later on the matter, I could certainly see how the doctrine of Jesus of Nazareth might hasten that happy day if all other nations adopted his views; but the Romans, who are eminently practical, refused to do so. Rome should in view of this certainly rejoice if the preachings of Jesus of Nazareth were spread among the Jews, the Persians, and the Germans. That was certainly something to bear in mind next time I had a chat with Pilate. Why not spread a doctrine of nonresistance and submission to all the world, while we Romans alone remained aggressive? The prospects were certainly exciting.

But to return to my manuscript. Philip had said that it raised more questions than it answered, so I asked him to list these questions and I would answer them. I brushed aside his objection that the answers should come out of the narrative, for that is just a matter of form and after getting Seneca's letter, I don't give a fig for form. Here are Philip's questions.

What is the Spirit, or Holy Spirit, that came in the form of a wind and tongues of fire and enabled the Apostles to speak in many languages in which they had no training?

Very simple. It is one of the manifestations of the god of the Jews. He appears in the form of a wind or tongues of fire or in the form of a dove.

Is the Spirit or Holy Spirit or the Spirit of Light the same god as the god of the Jews or is he a companion god of their god?

The Jews have only got one god, so the Holy Spirit must be the same god. But because he appears in the form of a dove or wind or fire does not mean that the Jews worship doves or wind or fire any more than we Romans worship a marble statue of a man with wings on its feet called Mercury. That is only the form in which the god appears to us and the statue only reminds us of his powers. (You will be surprised to know that it was Caballus who pointed this out to me. I once tackled him on the fact that the Germans worship trees and he said they did not, but merely regarded oak trees of huge size as places where their tribal gods lived now and then. Only the Romans, he said, were stupid enough to think that they actually were their tribal gods. This came as a great surprise to me.)

Did Jesus of Nazareth claim to be another form of the Jewish god; their god in the form of a man instead of in the form of a dove?

No. He said according to my friend Luke that the Jewish god was his father and his mother (Luke says) was

[95]

a woman called Mary who was impregnated by the Jewish god and bore him a son who was Jesus of Nazareth. So he couldn't be the same as the Jewish god, for a man cannot be his own father. He was a demigod like Hercules.

At this reply Philip asked me gently whether, if Jesus of Nazareth was a god (not a demigod), why couldn't he be his own father, since the gods have powers far beyond those of humans?

I am not going to try to answer that because it is a silly question. Once you get into a discussion of divine powers, anything is possible but discussion is not. For discussion must be based upon reason, and man cannot reason about what is divine, for surely the very notion of divinity demands that it be something beyond human reason.

I have put all this in to improve the manuscript to satisfy the objections of Philip and will now go on with the story of important matters which befell the followers of Jesus during the time I was absent from them.

Enmity soon arose between them and the Pharisees and Sadducees or at least the leaders of these two groups. (The followers of Jesus became known as Christians. That name was first applied to them in Antioch some years later, but it is a convenient word and I will use it when describing them from now on.)

The number of Christians had soon grown in Jerusalem to several hundreds. (Of the thousands who were converted when Peter first addressed the crowd most were from faraway places and not residents of Jerusalem.) The movement gained supporters from rich and poor alike and it had one remarkable custom. When Jesus was alive a rich man had come to see him and had asked what he must do to be certain of gaining paradise. Jesus told him he must not cheat or lie or steal, must honor his father, not commit adultery, worship the true god, and so on. The man said he did all these things and Jesus said to him that if he wanted to be perfect, he should sell everything he had, give the money to the poor, and follow him.

The rich man had very sensibly refused to do this and gone away. I would have done the same myself, and I have always noticed that the poor keep telling the rich to be poor. The rich never offer each other any such advice, so it is all based on envy.

Anyway, that suggestion of Jesus' was taken to the letter by all those who now followed his teachings. Luke assured me in his letters that everybody who believed Jesus to be the Messiah sold all his property and gave it into a common fund for his "brothers." All were fed out of this common fund. People took strangers into their houses and treated them as part of their family so long as they were Christians. They called each other "brother" and "sister" and if a man worked for wages he gave his wages not to his wife but to Peter or one of the other Apostles, who put the money into the common fund. (This led to some quarrels later.)

The house which Peter and John had now purchased for the Christian community near the Temple was no longer big enough for their gatherings, and so Peter and the Apostles would meet in the Portico of Solomon, which was on the east side of the Temple overlooking the valley of Kidron with, opposite it, the Mount of Olives. Here there was a big terrace which ran uninterrupted for two-thirds of the length of the Temple and adjoined the Court of the Gentiles so that non-Jews could come and talk to the Apostles. The two worked a great number of cures both of people who were sick and of others possessed by devils. They always worked these cures by calling on the name of Jesus of Nazareth and I do not doubt for a moment that this was so, for the very mention of that name had been enough to free the pythoness Tabitha from the spirits that possessed her. (She was a continuing expense to me.)

Of course the Sadducees, who differ from other Jews in that they do not believe in life after death, found this intolerable. Peter and John had already received a legal warning against mentioning the name of Jesus, and the

Sadducees then had Peter and John arrested and put them not in the Temple jail but in the jail in the city where thieves and others were confined. The two were out again the next morning, and were preaching in the Portico of Solomon shortly after dawn, saying that they had been released from prison by an angel. So they were sent for to appear before the Sanhedrin, a sort of council of priests among the Jews. Caiaphas was very annoyed. He would not even mention the name of Jesus himself, but said that John and Peter had both received a formal warning not to preach in *that* name. Instead of obeying they had filled Jerusalem with stories of Jesus and his doctrine and were working to put the guilt of the death of Jesus on the Sanhedrin and the High Priest. (That, of course, is where it belonged, as I myself knew. But that is beside the point.)

Peter was not in the slightest cowed by this lecture. He outright accused Caiaphas of putting Jesus to death and said that he and the Apostles must obey God before they obeyed man, and, ordered by God to preach the resurrection of Jesus from the dead, and cure people in his name, and spread his doctrine, they had to do so.

Caiaphas was so angry he wanted to have them put to death right then, but an older Pharisee called Gamaliel, who had a great following among the Jews and taught the interpretation of the Torah in his own school, cautioned against this. Gamaliel pointed out that when previous "messiahs" had been put to death, their followers were soon scattered and nothing more was heard of them. But matters seemed to be entirely different with the followers of Christ. Instead of being scattered after his death, they were more numerous and bolder.

"What I suggest," said Gamaliel, "is that you leave these men alone and let them go. If this enterprise is of human origin it will break up of its own accord, but if it does in fact come from God, you will not only be unable to destroy it, you may find yourself fighting God."

So the priests contented themselves with flogging Peter

and John and then turning them free after again warning them not to preach in the name of Jesus. They ignored that warning. I have given you this account to show what was the cause of the break between the Christians and the Jews of the Temple party. It was first: that the Sadducees did not believe in life after death and so abominated the story that Jesus had risen from the dead. Second: that the Pharisees (of the Temple only, for many others supported Peter and John and believed in them) having put Jesus to death for claiming to be the son of God or God himself, could not confess that they had done wrong, however many miracles and wonders they were confronted with. I have already pointed out that in this respect Caiaphas was in a very uncomfortable position and had my sympathy.

One further reason for giving you this account was to introduce the name of Gamaliel. For one of the scholars he taught in his Bible school was a man who became very important a few years later. His name was Saul or Paul—depending upon whether he was being Jewish or Roman at the time. He was a man of many parts.

I will now go on with my own story.

XIII

ALTHOUGH JOPPA is a port for pilgrims, the wind during the sailing season will scarcely allow a passage directly to Rome. The usual route is south to Alexandria and thence via one of the great corn barks, to Ostia, which is the port for Rome on the mouth of the Tiber. So I took a small sloop, comically named *Hercules,* to Alexandria and there arranged passage on one of my own corn barks to the capital. There were in any case several pieces of business to which to attend in Alexandria, concerning the coming export of the grain harvest, and when all these were attended to I paid a visit to my friend Tutmoshe, one of the remaining secret priests of Aten.

Tutmoshe was one hundred and eighty years of age at the time and had told me once when we were a little drunk together that he had decided to die on his two hundredth birthday. A sacred beetle which he had saved from being crushed under the hoof of a horse had promised him as many years of life as he wished, but he had decided that two hundred was enough.

"Life is a wheel which makes a complete revolution every sixty years," he said. "The first sixty years all is new and in any case, as infants and children, you do not recognize what is going on. The second sixty years you begin to detect certain things being repeated. The third sixty years these repetitions, or patterns, become so plain that you begin to lose interest in the world and turn your thoughts upon yourself. There is nothing more I can know about the world or about myself, and I will be content to join the gods and the divine pharaohs who have gone before me and live in the perfect order which they have established in the world above this world."

It was through one of the scribes of Tutmoshe that I had learned about the appearance of the phoenix in Egypt of which I had told Pilate. I naturally wanted to question him about this marvel and perhaps see the miraculous bird myself.

Tutmoshe lived in a large villa on the western side of Alexandria on the shores of a beautiful lake, among whose reeds the sacred ibis searched for their food. The villa was built of that green marble found in the mountains of Abyssinia, but the interior walls were plastered so that they could be painted with those charming scenes which delight the Egyptians. Of all the people in the world I think the Egyptians are the happiest. Their nature is mild and hospitable, they welcome foreigners, and their pharaohs and priests have many times been of foreign birth. They love music, dancing, and drinking, and indeed they excel in everything they do. They are happy to be known as grain growers to the world, and if they have one fault at all, it is that they cannot understand why everybody does not want to be an Egyptian.

When I arrived Tutmoshe was basking in the sun, lying in a small boat made of rushes such as the Egyptians make for river use, the boat itself floating on the lake. A sacred ibis stood on one leg at one end of the boat, guarding him, for he had long ago achieved divinity, and this was recognized by all wild creatures. They had no fear of him whatever. Fish came to his hands to be fed, birds often perched on his bony shoulders and told him secrets, and he could cause a lotus to bloom by holding his hand over the closed bud.

As soon as I arrived a tiny breeze, at his command, disturbed the placid surface of the lake and, caught in it, the light rush boat drifted to the shore and Tutmoshe left it. He was terrible to look at—nothing more than a mummy with the wrappings removed, for he was quite naked. I could not help but glance at his genitals and was comforted to find that they looked young. The thought of that failing power is for me the most terrifying prospect of old age. As for the rest of him, his bones almost pierced the skin and his teeth seemed to have grown entirely too big for his head so that he had difficulty closing his lips over them.

"Yes, at first glance I am very ugly," he said, for I couldn't hide my reaction. "Often I catch a reflection of myself in the polished moonstones in the hall or in the water of the lake and I am surprised for when I was a boy I was very beautiful. But that is the payment we make in return for the gift of time. In eternity, of course, no such payment is demanded and when I am free of time, I will be as beautiful as ever. Even you, Theophilus, will be without your big stomach and that sausage nose of yours which the phrenologists assure you is a mark of generosity."

One of his servants brought him a robe of saffron (that color sacred to priests of the sun) and he put this on and we sat together by a small pool into which the waters of a fountain fell with a pleasant sound. For so eminent a man I had, of course, brought a special present, though it is difficult indeed to think of what would be acceptable as a gift for a man who has lived almost two hundred years. But I had received from the Pretannic Islands a sphere as large as an apple of the black glass known as jet, held on a stand made in the form of a silver claw. Jet has always been precious in Egypt, and Tutmoshe received the gift with pleasure and great interest, inquiring the exact part of the islands from which it came and ordering one of his servants to place it below the sun disk which illuminated the wall of his bedroom.

"It is," he said, "a representation of night which is held captive in the claw of the stars until My Lord the Sun returns again to flood the world with warmth. How good and loving is My Lord. Even these old bones he does not despise, nor shrink from touching every wrinkle of my scaly skin. He pours his warmth into so foul an object as me as generously as he does into the pink and lovely interior of the lotus. He causes the great Nile to rise and everything to grow by the abundance of his love, and looks with equal tenderness on the newborn and the dying, on the criminal and on the just man. All creatures on earth are his children and he despises not one of them."

I was touched by this spontaneous outpouring of praise for his god, and when he was done, he surprised me by his ability to read my most remote thoughts and by asking a question which had nothing to do with his paean of praise for Aten.

"You come to ask me about the phoenix?" he asked. "You know that that holy bird dies and is born in Arabia, though it flies to Heliopolis, the city of the sun, in Egypt as soon as it is reincarnated. Did you not hear of its death and rebirth when you were in Judaea—for it is in those parts that this took place."

"No indeed," I said. "Nor anyone else who was there that I know of."

"Possibly it died and was reborn alone in the wilderness," said Tutmoshe. "Alas that no one should have been present. Yet that was undoubtedly the god's own desire. I saw only its flight at sunrise, coming from Judaea and surrounded by a host of other birds all joyously singing about it. The sky was full of them—swans, ibis, stork, flamingoes, peacocks, hawks, falcons, macaws, parrots, even the tiny sparrows of the streets. And in the midst of this heavenly host the phoenix, bejeweled in feathers of gold and scarlet, azure and turquoise, purple and emerald, and emanating around it a light as glorious as that of its father the sun. No pharaoh was ever more splendidly decked and attended than the sacred phoenix who, singing a song of triumph over death and of benediction for all, flew towards Heliopolis to pay tribute to his Holy Father in the sacred city of the sun."

"What does this portend?" I asked.

"The beginning of a new age," said Tutmoshe. "That is always the significance of the rebirth of the phoenix. The bird god dies and is reborn every fifteen hundred years. At its first recorded birth, three thousand years ago, the Old Kingdom of Egypt was founded under the first pharaoh. Records from that time are obscure and only partially translated, for our language has greatly changed since then. Much of the significance of this first recorded appearance of the phoenix is thus lost to us, yet the rise of Egypt was certainly foretold in that appearance.

"At its second appearance, fifteen hundred years ago, the portent had moved from Egypt northward to the land of Canaan. There our Father the Sun destroyed by his rays the evil cities of Sodom and Gomorrah, and the land of the

Canaanites was shortly afterward given over to the Jewish people, who till then had been but desert tribes without a homeland. Here in Egypt the New Kingdom also came into being and men turned from the worship of many gods to the worship of one true god, Aten, the merciful, the loving, the father of all. Aten, you know, revealed himself in a vision to the young Pharaoh Akhenaton, who built a new city, a paradise on earth, for the honor of Aten, but was murdered by the old priests. The age which started with the destruction of Sodom and Gomorrah, with the rise of the New Kingdom and with the worship of the one true god here in Egypt, is now ended. A new age is born and though it is hidden now, the whole world will know of it and be changed by it in the era which has just opened."

"Is this new thing hidden from you too, Tutmoshe?" I asked.

"No," said Tutmoshe, "it is not hidden from me. But you, Theophilus, are a child. And it is foolish to tell a child things which it cannot understand. So I will not tell you."

My disappointment at this reply was crushing. Believe me, I would have paid him ten million sesterces on the spot to have been told the secret although, on reflection, to a man nearly two centuries old, ten million sesterces is hardly an acceptable gift and it occurred to me that he would have found more acceptable one of the fragrant blue Nile lilies which grew in the fountain.

"You are quite right," said Tutmoshe, who could read thoughts without the slightest difficulty. So I reached and broke off a blue flower and put it in his withered hands. He took it, and put it behind his ear like a young boy in love and said, "See, it does not withdraw in horror because I am so old, but being a child also of My Lord, consoles and beautifies me." Then turning to the servant who stood always beside him, he said, "Bring a bowl of warm milk." A bowl was immediately produced and Tutmoshe, holding it in his lap and turning towards a small rock garden across the courtyard in which we were seated, said, "Come, sister, and drink."

You can imagine my horror when out of the rock garden there slipped one of the terrible gray asps of Egypt. It flowed in liquid menace across the terrace towards us, the head slightly raised and its awful hood extended. The sweat broke out on my neck and brow at its appearance, for even the look of these creatures, like that of the basilisk to whom they are related, is death. You are aware, I am sure, that the asp is foster parent to the basilisk, whom he hatches out of an egg taken from a cock, and it is from the asp that the basilisk inherits his fatal glance. I was then turned to stone as the asp, which was of great size, glided closer to Tutmoshe. It stopped when but a little distance off, raised its head higher and would have killed me with its death-dealing look had not Tutmoshe intervened to save me.

"Do not fear him, sister," he said. "He is your brother also. See how fear has set you two apart. Yet love could bring you together. Come. Take the milk from your brother's hand," and he gave me the bowl. I do not know how I did not drop it. Certainly my hand trembled as I held the bowl out to the serpent, so that the milk slopped about in it. The asp, weaving its hooded head from side to side, approached with fatal menace, and Tutmoshe, putting a hand on my arm to steady me, said, "Theophilus, which would you have—death or life?"

"Life," I managed to whisper. "Save me."

"You must save yourself," he said. "You fear her. Fear kills. You must love her. Love gives life. See how beautifully My Lord has shaped your sister. Every scale is a jewel and her hood as graceful as a pearl. Come, offer your sister the milk, in love, and not in fear."

Under the spell which he, being divine, could put about me, for a moment I felt an outpouring of love for the terrible serpent, a sense of intense and intimate involvement with it and of sorrow that it should be so universally feared and hated. The hood immediately collapsed and the asp gracefully dipped its head in the bowl of milk and drank. More than that, when it had drunk its fill, and with the milk still dripping from its jaws, it three times rubbed its cool head against my arm in a sort of caress and then moved back to the rock garden.

"When My Lord the Sun created earth, he brought order out of chaos," said Tutmoshe. "So the first of his laws is order. In obedience to this law, he caused the Nile to rise each year on the same day at the same hour, and to subside each year on the same day and the same hour. He caused the stars to take and keep their stations in the sky, and he himself, in his infinite love, appears each day with such regularity that we can tell exactly the moment when he will first lighten the eastern horizon, and the moment when he will be gone over the western horizon. He taught man, in his love of order, to count and to measure, and to organize, and to plan, and to work with his fellows, so that the Rule of Order, which is the first law of Aten, should be spread throughout the world for the good of all creatures on earth. Obeying the Rule of Order men out of chaos carved the fields and planted and irrigated them, and then men came together to govern themselves and cities were built and order was established everywhere by the aid of that grace of the one god which is called mathematics.

"The second rule of Aten is love—that all creatures should know and love each other as his children. This is a greater rule than the first, but it could not be applied until the Rule of Order had been established. Aten first revealed the Rule of Love to the Pharaoh Akhenaton (whose name means the Tool of Aten) in a vision. The Pharaoh tried to apply the Rule of Love by his own example and to this day you will find, here and there, pictures of the Pharaoh Akhenaton kissing his children and his wife and embracing animals and plants. But the older priests distrusted the Rule of Love and destroyed Akhenaton and his City of Love, contrary to the will of the one God. Therefore men were left with nothing but order and with the discipline and fear which, without love, order brought.

"Now tell me, Theophilus, who have just amazed yourself by feeding what you thought your deadly enemy, what rule will this new era, foretold by the rebirth of the phoenix, bring?"

"The Rule of Love—again," I ventured.

Tutmoshe shook his head. "That rule was brought once. God does not send his gift twice. Love is already here for men to use as you have yourself seen in loving your sister the asp. Think, Theophilus; think hard. The phoenix, you say, died and was reborn alone and unseen. Did you not see another die alone in Judaea—quite alone, deserted by his followers, unrecognized by others? Die and rise again?"

"You mean Jesus of Nazareth?" I asked.

"Yes. Jesus of Nazareth," said Tutmoshe. "Of what did he say he was king?"

"King of Truth."

"King of Truth," replied Tutmoshe. "So our most loving lord and god sent first the Rule of Order, then the Rule of Love (which was rejected), and now the Rule of Truth. And when these rules are established over all the earth, no one will die and all will live in the eternal happiness of the presence of god."

Tutmoshe glanced at the holy ibis, which now stood in the pool of the fountain. "The birds have known this for a hundred thousand years," he said.

XIV

To hear Tutmoshe talk of that Jesus the Nazarene whom I had seen reluctantly condemned to death by Pilate as the one who was to usher in the new age foretold by the rebirth of the phoenix came as a great shock to me. In a moment I saw again his face—quiet, strong, enduring, full of deep compassion—and the strong neck which supported his fine head. I recalled his words, "My kingdom is the Kingdom of Truth—it is not of this world." And his own words to me that he would be my friend all my life.

"Did you touch him?" asked Tutmoshe. "What else did he say?" It seemed to me that everything in that garden, the sacred ibis, the blue Nile lilies, and even the terrible asp, which now again approached, were straining to hear my answer. The ibis indeed put its head on one side and, moving closer, peered at me out of one jeweled eye. (It is said they are not truly birds but lesser gods in the form of birds. They cure with a look all those madnesses which consist in terror of water.)

"I offered him a cup of wine because he was a fine young man and because I have seen so many flogged slaves," I said. "But I scarcely remember much more of what he said. It was cold. And I had not had my breakfast."

The look of disdain from the ibis was unmistakable, but Tutmoshe smiled. "It is your blessing, Theophilus," he said, "that you never hide anything. It is your blessing too that Jesus of Nazareth offered you his friendship. No greater good fortune could come to you though you lived four times as long as I. He must have loved you."

This seemed to me nonsense and though I respected

[108]

Tutmoshe, who himself was divine, I told him so, for the gods are not served by lies but by truth. "How could he love me if he did not know me?" I asked. "I did not know him either. I only saw him before Pilate, talking about truth. He spoke very oddly about truth now that I come to think of it. He spoke of truth as a kingdom, which is part, I suppose, of the Jewish madness, for a kingdom is an extent of territory over which a king rules, enforcing his own laws. It is nothing else. One might as well talk of a kingdom of love or a kingdom of courage as a kingdom of truth."

"One might as well indeed," said Tutmoshe. "And do you not think these are kingdoms over which God must rule, for no man may ever command them? Can one man command all the love in the world, or all the truth, or all the order? Jesus of Nazareth was and is divine and the proof of that lies in his speaking of his kingdom as that of truth. What else did he say?"

"He said that he had come into the world to establish the Kingdom of Truth and all those who seek truth are of his kingdom," I said. "He said he was a king, but his kingdom was not of this world. It is my opinion that he could easily have escaped execution, but he was driven to death—as so many of the Jews are driven to death—by his own obsessions."

"His Kingdom of Truth among men is very small indeed," said Tutmoshe. "But man will change in the new age announced by the phoenix, and that kingdom will grow rapidly. Man will have to find something more valuable than riches. Consider, Theophilus, in that new kingdom how useless all your fortune will be. You have to get rid of it, Theophilus, and put some other value in its place. Do you think you could give away all your treasure?"

"The answer to that is very simple," I replied. "No."

"Not even to keep the friendship of the crucified Jew?"

"My good Tutmoshe," I said heatedly, "I don't want friends who would reduce me to begging. They are not friends but enemies. And I will tell you something more—from bitter experience—a poor man has no friends."

"You have only lived half a century," said Tutmoshe, "and so you are still a child in understanding life. If you had lived a hundred and fifty years you would know the opposite is true and only the poor have friends and know real love. For the friends of the rich are friends of their riches and the love given the rich is love given their treasure. Poor Theophilus. You are not going to live a hundred and fifty years, and so have only a short time to learn that lesson. Yet you have this in your favor. You love the truth. To that extent you are already one of the kingdom of the crucified Jew. Also you are not alone. All creatures, other than man, belong to the Kingdom of Truth which is the kingdom of Jesus of Nazareth.

"Consider, Theophilus—the wind cannot lie; the grass cannot deceive; the palm must be true to its nature and bear its own fruit and not another's; your sister the asp there cannot belie her nature, which is merciful, for though she kills, she does not kill for joy or fame, but only out of a true need agreeable to her creator. The flame cannot burn cold, nor ice sear with heat. When man can no more deceive than the grass in the fields, than the flame and the ice, then the kingdom of the Nazarene will have come and man will for the first time since his creation be free."

I stayed with Tutmoshe for a week and told him of the two times I had seen Jesus of Nazareth since his crucifixion. I also told him of how the mention of his name had been sufficient to expel the spirits from the pythoness Tabitha, who was now only a thin and unattractive young woman, added to my household against my wishes and to my expense.

"What do you think is the reason the Nazarene should show himself to me?" I asked. "To be sure, if he is as you think to establish a kingdom based on truth which will last forever, then it should certainly be to my advantage that he should have an interest in me. But he would do better for himself to appear to Pilate or perhaps Herod, for I think Pilate's star is setting. He is too hard against the Jews to last and it was Sejanus, you know, who got him his position. Sejanus is dead, and so I must go to Rome and mend my affairs."

"Find out all you can about the Nazarene," said Tutmoshe, ignoring all this. "He has work for you to do. That is plain. Whether you wish it or not, your future is bound to the Nazarene. Go to Rome by all means. But you will have to return to Jerusalem. You think yourself free, but you have become a subject now of the Kingdom of Truth of the crucified Jew."

To this I did not pay much attention at the time. One has to beware of those who are divine. Often what they say is not sensible, and therefore should be put aside as applying to them and not to mere mortals.

I have only one more incident to relate of my visit to Tutmoshe and this concerns him and Tabitha. Tutmoshe wished to see her and though I tried to dissuade him, saying that she was a young woman of no importance, he remained interested in her, so I sent Philip to get her from Alexandria, where she was lodged with Caballus and Cestus. Fortunately cotton clothing is very cheap in Egypt, so I was able to buy her, without too great an expense, a white cotton gown so that she would be decently clad for her interview with the old priest.

To my surprise, he took a fancy to her, and she was not at all repelled by his appearance, which as I have said was that of a mummy, but seemed immediately to be fond of him. When I saw how matters were between them (remembering also that Tutmoshe's sexual parts were by no means as withered as the rest of him) I berated myself for giving him that globe of jet from the Pretannic Islands when I could have pleased him far more by giving him Tabitha, whom I certainly did not want myself. However, I have always made it a rule to consult my slaves on their own feelings before giving them to another. So I took

[111]

Tabitha aside and asked her whether she would be willing to enter the service of my friend Tutmoshe.

"He is a hundred and eighty years of age," I said. "And so his sexual demands on you are not likely to be great though you must expect some activity. After all, while there is life, there is life and you will not be so cruel as to deny an old man a few fleeting pleasures. Also you are ugly and will scarcely find any young men around here to sport with, but you will be well fed and properly clothed and if you close your eyes and think of others, you may find it possible to enjoy intercourse with him. Reflect again that food and clothing are not easy to come by and many sacrifices of self can and should be made to obtain them."

"I will do whatever you wish, my lord," said Tabitha.

That was exactly like a woman, leaving the decision up to me, but I am not a man to be thrown into a quandary by such wiles. "Then since you have no objection, I will give you to Tutmoshe," I said. "He is to live another twenty years, which will give you time to save some money against the days of your freedom which he will certainly grant you when he dies."

So I was rid of Tabitha, but to my surprise Tutmoshe did not thank me for the gift. "You are surprised that I do not thank you?" he said. "You have given me nothing. You did not want the girl yourself. That is no gift which does not involve sacrifice."

However, when I left Tabitha, I had a twinge of sadness at parting and, remembering how she had kissed my feet when the spirits had left her, I almost resolved to ask for her back. But a bargain is a bargain and must be adhered to. Otherwise no business is possible in the world. So I did not ask for her back though Caballus, when he learned that I had given Tabitha to Tutmoshe, told me I was a fool.

"She was worth more to you than you know," he said. But the Germans are a hot-tempered people and although he was devoted to his wife, I imagine he had been amusing himself with Tabitha in my absence. He sulked for several days after we left Alexandria but part of that may have been the effect of our sea voyage to Ostia, for the Germans, as I have said, loathe the sea.

XV

WE HAD A POOR PASSAGE on the corn bark *Gatherer* from the Nile to the Tiber. A southerly wind favoring the voyage became on the second day a westerly gale. The seething seas battered the hull and so strained it that we had to turn our stern to the wind and run for shelter to Cyprus. Here at Limassol the damage of the storm was repaired, and the cargo restored. This not being the season of the grain harvest we carried a mixed cargo of dates, honey, and cotton together with a number of curios and precious articles taken from Egyptian graves for which there is a great market in Rome. (The scrapings of mummies, particularly from the dried fingernails, drunk with a little wine, are held a certain cure for baldness, though the divine Julius, who first learned of this remedy in Egypt, was bald to the day of his murder.)

At Cyprus, turning misadventure to good account, we took on a cargo of copper ore from the mines, and since this stuff when being loaded or unloaded gives off a poisonous dust, I moved ashore and called upon the Proconsul, Sergius Paulus, to pay my respects. He received me with warmth and begged me to stay longer, pointing out (which I well knew) that many vessels were now calling in this sailing season at Cyprus so that I would not be held up unduly if I left the *Gatherer*. But I said that my business in Rome was urgent and he did not then press me.

I gave him the news from Judaea as it concerned Pilate and Herod, but there was little I could tell him that was new, for he had excellent communications with Judaea, Egypt, Cyrene, and Rome, Cyprus being an island at which almost all ships call.

He introduced me to his magician, a Jew named Bar-Jesus who performed many wonders for me; for holding his hand in a beam of sunlight in a darkened room, he split it into many colors and taking a piece of rock out of a jar of water, he held it a few minutes in the air in iron tongs whereupon it immediately burst into flame. Also he picked up a small stick from the ground and it was transformed into a snake. So there was no doubting the man's powers.

He was skilled also in astrology and assured me that he could foretell my future if I could give him the exact date and minute of my birth. But who knows the date of the birth of a former slave? I could give him no details at all, but he by an examination of the characteristics of my face and certain of my mannerisms, and being acquainted to a degree with the outline of my life (with which I will not trouble you) pronounced me born under the sign of Leo and likely on the twentieth of July about the eleventh hour. Such were the powers of this remarkable man who was the chief advisor of the Proconsul Paulus. The Proconsul himself, a man of great intelligence, did not rely entirely on the advice of his magician, but having learned from him what forces were at play among the stars, also acquainted himself with all the facts involved in a particular problem and, meditating on these, produced his solution. I asked him whether he did not think it sufficient in managing his affairs to merely consult the magician Bar-Jesus who, since he could foretell the future, could save him the trouble of investigation and thought.

"I have meditated long on that question," he said, "and I believe that the future is not a settled matter as is the past. We are not destined to particular ends. All the stars can say is the fate that is likely but not certain to befall us. What happens is to a great degree in our own hands and depends on the clarity of our thinking and the manliness of our resolves."

"That would make each man the master of his own fate. Do you think this is so?" I asked.

"He is the master of his own fate to the degree that the captain is the master of a ship. The captain may keep his ship afloat by skill, by courage, by clarity of thought, by talent, and by determination. But he cannot control the unexpected blast that rolls it over or the vast wave that engulfs it. Nor can man control the blows the gods may direct at us in their anger. But if we know that such a blow is coming, then we can seek to appease the gods by sacrifice and by honest living. And if we live honestly and deal fairly with our fellows, then the gods are not likely to be angered by us."

"The gods themselves play tricks on each other," I said.

"I do not believe this is so," said Paulus. "It is only that men, making up stories about the gods, say it is so. But men know little of the gods, and in their ignorance have made the gods in the likeness of men. Yet the gods are not made by men and exist separate from man and independent of man, and have no likeness to man."

A remarkable man then, Sergius Paulus, yet I have to say that under Tiberius all the Roman administrators were good men. "I do not envy Pilate," he said when we discussed Judaea. "I have many Jews here and find that, left to themselves, they are peaceable enough. But to rule Jews in that land which they claim as their own, given to them by their god, is an impossible task, for they will not be ruled. All that may be done is to banish them entirely from Judaea."

Bar-Jesus was of course a Jew and though he remained silent, his face blazed with anger at such a thought and the anger was not lost on Sergius Paulus. "You have something to say on the subject?" he asked. "Speak without fear."

"Why should my people be banished from the land given them by God?" he demanded. "Why instead should Rome not leave Israel?"

"Because power has its own right and there are demands which are made on powerful nations which they must meet if they are to remain powerful," replied the Proconsul calmly. "Rome has built a strong wall about herself, stretching from the Gates of Hercules to Judaea. Are we to knock a hole in that wall to please the Jews? We might not survive that hole, my friend, and then our empire would crumble and the loss to the whole world would be terrible. Do you think Gaul would enjoy returning to tribal rule, to human sacrifices, and blood feuds? Or Spain whose agriculture and mines now prosper would happily return to rule by brigands? Or Egypt to rule by murderous priests? Power once assumed becomes not an exaltation but a duty and he who carelessly throws it aside deserts mankind. Should Rome fall, my friend, the world will mourn her loss not for years or decades but for centuries, and in the darkness that follows we who were of Rome will appear not as men but as demigods."

It warmed my heart to hear a man speak so staunchly of Rome, for as you know I am myself a Roman and I deplore that modern fashion which holds love of nation barbarous and delights in extolling the vices of inferior peoples over the virtues of one's own country. How can anyone say or hint that Rome is not superior to all nations, when Rome rules the world? How can it be maintained that others are the equals of Romans when they are ruled by Romans? Are men ruled by their equals?

But such arguments will not persuade those who are determined to think fashionably rather than sensibly; to believe that culture consists in denouncing that noble state which gave them birth and bread and protection.

I had time enough ashore to attend for an hour or two the gladiatorial games which were held in honor of the birthday of a niece of Paulus. Although this was but a provincial showing, yet it was well arranged, and two gladiators agreed to fight to the death—swordsmen both. The victor was a Scythian who, brought to his knees by a thrust to the groin, nonetheless retained sufficient control to slip his sword into the unguarded armpit of his opponent and so dispatch him. He fought with the long Spanish sword, while the other from Cisalpine Gaul, fought with the shorter Roman gladius, designed more for cutting than thrusting since it must batter down shields.

Caballus, who had been sulking since I got rid of Tabitha (*he* did not have to pay her expenses), begged to be allowed to take part in the games, and since I had full confidence in his ability, I permitted this. He was given a short spear and matched against a bear which he enticed before Paulus and me and then after dodging several blows which could have taken off his face, killed it. I was surprised to see how the bear, with the spear entering its breast, gripped the shaft between its powerful and bloody paws and turned its eyes towards us in agony, just like a man, which of course brought cries of delight from all.

Caballus indeed covered himself with glory but became very sick a little later through drinking a gallon of cold Egyptian beer while still streaming with blood and sweat. He would not have behaved so if his wife Erithus had been with him, and indeed I think all men would be wiser if, traveling about the world, they took their wives with them.

From Paulus I learned much more of conditions in Rome, for Cyprus, as you know, is the ear of the Roman Empire. It appeared that Caligula, the last surviving son of Germanicus, who had been invited to visit Tiberius at Capri, had been charged to seek among the Praetorians an officer of great popularity who could replace Sejanus, of whom Tiberius had been suspicious.

Caligula went about this commission with commendable prudence. He certainly did not ask questions of this one and that one, which would have immediately aroused the suspicions of Sejanus, but instead, disguised as a madam, with his cheeks painted and his eyelashes smeared with kohl, he visited all the stews where the Praetorians gathered to drink and riot. There, by supplying prostitutes to the men, buying them drinks, and arranging licentious shows he soon discovered that no officer was more popular with the Praetorians than one Macro, who had a pretty and available wife, Ennia Naevia. Caligula recommended Macro to Tiberius, who, having found a successor, then denounced Sejanus to the Senate and had him arrested. Macro and his men murdered Sejanus, their former commander, and now Macro was the power to be dealt with in any approach to Tiberius.

This information I did not, of course, get directly from the Proconsul Sergius Paulus, who was too honorable a Roman to deal in such gossip. He gave me only the facts of who now held the power under the Emperor, of whom he spoke with reverence and affection. But every ruler has a court and from the courtiers and the slaves and attendants of the court I could readily piece together the whole story.

I could not avoid visiting the capital, dangerous as this was because of my friendship with Sejanus. I had to make myself known to Macro; to congratulate him and give him such presents as would assure his friendship. Not to do so would be taken as a sign of hostility on my part, and tardiness in doing so would be taken as secret sympathy with Sejanus, whose favorites (Pilate among them) were doomed unless they could succeed in convincing Macro and Tiberius of their loyalty and love.

I gave much thought to the presents which I would send to Tiberius and Macro and also to Caligula. Macro, I learned, had a love of silken clothing and for Caligula money was all that was required, for he used every penny he could find on his debauches. For Tiberius a remarkable present other than money was suggested by Bar-Jesus, who as a magician was in touch with Thrasyllus, the astrologer and advisor of Tiberius. "You cannot fail to please the Emperor if you send to him several dozen white mice," he said.

"Such an insignificant and insulting gift would only result in my death," I said.

"Not at all, sir," said Bar-Jesus. "Reflect that Tiberius has everything that he could desire, so whatever is sent him must show great thought for his person and knowledge of his pleasures. His greatest pet is now a large snake, which he delights in feeding personally. Several dozen mice for the snake would show thoughtfulness and help to win you his favor. Also if you should find any strange reptile, that also would be a very acceptable gift. He loves reptiles. I know where there is a lizard to be had which has two heads," he added. "Five hundred sesterces will secure it."

I examined the lizard but it seemed to me that one of the heads was diseased and so the creature would soon die. But a small snake also with two heads was brought me and I bought that and gave it to Philip to take care of. The Macedonians have a love of snakes and regard it as the greatest good fortune if a snake will share their bed with them from a belief that snakes are gods in disguise. Philip then assured me that he would keep the snake in good condition, which he did. He did not, however, reverence it, and remarked that the right head seemed to have dominance over the other, which had assented to play the inferior role.

"It would be interesting to discover whether this snake has more intelligence than others. With two brains, that is possible."

"Let us leave that to Tiberius," I said. "For myself I would point out that two men are not necessarily wiser than one, but often more timid and more foolish."

Before I left Cyprus the magician Bar-Jesus took me aside and asked me privately what I knew about his namesake, Jesus of Nazareth. The story of his crucifixion and resurrection was already well known on this island. That is not really to be wondered at, for it had been spread by Jews leaving Jerusalem to return to their homes after the Feast of the Passover. In any case, the Jews are the greatest travelers in the world. If you want to spread a tale from one end of the world to the other in the shortest time, tell it to a Jew. He will tell it to another, and your tale will soon be known everywhere.

Bar-Jesus was interested in the resurrection of Jesus, for these magicians like to hear of the feats of other magicians and will offer large sums for the secret of performing. such feats. But I did not like Bar-Jesus and told him merely that I had heard of the story of the resurrection but did not say that I had seen the resurrected Jesus myself. Nor would I tell him anything more, though I knew he did not believe me.

"You were present at his trial, I hear, and gave him a cup of wine," he said. "It is rumored that he gave you magical powers in return." You see, he had already heard from that rascal in Joppa about my casting out the spirits which dwelt in Tabitha.

"That is only a rumor," I said. "I am only a merchant, not a magician." But he did not believe me.

XVI

ROME IS not only the greatest city in the world but it is
also the most splendid and the gayest, the noisiest and
the fullest of movement, the richest in terms of commerce,
and the wisest in terms of government. If all the world
could see Rome, so splendid is she, none would rebel
against her, such is her majesty. Her greatness lies not
only in her temples and buildings and open places, but
also in her traditions and her history, which Philip has
been teaching me. I say with pride that whatever there
is that is noble in the world had its source in Rome.
Philip reminds me that the Greeks led the world in
philosophy and the arts, and this was undoubtedly so
for a while. Yet I doubt they were ever as manly as we
of Rome, and certainly they fell through treachery, which
is hardly a virtue of philosophers. "You Greeks are but
teachers," I once told him. "We Romans are the doers."

Rome is a city of green, white, and red, the green of
the many open spaces and trees and flowering gardens,
the red of the pantile roofs which cascade down the sides
of the hills and are ever in view, and the white of the
buildings and great temples. The whole world looks to
Rome as its home, and it is remarkable that this is true
not only of men but of birds as well, for eagles often
perch on its buildings and monuments and flocks of starlings and pigeons, thrushes and blackbirds flit about the
city. Even the shy wren visits Rome and one was set upon
by starlings and plucked to death on the eve of the assassination of Caesar, a plain warning which the divine
Julius ignored. At dusk and at dawn the chattering and

chirping of birds drowns out all the other noises of the city. You may add to these sounds the lowing of cattle brought to be slaughtered, the baaing of sheep and the neighing and clatter of horses, whose droppings are carefully collected by the poor for winter fuel.

All nations have their quarters in Rome and you will find there Ethiopians, Indians, Scythians, Persians, Germans, Greeks, and Jews, though at the time of my visit the Jews had been banned from Rome by Tiberius because they are so contentious and stiff-necked. However, as the saying goes, "It is easier to ban the wind than the Jews," and so there were many Jews in Rome despite the ban, living some in very comfortable villas and others in rooms below the ground or in the catacombs where the dead are buried and where it is rumored their magicians torture stray children to death in the service of their god who hates all who are not Jews. (But who would believe all that is said about the Jews?)

I left the *Gatherer* at Ostia and moved ashore to the house of Gratius Porcus, who is the superintendent of my warehouses there and has under him a staff of forty accountants and tallymen as well as a force of police, for stealing while loading and unloading ships is the greatest source of profit to thieves and loss to men of business. The head of this police force is none other than the infamous John the Hammer, certainly the most notorious brigand in the whole of Latinum, who at one time controlled an organization of thieves, murderers, and bullies which terrorized the countryside until he was caught and sentenced to the galleys.

There he served on the same bench as I and indeed ruled the bench and, such was his genius, soon had an organization among the galley slaves whereby every one of them was in a degree subject to him and gave him the best food and dared not deny him a favor. When I obtained my own liberty—I was but three years in the galleys—and, having prospered, needed a watchman, I arranged to buy John the Hammer out of the ships.

This is the best way to arrange business matters; to go always to the expert. What after all is an evil reputation? Is it not actually only a measure of a man's luck? Those who are unlucky or careless go to the mines or the galleys while those who are more fortunate parade the streets as benefactors. So I have found it to be. When then I needed a watchman, I purchased John the Hammer for a large sum and put him in charge of my warehouse.

"Have you lost your wits?" he asked when he was brought to me. "Surely you are not going to trust me among your goods? I would regard it as a crime not to steal from you with so many fine things about."

"One thief I can survive, as a granary can survive one rat," I replied. "Just keep the other thieves out." This John the Hammer did to perfection, and I have this advice to offer you—in guarding against thieves hire a thief, for honest men are no match for them. John the Hammer was not a man of great size as those who never saw him say, but a small man and got his name because he carried a stonemason's hammer on any enterprise and cracked many skulls with it. He was quite without mercy.

From Porcus I learned not only the condition of my business, which prospered as usual, but the latest news of the economic situation in Rome, the amount of food distributed and in storage, the state of the salt payment, the supply of clothing, the condition of transport, the amount of money sent abroad to the legions, and such matters which are, after all, only of interest to a man of business. Employment in Rome and throughout Italy was as ever in a poor way, for with so many slaves brought in by the legions, no freeman could find honest work.

Even the crafts were now all invaded by slaves so that shoemakers and saddle makers, stonemasons and carpenters were all slaves working in their own shops and able to undersell free tradesmen. A few months previously, Porcus said, there had been a riot in which a great number of these artisan slaves had been killed and their shops burned to the ground. The fire had spread and burned several streets of shops before the fire brigade got it under control. It was the old story of the Tiber pumps having parts missing when wanted, and the usual bucket line being impeded by that mob of sightseers who always gather about a fire. The two things of which I am most afraid in my business are the Emperor and fire—fire second, of course, since some measures may be taken to control it. But one word from the Emperor and all is lost.

My most valuable information regarding affairs came not from Gratius Porcus but from John the Hammer. As I have a network of informers among slaves and former slaves (men like Pallas and Narcissus now holding high positions) so John the Hammer had a network of informers among thieves, brothel keepers, sellers of drugs, tax collectors, and other malefactors.

"Don't worry about Colonel Macro," he told me when I mentioned my anxieties over the successor to Sejanus. "He won't last long. He is just a big wine-swilling, woman-using tub. Little Boots"—by whom he meant Caligula, of course—"is the one to watch. He's as lecherous as a goat in March and as cunning as a three-legged dog. He'd cohabit with a dead camel and twist the arm of a starving baby. Of course he can't help it, poor fellow. He's mad."

"The son of Germanicus?" I said, surprised.

"Yes, the son of the noble muckhead Germanicus—the only one who survived. How do you suppose he managed that, you blind old bastard. By virtue? And as for being mad, I don't mean howling like a dog when he sees the moon," said John the Hammer. "That kind of madman doesn't do anybody any harm. I mean really mad like a Carthaginian god. Do you know how he spends his mornings? He goes down to the butchers' shambles by the Tiber, the big one below the bridge where the fishing is so good, and pays the butchers to let him kill the animals. His favorite method is to tie a sheep down, take a red hot sword and stick it up its behind. Little Boots Barbecue Special, he calls it.

"You know what he said when he learned that his mother had been flogged until she was blind and his two elder brothers starved to death? He said, 'What is for dinner tonight?' You know the far end of the Field of Mars where there are all those thistles in summer? Well, one day when he was exercising with the cadets, he saw a starving donkey there eating thistles, and he laughed so long they thought he was going to have a fit and held him and took a pint of blood from his arm. That's the only time anybody has ever seen Little Boots laugh."

"This isn't madness," I said. "If you knew anything of philosophy"—Philip had been instructing me—"you would know that that is merely his attitude. What about his reason, his judgment? Is that affected? Does he make decisions that are against all reason?"

"How would I know?" asked John the Hammer surlily, for he had plainly hoped to impress me with these horror stories of Little Boots. "How much reason does a man use in a brothel, which is where he spends his evenings and nights? Either that or going with a gang of bullies and beating and robbing people. He likes to rape old women. He's like Mallus, only worse." (Mallus was the slave overseer on the galley. He had many curious tricks, such as putting a noose of fishing twine around a man's testicles, tying the other end to a ring in the deck, and then making him castrate himself by scourging him. Again Mallus always threw the ship's slops overboard to collect sharks before sending after them such slaves as were too sick to be of any more use. He liked to watch the sharks take them. He was finally drowned by being held, head down, in a bucket of urine, for which those responsible were impaled.)

"I will tell you something else about Little Boots, the son of the noble muckhead Germanicus," continued John the Hammer. "He had a friend, the son of a Senator, who had the trots and had to go constantly to the lavatory. One day Little Boots said to him, 'Your backside will be the death of you.' 'Oh, no,' said his friend, 'I am getting better.' But the next time he came out of the lavatory Little Boots denounced him for insulting Tiberius. He had put a coin with the image of Tiberius in his friend's pocket and it is, of course, death these days to go into a lavatory or a brothel bearing a coin with the image of Tiberius on it. When his friend was taken off to be strangled, Little Boots called after him, 'I told you your backside would be the death of you.' But this time he did not have the last of the joke, for his friend replied, 'Alas, that I should have squirted into the Cloacha Maxima so much that was infinitely superior to you.' "

John the Hammer had a score of these tales concerning Gaius Caligula which were quite contrary to his public reputation, for all knew him only as the son of the noble Germanicus and expected, should he succeed Tiberius (though none dared even whisper of the possible death of Tiberius), that justice and wisdom would prevail throughout the whole Roman world.

After studying the reports of Gratius Porcus and of John the Hammer and various other reports which had been sent to me in correspondence awaiting me at Ostia, it seemed that Caligula was certainly the man of the future if not of the present. Meanwhile Tiberius, living in Capri, had with the murder of Sejanus restored his own authority and Colonel Macro was but the tool of these two, though, of course, as Chief of the Praetorians, he wielded a great deal of power himself.

It would not, I reasoned, be to Macro that I must turn ultimately for that favor which would enable me to prosper in my business as chief shipper of grain to Rome, but to Tiberius himself. I sent then, when I had arrived in Rome, a large gift of money to Caligula with my earnestly expressed good wishes for his health, another gift of silks and a small chest of jewels to Colonel Macro with my profoundest hopes for his continuing success as a great soldier of Rome, and to Tiberius an even larger gift of money and (with much misgiving) several dozen white mice and my little snake with two heads. With these I sent my hopes that he would continue in strength to give to the whole world the protection of his wisdom, his justice, and his love.

Macro replied by summoning me to the Praetorian headquarters and issuing me with a pass for all hours and into all places whatever the hour and also freedom from search. He was a vast man, young, but with the red tendrils of the vine, as they are called, already creeping across his cheeks and nose. He inquired about a certain Egyptian cloth which has but the weight of a cobweb and is used exclusively by priests, and I arranged to have a hundred yards of it in white, blue, and gold sent to him immediately.

Caligula replied to my gifts by sending a note in which he said that he heard I had been long away from Rome and would undoubtedly be in need of new furniture since that in my house would be out of date. He was therefore sending me some and I could make whatever payment for it I thought fit. It is the custom in Rome, on a certain day, for people to throw out of their houses the broken and useless furniture which they do not wish, and it was this discarded furniture which Caligula sent me—beds with broken frames and no legs, chairs without seats or backs, and so forth. I thanked him fervently for his generosity, hinted that I was also in need of carpets and drapes, and sent him a purse of gold pieces. The next day a moldy piece of rush carpeting arrived, for which I paid a princely sum.

But it was from the Emperor at Capri that I received my most frightening response. This came in the form of a visit from a centurion of the Praetorians summoning me to the Emperor's presence, and I immediately bitterly repented that gift of mice and a small snake which the

wretched Bar-Jesus had suggested I make the Emperor,
for I was sure these ridiculous offerings had angered him
and I was a doomed man.

"Master," said Philip, "he has not ordered you to
kill yourself." But somehow I did not find that comforting.

XVII

ON RECEIVING THE SUMMONS of Tiberius I made my will
very carefully. That gave me some difficulty, since I had
a large fortune and neither wife nor children, mother
nor father nor any blood relation to whom to leave my
money. Of course I had to make the Emperor one of my
heirs. This is always done so that his wrath will not be
directed against the other inheritors. To Tiberius I gave
one-third of my fortune, and the rest, after careful reflection and consultation with both Pallas and Narcissus (you
will learn more of them later; they were at the time
freedmen like myself and stewards in the household of
Claudius, the idiot nephew of Tiberius), after consultation then with these two, I put into a trust fund. Philip
was to receive twenty-five hundred sesterces a year, to be
increased by two hundred sesterces a year for each child;
the money again to go to their children, and Cestus and
Caballus were each to receive one thousand sesterces a year.

I made other generous bequests to Gratius Porcus,
John the Hammer, Basil Chrysanthus (my chief agent in
Greece), and my other agents and stewards so that they
would not contest the will and also to reward them for
their services. To my little immediate family I also gave
their freedom and a further bequest of five thousand
sesterces to be paid from the trust fund should they seek

Roman citizenship. This was a secret provision of the will, to be fulfilled only after they had made serious efforts to become citizens, for to be a citizen of Rome is a noble thing and should be sought for the honor itself and not because of a money reward. (The five thousand sesterces would, of course, help them to buy citizenship, which is alas often for sale. But there is nothing, however noble, that falls within the gift of man which is not eventually for sale, and one must learn to live with the world and accept its ways.)

I debated some time whether the gift of twenty-five hundred sesterces a year to Philip was not overgenerous. I could certainly be forgiven if I had given him less, for he constantly criticized my literary style and stubbornly insisted that the Greeks were superior to us Romans and often had an air of pious suffering when shouted down. But I decided to be generous because of his crippled feet and because as a scholar he certainly needed money, it being almost impossible to earn money by scholarship, since, as I pointed out to Philip, nobody either eats learning or wears it. It is in fulfilling those two latter needs that the greatest fortunes are to be made.

Before leaving Rome I made sacrifices to Jupiter the Greatest and Best and to Apollo the Merciful and also to Mercury. But at none of these sacrifices did I receive any degree of interior comfort as in the past. The statue in ebony and ivory and gold of Jupiter the Greatest and Best looked more dead than any corpse I had ever seen—dead as a stone which has never, of course, had life. The priests could give me no assurance regarding my future and Gaius Caligula, whom I met unexpectedly as our litters passed in the streets, cried out to me, "Goodbye, Furniture Lover, alas that the dogs and the birds should have you all for their feasting," which Philip, in the litter with me, said was a line from the *Iliad* when Achilles addresses the doomed Hector.

Indeed everybody looked upon me as a man dead and avoided me, believing some rumor which had been spread about that I had fallen into the ill favor of the Emperor. Only John the Hammer was cheerful.

"Just think of it, Theophilus,' he said. "You, a former galley slave, are going to see Tiberius. Would you ever have believed such a thing when you sat sweating at the oars?"

"I wish it were you who were going to see him and not I," I replied fervently.

"Have you not died already twenty times as a slave?" he said. "Why fear another death? Anyway, don't worry, you still have a friend or two for all your money." Is it not strange that so notorious a man should be the only one to offer any comfort in my peril? He offered to accompany me to Capri; but I could not even take Philip or Caballus with me, for I was escorted on board the appointed vessel at Ostia by the centurion, and so taken to that beautiful but terrible island where the Emperor lived.

I did not see Tiberius right away when I arrived at Capri. Far from it. Instead I was lodged in one room of a small villa some distance from the Emperor's palace and refused permission to leave this little prison even to get a breath of air. As time went by my anxiety mounted and I went over a thousand times all my dealings in the past with the Roman state in the supply of corn to see in which of many areas I could have offended.

Of course, it is possible to bring a case of treason or bribery or conspiracy at any time against a man in my position. When you have reached such a place as I in public affairs, whatever you do or do not do can, with slight manipulation, be made treasonous. Yet I could honestly say that although I had had my profit out of the corn supply and also out of the construction of several aqueducts and the supply of stone for military forts of a permanent kind, these profits were not more than they should be, and my bribery of officials had never had the end of persuading them to neglect their duty to the state. If a colonel or general is given gold to order stone from one quarry rather than from another, can it really be held that he is less a soldier or less loyal to Rome and his men for accepting? Of course not. He shows only that he is a man of affairs, and such men, in the pinch, are to be trusted above those who make a show of being incorruptible. Beware of incorruptible men. The price you will pay for that virtue will be disastrous, and will be measured in freedom rather than money. Men of great virtue are the natural enemies of mankind, who are not at all virtuous in their natures.

Well, I spent four anxious days in that miserable prison of a villa and my terrors were augmented by many fearful screams and noises during the night, at times waking me from a sound sleep. Once shortly after dawn, hearing a terrible bellowing nearby, I beheld in the thin light a black bull with, strapped beneath his belly, legs astraddle and screaming in agony at being impregnated by so huge a beast, a young girl. The bull, much aroused, was thrusting with all his might and the girl screaming and there was the Emperor himself in a most shameful position with two young boys. Such unnatural acts were often practiced in Crete and also at Thebes in Egypt where the sacred bull was once a year offered a young girl for his satisfaction, who always died after being so violated.

What added to my sufferings was the food which was served me. It was horrible—leavings from another's plate for the most part, chewed and spat out—and the wine was so bitter that I thought it poisoned. Food has always been a great comfort to me and I now ate as poorly as when I had been a slave. Nor was any of the philosophy I remembered from Philip's instruction any comfort. I quickly found that the prospect of death is a complete counterargument to philosophy. What fine philosophical presentation can comfort a man who stares at his own grave? Confronted with this reality all the wise sayings of the philosophers are as worthless chaff.

At the end of a week, I was in such a state that I expected every time footsteps approached that a centurion had been sent to cut my head off. But the first visitor I had, other than the tongueless servants who waited on me, was none other than the great astrologer of Tiberius, Thrasyllus.

He was a very old man, thin, small, withered. His head was completely bald. There was not a vestige of hair left on it. He had no beard either, though astrologers affect beards, and his eyelids were red with age though the eyes themselves were bright.

"You did right to follow the advice of Bar-Jesus in the matter of gifts," he said by way of greeting. "The Emperor was pleased."

Imagine what a relief it was to hear that! I blurted out all kinds of happy nonsense in reply and Thrasyllus smiled in a distant way and silenced me with a bony hand. "I am to take you to the Emperor," he said. "Be sure to answer him truthfully. Come."

Would you believe that it was only then that there flashed into my mind the one incident regarding the corn supply about which I was immediately convinced the Emperor wanted to question me? It concerned the corn bark *Spica* which had been wrecked five years previously off the island of Rhodes. Yes, Rhodes. That island where Tiberius had lived during the reign of Augustus in banishment, where he had been treated first with respect and then with contempt as his influence with Augustus dwindled. Livia, the wife of Augustus, had rescued Tiberius from that island, where Thrasyllus had been his sole companion and comforter (though Tiberius at one time, thinking him an imposter, had, the story went, planned to fling him off a cliff). Well, then it suddenly occurred to me that Tiberius had a special interest in Rhodes and many informers there and the wreck of the corn bark *Spica* would have been reported to him and with Sejanus dead he had undoubtedly been reading over the state accounts, for he took, even in his old age, the greatest concern over the Roman corn supply.

So you ask how is a man to prevent a shipwreck? Are not a dozen corn barks lost every year? That is indeed so. But when I had gone over my accounts for that year, I found that I had been credited with a payment from the Roman treasury for the cargo of the *Spica,* which, of course, had never reached Rome. I took the matter up immediately with Gratius Porcus, who, as I have said, handled the tally at Ostia. It was nothing but a bookkeeping error, he said. A secretary had written the name *Spica* instead of *Spera* in crediting a shipment. I told Porcus to see that the record was changed before any treasury money was accepted. But now I realized that Porcus had been lax. The record had not been changed. It stood in the state accounts that I had received a payment of Roman gold for corn which had never reached Rome—evidence that I had cheated the Senate and the people of Rome. The penalty for that was death. I did not for one moment doubt that Tiberius had now found that ill-omened entry and that was the reason he had sent for me. I believed myself a dead man. Many headless bodies have indeed been flung down the Stairs of Mourning in Rome for less than that as a warning to others not to cheat the Roman state.

It was in this condition then, trembling, indeed sweating, and expecting death, that Thrasyllus brought me into the presence of the Emperor, who was seated on the terrace of his villa (it was really a palace, the walls on this side covered with Greek frescoes, for Tiberius was a secret admirer of the Greeks). With him, within call, were four of those huge Germans who formed his bodyguard, golden-haired bulls with moustaches and beards as thick as bushes. They were armed with short stabbing spears and had axes in their belts, for the German prefers the ax or the hammer to the sword in hand-to-hand combat. What ugly brutes they were. I believed immediately the story that their whole race resulted from the rape of a young maiden by a bear.

"Here is Theophilus the grain merchant and shipman for whom you sent, Caesar," said Thrasyllus.

Tiberius, leaning back in his chair and chewing something between his big jaws, very slowly, was looking out to sea and did not give the slightest indication that he had heard a word or was aware of our presence. I had heard that Tiberius possessed many remarkable abilities, among them that of seeing distant objects invisible to others. Also he had such huge strength in his hands that he could, with a sudden jab, poke his forefinger clean through an apple, or through a boy's head, which he had done once for his amusement. It is possible that on this occasion he was watching some ship going by. All shipping, as I well knew, had orders to keep ten miles distant from Capri in passing. Possibly he was watching one which had not obeyed this rule. Whatever engaged his attention, it was some time before he slowly turned his head to me (all the movements of Tiberius were slow, like those of a tortoise) and examined me with his pale blue eyes.

"Hail, Caesar," I said in a voice which certainly did not belong to me.

"Why do you not bow?" he asked.

"If you require it, Caesar, I will," I replied. "But I am a citizen of Rome and as you know Romans do not bow." Really it was not courage that prompted so foolhardy a speech. I was at my wits' end trying to find an explanation for why I had not bowed and that was the reason I said what I said, not out of boldness then, but out of fear. But the reply was exactly the best one to make to please Tiberius. Whatever his faults he did take pride in the traditions of Rome even to the extent of carefully eliminating all Greek words or constructions from his messages to the Senate.

"You are Roman then?" he said. "I thought from your name you would be a Hellenized Jew. There are none worse. You may sit since we are both Romans together," and he pointed to a chair. Tiberius was a big man for a Roman. In fact, he was a little taller than those bears of Germans who guarded him. Even though he was old at this time, his broad shoulders had not stooped and his spine was but a little curved throwing his big head forward. His face was bronzed and in that bronzed face his pale blue eyes had a merciless and calculating appearance. He wore his back hair long—a characteristic of the Claudians. He wore soldier's sandals on his feet and I noticed that his toenails were thick and rounded and brown as if made of horn as is the case with all men as the years go by. He was naked beneath his toga, for the day was hot and humid, though it was cool enough in the shade of the terrace.

"You have returned from Judaea, Egypt, and Cyprus," he said. "What temper did you find among the people? How are the roads? What did you find wrong that should be righted?"

I had expected to be asked about the corn bark *Spica* and these questions took me by surprise. They would have surprised me in any case. Surely Caesar did not have to turn to mere travelers to find out how matters stood in the dominions of Rome?

"Caesar," I replied, "all is excellent. I was able to travel with but one man for a bodyguard and at no time was I in danger on the roads or in the inns at which I stayed. I could find horses when I wished and I was never more than three weeks in getting letters from Rome. Throughout the provinces I found people blessing your rule," and I told him of that fine innkeeper at Emmaus whose business was in such a prosperous way because of the suppression of brigandage under the Emperor.

He showed not the slightest pleasure at my glowing report. Those slow jaws moved regularly, chewing whatever he had in his mouth, and his slow mind seemed also to be chewing what I had said. There was a long silence when I concluded and then he said, "Did you see Pilate?"

"I did, Caesar," I replied. "At the time of the great Jewish feast which they call the Passover. . ."

"I know of it," said Tiberius. "Why is it that those Jews are so devout, whereas in Rome the temples are empty and the priests themselves petitioning to be released from their duties to go holidaying in Spain or Gaul? Rome will pay for her impiety. Pilate hates the Jews, and I protect him. But I have had a report that recently on a public occasion and while you were present, he wavered in his loyalty to Rome in favor of a Jew who plotted against the Roman state."

I said nothing. I have not survived among so many perils by going to the rescue of doomed men, and Pilate was doomed. It was his fault. It does not do to hate those you rule or stir them up against you. Of course, who can rule the Jews? Whoever attempts to rule them will not come out of it with a good reputation, that is certain.

"I have heard that Pilate was loath to put to death this enemy of Rome," said Tiberius. "You were at the trial of this man. Tell me what happened."

Now I realized how wise Pilate had been to summon me to that trial as a witness and I cursed him for involving me in the affair to save his own skin. Let whoever doubts the power of the Jews reflect that, banished from Rome, they still had the ear of Tiberius and had given him every detail (from their own viewpoint) of this case.

"Caesar," I said, "although I was present at this trial I know little of this man or this matter. The man was tried at the insistence of the High Priests, headed by Caiaphas. But there was no evidence at the trial to show that he plotted against Rome. He said he was a king.

[136]

That is beyond doubt. But he added that his kingdom was not of this world, that he had no earthly followers, and that if he had he would not be standing there shivering before Pilate. It was very cold," I added. "It was early in the morning. I had not had breakfast."

That last remark brought a glint of a smile to the face of Tiberius. He turned those pale blue eyes on me, and the corner of his thin mouth was upturned in the kind of grin one sees on the face of a dead dolphin. I have marked that grin many a time and wondered whether the dolphin, dead, had discovered some huge joke on us who remain alive.

"Have you dined well here?" he asked, leaning forward a little in his chair as if to press the answer out of me.

What was I to say? Thrasyllus had warned me only to speak the truth and with that warning in mind I replied, "Horribly." At this Tiberius neither started nor frowned but just stared at me, his big jaws moving slowly. Then he leaned back in his chair and after another of those silences he said, "I am assured that this man, Jesus, was an enemy of Rome and he planned a rebellion." Again silence. Tiberius' next words sent a chill through me like death itself.

"I am told that you gave this man a cup of wine," he said.

Was it really possible then that that forgotten gesture was the reason for my being summoned before Tiberius? Not the grain bark *Spica,* but a cup of wine I had given a shivering Jew being tried for conspiracy against Rome? How true it is that we are all trapped by tiny threads spun by Ariadne, the spider goddess.

"Well," demanded Tiberius. "Did you give him a cup of wine?"

"Caesar," I replied, "I did."

"Why?"

"I felt sorry for him, Caesar. He had been scourged.

His nose was half torn off, one eye almost blind. He shivered in his pain, and he was a young man."

"That does not impress me," said Tiberius. "Such sights are not unknown to us Romans. You have been to the gladiatorial games and you have enjoyed them, I suppose. You were a slave yourself and saw many men scourged and crucified too, or put on the rack or condemned to the stone. Why did you pity him, Theophilus? Is it not true that you were one of his secret supporters? Do not lie to me. I know of your interest in him. I know of your correspondence."

"Caesar," I cried, "I had never heard of this man until Pilate bade me attend his trial. That I swear before the immortal gods. Why should I, who have received so many benefits from Rome, plot against the state which has been both my mother and my father? What could I hope to gain that I have not already received? And, Caesar, though this man had followers, as I later learned, they had all fled in fear and left him alone at his trial. Now, if I were one of his followers, would I not also be afraid to see him brought for judgment? Would I offer him publicly a kindness—offer him a kindness before Pilate and Annas and Caiaphas when he was doomed and alone?

"Caesar, I am not a brave man. Also I am not a foolhardy man or I would not have survived the many perils of life. Had I been a follower or supporter of this man Jesus, I would, I assure you, have been the first to denounce him and the last to offer him a cup of wine."

"And yet you were present at his trial," said Tiberius. "Why? Was it not so that Pilate himself, as your friend, could warn you of the danger of associating with such as he?"

"Far from that, Caesar," I said. "Again I swear by the gods that I did not know this man until the moment I met him before Pilate. And Pilate summoned me to the trial because he wanted me as an impartial witness to those proceedings—someone utterly strange with no bias on one side or the other, for Pilate knew that whatever he did, a report would be sent to you which would attempt to discredit him because the Jews hate him so."

Again a long silence; but this time those big jaws stopped chewing.

"What is your view?" said Tiberius at last. "Was the man an enemy of Rome or not?"

"He was no enemy of Rome," I said. "No witness could testify against him that he planned a revolt against Rome."

"You are wrong, Theophilus," said Tiberius. "His followers are now numbered not in hundreds but in thousands. Wherever he went during his life great throngs surged around him. Now he is dead, the throngs are greater. Do you think, Theophilus, that Rome can tolerate loyalty to such a man in Judaea, where every twenty years a rebel rises to lead the people against us? A rebel always sent by their god. Annas and Caiaphas were right to denounce him. They have been rewarded. You were wrong to befriend him."

Thrasyllus interrupted now. "A question is permitted, Caesar?" he asked.

Tiberius turned his fish eyes on the astrologer and nodded.

"There is a story which I have heard from many sources that this man after he had been crucified and his death certified by the attending centurion to Pilate, this man, it is said, rose from the dead," said Thrasyllus. "This story is believed by his followers and I know that you have been in touch with them. Do you believe this story?"

"What man can rise from the dead?" I asked.

"You have not answered," said Thrasyllus.

Well, what was I to answer? There was only one reply I could give and save my life and that was that I did not believe that Jesus of Nazareth had risen from the dead. I resolved to give that reply and intended to give it but when I spoke I said instead, "I have seen him twice alive, since he was crucified."

How could I have said such a thing? As soon as the words were out of my mouth I regretted them. I assure you I had no intention of saying them. I would have cut out my tongue rather than utter them and yet I said them.

Thrasyllus looked at me with deepest interest. There was a glitter of excitement in his eyes behind his red-rimmed lids so that I knew that he believed that what I had said was true, confirming his own conclusions and magical investigations. It occurred to me then that Thrasyllus himself was behind this summons to Tiberius, for like all magicians he wanted to know above all else whether it was true that Jesus of Nazareth had raised himself from the grave. But I had no time for this line of thinking. Hardly had I made my unwilling testament to the resurrection of Jesus of Nazareth than Tiberius beckoned to those beasts of Germans behind him and as he turned one of them went for the ax in his belt.

"Our guest should return home," Tiberius said. "Let him swim. First he should dive from the cliffs, and then swim home."

As in a nightmare I was dragged off by the Germans, who hauled me by my feet across the garden to where the bold edge of the cliffs towered over the sea below. My robe slipped over my head and my naked back was lacerated on the rocks and earth. I squealed like a pig on the way to the slaughterhouse and flayed about me with my arms to the amusement of the guards and of Tiberius, who followed along, for he enjoyed such sights.

At the cliff edge one of the Germans seized my wrists and the other my ankles and then they swung me between them, waiting for the signal from Tiberius to let go and fling me over the cliff to my death a hundred feet below. How lovely the sky looked then in those last glimpses and how dear the earth and the flowers which

I saw for fractions of a second as I waited to be flung out into the empty air!

And then, when swinging higher and higher, I expected at any moment to be flung over the cliffs, I was saved. As the arc of the swing grew higher and Tiberius stood by enjoying my screams, there came from far out to sea a rumble of thunder. It was heat thunder—nothing more than that. We who have been sailors know such disturbances well. I did not hear the first rumble. But I heard the second, and the third ended with a sharp crack and a flash of lightning. And in a moment Tiberius had thrown himself on the ground with his toga drawn over his head and his behind naked to the world. I saw him because the Germans stopped swinging me. Tiberius who, like all the other Claudians, believed himself descended from Jupiter, feared only one thing in the world and that was thunder. In a thunderstorm, he was always seized by panic, believing the great god was about to destroy him.

The Germans put me down. They were frightened too. Tiberius was shouting, "Stop it. Stop it. Stop it." But the thunder rumbled on and on until the island shook. Thrasyllus just stood there staring at me. What caused me the most wonder was the sight of Tiberius on the ground, his white backside exposed and writhing in fear, because I had never expected to see an emperor's behind.

The thunder ceased in a moment. It was not a real storm, nothing more than heat thunder, as I have said. Tiberius recovered himself and the Germans prepared to fling me off the cliff again, but Tiberius slapped one of them so hard across the face that his beard in a moment was smeared with blood and snot.

"Let him go, idiot," he said. "Didn't you hear my father speaking? Send him away from here and never let him return."

And so, by the sheerest good luck, I escaped death. One has no right to expect that kind of luck, and yet every man has his share of it, and there is no man who has reached fifty years of age who cannot look back on his life and see how many times he has been saved by such undeserved good fortune.

When I got back to Rome, you may be sure I sacrificed four bullocks and five ostriches (they are very expensive) to Jupiter; I did that just in case the god had saved me but I think it was just luck, for what god would ever be interested in me, Theophilus?

XVIII

THE NEWS that I had been saved from death on Capri by a thunderstorm brought about a most fortunate change in my position in Rome. I have already told you that before I went to Capri people avoided me as having fallen into the Emperor's ill favor, and Gaius Caligula had made a mocking reference to my imminent death. When I got back, my survival was held due to my piety and the intervention of the gods, and many eminent callers came to my house to inquire the details and give me gifts and their best wishes.

I knew myself, of course, that my salvation was just a matter of luck. You will not deceive a sailor on the subject of a thunderstorm. However, Romans and landsmen live on superstitions and all now took it that I stood in the special favor of Jupiter and would live a long and happy life. Even the priests of Jupiter visited me, and so as not to appear impious, I was obliged over and above the bullocks and ostriches to spend far greater sums in sacrifices to that god, and in offerings as well, than I had intended. However, I was not going to quarrel overmuch about public expenditure in gratitude to a god whose attention I certainly could not claim to deserve. It is very comfortable, for a while, to be thought pious, and this view never having been taken of me before, I enjoyed the novelty of it for a time. Even John the Hammer came up from Ostia to congratulate me on my escape. To my surprise (for he was an eminently practical man) he said seriously that my escape was undoubtedly owing to divine intervention.

"There was always something odd about you, Theophilus," he said. "Plainly you have found favor with whatever gods there are. Jupiter is an old lecher and nobody cares about him except children and a few old women. As for Apollo, with that good-looking face and smooth behind, he wouldn't survive five minutes in half the baths in Rome, god or no god. But whatever god there is above the race of men has his eye on you. You're lucky. Maybe I ought to worship you except that I've seen you whipped too many times. Here. Let me touch you," and he reached out to touch his hand with mine.

"Why?" I asked.

"For luck," said John the Hammer. "Also I had a young soldier the other night—a lovely little boy from Calabria—and the centurion is getting angry, for he wanted him for himself." And then he gave that raucous laugh of his which is half madness and half a challenge. He used to laugh like that on the war galleys when we engaged in battle, and under the whip shout prayers to the gods of the Carthaginians that the Romans would be defeated, even though that meant his own death. You are not to think that John the Hammer was not afraid of death. He held that fear of death which is common to all but glory hunters and other lunatics. But when in danger he shouted at Death as if it were a person and dared it to come for him.

I have referred to eminent callers. Half-a-dozen Senators came to pay their respects (all had avoided me when I first arrived in Rome). They came at night, of course, and in disguise, for Tiberius was always suspicious of individual Senators, though he held the whole body of the Senate in the greatest reverence. They were very old men, helped up the stairs and in and out of litters by their slaves, and one of these, who could remember from his earliest childhood stories of the assassination of Caesar (no other in fact than Gaius Maximus Leguma, whose family traced its descent from the goddess Minerva), wanted to know whether Jupiter had not appeared in the form of a bull at the height of the thunderstorm.

When I told him no, he was disappointed and went away saying that it was probably not Jupiter at all who had saved me, but some inferior diety.

Another caller was an old colonel of the army of Germanicus—that is, the army which had avenged Roman honor on the terrible frontier of the Rhine. Such a man you may be sure I received warmly, pressing him to stay with me and giving him many gifts besides entertaining him with wine and good food. The poor fellow was quite surprised, for he and his fellow officers had, since the murder of Germanicus, become military outcasts in Rome. He had no employment and no pension and subsisted on a farm in the hill country which scarcely produced enough for himself and his family. Still he called on me, not to congratulate me on my escape or my favor with Jupiter but to ask after the health of Tiberius.

Yes! He dared talk of the health of Tiberius, which was certainly a forbidden topic in Rome lest an accusation be leveled of wishing the Emperor's death. Poor Colonel Servius, however, had no sensitivity at all and his rough tongue was without a doubt one reason why there was no place for him in the army and only a starvation farm available for him and his family after all his years with the eagles.

"Little Boots will change everything," he said, taking a good manly gulp from his wine cup. "Oh, never mind that he plays a little rough now. A boy brought up in a

Roman camp is not going to have good house manners, I can tell you. But his heart is sound, never fear, and he will not forget the old soldiers and officers who were his nursemaids on the Rhine. When he is Caesar, we who knew him will have our rights."

A little later when he had had a few more gulps he told me the full story of the campaign which had won back the lost eagles of Varus' legions and the finding of the place where the survivors of the legions had made their last stand.

"Bones all about," he said. "Horse bones and men's bones and skulls nailed to trees or stuck up on poles. A lot of the troops had been impaled—you know how it is done. A sharpened pole is put in the ground and well greased with beef fat and then a man is lifted up and sat on it so that the pole is driven right up his behind, and the more he wiggles and screams the lower he sinks on the stake. Well, we found a lot of skeletons on poles like that, and some of them burned in pits so they were burned alive. You know what I say? I say it serves them right for surrendering. A soldier's always got his sword after all, and when things are bad and going to get worse, a good man will fall on it.

"But the army isn't what it used to be. Soft. All of them. That's what's the matter. Soldiers ask, 'What's this war all about anyway?' as if it was any of their business. And then they get so they don't hate the enemy and that's always a mistake. Well. They lost the eagles and those that survived were impaled and crucified and burned alive and serves them right. But when we have Little Boots as Caesar things will be different. Little Boots was brought up a soldier."

I had my doubts about Little Boots from what I had heard of him from many others besides John the Hammer. But this bluff old soldier, living in the country, either would not believe such tales or had not heard them. He praised Tiberius but gave it as his opinion that he was misinformed by his ministers.

"That Macro is a palace soldier just like Sejanus was," he snorted. "All wine and shout. But when the legions move out in the German mists to make their stand and the ravens start crowing overhead expecting a feast, you won't find men like Macro around. Tiberius should have more sense than to trust him. He's seen the ravens and crows feasting many a time."

Altogether I enjoyed the old colonel's company. He had a Roman's point of view: sacrifice, loyalty to the old gods, belief that the worship of Mithras, now prevalent in the legions, was softening up the men and destroying their spirit. He hated the Praetorians and, referring to the black horsehair plumes of their helmets, said that all you ever found under a horse's tail was a horse's ass. He also resented the fact that the Caesar's bodyguards were all Germans. When he was a little drunker he sang some of the old army songs—the one everybody knows that Caesar's legions, Rome-bound, used to sing, warning the men at home to lock up their wives and daughters, for the old baldheaded lecher was coming to make play with his weapon, and another of which I remember the following lines:

> *I've been a soldier since I was born*
> *And me dad was a soldier before,*
> *He won half of Gaul on a handful of corn*
> *And chose for me mother a whore.*
>
> *A big-breasted whore from a good Roman stew*
> *Who'd welcome a maniple an hour,*
> *She gave each her all for a minute or two—*
> *Such seeding brought me as the flower.*
>
> *So watch out, old Herman, you big-butted German*
> *A-lolling on Father Rhine's shore,*
> *You'd better run faster, you're facing disaster*
> *From five thousand sons of a whore.*
>
> *Heigh ho,*
> *From five thousand sons of a whore.*

It was a much better song than the one Caballus sang with its interminable *hoch hoch hoch* chorus. Philip does not approve, of course, of my including it in this testament, saying that it is vulgar and has no bearing on my tale. But I want to show the kind of soldier that once served Rome before the present rot set in. They were staunch men. There should be a tribute to them somewhere.

I was telling you, however, about the distinguished visitors my escape from Capri brought me—priests from the temple of Jupiter the Greatest and Best, Senators of some of the oldest families in Rome, the fine old colonel, and most surprising of all, Gaius Caligula.

This time he didn't bring with him a lot of old furniture. He came disguised as a woman accompanied by an older man posing as her father, but who was actually Cassius Chaerea, a senior centurion transferred from the army of Germany to Rome at the request of Caligula. Caligula had a mania for disguises and playacting. He disguised himself as a madam, as I have told you, and actually ran a brothel on the Tiber while plotting against Sejanus. He disguised himself as a Thracian gladiator (he liked Thracians) and was very nearly killed in a street brawl as a result, for he was a poor hand with weapons. He disguised himself as a barrel roller, as collectors of liquid garbage were called, and once as the god Mercury, running through the city in the dawn hours naked except for an athlete's skimpy short tunic and with gold wings tied to his sandals. He was met by a party of revelers on that occasion and beaten, for drunk as they were, they were not going to be deceived into confusing the hairy spindly legs of Caligula with the magnificent limbs of the great messenger of the gods.

The strange thing is that Caligula always expected everybody he met to believe these deceits which he practiced on himself and yet at the same time recognize that beneath the disguise was the great Caligula. He thus both denied and asserted himself at the same time. But then he was rumored mad even in those days among those who knew him. A glimpse of that madness was given me when he called on me in the disguise of a woman.

"Do you not know me, Theophilus?" he asked as soon as he was brought into my presence. "Do you not sense some aura about me?"

Now I recognized him immediately not only because I knew about his disguises from John the Hammer, but also because it was impossible to mistake those sunken eyes, that broad forehead, and the pronounced hollows of the temples.

"Indeed, I recognize you, Gaius Caligula," I said. "And I am honored that you should come to visit me."

"You see?" he said, turning delightedly to Cassius. "It shines through. It gets stronger every day. However I disguise it, it is stronger. That is why Ennia"—she was the wife of Macro—"has to close her eyes when she is copulating with me. And I have the divine disease, you know, like Julius Caesar. I have fits and am thrown to the ground by the jealous gods."

I soon learned the reason for Gaius Caligula's visit. Although he was often now summoned to Capri, as the sole heir of Tiberius, whose only son Drusus had choked to death on an apple some years before—he had thrown it up in the air and on trying to catch it in his mouth it had lodged in his throat (that was the story)—although, then, often summoned to Capri, Caligula had not been there during my visit, remaining in Rome. But he had had news of what had happened (as had all of Rome, as I have said). He had not, however, come to congratulate me on my escape, nor congratulate me on being so deeply in the favor of Jupiter. No. Caligula wanted to hear what Thrasyllus had wanted to know—he wanted to know about the Nazarene, Jesus.

The last thing in the world I wanted to talk about was the Nazarene. How malicious of the gods, I thought, that they should have thrown me and this Jew together—two people who had nothing whatever to do with each other and nothing in common. But Gaius Caligula was merciless in his questioning and even dragged out of me a confirmation of the story of how the spirits had left the pythoness Tabitha at the mention of the name of Jesus. (That story he knew, anyway. Thrasyllus had told him, and the keeper of Tabitha at Joppa had written the details to Thrasyllus, for, as I have remarked before, all these magicians keep up a correspondence with each other.)

Then he wanted to know all the details concerning the birth of Jesus, the signs that had accompanied his birth, and the wonders he had performed while alive. Of course you may think that he would have done better to have written to Herod or to Pilate for these details. But, as in the finding of a successor to Sejanus, Caligula had proceeded by guile and indirection, so now, in finding out about Jesus, he went to neutral and not to official sources. He had already, I learned, questioned many Jews returning from the Pasch in Jerusalem about Jesus and believed him to be, as I did myself, a demigod at least.

In the end, to get rid of him, I promised to dictate a written account of the life of Jesus. That was easy to do. I merely borrowed passages from the account sent me by Luke, and sent that to him—a very much shortened version.

Caligula studied it and appropriated episodes from it. He was soon suggesting that he had been born in a cave in Antium and that at his birth three stars had stood over the cave in the form of a sacred triangle and that the gods disguised as shepherds had visited him and given him gifts.

Sometimes he said his father was Jupiter and sometimes Mars, and he said that Germanicus was no more his father than a cup is the father of the wine that is poured from it. For a while also he went about touching sick beggars and pretending to cure them. Some he bribed or frightened to say that they had been cured by him. But once when he was pretending to cure a blind woman in the Forum, an eagle which had perched for a moment on the temple of Janus suddenly swooped down and struck his baldish head with its claws, ripping his scalp. That so frightened him that he stopped his cures.

However, as he was always short of money he took to selling divine medicines and became in a little while an expert poisoner.

XIX

ALTHOUGH I HAD DREADED going to Rome, which is always full of dangers for a man of wealth, and temptations as well, I found it difficult to leave at first. We Romans live our fullest in Rome and, removed from the city, ours is only a partial life full of longing to return. Perhaps the danger itself is part of the attraction, for who wishes to live like a cow, devoid of love or of fear? Besides I soon had several agreeable mistresses in Rome, one the wife of a knight who, since he was devoted to pederasty himself, raised no objection. Indeed he had married Flora Panae only to escape enslavement for debt, divorcing his first wife who was as avid a spender as himself.

For Flora, the arrangement was entirely satisfactory. She was an open, generous, happy woman who loved to copulate and did not wish to be restricted to one bed. I met her at a party in my honor arranged by one Vitellius, a close friend of Gaius Caligula, of whom I will perhaps say more later. Vitellius had made an art of flattery and, sickening though it was to see him practice that art on others, I have to confess that it was very gratifying, though expensive, when he practiced it on me.

At this party, for instance, everything had been arranged

to pay tribute to my eminence in the world of shipping, as chief supplier of corn to Rome.

Imagine the splendor of the setting.

There was a vast dining hall before which had been constructed in a few days a huge artificial lake representing the Great Sea with two small islands representing Crete and Cyprus. A jetty covered with flowers at one side of the lake represented Ostia, and the dining hall itself, decorated with flowers, with banners, with statues of gods and warriors, Rome.

The dining hall was lit with a thousand torches in polished brass holders when we arrived for the feast, but the tables (of polished Nubian ebony) at which we were to recline were bare of anything but flowers. A huge Parthian, painted all over with gold, at the striking of a gong, arose from the water of the lake and, dressed like the god Neptune, sounded a conch shell (it was full of water and gave, until emptied, a miserable blat), and then out of the darkness which enshrouded the other side of the lake came a flower-bedecked ship, rowed by slaves but with sails of silk, and containing all the foods for our feast—oysters (each containing a pearl), fish of every kind, roast pigs, roast beef, cascades of fruit including the wonderful purple figs of Judaea and the tart apples of Syria, and also mounds of the yellow sausage-shaped fruit of wisdom beneath whose delightful fronds, it is said, the sages of India rest, cogitate, and eat. There were wines of every kind and honey and bread and pastries and on the sail of the ship as it approached were the words, "Theo Provides All." This was received with thunderous applause by the several hundred guests who attended and I, thinking that they were praising my work in supplying Rome with her corn and many of her other necessaries and luxuries, was highly flattered and made a fine speech which was interrupted by a few ruffians demanding food.

Later, however, I found that the message on the sail was to be interpreted literally rather than figuratively, for the bills for all this splendor were presented to my stewards. They had paid a great portion before the matter was brought to my own attention, whereupon I stopped payment and demanded of Vitellius an explanation.

"My good friend," he said, "believe me, I only wanted to give you an opportunity to show your fellow Romans the amount of your love for them and your generosity towards them. Already your name is being praised in every corner of the city, and a proposal is to be brought forward in the Senate for the erection of a statue to you in the Forum—to be put, in fact, in the very place once occupied by the statue of Sejanus, which, as you know, was thrown down. Beneath is to be the inscription 'Theophilus—Lover of Rome and of the People.'

"I was quite sure," he continued, "that, in making all the arrangements for the tribute in your honor, you would not want your friends, needy as they are, to bear the cost of their good wishes. However, if you find the tribute too lavish, a public subscription can perhaps be launched to pay the cost of the tribute, but think what harm that would do to the reputation for generosity and love of your fellow citizens which you have now gained in this city."

Caballus also, when he heard I objected to the payment of the bill for a feast given in my honor, turned angrily on me. He was not, of course, a Roman, but a German, and even if he had been given citizenship, he would have remained a German, for that is the way with his people. Citizenship is wasted on them. As it was, he judged the whole event by his German standards and said that among his people, who were regarded as barbarous, it was held a matter of honor for the chief to pay for a feast, and furthermore that these feasts lasted not two or three days, as was the case with mine, but several weeks, and there was never a single case of the chief complaining about the size of the bill. He said he would certainly leave my service if I did not wipe out the stain to his name (yes, *his* name, not mine) by immediately agreeing to settle the full account.

I have told you that Caballus, since I had removed the iron collar from his neck, regarded himself as a free man, so his threat to leave my service was not idle. He could be replaced, of course. Yet I have to confess I had become fond of him. It is certainly true that the master is owned by his slaves (I speak of those who are members of his household) for to have dismissed Caballus would have been to hurt myself.

I do not pretend that his attitude persuaded me to pay the bills. I mention it only as a surprising view which I found widely shared. In the end not only did I pay all the bills, but also was persuaded to provide three weeks of free admission to the hundred and thirty public baths which I owned about Rome. But I was wise enough to dissuade the Senate through friends from proposing the erection of a statue to my honor. Not only was Tiberius known to be insanely jealous of all those to whom such honors were proposed, but in walking about the streets and public places of Rome, I could not fail to note that the base of almost every statue in the city was used by the wags for writing uncomplimentary comments and little verses. Even the statues of Tiberius were not exempt. Of course it was death to even let your eyes fall upon the uncomplimentary verses which (despite attempts at removal) still defaced the statues of the Emperor. Yet one could read them out of the corner of the eye. One said:

> *The old goat prefers to lick*
> *Instead of using Nature's stick.*

Another, referring to the habit of Tiberius of drinking his wine neat when he was a young man, said:

> *Neat wine won't do*
> *To offset the cold,*
> *He drinks men's blood*
> *Now that he's old.*

In the time of Sejanus the number of executions in Rome had been kept within reasonable limits—two or three a week; no more. But the Stairs of Mourning were never empty now, strangled bodies being thrown down them at all hours. I heard it said that as many as half a dozen a day were dispatched, some of them young girls. Since it is contrary to piety for a virgin to be strangled, such victims were always first raped by the executioner so that the gods would not be offended. This, by the way, was done with Sejanus' daughter, who was twelve at the time.

Alas for Rome! Beneath all her gaiety and her activity, her fine displays of gladiatorial games, her public baths, her bustling Forum, her great feasts, her busy shops and gossiping people (for two Romans never meet but they discuss the world) beneath all this I found after a while not wholesome content but nagging fear. Yes—a rising fear which convinced many that the end not only of Rome but of the world was approaching fast.

The temples, as the stranglings mounted, were now rarely without people offering sacrifices, though in peaceful times they are, as the world knows, neglected. When things go well, what after all is there to pray for? Also many foreign gods now had their secret temples and priests; gods of the eastern peoples, who lacked the strength of the gods of Rome and appealed to a people grown soft and fearful.

There were many secret religions which had not the approval of the Senate and the Emperor and whose worshipers gathered in the basements of houses or in the underground cemeteries or catacombs or even built entirely secret underground buildings, whose entrances were unknown except to the worshipers.

It is said that the Jews first started this practice of secret worship. That may be so. However, I think other eastern religions first started the underground mystery shrines, particularly those of Persia.

Astrologers abounded. So many managed their affairs under the direction of these stargazers that the practice of astrology was now subject to strict controls. All who claimed the lore had to register with the authorities, and no prediction might be made except in the presence of witnesses. Their booths, however, with drawings on the walls of the sun and the constellations, were to be found in every street and some had a license to erect booths on the edges of the Forum, where they plied a brisk trade.

There was not, I think, a Roman who did not carry some charm or amulet to ward off evil, a favorite being the dried foot of some bird or beast such as a rabbit or a dove. A piece of wood from a cross on which a man had been crucified was thought to bring good luck, as was also the leather noose with which most criminals were strangled in the underground prison adjoining the Forum. Both these charms protected the owner against a similar death as well as bringing good influences into his life.

Although the number of gladiators private citizens might own had been limited to three hundred and twenty pairs (and few indeed could afford such an investment, for the cost of feeding them was huge) nonetheless no man of substance walked the streets of Rome without a bodyguard of half-a-dozen men, which enormously added to the congestion. Caballus customarily hired some of his countrymen for my protection.

It is well known, of course, that all wheeled traffic in the city was forbidden until the middle of the afternoon, but even so the throngs in the streets were thick and clashes between gladiators brought many riots which the Praetorians were not always anxious to quell. A major source of these riots was the rivalry between the fans of chariot racing, to which Tiberius was devoted and in which Caligula was now showing great interest. (He had driven a chariot himself in a race, but not having paid enough money to his rivals, had been ignominiously beaten, whereupon he had had the horses destroyed for not doing their best for him.)

The Green faction was the favorite and the one supported by Tiberius. But sometimes the Scarlet won and then there was rioting and heads broken and many killed. A group of Green supporters had only to meet a group of Scarlet on any feast day for a riot to result and the authorities only interfered when property was endangered, for it was rightly felt that it was proper to encourage a martial spirit among the citizens of Rome.

You will have to bear with me while I deal with these matters. They touch the heart of a Roman deeply and you must remember that although born into slavery, I achieved citizenship and hold that as the greatest of my treasures. It grieved me to see that which I cherished brought so low and find free-born Romans, fearful of having to serve with the legions, hiding in slave barracks and indeed becoming slaves to avoid service—thereby completely reversing the path which I had followed with so much hardship.

A few words more then, and I am done. What I have not put down here in words, you may deduce for yourself from what I have said. For all her business and her activity and her outward gaiety a deep uncertainty and fear lay below the surface throughout Rome, fed by the predictions of astrologers, the riddles of soothsayers, the superstitions of idle women, prophecies of the end of the world, the interpretation of omens and uncertainty of daily living owing to the number of police informers everywhere—even at feasts. Insults to the Emperor or to the gods, alleged by political rivals or rivals in love or business, destroyed many a man and his family in Rome. When I was a galley slave I gave no thought to those who might die of exhaustion or under the lash or on the benches except to curse their weight on the oar. That is only natural. Agony knows no sympathy for anyone else. But it was a new experience for me, at a gathering in Rome, to have someone arrive and say that another, well known to all, had been condemned to death and have those around, beckoning for more wine, inquire languidly, "What else is new?"

That was the way matters were, as I discovered after a while. Each man sensed his own danger. None would go to help a friend. Myself, summoned to Capri, found not a consoler in Rome but John the Hammer as I have related.

It is not enough to blame Tiberius for this atmosphere of fear. One word from him, all knew, meant death and he was old now and full of suspicions. But was Tiberius to be blamed for a panic lasting several days resulting from a rumor that a new Arminius, at the head of a German horde, had crossed the Rhine and was headed for Rome?

In the time of the Republic, such a story would have brought a host of young men crowding the recruiting camps of the legions, particularly the beloved Twenty-ninth. Now all men of military age suddenly disappeared, until the rumor was proved untrue and the originator, a demented old man whose two sons had been killed on the order of Tiberius, was flung to his death from the Tarquin Rock.

"Rome fears Rome," Philip said. It is the kind of silly answer one gets from Greeks, who are always dabbling in philosophy instead of in practical matters.

"How can one fear oneself?" I demanded. "That is nonsense."

I mentioned this saying to Seneca. Although he had been uncomplimentary about this testament, as I have told you before, I still employed him in business disputes, though I had naturally reduced his fees.

"How can Rome fear Rome?" I asked. "You see the absurdities to which philosophy reduces those who practice it?"

Like all philosophers he did not reply with an answer but with a question. That is a technique of theirs to make them appear wise. He said, "My dear Theophilus, what will it profit Rome if she gains the whole world and ceases to be Rome?" What kind of sense is there in such a question? How could Rome cease to be Rome other than by her destruction? And how can a state be destroyed by world triumph since destruction by its very nature comes from defeat?

I pointed this out to Seneca. Our conversation took place on the porch of Pompey's library, where he did much of his business. "Triumph brings triumph," I continued. "Triumph cannot bring defeat and destruction."

"Tell me," said Seneca, pulling at the end of his pointed nose, which he always did when about to make a sly point. "Is Greece an independent nation?"

"It is not," I said. "It is a dependency of Rome."

"Very well. Greece was, however, once an independent nation?"

"That is so."

"And at one time the Greek king, Alexander of Macedon, had conquered the known world?"

"Except Rome," I said.

"I will grant you that. But at that time the Greeks were the greatest power on earth and had even defeated the Persians against whom our arms are, alas, inconclusive."

"No one can deny that," I replied.

"Good. Now at that time were the Greeks greatly respected for their intelligence and their learning and the love of the arts and of wisdom?"

"I am told that they were respected for their arms."

"Were Greek teachers everywhere sought?"

"I think not."

"Were Greek fashions everywhere copied and Greek art everywhere admired?"

"I do not believe so."

"It was only after their empire fell and Rome defeated the Greeks that they gained their present prestige in the world."

"Perhaps that is so."

"Can you not say definitely whether that is so or not?"

"All right. That is so."

"So do you not now see that it was only in defeat that the Greeks achieved greatness, and only when Greece had gone that Greece achieved her great glory? In short it was in defeat that Greece found herself and in victory that Greece lost herself?"

"What lesson am I to receive from this?" I demanded. "That Rome will not be truly great until her legions are conquered by the Persians or by the barbarians?"

"The lesson you are to learn from this is that you are to start thinking of something more than tons of shipping, storehouses of grain, warehouses of amphorae, the construction of aqueducts, of forts and barracks, and of public baths and roads. For, my dear Theophilus, I will now slightly change the question of my prologue to provide the epilogue and will ask, 'What will it profit Theophilus if he gains the whole world and loses Theophilus?' "

"And to your epilogue I will reply that all men must die and so all men must be lost in the end," I said.

Then Seneca looked at me earnestly and said, "If then, as you say, we have only this life to live, should you not consider deeply, Theophilus, how you should *best* live it so as not to waste one moment of it? Is not that the most important question which confronts you and in fact confronts every man?"

Now I can truthfully say that up to that moment I had not the slightest doubt of the purpose to which I should direct my life. I wished for wealth and power above all else, and bent every effort as the world well knows to attaining both, and with great success. I am entitled to boast of that success. No man may take it from me. All that I achieved, I achieved alone, and it is ridiculous to pretend that among men of affairs my name is not known and respected all over the world.

Nor am I going to pretend that those words of Seneca's had any immediate effect on me. Not at all. I dismissed them with a shrug, putting them down to envy and asking myself how a man who was so good a lawyer could at the same time be so mistaken about values; for Seneca clearly held the accumulation of wealth and power a waste of life. That, of course, is a view often held by those who have neither wealth nor power and the sudden death of a wealthy man in unhappy circumstances is always a great comfort to the poor as showing the retribution of the gods—as if the gods did not love the rich.

No. Those words of Seneca's had no effect on me at the time. But like the little shipworm which can sink a ship, though when it first enters her planking it makes a hole too small to be seen, so Seneca's words bored into my mind. They would return to me when I lay in bed at night and thought mournfully of death as all men must do. They would come to me on some pleasant occasion, when drinking with my friends or making love to women. Nor was it an effective antidote to curse Seneca as a fool and a failure and drink more deeply. I began to examine the quality of my pleasures and found many not as enjoyable as I had thought. (I wish I had never got into such a miserable habit. I advise you strongly against it. That way lies the road to misery.)

Philip noticed a change in me in the months that followed, and Caballus begged me many a time to go with him and his friends to the German quarter of the city and drink vast quantities of beer and eat sausages and pickles and sing their interminable *hoch hoch hoch* songs. I did go several times, but not with the same old gusto. Seeking to overcome my depressions I gave a gladiatorial exposition at Caesar's old wooden amphitheater close to the Field of Mars, at which two hundred pairs of gladiators fought, Samnites and Thracians, single and in groups of half a dozen, with a wild-beast hunt beforehand, and although these combats have always delighted me, I found no real pleasure in them, though there was indeed for a moment the old exaltation when the crowd roared at the death thrust and Thracian or Samnite went to the ground, blossoming blood.

In the heat of the summer I moved to the country and returned to Rome in the winter. Now I did not want to remain in Rome, yet found myself indecisive and so stayed throughout the winter. Then in the spring something remarkable happened. I rose early one morning and went out of the city on the Appian Way. It had rained lightly during the night and in the newly risen sun a thousand diamonds sparkled on the grass among the tombs. A few people were out picking mushrooms and one or two carts had begun to move along the road. I came unexpectedly on an old wild-plum tree, its roots thrust into a moldering wall. It had been struck by lightning, but on one branch and one branch only, a few delicate pink blooms smiled against the sky.

And when I saw them, for no reason at all, I burst into tears and thought of the road to Joppa and the pleasant clopping of the horse's hooves as Cleophas told me of the Nazarene.

I decided immediately to quit Rome and to return to Judaea—to see again the quiet sunlit hills and the wild lupine. Or so I told myself.

BOOK III

XX

IN PUTTING MY AFFAIRS IN ORDER to return to Judaea, I completed plans to convert all my interests to shipping, for Rome now imported everything, and by sea, and a single voyage could turn a profit of 200 percent. My stone quarries and clay pits, my public baths and other investments were sold and the money used in the construction of more ships. In recognition of this change I added an anchor to my signet ring, placed below the amphora which was my previous sign.

All being then in order, I went back to Judaea, visited the innkeeper at Emmaus and saw again the lily-strewn fields and the sheets of lupine. (I had lost money on my previous purchase of seed for slaves, but recouped the loss by selling the seeds to farmers for winter cattle feed.) And then I went on to Jerusalem and from Jerusalem to that magnificent Temple of white stone, standing on its hill in the city and surmounting it like the snowy cap of a great peak.

All through the day that Temple shines in the sunlight, visible from afar, so excellently was it designed by Herod the Great. At night it has a moth glow in the starlight above the dark of the city, where at dusk every door is shut and every window shuttered. Having been put in such peril because of my knowledge of Jesus, and remembering the advice of Tutmoshe to find out all I could of him since he was certainly a demigod, and interested in me, I sought out Peter, the chief of his Apostles or messengers who preached in his name.

It was not hard to find him. He was as well known in Jerusalem as Caiaphas. He went every day, at the first summons of the priest, "Hear, oh Israel . . ." to the Temple to make his sacrifice and to pray. He remained for some time on the Porch of the Gentiles and preached to the throngs who gathered around him. Of course, he was not the only one preaching around the Temple. Not at all. The Jews are forever ready to talk and argue about their religion. Their beliefs, like those of the Egyptians, are written down for them in a series of five books telling the story of the creation of the world, and giving the laws which they must follow in the worship of their god and so on. The Egyptians are quite content to leave the interpretation of the laws of their gods to their priests. But the Jews are constantly arguing about the interpretation of these laws and the interpretation of the words of their prophets. Many then preached about the Temple, but the biggest crowd gathered around Peter. This was a great annoyance to the High Priests, to Annas and Caiaphas, the more so because Peter and those with him—that is to say, one James of Zebedee and his brother John, and also a man called James, who was himself a cousin or some such relative of Jesus of Nazareth—insisted that Jesus had been the Messiah and that he had been put to death by the High Priests. After listening to what Peter said (for I did not intrude myself on him immediately on arriving in Jerusalem), I was surprised by the tolerance of Caiaphas. But then since these men attracted huge crowds, it would have been difficult to seize Peter without a tumult.

I was not impressed by what Peter said in his preaching at all. Really it was all nonsense to me. To understand the religion of the Jews, one has to devote years of study to their books and even that won't do, for you have to have a teacher explain what the books mean. There were many references by Peter to Isaiah and to David and others, but not knowing really who these people were or what was their significance in the Jewish religion, I found it all beyond me. Besides, as a Gentile I stood out among the crowd, who were almost all Jews, with their ringlets of hair falling down the sides of their heads, their prayer shawls and skull caps, and their air both of curiosity and of secrecy.

Every now and then one in the crowd would cry out something and strike his breast or his forehead. Some fell to the ground in an ecstasy or agony and some tried to kiss the feet of Peter or John or James or whoever was with him, which disgusted me for, as you know, I had myself, a Roman, refused even to bow to Tiberius.

The only friendly faces in that crowd were those of one or two Roman soldiers who stood by to keep an eye on things. Strictly speaking they had no business there, for there were Temple soldiers in the control of the priests to keep order. Being on Temple grounds they were compelled to leave off ornamental breastplates or helmets which might show the Roman eagles or any other image, and even the scabbards of their swords were plain and the pommels of the swords (on which often the head of Hercules or of Mars or perhaps of a bear or lion is carved) had to be the unadorned regulation issue. It was only natural that I should stand close to my countrymen in listening to Peter, and exchange a few remarks about what was being said.

I expected scorn from the soldiers, but found them respectful instead. In fact, instead of egging on the dissidents in the crowd against Peter and the others, which was what one would reasonably expect, they quieted a few of them with a stern look or a move towards them.

"What do you think of all this?" I asked one of them.

He was a tough old man of sixty years or more. The corners of his eyes were lined by decades of squinting in the glare of sun and of snow, and his shallow cheeks were sunk in both by age and the lack of teeth to support them. These are the best men of Rome, I assure you. Alas, that they are so few, for the ranks of the legions are filled more and more with Syrians and Parthians and Gauls. But here was a Roman of Rome and a man of forty-five years of service.

"I don't understand all that Jewish stuff any more than you, sir," he said. "But there's something to what he says all right. The Jews have always known more about the gods than anybody else. That's my opinion. Now you take this man Jesus they're talking of that was crucified. They say he rose from the dead. Well, this very evening that Peter of Capernaum—it's a little town on the Sea of Tiberius, sir; that's where he comes from—well, him and them others will start healing the sick right here; cripples and blind and such like, in the name of that same Jesus. And make no mistake, they really cure them. No fakes at all. I've been here five years and some of them as is cured, I've known myself. You know how it is. They sit outside the barracks or wherever people pass by and beg. Their friends bring them in the morning if they are blind or lame and then take them home in the evening, though I've known some what was left there all night. To punish them, I suppose.

"Well, you get to know particular beggars, passing them every day, and they aren't too proud to take a penny, even from a Roman soldier. Usually I give to the blind ones. There's a lot of blind in this country. I think it's the sun, or the dust. But to get back to what I was saying, sir, if that same Jesus didn't rise from the dead, and that story is all a lie, then how can they do all these cures calling on his name? And if he did rise from the dead, who was he? Not a man like us, sir. That's for sure."

"Always supposing that he *was* dead," I said.

It was a ridiculous thing for me to have said, of course. I had seen Jesus half dead after the flogging, and the report of his death had been brought to Pilate by the officer in charge of the execution. He dared not lie, for the Roman law, as you know, is this—if a condemned man escapes death, then the officer responsible for his execution is to die in his place and in the same manner—crucified, in this case.

My soldier friend looked at me oddly and said, "You heard that story too, eh? That he wasn't dead but unconscious and was taken down in a hurry and revived in the tomb? Well. That's a lie. Because I'm the man that nailed him up. And I watched him die, with that crowd around wagging their heads and sticking out their tongues and telling him to come on down and save himself.

"And I was right there when the centurion Longinus—he's still about here—took my stabbing spear (we infantry as you know use the short ones now, following the German style for close fighting) and rammed it into his heart. Nothing come out but a little blood and water, which ran down the shaft. There wasn't enough blood left in him to feed a gnat.

"I thought then that he was what they call kosher—that's the way they dress their meat to eat, sir. Drained of blood. They bleed it to death. Just like this Jesus. So he was kind of food for them. You get these queer fancies now and again," he added lamely.

Certainly I believed this old soldier of Rome, who for all his years' service in the legions was not even a senior centurion, but an ordinary legionnaire. Still, Rome was not to be blamed for that. He had many times, he told me, been promoted to command of a maniple and then of a century. But he had uncontrollable bouts of drinking, to which he confessed cheerfully, and was always demoted. His name was Balbus and I would think him the world authority on the beers and the wines of Gaul and Germany. He had served even in Britain and drunk a fiery drink called "aquavit" or "water of life" which he had found among the Pictish tribes of the north part of the island. "Goes down your gullet like rusty hooks," he said. "But it makes you surprisingly cheerful in a minute."

That evening, prompted by Balbus, I came to the Temple to watch the cures. Several thousand people had gathered even before I arrived, bringing the maimed and blind and sick with them. There were half a dozen Apostles about, eyeing the array. Everything was very orderly. The sick were put in rows on the steps of the Temple. The Temple was now all gold in the westering sun, and the shadows of the columns made lines of indigo on the marble pavement.

Peter and his companions, having made their evening offerings, came out and began to move around among the sick people.

I had brought Philip with me. I am after all a man of business and Philip's feet were crippled. Why shouldn't I, even though a Gentile, try to profit from such an opportunity by having him cured? Those who are defeated in life defeat themselves, saying that there is no use trying such and such a thing for it will not succeed. Well, my practice is to try it anyway. Let the world defeat you, but be on your own side in all matters. That is my advice.

Philip was excited. He was deeply interested in Jesus of Nazareth through reading Luke's account of his life, together with those letters Luke had sent relating some of the occurrences among the Apostles—the great wind and the tongues of fire—of which I have told you. To walk without crutches was his dearest wish, and despite his Grecian pretenses to superiority over us Romans, I had spent a lot of money hoping to help him regain the use of his feet, but to no avail. Of course since he was not a Jew, he could not lie with the Jewish sick, but I obtained a good place in the crowd where one of the Apostles must pass by, when I would ask him to cure Philip for me, and offer a generous payment as well.

I had expected pushing and shouting and scenes of hysteria but instead everything was subdued, as if for a religious service. Peter stood for a while on the top of the flight of steps on which the sick were waiting and said that they should pray the prayer they had been taught by the master. I have heard it many times since and indeed there are many parodies of it about, now that the followers of Christ have become an object of scorn.

Here it is: "Our Father, who art in heaven; may your name be blessed. May your Kingdom of Truth and Righteousness come. May your will be done on earth by men as it is in Heaven among the angels. Give us this day the food we need. Forgive us our offenses against you in the same measure as we forgive the offenses our brothers have committed against us. Lead us not into judgment but deliver us from Evil. So may it be." Most of the people seemed to know it, and I saw the lips of the soldier Balbus moving.

When the prayer was over the Apostles went around among the sick and I watched them closely to learn their method. They made a magic sign over each one with their right hand. Balbus said it was the Sign of the Cross, and more and more of the believers in Jesus used it during prayers or in greeting each other. After the magic sign had been made, the sick or infirm person was questioned (if he was not deaf) and then the Apostle put his hand on him and said something. The questions and what was said I did not hear until Peter got close to me. The question was this: "Brother, do you believe that Jesus of Nazareth who was crucified was and is the son of the living God, the savior of the world?" Sometimes the reply made was merely a nod of the head. When the reply affirming belief had been given then Peter would say, "In the name then of Jesus, the son of the living God, and according to the faith that is in you, may you be made whole."

I saw several lame people and one blind man cured. No doubt about it. The formula worked. And yet not all were cured by any means. Many cures failed and when this happened Peter would say, "Brother, you must receive the son of God more fully. You have the door but halfway open. Open it with abundance. Pray for belief."

"But I *do* believe," cried one on whom the cure had been ineffective. "Why am I rejected?"

Peter tried again with this man, who had a withered arm, and again failed.

"Why is it not cured?" asked the man in amazement, staring at his arm.

"Because the Messiah wishes you to bear that affliction for him, brother," said Peter.

"Why should I?" demanded the man fiercely. "I have borne it all my life."

"Is it really so much?" asked Peter. "Didn't he die on

the Cross for you? How much does a withered arm weigh against such a death?"

I wish we had not overheard those words. They undid all my plans for Philip. The love of philosophy is certainly the ruin of the Greeks both as a nation and as individuals. For when Philip heard Peter ask the man whether he could not bear a withered arm, when he who could cure him had borne death by crucifixion for his sake, Philip turned and rushed away on his crutches down the Temple steps. It was useless to call him back. He would not listen to me, but went off and was soon lost in the crowd.

Peter saw Philip go, heard me calling and turned to look at me. He had a good seaman's look. There is no mistaking that look anywhere. It is open, simple, and yet wise. I had thought he might be pious, which is what divides me from priests other than my good friend Tutmoshe. But he was wholesome and plain and there was almost a smell of salt air about him. I would have put to sea with him without a moment's hesitation.

"Why do you stand here among the Children of Israel?" he asked mildly.

"I hoped you would cure my slave," I replied.

Peter turned to the others and said, "See, my brothers, how the Master loves and serves his servant. So Jesus told us we must do when he himself washed our feet. He told us none should set himself above his brethren, and he that was last, would be first, and he who was first would be last, and he who was placed in authority must be ready to do the most lowly work for his brothers. Bear that well in mind, remembering that it is through pride that the angels fell."

Then, addressing himself to me, he said, "Send your slave to the brethren at their house and if it is the will of God, he will be cured."

With such a promise I went off to find Philip.

XXI

PHILIP REFUSED to be cured. He decided to bear his crippled feet for the crucified Jew, and no amount of pleading, coaxing, or even bullying on my part could make him change his mind. It was really frustrating. Perhaps you think I talk too much of madness in connection with the Jew and the followers of Jesus of Nazareth, yet can you deny that a cripple refusing to be cured is out of his wits? And is it not frightening to reflect that this insanity was now spreading from the Jews to non-Jews like Philip? It was a contagion and I was afraid that I might be, unwittingly, coming under the Jew's influence myself. After all, what was I doing in Judaea anyway? Is it sensible for a man to make such a journey, impelled to it by a sight of a blossoming plum tree, itself perhaps an enchantment of Jesus?

I reflected deeply on my relationship to him and wondered whether when I gave him that cup of wine during his trial before Pilate, he had not put a spell on me. I had ample proof that he was a great magician. Indeed, I half-expected to see the Jew again in Jerusalem, standing perhaps in the shadow of a doorway or walking through the gardens on the eastern side of the city. I found myself looking for him in alleyways and bazaars and around mason's yards, where I thought he might be since he had followed the trade of stonecutter. Once I saw a man who looked like him, and touched him, but when he turned around it was a stranger.

"Who are you?" I asked.

"Barabbas," he replied.

"I thought you were another," I said.

The man drew the Sign of the Cross on his breast with his forefinger, questioning me with his eyes.

"Yes," I said. "Him."

"It is strange," he said. "Many think that."

"Were you at Emmaus a year ago?" I asked. "At the inn there? Was it you I saw with two others—Cleophas, a shepherd, and a friend?"

"No," he said. "I have never stayed at the inn at Emmaus. I was at Antioch."

Still, having seen one who looked very like Jesus, it certainly occurred to me that there might be others and there might be, as Caiaphas maintained staunchly, a conspiracy among the disciples of Jesus to have one or another of these look-alikes appear here or there, so that the rumor of the resurrection could be spread around. The man at the inn at Emmaus I had not clearly seen at all. I only had seen three, where others were prepared to testify there were but two. And whoever it was that had appeared over the tomb, when I visited it, might have been someone who had stood there watching me examining the empty grave and the broken stone. You see I was fighting against the contagion of the Nazarene, and it was a great relief to have these explanations, for I am a man of business and of reason.

Mixed with this relief at the sensible explanations of the resurrection, there was also a feeling of sadness. Examining this, I found it came from a desire to believe that Jesus had triumphed over death. I remembered his face, so fine and strong and young. Was it now only a moldering skull, lying in some hole where his body had been put when it had been stolen from the tomb?

I was annoyed to find on reaching Jerusalem that Luke had gone to Antioch, taking with him Mary, the mother of Jesus. She had been put by Jesus in the care of John of Zebedee, but he, filled with what was called "the Spirit," was preaching in Jerusalem. The rising emnity against the Christians (of which I will say more later) made it unsafe for Mary to remain, and so she had been sent to Antioch with Luke, who had become her very good and trusted friend. (All that he knew or wrote about the childhood of Jesus, he had got from the mother Mary. The Apostles knew very little of it, and weren't interested either.)

The Apostles had bought the large house with an upstairs banqueting room in which they had eaten their last meal with Jesus. It was now their meeting place, and it was here that I went to find out at firsthand, as Tutmoshe had advised, more about Jesus. It was here that I was able to question Peter about him, putting aside for a while all that Luke had written me. It is best, after all, to get a story from more than one source.

Peter talked to me in a small courtyard attached to the community house. He was already the one with authority among the others, because Jesus, in his lifetime, had made him their chief. Peter was a short, broad-shouldered man, seeming to have a very big head, but this was because he allowed his hair and beard to grow. He would be about forty years of age, but his hair, naturally black, was streaked with white. He had a simple almost humble way of talking, which I have found to be the way of talking of two classes of people—very cunning men, or very honest men. I judged Peter honest, for although he had many opportunities of enriching himself, he never did so.

I told him I thought I had twice seen Jesus, his master, as he called him, since his crucifixion and gave him the circumstances. He knew of the incident at Emmaus both from Cleophas and from Luke, so of course he knew of me. I told him too how I had met Barabbas and taken him for the Nazarene, so closely did they resemble each other.

"Now," I said, "it seems to me that I was perhaps mistaken and I did not see a man who had raised himself from the dead, but rather someone who I thought was he."

"As to Emmaus," said Peter, "Cleophas says it was the Master who was with him at the inn, though he had not recognized him at first and thought him just another traveler. He has appeared to the brethren many times—single

[175]

and in groups. We have seen him eat. We have touched him. This is no delusion. If it is a delusion, then the ground you and I stand on at this moment is a delusion.

"But what amazes me is that you, a Gentile, should have seen him. For none have seen him who are not Jews. We find it very hard to believe that you have seen him. I wonder whether you have not deceived yourself. I wonder why he should have shown himself to you—and only you among the Gentiles? For a while, when Cleophas told us that you had seen the Master, and were a Gentile, we thought he was lying and had himself not seen the Master."

Would you believe that hearing Peter doubt that I had seen Jesus, I was annoyed and was on the verge of asserting strenuously that I had, when I recollected myself and remembered that the object of my interview was to find out whether the story of his resurrection was not, after all, a conspiracy to discredit the Temple? So swallowing my resentment I questioned Peter further. "No doubt your master was a good man and a great magician," I said. "But I have heard stories that his resurrection is a plot agreed on by his followers to avenge yourselves on those who crucified him and discredit Caiaphas."

"Sir," said Peter, "I have a fine boat for seine fishing on the Sea of Galilee and so have James and John. Others among us have vineyards and olive orchards. We have wives and children. We have left all of these to follow our Master. Would we desert everything we have to support a lie? Even if some of us were foolish enough to do so, would all of us do this?

"Could there really be a common agreement at such cost, to support a pretense? Again, can good come out of evil? Can men be cured, as you have seen them cured, in the name of a lie? Does God support liars and shams with his power? And lastly would we endure scourging and the anger of our priests for a lie?"

He then undid the ties of his garment about the neck. His shoulders and his ribs were crisscrossed with scars, some not healed.

"What kind of a fool's bargain would that be, brother—to give up my fine boat, which it took my father and me fifteen years of work to buy, to leave my wife and my home, and to accept scourging for a lie? Men will only do such things for the truth and this truth I tell you. Jesus of Nazareth was and is the son of God. He was God come to earth as a man. He came to save men from their sins—to show them the way of right and of truth which would lead them all to union with his father. Those who did not believe him put him to death. Dying he begged that they be forgiven, saying those who condemned him did not know what they were doing. Since he forgave them certainly we forgive them. We have no enmity towards Caiaphas. We only want to show him his error in not recognizing the Messiah because he did not appear in the form Caiaphas expected.

"We do not condemn the priests when they imprison us and scourge us. But that Jesus rose from the dead, that he is the son of God, that he will come again at the end of the world, which is almost at hand, we know to be true and we must assert and preach these truths openly. Beside these truths, the loss of our families, of our businesses, and the blows and stripes we suffer are nothing. We will gladly accept death in the service of the Messiah. We fear only that we may fail him, but he, knowing our weakness, has sent us the Holy Spirit to help us and so we cannot fail."

He spoke passionately, as you can see, but it was not the sincerity of his words that convinced me. No. It was the scars of the scourging on his back and chest that persuaded me. "The blow is the father of truth." That saying is a true one, for I can testify that no man will cling to a lie under blows, which is why torture is the only reliable questioner.

I was convinced by those stripes, but that does not mean that I believed what he believed, namely that Jesus of Nazareth was a god or the son of a god. I believed him a magician and a powerful one, and a good man, and perhaps a demigod. I have known many magicians. Do not forget that Tutmoshe had been able by magic to coax that terrible asp of Egypt, whose glance is death, to feed from my hand. Magic is not so rare in the world. It impresses me, but it does not overwhelm me. As for rising from the dead, the trick has been done before. I do not say that it is a common form of magic, but it is done in India by certain holy men who die and are buried and then are dug up not three days but three weeks later; and when their tongue, which they have swallowed to perform this feat, is pulled back from their gullets, they return to life. Of course they are not crucified and then speared through the heart, which calls indeed for a very powerful form of magic. But who is to put a limit to magic?

What was striking, however, about the magic of the Nazarene was that it worked on an entirely opposite principle from that of Bar-Jesus and Thrasyllus and others who had such powers. These magicians thrived on disbelief. "Can I turn this stone which I hold in my hand into a piece of bread?" Bar-Jesus had asked me at Cyprus. Of course I said he could not. Whereupon he opened his hand and the stone had indeed become a piece of bread, moist and of quite a different shape from the stone he had previously held.

But the Nazarene worked his magic in the opposite manner. He did not require disbelief but belief. If the beholder did not believe that some wonder could be performed, then it was not performed.

This difference was striking and you will ask, and rightly, did the power to perform miracles rest in the Nazarene, or did it rest in the person seeking the miracle? Now you will understand why I gave you that tedious description of how Peter and the other Apostles cured the sick and the maimed on the Temple steps. I could have been much more dramatic. I could have described the exultation, the tears of gratitude, the cries of praise to Yahweh, the kissing of the Apostles' robes and their hands. But all that would have been beside the point. The point was that the miracle depended not on the power of the Apostle but on the faith of the petitioner, who, if he did not believe, was not granted the miracle he sought. Furthermore, on rereading Luke's account of the life of Jesus I found these words said by him to his Apostles, "Listen carefully to what I have to say. If you have faith as big as a grain of mustard seed"—which is the smallest of all seeds, even the seeds of grasses—"you can move a mountain."

Now I began to ask myself whether there was not a key here to the possession of magical powers. If I could convince myself that Jesus of Nazareth was not the son of a builder, but the son of the Jewish god, and himself divine, would I be able to move a mountain? Would I (which was far more to the point) be able to summon up for my ships the southerly winds they needed to carry their grain to Egypt, or, equally important, still those autumn storms which whirl unexpectedly out of the Greek mountains and wreck many vessels? I had seen the sick cured and I had seen blind men have their sight returned to them. Also, even without believing in Jesus or knowing very much about him, I had, just by the mere mention of his name, cast half-a-dozen spirits out of Tabitha (costing me, as you know, a lot of money).

When I left Peter then, after my first interview in which I established the fact that the resurrection was not a fraud, I thought the whole thing over, considering how it might be put to use. I saw plainly that nothing would profit me so much as to be able to believe that Jesus of Nazareth was the son of the Jewish god, and then be able to work whatever wonders I wished in his name. Therefore, I returned on the next day and asked Peter to give me whatever instructions I needed to secure this belief, which I assured him I earnestly desired.

"You must first be instructed in the Law," said Peter, "for you are a Gentile."

This was something I had overlooked. "Cannot I just believe in Jesus?" I asked. "Do I have to become a Jew?"

"You have to become a Jew, Theophilus," Peter said

without hesitating. "We are all Jews. The Messiah was promised to the Children of Israel. By becoming one of us, you can gain eternal life. What is that compared with the study and instruction involved?"

I did not tell him that it was not eternal life I was interested in but corn from Egypt. But I had a question that shook him. "If Jesus, your master, was concerned only about the Jews," I said, "why then should he have appeared twice to me who am a Gentile, and why should I have been able to cast out spirits in his name?"

That puzzled him so much that I was embarrassed to have asked the question. "There are many things I do not understand," he said at last. "I cannot give you an answer. I can only repeat that to be received by the Master, you must become a Jew."

XXII

IT IS WELL ENOUGH for a Jew to become a Roman, for all men desire citizenship in our great empire, and that desire is certainly honorable and profitable. But is it right for a Roman to become a Jew? Is it right and honorable to turn to a foreign god and foreign customs; to accept what the Jews claim—that there is only one god and that of all the people on earth, that god loves the Jews best, making Romans people of the second rate? How could any true Roman accept that? In the end I told Peter that I would not become a Jew though I wished to believe in Jesus as the son of the Jewish god and whatever else was required.

"You have not received the Holy Spirit and so it is impossible for you," said Peter. "If you receive the Holy

Spirit then all these difficulties will go. However, if you earnestly desire to be received by the Master, that will certainly happen. 'Seek and you shall find,' he told us. 'Knock and it will be opened to you.'" That sounded good, but was of course nonsense. Where do you seek? On what door do you knock? That red door which I had not found in Rome but which the spirit in Tabitha had told me I must find? The door to the Apostles' house was white, and of their Temple, gold.

I was disappointed. What a fool I was to have come so far on a glimpse of plum blossoms and a weariness of Rome. I rose to go, disliking the Jews. Certainly, I told myself, this is a nation which despises mankind, and regards all who are not like them as inferior.

Peter looked sad. He sensed undoubtedly that he had answered me like a fool and driven away from his fold a man of great influence and vast wealth. That was a mistake. How many citizens of Rome, he could reflect, wished to be followers of his master? Possibly I was the very first and he had laid down conditions impossible for me to accept. I was halfway across the courtyard when I met the man with the withered arm whom Peter had not been able to cure. He was as unhappy as I.

"Friend," I said, "I cannot cure your arm. But here is some money which may comfort you. It comes from a Roman and a Gentile, as you see." I was angry and wanted to show Peter up, with his empty philosophy which certainly could not stand up against a gold coin given to a poor man.

The man hesitated to take the money. Alone he would have accepted it, but between Jew and Gentile the Jews have erected a wall which even rebuffs charity. "Come," I said, "I have money and you need it. Is not that enough doctrine between us?"

The man then took the money and asked his god to bless me, and I left.

When I told Philip about my interview with Peter,

he took on an attitude of patient piety which infuriated me. You have heard enough of Philip to know that for all my tolerance towards him he delights in opposing me. Whatever argument I advance, he takes an opposite point of view. Whatever action I decide on, he suggests alternatives. But I am tied to him because he is my slave, and although I could set him free in a moment or sell him to another, yet I cannot.

"Come," I said, "admit for once that I was right. I went there prepared to believe whatever he wanted me to believe, and instead Peter wanted me to study and become a Jew. But if the study of their laws could only lead to the belief which I offered him anyway, why should I study? Also, it is beneath his dignity for a Roman to become a Jew. So. Was I not right?"

For answer Philip rose and, getting his crutches, got the rod with which I sometimes beat him. "You will need this, master," he said meekly.

You see how infuriating he is? Certainly I have beaten him. What else would you do with a critic who says your writing is bad and dull, and your usage of language violates all the established rules? But when I have beaten him in the past, I have always felt more wretched about it than he under my blows. I would gladly have taken every one of those blows on myself than have suffered the remorse which always followed them. Can you believe that I have gone down on my knees after such a beating and begged Philip to forgive me and even got dishes of fruit for him and bought him new clothes? Well, it is true. In cooler moments I have wondered whether when Philip wished a new undershirt or cloak he did not goad me into beating him in order to get it. That is the way with Greeks. They are devious by nature.

On this occasion, however, I contented myself with flinging the rod out of the door. "What did I do wrong?" I demanded, seating myself a good distance from him, so that he could be assured I would not become physically violent.

"Master, you went there for the wrong motive—to use the power of Jesus of Nazareth to make money."

"What in the name of Great Jupiter is wrong with that?" I demanded. "Pray tell me what else is power for? For childish tricks? To turn mountains into eggs and eggs into women's hair combs? Let me tell you something, my dear Macedonian. If you have read Luke's account of the life of this Jesus, one very important point could not have failed to escape you. Do you know what that point is?"

"No, master," said Philip with that quiet modesty which at times makes me want to kick the crutches from under him.

"There are you," I stormed. "For all my kindness to you, you are not really devoted to my affairs. If you had read that account carefully with your master's needs in mind, you could not have failed to note that Jesus had a power of particular concern to me—power over the seas and the winds. He was able to walk on water, and gave that power to Peter for a short time. And he calmed a storm which threatened to wreck their boat on the Sea of Galilee. And let me tell you something. Storms on inland seas are nothing to be sneezed at. The waves pitch up steep and high and the bottom is all mud so no anchor will hold.

"Now is it wrong that I should seek this power? Is it really a crime—something unholy—to make a profit? Is it really unworthy to wish to save my ships and my seamen and feed the hungry of Rome? Come, my good philosopher. Propound to me on the uses of magical powers. Are they rightly used when a man turns a stick into a snake, and wrongly used when a man saves a fleet from destruction?"

I had him there, of course. These fine arguers cannot

stand up against the plain sense of a businessman, and Philip had no reply that he could make.

Later he said I had misunderstood him. That is always the plea of those who are wrong. He said that it was certainly a correct use of magical powers to save a grain fleet threatened by a tempest. Indeed, Jesus of Nazareth had done something similar when, finding five thousand people around him in the wilderness, he had taken a loaf or two of bread and a few fish and turned them into enough food for everybody with plenty left over. The difference was that he had not charged them for the meal—he had not done it to make money.

"So," I said, "if I would feed Rome for free, I might have the power to control storms. But if I make a reasonable profit out of feeding Rome, then seamen must be sentenced to drowning and ships to being wrecked. That would certainly seem to me that making a profit is sinful and Jesus of Nazareth is an enemy of capitalism. And, I might add, of good sense."

XXIII

I WENT TO SEE Caiaphas and Annas, who, of course, had their informers throughout the city and they warned me against the company of the Apostles.

"You should not mix with such lunatics," said Caiaphas. "Really a man in your position ought to be more careful. In your business, my dear Theophilus, do you need friends among the rabble? Would it not be more to your benefit to align yourself with established Judaism, which in its friendship for Rome is always the first to denounce these imposter Messiahs?"

There was in this a hint of who had told Tiberius about my offer of a cup of wine to the shivering Nazarene during his trial. I certainly did not blame Caiaphas or Annas for conspiring against me, for if they could profit by bringing about my fall, were they not entitled to try? And they feared my friendship with Pilate.

"My dear Caiaphas," I said, "we are both men of business. Your business is your god, and you have made a fine thing out of being one of his High Priests. I don't criticize that. I scarcely know what a god is for if not to help men make a lot of money and stay healthy enough to enjoy it. My business is shipping. You fear perhaps that I will put my wealth and my power and my influence behind these Nazarenes and so harm your position? Not at all. Reflect that I am a Roman and Rome rules Judaea through Pilate on the one hand and through you on the other. Roman sovereignty over Judaea is a matter of both need and pride. It is something I seek to support, not destroy."

That reply angered Caiaphas because it was true. He was a High Priest because Rome wished him to be and as such he was as much a tool of Rome as was Pilate, whom he hated. However, he controlled himself and said smoothly, "Nonetheless, my dear Theophilus, you have been seen openly associating with Simon of Capernaum and James, the relative of the crucified Jesus. Why?"

I would not tell such a man as Caiaphas of the plum blossoms, or of the spell which the Nazarene seemed to have put upon me. So I took a leaf from the book of the philosphers and replied to his question with another question. "Why did you have the man Peter of Capernaum scourged?" I asked.

"I did not do that," said Caiaphas. "It was done by the Sanhedrin—the council. It was done because the council had itself forbidden him, under pain of scourging, to preach in the name of Jesus of Nazareth."

"Why was he forbidden?"

"Because Jesus of Nazareth was an imposter."

"You know that is a lie, don't you?" I asked.

He did not reply.

"Come, Caiaphas, just between you and me," I said, "is it not a lie that Jesus of Nazareth was an imposter? Because if he were an imposter, would it not be impossible to perform miracles in his name?"

"Not at all," said Caiaphas. "Miracles have been performed by that Lord of the Flies, Beelzebub. The blind have been cured by him—and devils cast out. We all know that. Jesus of Nazareth casts out devils and cures the sick and the halt in the name of Beelzebub, the prince of devils."

"Does the devil then come to your Temple to pray?" I asked.

"What are you saying?" he demanded, outraged.

"You must pardon it in an ignorant Gentile," I said. "But if Jesus of Nazareth was a devil or was possessed by a devil, how could he come to make sacrifices in the Temple, as he did? Any why do his followers come to the Temple every day to pray?"

"You are dabbling in matters which are beyond your knowledge and desperately dangerous for you," said Caiaphas angrily. (I really had him by the hip.) "I advise you to stick to your shipping. In these matters you, a Gentile, are like a child playing in a nest of scorpions. You can only be stung. So far only the Sanhedrin, in its wisdom, has acted against these men. So far the punishment has been only stripes. There are other punishments. Do not meddle here, Theophilus."

I have told you that I really liked Caiaphas. He was as devoted to his god and his Temple as I was to Rome, and that is always admirable. But he was beginning to have doubts and that was evident in his anger and his threats against the followers of Jesus.

"Will you have to kill Peter too?" I asked. "And then James? And John and the rest of them? How many?"

"It is you who speak of killing, not I," said Caiaphas, recovering himself. "Since you are a Gentile, life matters little to you. But to us who are Jews, life is holy—God's great gift of love. We take it only when God, the origin of the gift, is blasphemed or profaned. But if one or two of these should be put to death—because of their perversity and against the will of the priests—then the others will learn wisdom and the sect of the Nazarene will vanish."

"If you put Peter to death and he is raised from the dead by magic," I said, "what then?"

"If even Jesus was raised from the dead, I would believe in him," said Caiaphas. "He was not. The story of the resurrection is being spread by imposters who appear here and there and is enormously profitable to his disciples: Every day people bring them gifts of money and of food—far more than they could ever hope to earn in all their lives as fishermen. You say my business is the Temple and yours is shipping. Well, theirs is Jesus of Nazareth, and they are making a very good thing out of it indeed. Already they own a fine building which they could never have bought before, and if you want to see how much they make in a day, stay with them at the times when offerings are brought. You will see so much wealth poured in that you, as a businessman, may consider becoming one of the followers of the Nazarene yourself."

I did not ask him whether the wealth brought to Peter and John matched the wealth brought daily into the Temple.

The great doctor of the Jewish law in Jerusalem at this time was Gamaliel. His name was always mentioned with the greatest respect, and if any matter concerning ritual was in dispute—even among the High Priests—Gamaliel was always consulted and his advice often accepted. It is a good rule in business to go to the slave in small matters and to the master in big ones. While I had no intention whatever of becoming a Jew, I decided I would still find out something more about Judaism than I had learned in the course of gossip with Jews and Gentiles, and plainly the best source would be Gamaliel, who was renowned as a teacher in Alexandria as well as in Rome, though the Alexandrian Jews, under Philo Judaeus, had a different interpretation of their law from those who were under the influence of Caiaphas and Gamaliel.

First I sent Gamaliel a gift. That is the best approach to anybody. I could not send him food, which I knew would be held unclean, so I sent him money, which no religion in the world ever pronounces soiled, whatever its source.

To my astonishment Gamaliel sent the money back, but said he would receive me, since he knew of my name and my growing interest in Judaism. I visited him at night, as a matter of discretion, and found him a generous, open-minded man, with views so tolerant and so just that he would have made a good Republican Roman. He was a man of about my age, but the Jews, through their custom of not cutting their beards and their hair, give the appearance of being older and appear to have large heads. "Big as a Jew's head," is a common expression in praising a fine melon.

I told him what I knew of Jesus of Nazareth, of my visit with Peter, of my desire to obtain magical powers, and of my disappointment at discovering I had first to become a Jew.

"Frankly," I said, "apart from the amount of study involved, it would be bad for my business to become a Jew. Many people do not like the Jews."

Gamaliel enjoyed my presentation and approved of it. "My dear Theophilus," he said, "if honesty would win you Heaven, you have nothing to fear. You are one of the most honest men I have ever met."

"Honesty has been forced upon me by experience," I

said. "If I had the wit to conspire with cunning, I assure you I would do so. But I have not, and therefore deceit is more dangerous for me than those I might hope to deceive. But although I do not want to become a Jew, can you clearly tell me what is required of those who do?"

"If only it were that easy," replied Gamaliel. "I am fifty years of age and still studying the Law. For us the Law is like a field in which the more we delve, the more is produced. The Law is the manifestation of God, and the more we study it the more we enter the mind of God and the closer we come to Him. One lifetime is not sufficient, Theophilus."

"Then no one can ever say that he has succeeded in becoming a perfect Jew," I said.

"There will be one who can say that—the Messiah," said Gamaliel.

"And Jesus of Nazareth was not the Messiah?"

Gamaliel hesitated. "I will not judge," he replied.

"Come," I said, for this Jewish deviousness, so like that of the Greeks, always irritated me. "Let us get a few facts. Certainly I am never going to be the master of your law and it seems to me that no man will ever be. For if a man knew all about God, then he would himself be the equal of God and would then be God. But to get down to fundamentals. To become a Jew it is necessary to believe in one god and only one god?"

"That is so."

"And you must believe that that god laid down a number of commandments which must be obeyed?"

"That is so also."

"How many commandments?"

"Ten. They are in three sections. The first section deals with man's relationship to God. The second deals with man's relationship to his family. The third deals with man's relationship to his neighbors."

"All that in ten commandments?" I said, for I was certainly surprised.

"You must remember that they were laid down by God," said Gamaliel. "Had man undertaken the task ten thousand commandments would not have been sufficient."

I ask then what were the commandments and he knew them by heart and gave them to me. The first two sections I found did not apply to me. I had no family and other than the great gods of Rome, I knew no god. The third section I found that I had very largely complied with in any case. They dealt with robbing, killing, bearing false witness, and so on. I told Gamaliel that I was quite a good Jew regarding this last section of the law, but added that in the matter of coveting my neighbor's wife and my neighbor's goods—both forbidden by the Jewish God—I was certainly guilty.

"It is often highly profitable for a woman, for her husband, and for her children as well, for her to share another's bed," I said. "If the widow of Germanicus had gone to Tiberius her children might today be alive," I pointed out.

"It is unchaste," said Gamaliel. "Among the Gentiles these things are done, for their marriages are not blessed by God, but among us infidelity is punishable by death."

"In that respect you are like the Germans," I said. "But what about all these other laws of the Jews—circumcision, not cutting the hair, the clothes that may be worn, the foods you may eat and not eat, the washings, and so on? There is no mention of those among the laws laid down by your god."

Gamaliel said that these laws had been revealed to their prophets and their priests, who had put them down for the guidance of the people. There were a great number of them, and there were very many of the Jews who observed them in the strictest fashion and believed that by so doing they were serving god and would be assured of going to Heaven when they died.

"I do not mean to be irreverent," I said. "I am really

inquiring quite honestly. I do not understand how any god could be interested in the length of a man's hair or the food he ate or the clothes he wore—not to mention so astonishing a matter as cutting off his foreskin. The ten laws you have told me, with the exception of the matter of fidelity in marriage, seem quite reasonable to me. But these others are scarcely reasonable at all, and to a non-Jew, laughable."

"It is often the case that the things men do become more important in themselves than the reasons they are done," said Gamaliel. "Then the thing that is done, having lost its reason or its significance, becomes as you say incomprehensible and ridiculous. The Laws regarding food and dress and other observances were laid down for reasons of health, for self-discipline, and as an antidote to pride. Many of us, washing our hands before we eat, lest we contaminate our food, do not stop to think whether the spiritual food we eat may not be contaminated, but that is one of the objects of our purification.

"Again, regulations regarding dress—the length of fringes and the number of tassels, the kind of clothes that may be worn—are intended to keep our people from lavish expenditure on dress, in which the Gentiles in their pride indulge.

"Yet the very observance of our rules regarding dress becomes a matter of pride among us, and those who observe the rules scrupulously tend to despise those who don't. That is a worse demonstration of pride than dressing like a peacock. And so the matter goes. The food that drops freely from the trees we are commanded to leave for the stranger. But many send out to shake and beat the trees daily so that nothing may be said to have dropped freely from them.

"We Jews, though chosen by God, are human too. We bear a load that no other nation bears—the load of being the Chosen Ones, and yet being as willful in our natures as our fellowmen. For that we have been greatly punished in the past. For that same willfulness, which we persist in now, we will undoubtedly be punished in the future.

"We Jews are blessed but we are also cursed. Our blessing is that God is our Father, and we are all His children. Our curse is that our minds will not leave matters to God, but we insist upon inquiring and looking for definitions of definitions. We look for assurance in the meanings of words and ignore the meaning of God, which He doesn't withhold or hide from those who love Him.

"We must know exactly, to the last scruple, what is permitted and what is forbidden—in human terms. I will give you an example. We are forbidden to work on the Sabbath. But if a man's house burns on the Sabbath he is obviously entitled and indeed commanded to save his life by leaving it. However, can he save his property? Is removing his furniture from his burning house work? If he may remove what is necessary for the support of his wife and of his children (and he is commanded to preserve them) then what is necessary, under that definition, and what is not?

"You see how we are tortured by this scrupulosity of ours? You see how we are torn all the time between serving ourselves and serving our God and to what wiles and hair-counting arguments we are driven to justify ourselves to ourselves? No other nation on earth bears this intolerable burden, for no other nation on earth has been chosen by God and addressed directly by Him.

"So we produce definitions of definitions of definitions and refinements of refinements of refinements until the whole nation groans under the weight of the Law, and men, driven to despair of salvation, become apostates, as thousands have done in Antioch and in Ephesus and in Alexandria and in Rome itself.

"We need now, not the refinement of the Law, but its purification to its essentials. I assure you, my dear

Theophilus, I devote my life now to relieving men of the burden of the letter of the Law, by a return to the spirit behind the Law and a generous interpretation. But what we need is one who will so simplify it, while preserving it, that it will be acceptable to the whole world. Then, Theophilus, it will be quite easy for you to become a Jew."

When I mentioned this conversation later to Philip, he said quietly, "There was a man who did simplify their law. He reduced it to two principles. They must love and honor their god. They must love their neighbors as themselves."

"Who was he?" I asked.

"Jesus of Nazareth," said Philip. But I did not remember reading that passage, being more concerned with magical powers, which are, after all, more profitable.

XXIV

Despite my natural repugnance at becoming a Jew and so deserting the traditions and gods of Rome, I still thought it might be possible to become a follower of the Nazarene.

I have told you I wanted to become a follower of the Nazarene for the immense power it would give me. Certainly that power was not to be put aside lightly. Every day I had proof of it, and Balbus, that fine soldier whom I had met on the steps of the Temple and with whom I became friendly, produced further proofs.

He had established a little household for himself with a wife who, having formerly been a prostitute and thus rejected by all, had happily settled down with him. Her name was Naomi, for she was a Jewess, a buxom, easy-going, frank woman who knew from her profession how to make a copper or two go a long way. Really she was as fine a wife as a man could want, and if you should ask why should a man marry a prostitute, then I must ask is it not better to marry a woman who put some value on her favors and sold them, rather than marry one who valued them so lightly that she gave them away free to all who sought them as the fancy took her? If fidelity is important in marriage (I am open-minded on the matter) then a prostitute is not likely to be as adventurous and curious after marriage as one who is not a prostitute, or a girl whose sole experience of intercourse has been with her husband. Naomi was also an excellent cook. Really no one in the world can roast lamb like the Jews; the particular mixture of herbs and oils with which they garnish it sets my mouth quivering now. Seneca once asked me what good had come to Rome from her conquest of Judaea, and when I replied "roast lamb" I got the name of a wit in Rome for some little time.

But I was talking about the powers of the Nazarene. Balbus, who received me in his little house often, produced many proofs. He introduced me, for instance, to a certain Lazarus, who had been raised from the dead by the Nazarene. The two had been very close friends. There is a kind of love among Jewish men, which is not sexual but which differs entirely from that between brother and brother and father and son. It is warmer, more trusting, more generous. This kind of love had existed between the Nazarene and his follower John of Zebedee and the Nazarene and this man Lazarus.

Well, Lazarus had died of a flux and had been buried hurriedly after anointing. He was three days in his grave when his friend Jesus appeared, to be told that he was dead. When he heard the news he wept, for the Jews are not ashamed of their tears. Then he told the sister of Lazarus to give orders to have the stone covering the mouth of the sepulcher removed. But she objected, saying that her brother, having died of the flux, would already be stinking, for so it is with those who die of that disorder.

Then he asked her whether she did not believe that he, Jesus was the son of God, and whether she did not believe that he could raise the dead. She replied that she believed both these things and at his command the stone was rolled aside. Then Jesus called Lazarus by name, and Lazarus came out of the tomb, alive and well, but still wrapped in his burial cloths.

Balbus took me to that same Lazarus, and he was certainly alive and no ghost, for he ate the white foods of the living. But afterwards I heard rumors that he had never really been dead, as I now heard many rumors that Jesus had not risen from the dead, but a number of imposters, including his own brothers, were posing as him. That trick has been tried before and sometimes with success. It is not so long ago since all Rome was shaken by the news that Postumus, the reputed son of the divine Augustus who had been killed on the death of his father, was alive and had landed at Ostia, where he was welcomed by jubilant sailors who always loved him. Only later was it found that this was the work of the imposter Clement.

"Well, sir," said Balbus, "believe what you will. But you cannot deny the evidence of your own eyes and you have seen many cured in the name of Jesus. And me, sir, that helped nail him to the Cross, he even cured me."

"Cured you of what?" I asked. "You never said anything about this before."

"Well, it wasn't very much compared with some of the other cures, but it was a lot to me and a great kindness and I can't say I deserved it. I mean some of these beggars he cured never did any man any harm. But a soldier now. Well, the whole life of a soldier is harm, in a manner of speaking, and when it comes to looting—well, I don't have to go into those things, I don't suppose. Anyway, for a long time my sight had been going. I think it was from a blow on the head I got in the German wars. But whatever it was, I couldn't see anything that was much more than three or four feet from me.

"Of course, it may have been wine. I drunk a lot of it in those days, sir. Well, when he was being crucified, I had to nail him and I put my knee on his wrist and drove the spike in—three or four blows was all it took and he didn't even clench his fist like most of them do—which breaks their fingers, of course. He didn't cry out nor nothing. I felt sorry for him and I admired him. You saw what he was like, didn't you, sir, with his nose half off and his beard all blood and one eye blind from the scourging?

"In those days I always carried a little strong wine with me, and I was going to take a swig when I thought maybe he needed it more than I did. Now I don't know why I did it. I've seen a lot of men die and I'm used to it. But there was something special about him. Anyway, I held my sponge full of wine to his mouth but he turned away and then he looked at me most peculiar. Kind of tender as if he was sorry for me instead of me being sorry for him. And then I had a terrible pain in my eyes, sir, and cried out and held my hands to them. And when I opened them, I could see everything as sharp as a needle. I never realized how blind I had been until I could see real sharp again.

"So he cured me, you see, sir. It wasn't any great miracle —not like raising Lazarus nor raising himself from the dead. But a miracle it was. And all because I gave him a little wine.

"Other things changed for me too, sir. Of course I'm still a good soldier and always hope to be. But I'd hated the Jews up to then, sir, and hated anybody that wasn't a Roman and among the Romans I hated anybody that wasn't a soldier. Natural enough after forty-five years with the legions. But now I love the Jews. It was like I had never seen 'em before. Zeus, how I laugh at their jokes now. They've got some good 'uns. And I've been to their funerals and their weddings. And I'm not ashamed to say that I've cried when some of them died.

"Of course, me being a soldier and Naomi what she was, they're not all friendly. Can't blame them for that, sir. But ever since my eyes was cured, the world doesn't seem to be full of enemies anymore. You know, I look at someone else and I see myself. That's the best way I can explain it.

"You've seen how these Jews stagger around under big loads, haven't you, sir? They carry more than a donkey does in Rome. Well, in the old days, we used to wait until one came loaded down and just give him a little push and that was enough to make him stagger and send him sprawling. Got many a laugh out of that. But now, I look at them and I think, 'That might be me under that load,' and instead of giving them a shove, sometimes I help them.

"I don't know whether this is making much sense to you, sir. But there was a lot more to that crucified Jew than just miracles." And then he made that magic sign on himself—the Sign of the Cross.

"Why do you do that?" I asked.

"Out of respect, sir," said Balbus.

Now I have said at the beginning of this discourse that I had told myself that the reason I wanted to be a follower of the Nazarene was because of the powers I might look for over the wind and the sea. But you will now have guessed that this was not all the reason, but rather the part of the reason I advanced as being acceptable and sensible in the judgment of others. For it was the something else about the Nazarene that fascinated me, and which had also interested that excellent soldier of Rome, Balbus. That something else was the Nazarene's own form of madness, which was entirely different from the lunacy of other Jews.

What are you going to make then of such laws as these —all preached by Jesus? "If a man strike you, turn the other cheek. If a man steal your cloak, give him your shirt also. If a man makes you walk a mile with him, go with him another five miles. Bless those who curse you. Pray for those who hate you. Give to all who beg from you. Love your enemy. Lend money without expecting repayment." And so on. If you doubt that the Nazarene ever laid down these laws, I can show them to you in the account I have of his life prepared for me by Luke. As I said at the beginning, I have put nothing in this testament which I do not know to be true either on my own witness or on the witness of others who are equally reliable.

There are many lunatics in the world and they are soon so identified and ignored. But this lunatic had died for his lunacy; yet now he had a bigger following than when he was alive and, what was more, all his followers believed in his lunacy as the only real sense in the world and had given up everything they had in the world to follow and obey him. Nor were all his followers simpletons. Peter was a plain seaman but with a lot of sense. Balbus was no man's fool; and my interest in the Nazarene was certainly intensified when I discovered that the senior centurion who had officiated at the crucifixion, Longinus, had made a large money offering to Peter in the name of the man he had crucified, who, it appeared, had once cured his old servant who was dying. To go on, Nicodemus the Pharisee was a very intelligent man, and so also was Joseph of Arimathea, and I found later that Gamaliel (yes, the great Gamaliel) had advocated leaving the Apostles and followers of Jesus alone, since it was just possible that Jesus had been sent from God.

So now you will see that it was not altogether the hope of obtaining magical powers that attracted me to the Nazarene, but curiosity about his upside-down philosophy as well as his growing influence among men.

Yet, to be honest, which I hope I am, there was also something more. It was what he had said when I foolishly offered him, out of pity, that cup of wine.

[198]

"It is not from the cup of comfort that I must drink now," he had said. And then, "I will be your friend, Theophilus. I will never leave you."

That was it. He would not leave me. That, I think, was really why I came back to Jerusalem. Wherever I turned, I suspected, I would find him in one form or another—in the plum blossoms outside Rome, in the stumbling sentences of Balbus, in the casting out of the spirits of Tabitha, in the flowers on the Judaean hills, in the slant of a sail in the wind which must always delight a seaman, even in Philip's offering me a stick to beat him. The Nazarene would always be there. I wished it were not so. I wanted life as it used to be before that accursed day when I met him—a life of business, of activity, of shrewd deals, of increasing wealth and power.

Was ever so much lost, I ask you—women, gladiators, feasts, and all the delights of wealth and influence—with the gift of a cup of wine?

XXV

ANGER AGAINST THE FOLLOWERS of Jesus soon began to mount in Jerusalem. Caiaphas, it must be admitted, had shown himself my friend in warning me to stay away from Peter and the other followers of the Nazarene. He knew in advance of the coming anger, and without a doubt he used his agents to stimulate it. Still, he did not wish me to suffer from it. Pilate also knew of the mounting wrath, and welcomed it. Nothing delighted Pilate, now withdrawn to Caesarea, as much as bloodshed among the Jews.

However, the anger did not all originate in the Temple. Not at all. But to tell you how it did arise I have first to describe how these Nazarenes lived, and I have to warn you that they were not the only ones among the Jews who lived in this fashion. A sect called the Essenes lived in a like manner and so also did a sect called the New Covenanters, who, from their astrological calculations, had decided that the time for the appearance of the Messiah had passed without his appearing (they did not recognize Jesus of Nazareth as the Messiah) and so believed that God had entered into a new covenant with them, setting a new date for the coming of the Messiah.

These sects lived out in the deserts in communities of their own, in that wilderness area which is full of caves on the western side of the Sea of Galilee. (These caves were once inhabited by monstrous men, whose terrible skulls with thick ridges of bone over the eyebrows are occasionally found. I had such a skull once. These monsters are said by learned Jews to have been the descendants of Cain, who killed Abel and on whom God put the mark of ridges of bone over their eyes. I sold the skull I had to a physician in Crete who, using scrapings of it, was able to cure toothache.)

The Nazarenes differed from these other sects in that they lived in the heart of Jerusalem, a few yards from the Temple, so that all they did was known to and affected the whole city and not merely witnessed by wild goats, stray donkeys, and ragged flocks of sheep.

Very well. Now the principal feature of their living, in which they differed from their fellow Jews, was that the Christians, as they came to be called later, owned everything in common. They did this because their master Jesus had once pointed out to them that the birds of the trees had nests, and the foxes had holes in the ground, but he had nowhere to lay his head. I think that at the time he was merely feeling peevish.

Jesus once said that it was harder for a rich man to get into Heaven than for a camel to go through the eye of a needle, so I hope I have said enough to show that Jesus had taught his disciples that wealth was an evil thing and a tremendous handicap in reaching Heaven after death, for which they all hoped. And I hope also that I have said enough about the Jews for you to know that they take everything literally even if it is only intended figuratively, and so had burdened themselves, as Gamaliel had told me, with a thousand laws, all quite absurd, whose significance had been forgotten.

Well, the Nazarenes did exactly the same. Remembering the words of Jesus, Peter, John, James, and the rest of them went about preaching that if people wished to be saved, they must sell all their possessions and give the money to the poor. Plainly Jesus was not a businessman, or more likely he did not intend to be taken as literally as his followers took him. If Jesus had been a businessman, he would have realized that for every seller there must be a buyer, so whoever gained Heaven by selling his property did so at the expense of another who lost Heaven by buying it. But, as I say, I do not think he intended to be taken literally, and he would have done much better had he addressed his teaching to the Gentiles (particularly the Romans) who know how to be moderate and not take everything that is said in its literal sense.

However, all the Jews who believed in Jesus as the son of God and as God himself in human form (and also as the Messiah) sold their property, and to be sure that the money got to the poor they gave it to Peter. It was really amazing the amount that was brought in, in this manner, every day and it was pathetic to see a widow come in, withered and stooped, as many of them were, and put into Peter's hand the few pieces of silver she had received for her little plot of ground or her share of an olive tree. (The olive is so necessary to the Jews that shares of the harvest of a particular tree are handed down from one generation to another.) With what fervency these poor creatures expressed their gratitude that God (in the person of Peter) had accepted their offering. With what tears did they seek to kiss Peter's hands or touch his washed-out clothes, and with what love did they follow him with their eyes whenever he passed.

Sometimes they cried out some ejaculation in an excess of emotion such as, "Blessed art thou, Bar-Jonah, who have touched the person of God. Blessed art thou who have eaten with Him. Blessed art thou who have heard the Word from His own mouth."

The whole atmosphere around Peter and the others was one of zeal and great emotion, but also of enormous happiness as if the widow, putting her few coins into Peter's hands, had been relieved of every pain, every care, every anxiety, every fear, both of the past and the future. I can say only that they appeared to have been born again and to have become creatures such as they never were before. This change was called "baptism of the spirit" or "receiving the spirit." I, myself, witnessing such scenes, wondered whether I ought not to sell everything I owned, give it all to Peter and be rid of every trouble I had in the world, and at the same time be assured of eternal happiness. Lunacy, I warn you, is as infectious as a cold. If I might have sold everything I had at one word, if it could have been done as simply as that, then I might have been guilty, in the hysteria of a moment, of this appalling folly. But fortunately all I possessed could not be sold at one word, and fortunately also, since I was a Gentile, it would have been no use anyway. But I envied the exultation and the happiness the old women achieved by the sale of a miserable donkey, or the gift to Peter of their last two battered earthenware crocks. Seeing such things I felt a sense of loss, of isolation. It was soon gone, to be sure, but it returned at unexpected times thereafter.

I was accepted among the Christians because it was known that I had seen the Nazarene at Emmaus on the road to Joppa. I was not, of course, the only Gentile with whom they would converse, for their master had told them that they must preach his doctrines to the whole world though it was first of all necessary for everyone to become a Jew if he wished to be saved. But I had a special standing with them and often talked with Peter and with John of Zebedee and his brother James.

John was charged with the care of Mary, the mother of Jesus, who when he was dying had made John the son of his mother, which is a special token of love among the Jews. The mother, Mary, however, was not in Jerusalem when I was there this time. She was about fifty years of age and she had gone with Luke to Antioch, as I explained. With her son crucified as a criminal she could not go back to Nazareth, which was her home, for who is neighbor to the mother of a criminal? She would have been subjected to many insults and hardships in Nazareth. She might have stayed in Jerusalem, but after Peter and John had been scourged at the orders of the Sanhedrin, John became concerned lest any affront or harm should come to Mary. Luke, having quit Herod's court, suggested that he take her to Antioch (which was his home city) and she was very fond of Luke, who alone among the Apostles could make her smile.

John could make nobody smile. He was like a thunderstorm either about to erupt or erupting. But Luke was a Greek and had the subtle and effeminate mind of the Greeks and had all kinds of pretty tales and fancies. Like many in Herod's service he had studied Judaism and had become a Jew, so there was no bar at all to his becoming a follower of the Nazarene.

In discussing the teachings of Jesus, John went deeper into the meaning of things than Peter, whose mind was often frustrated by subtleties. I will give you an instance of this. Of all the miracles which Jesus performed in his lifetime, there was one which seemed to me markedly different from the rest. As you know, I am not impressed by miracles, for I have seen many and they prove nothing except that there is a magical power and that some people possess it. That one miracle Luke did not include in his gospel though it was one which was performed at the request of Mary, the mother of Jesus. The family had been invited to a wedding at Cana, and the father of the bride was ashamed to find that he had not enough wine to serve his guests. Mary, a close friend of the family, had learned of this and she told Jesus of it. He was a little irritated and said sharply, "Woman, how does this concern of yours involve me? My hour has not yet come."

However, she told the wine steward to do whatever Jesus said and he, with a glance at his mother, relented, smiled, and told them to fill the big water jars at the front of the house to the brim, and then draw off some of the water for the wine steward to taste before serving it to the guests. When the wine steward tasted it, he found that the water had been turned into the finest of wines—far better than that which had been first served.

As I say, Luke in his account did not make any mention of this miracle, which annoyed me, for here certainly was a most useful piece of magic for a businessman such as I.

"Now, Theophilus," said John when he told me of it, "remember that the Master, who was and is the son of God, did nothing without reason. What do you think was the reason for that wonder of turning water into wine?"

"The reason is quite plain," I said. "It was to show his love for his mother and to save his mother's friends from being ashamed."

"That is man's reason," said John. "But he was the son of God. What was God's reason?"

"To prove his powers," I replied.

"If it was to prove his powers," said John, "why would he limit himself to so small a thing? He could have taken the city of Jerusalem and raised it fifty cubits into the air and left it there for a year or forever, but he did not do that. Instead he did a comparatively little thing. He turned water into wine. Again I ask you, why?"

I was forced to admit that I did not know.

"It was a sign that as the water was turned into wine,

changing its nature into something richer, so men must be turned into something better than themselves by the word of God. This was the first of his miracles and it announced the purpose of his coming among us; to change us into better creatures, to mold us, with our own free consent, into the children of God. We, however, were blind and could not see, and deaf and could not hear, until he sent the Holy Spirit to open our eyes and our ears and make the meaning of this and other miracles clear to us.

"Furthermore, in turning the water into wine at Cana, he foreshadowed the miracle which he now performs daily when in memory of him we bless wine and say the words, 'This is my blood,' when the wine indeed becomes his blood and gives us life."

"Is it really turned to blood?" I asked, for as you know I am a plain man and like plain answers. It was the wrong question to put to John. He snarled at me, "Roman, do you think always in coins and amphorae and ships, and think only these are real? What is real about things that are fated to crumble and be gone? The only reality is eternal. What exists in time is an illusion."

So he did not answer me plainly, but then you can never get plain answers from philosophers or magicians. For them there is no "Yes" and no "No."

When John recovered from his outburst, he said, less severely, "Remember, Theophilus, Jesus of Nazareth was and is God, and so did nothing without divine reason."

That made me nervous indeed. If Jesus did nothing without a deep and divine reason, what was his reason for twice appearing to me? I very much wished he hadn't; for the farther away a man can get from the gods—Roman or Jewish or any sort—the less misfortune is likely to befall him. A happy man, and fortunate, is one of whom the gods are not aware, for while the gods will often do good, they will just as often, indeed more often, do harm.

John always made me nervous. You could not be long with him without having him dissolve into something greater than himself and something fearful too. Also when he performed any miracle (which he did quite often), he did so casually, as if the miracle was an interference with something deeper that was going on in his mind—some conversation with the terrible Jehovah or Yahweh, who is the god of the Jews.

Sometimes John sat, unmoving, and without eating or drinking for a long time in that courtyard, his eyes open but seeing nothing in this world and his ears unstopped but hearing nothing and his body feeling neither the heat of the sun nor the chill of the night. People knelt and prayed around him when this happened, even Peter, and they brought flowers and made a carpet of them on the pavement before him, so that I thought John, at such times, might be in the process of becoming a god—as did, you recall, the divine Augustus and the divine Caesar, though only after their deaths.

When I mentioned this with greatest respect to Peter he was so angry he took me by my clothing and shook me. "Pagan," he roared. "There is only one God. No man can become a god. Can't you get that into your thick Roman skull?"

Afterwards he came and apologized. I liked Peter, but of John I was always a little afraid. That terrible communication he had frightened me. John was definitely a greater magician than Peter—of that I had no doubt. But he seemed at times very much closer to the source of his magic and seemed as if he were going to be absorbed into it. That would have frightened even so great a wizard as Thrasyllus, though it would, I think, have seemed very natural to Tutmoshe. Of course I wanted a measure of magic myself. But I did not want to be absorbed into it like a man drowned in a pool from which he only wished a drink.

XXVI

I WILL RETURN NOW to telling you of the anger against the Nazarenes in Jerusalem of which I have made mention. It came from many sources and not solely from the High Priests. You will readily understand it. Who after all is to blame the doctor, the seller of herbs and remedies of many kinds, if he suddenly finds himself without clients? The herbalists of Jerusalem, the doctors, the sellers of pieces of parchment with a sacred word or two written on them to ward off evil, the surgeons and bloodletters, the menders of bones and those paid to be nurses to the infirm; all were soon suffering heavy losses of clients and of fees as a result of the miracles of the Apostles.

Are these people to be blamed that they turned against Peter and John and James and Matthew and those others— not a dozen but a hundred or more—who without fee cured the sick?

Then again what about the baker and the butcher and the tailor and the landlord and the seller of oil? Who will buy meat or oil or clothing or bread when it is handed out free? Well, the Christians, taking the money brought to them, were feeding hundreds for nothing, and since they bought in bulk at wholesale prices, the retailer found his little shop empty of customers or, if not empty, but half as busy as it had once been. Yet he had to pay the same rent to his landlord, and matters getting worse daily he could do one of two things: he could follow Peter's injunction and sell everything and become a Christian, or he could unite with others in a similar plight and drive the Christians out.

I have said before that Jesus of Nazareth was no businessman; otherwise he would not have advised people to sell all they had, give the proceeds to the poor, and follow him. The matter strikes so hard at my own case that I must dwell on it further. For instance, if I sold all my ships and gave the money to the poor, a few million people would have a sesterce each for a day or two and in a year Rome would then starve and starving men, killing and looting for food, would tear down society. Without a doubt Jesus would have done much better had he, among his followers, picked one man with a head for business. Of course it might be argued that instead of selling my ships I should use them to freely transport corn to Rome. But who then would pay my sailors, the stevedores and the warehousemen and the clerks keeping their unending tallies? And if all these were to donate their services free, or in return for being fed and clothed, is not that exactly the condition of the slave? Who (other than miscreants wishing to avoid service in the army of Rome) would willingly become a slave?

So it seemed to me that Jesus, knowing or caring nothing about business, had embodied in his preaching a doctrine which must destroy it.

The first effort to destroy it took place in Jerusalem. To be sure, the outward cause of anger was alleged blasphemy and sacrilege. A young Greek converted both to Judaism and to the sect of the Nazarene, and one employed in issuing food and clothing to others, by the name of Stephen, was accused of blasphemy. He was accused, however, not by the High Priests or their party, but by a group of Jews calling themselves The Synagogue of Roman Freedmen. They were Jews who had been taken captive to Rome or were descendants of such captives, who had obtained their freedom and Roman citizenship in some cases.

They came from many parts of the Roman empire. They were all merchants. I knew some of them. They undertook to engage Stephen in debate concerning the teaching of Jesus and, knowing more about prices than about the law, they were badly worsted in this debate. So they went to the Sanhedrin and accused Stephen of blasphemy. The case was of tremendous importance. All Jerusalem was concerned with it. Despite all the cures and the free food which had been handed out by Peter and his followers, most of the people were incensed against Stephen and the Apostles; and in a religious fury, they denounced them as blasphemers, spat at them, and threw stones at them whenever they appeared in a part of the city far from their headquarters. I saw all of this myself. I warned Peter that he should charge money for his cures and for the food he was handing out or matters would go very badly for him. You see, people will often denounce on religious grounds those who have hurt them in business or political matters, for a charge of impiety is the quickest way of turning an honest man into a knave.

I warned Peter of this—it was hopeless to warn John. "Believe me," I said, "if you deprive a businessman of his profit you will be denounced and persecuted however much good you may have done, for the greatest of all sacrilege is to deprive a merchant of his take." Well, Peter would not listen to me, and so Stephen was tried by the pious merchants for blasphemy and, being condemned, was stoned to death.

After he was condemned he was dragged to a pit, where the stoning took place, and flung, bound, into the bottom of it. The mob which followed him now went through a very peculiar custom. They removed their outer garments and laid these carefully at the feet of a rabbi who was most scrupulously clad in the manner decreed by Jewish law. Now the reason for taking off their outer garments was not, Balbus said (he was with me) to give them greater freedom of movement, but so that ritual robes should not be defiled in a killing. Come, you say, this is nonsense. Is it not more important that the man should not be defiled? Well, I can only tell you what Balbus told me and ask you to remember what Gamaliel had explained, that the act had become more important than its significance. Whatever the real significance of removing the outer clothing may have been, I do not know. Perhaps it was that nothing holy or dedicated to their god, or worn to please their god, should be defiled by execution.

Anyway, they took off their outer robes and piled them at the foot of this very orthodox rabbi, and said something to him which I did not hear and he said something to them which was plainly an encouragement and an assurance that what they were about to do was right. The stoning started with little stones, perhaps no bigger than boys throw at each other in the streets. These came in a shower from all sides of the circular pit and there was no dodging them. I was surprised that in a matter of moments, the face of the condemned Stephen was a welter of blood, and dark patches of blood began a little later to show through his thick hair and beard. I have forgotten to say that he had been stripped of all his clothing except for a loincloth, so his body showed these welts and blue marks but did not bleed as much as his face.

Then, when I suppose everybody had got his aim in or enjoyed the shower of small stones to the fullest, bigger ones were thrown. These, about the size of a child's ball, did tremendous damage. One eye was blinded in a moment and a well-thrown rock knocked out Stephen's teeth and split his lips. He meanwhile was praying in a loud voice for those who were stoning him.

These larger stones put an end to the prayers. They knocked out his teeth, broke his nose, and raised vast lumps on the cheeks and forehead and brought him to his knees. But he was in an ecstasy and I do not think he suffered. He made no attempt to dodge the stones, though that would have been futile in any case. When he was knocked to his knees a huge cheer went up and the mob turned now to boulders. One hit him in the back, knocking him to the ground, and another following immediately split his skull from behind. He still moved and twitched, and in an effort to save itself, his body voided the contents of the stomach in a great spew of vomit, and of the bowels in an equally great spew of feces. In a little while he was entirely covered with stones and boulders and whether he was still alive or dead I do not know. No one entered the pit to make sure. The stones piled higher and higher and one by one the executioners moved off, got their clothes from the rabbi and went back to Jerusalem. They had come out a raging, god-stricken mob. They went back quiet, as if unsure of their justification. One or two stared at the pit with its mound of stones in the bottom and seemed fearful. On the face of the rabbi, however, was a look of exultation.

"This day the Children of Israel have defended their God," he said. "This day they have crushed the blasphemer and exalted the Law."

Then a group who had not come to reclaim their garments approached the rabbi. They were women and they had come to get the body. Among them was Mary Magdalene, who perhaps you will remember was a follower of Jesus, and had been a prostitute. As she came near, the rabbi moved his garments closer to him lest they be touched or defiled by her.

"Why are you here?" he asked.

"We have come to anoint the body for burial," said one.

"He is to be left for a day," said the rabbi, "that we may be sure he is dead."

"Rabbi," said the former prostitute, "is it not forbidden under the Law to let a man die on the Sabbath? And is not this the eve of the Sabbath?"

She had him there. In his anger I think he would have struck her, except that to do so would be to defile himself.

He had to permit them to get the body to be sure it was dead, and the boulders being heavy, Balbus went to give them a hand and so did I, though I cannot tell you why.

We carried the body covered with blood and smelling of excrement and vomit out of the pit. The rabbi, as we went by, did not look entirely triumphant.

"What is your interest in this matter?" he said to me. "You are not a Jew."

"Since I am not a Jew, what is your interest in me?" I replied.

But the former prostitute, Mary, looked boldly at the rabbi and said, "Saul of Tarsus, you have thrown a stone. But God will throw a mountain and beat you to your knees."

XXVII

I WAS NOT THERE when the god of the Jews threw a mountain at Saul. I was given the story by Luke, and he was not there either. Luke, however, got the story himself from Saul, with whom he later became very friendly and whom he accompanied on many journeys. But before I tell you the story I must tell you more about Saul of Tarsus and what happened in Jerusalem after Stephen had been stoned to death.

The first thing that happened was that panic spread among the Nazarenes. They all knew of the trial before the Sanhedrin and of how Stephen had been condemned to death for blasphemy on the evidence of witnesses who they said testified falsely. They now expected a miracle. They had expected originally that in some manner Stephen would be saved and some of them went to the stoning pit to see this happen. They had expected that not a single stone would touch Stephen, or the stones would leave him entirely unharmed.

Nothing of the sort happened, of course. Stephen died naked and in ignominy, covered with his own blood, vomit, and excrement. What was more natural then than that the Nazarenes should ask each other, "If this is what happened to Stephen, who was so close to Peter and was without sin, as we all know, what then is likely to happen to us? Are we not just as likely to be scourged and stoned to death or perhaps even crucified without Jesus stretching out a hand to save us?"

Many felt that Stephen had been betrayed by his faith in Jesus. They stopped believing in the divinity of Jesus, disassociated themselves from the Apostles and listened without anger to people saying that the miracles they performed were cures which would have occurred in answer to long prayer without intervention of the Apostles.

Many went immediately to the priests and assured them that they no longer believed that Jesus was the Messiah. After making certain offerings in penance they were promised that nothing would happen to them.

Others, however, though surprised that Stephen had died, argued that he would be raised from the dead on the third day. You will recall that Stephen, like Jesus himself, had been stoned on the eve of the Sabbath. When the Sabbath was over then, they hurried to the sepulcher in which the body of Stephen had been put. But they found the body still there and although there had been time to anoint the corpse and wrap it, the flies were already exploring the wrappings. I know what I say here, for I went there myself to see the body. Really I would have been disappointed if it had not been there for that would have made Stephen the equal of Jesus. But others did not see the matter in this light and so deserted the doctrines of the Nazarene.

Many fled. They were convinced that Jesus was divine,

that he had been raised from the dead. They were sad that he had not saved Stephen, and puzzled. They understood that Jesus would not save them either in a like case. So to avoid persecution they fled north to Syria and Damascus, and to Beraea and to Antioch, and some into Egypt and Cyrene. Those who remained were indeed persecuted vigorously by Saul.

He dragged them out of their houses (he had the Temple guard to help him), put them in prison, had them beaten with rods or scourged, so that the name of Saul of Tarsus was one of terror among the Christians in Jerusalem.

But what irritated Saul as much as anything was that these same Christians kept asking their god to forgive Saul. "May God forgive you, for you do not know what you are doing," they would say when sentenced to the rod or to be scourged. And this infuriated Saul, for it implied that those who were being flogged were closer to Jehovah than he, and in any case nothing is more annoying than to be forgiven for your virtues.

Annas and Caiaphas, however, found in Saul exactly the man they needed to scatter the Nazarenes without jeopardizing their own position. But Caiaphas later became worried and said that the kind of zeal Saul was showing was often as much a danger to the faithful as it was a scourge to the faithless.

"The last thing we need is another breather of fire," he told me. "Things are in a delicate state of balance. Tiberius grows old. Herod sickens. Pilate has made the mistake of indulging in a slaughter among the Samaritans. We have only to be still to win." Really I had to admire the man. He was always thinking and always able in the end to get his way. Many rulers are fools but Caiaphas was not one of them. He deserved a bigger arena.

One group of Christians, however, Saul did not touch and that was the group around Peter and the Apostles. Caiaphas was troubled about Peter and John and the others because of the undoubted miracles they worked and their tremendous influence. For all his Greek sophistication, Caiaphas believed in miracles. The people who were persecuted then were the non-miracle workers who were just the humble followers of Jesus. These fled.

One day, however, one of the Apostles, Philip, was missing from the community. It was feared that he had been seized by Saul's guards in the streets and put secretly into prison—perhaps the prison of Herod, into which many disappeared. Inquiries were anxiously made, but no trace of him was found. Then some weeks later he appeared preaching in a synagogue in Caesarea and he gave this explanation of his absence. An angel had appeared to him, he said, and told him to leave Jerusalem and walk along the desert roads towards Gaza. This he had done and had found a black man who was a minister of Candace, Queen of Ethiopia, studying the Jewish scriptures while traveling in his carriage back to his own country.

The black was puzzled by the passage he was reading, and seeing Philip (whom he recognized immediately as a Jew by his ringlets and his dress) he asked him to explain the passage to him. The passage contained a prophecy of Isaiah, one of the great oracles of the Jews. It was, "He was led like a sheep to slaughter; and just as a lamb dumb before its shearer, so did he not open his mouth. In humiliation his judgment was denied him; who shall declare his generation? for his life is taken from him."

The Ethiopian man, who was a eunuch (for it would have been indiscreet of the queen to be served by any other), wished to know whether Isaiah had been referring to himself or to another in that passage, and Philip explained that he had been referring to Jesus of Nazareth. He then spent some time going over all the prophecies concerning the Messiah which had been fulfilled by Jesus of Nazareth and the result was that the eunuch became a Nazarene and believed Jesus to be both divine and the son of God. He was cleansed with water from a nearby stream and immediately afterwards, Philip said, an angel took him (Philip) by the hair and carried him through the air in a moment to the city of Azotus, from where he made his way to Caesarea.

This story, of course, was not by any means difficult for me or for any merchant trading with Abyssinia (the copper of Abyssinia is purer that that of Cyprus) to investigate. The reports I received back were to the effect that not only had the eunuch been converted to belief in the Nazarene, as Philip said, but Queen Candace herself had also become a Christian, as these people were called when they had fled to Antioch. (The word comes from the Greek *chrystos*, meaning anointed, as the Messiah, Jesus, was said to be anointed by God.)

I was surprised to hear at the same time that the prestige of Pontius Pilate was now soaring in Abyssinia. It was held there that in condemning Jesus to death, he had faithfully fulfilled the prophecies of Isaiah and so was not only guiltless of offense, but worthy of honor as the instrument of Jehovah. Statues of him were now in demand in Addis Ababa, for the religion of the queen soon became the religion of her subjects, as is indeed right.

Pilate was not pleased when I told him the news. "If Tiberius hears of that, I may lose my head," he said. "A statue of a man living is the first step to a monument on his grave. How long do you think we must wait before we can worship him as a god?"

"My dear Pilate," I replied, "when he was about to have me hurled off the cliff, he seemed in excellent health. I am sure he will be with us for another ten years."

I will report one more detail concerning the death of Stephen and then go on with my story. When it was plain that he was not going to be raised from the dead, and without telling either Peter or John, I decided to test whether I might not unwittingly have received magical powers from the Nazarene. Remember the spirits had left Tabitha when I mentioned his name. So I went quietly, having only Philip my secretary with me, to the sepulcher where Stephen's body had been put and, making the magical sign, I said, "Stephen, in the name of Jesus of Nazareth, I command you to come forth."

But not a thing happened, so plainly I had not got the magic. If I had, I would immediately have cured Philip's feet, whether he wished it or not. But at least he was saved the disappointment of my trying my powers on him first, and Stephen, of course, was beyond hurt by my failure.

XXVIII

CIRCA A.D. 36–37. Now I will tell you how the mountain was hurled at Saul as the former prostitute Mary Magdalene had foretold. When the Christians had fled from Jerusalem, and when none dared to become even secret followers of the Nazarene in Jerusalem for a while, Saul found that he had done exactly the wrong thing in driving them out. Wherever they went, they continued to live in exactly the same way, that is, communally, and to preach the doctrines of Jesus, and to hold everything in common and at their meals to break the bread and drink their wine in memory of him, saying of the bread, "Behold, his body," and of the wine, "Behold, his blood."

Instead then of stamping out the sect with the death of Stephen, Saul had actually spread it. Soon, armed with letters of authority from Caiaphas, he was rooting out Christians among the synagogues of Judaea and Galilee, outside Jerusalem. (He dared not, however, enter Samaria on the same mission because of the enmity between the Jews of the Temple and the Samaritans, who mocked at the Temple as a monument of Herod the Great rather than the House of God.) Whoever, standing in the synagogue to read from the scriptures of the Jews, made any reference to Jesus of Nazareth was dragged out, beaten, taken to prison, and tried before the Sanhedrin so that the name of Saul was feared throughout the land among the Jews.

Saul made a great mistake in not going to Samaria, for Philip, who you will remember had been transported by an angel, had preached the doctrine of Jesus in Samaria and had been very well received there. Not only did he perform many wonders among the Samaritans, but he assured them that Jesus had many times said that God was not confined to the Temple but was everywhere and in every part of the world, which exactly suited their own beliefs. So there were soon more Christians in Samaria than had been in Jerusalem.

However, Saul, knowing how the Samaritans felt towards those who exalted the Temple, avoided their country and at last got letters from the High Priests authorizing him to look for Christians in Damascus, which will show you how far the belief in Jesus of Nazareth had already spread. But then the Jews are great wanderers about the earth, as are the Arabs whom they hate and who worshiped stones and trees and wells, which they believed inhabited by particular spirits. I could understand the Arabs better than the Jews, for we Romans worship the Tiber and a certain tree which had grown since the days of Romulus in the center of Rome and from which he ate the fruit, and there is no ship entering Ostia which does not dip her sail to that white rock which Pollux caused to rise from the sea to make the entrance to the port of Rome. Also the Arabs are very open and laugh often whereas the Jews are secretive and live sadly under the fist of their terrible god.

Now, as I warned you, I have to tell you this story in the words of Luke, who wrote it down for me, having himself got it from Saul. I later questioned Saul and he told me the same story, and to show you that I am not twisting matters to make my testimony seem consistent, I will give you the story as Saul told it to me also.

Luke first, however, and here are his words:

"My dear Theophilus, I send you my greetings and also my deep respect and also my love and with it again some herbs from the highlands of Syria to cure your ailment. You are to steep as much, crushed, as you can hold in the hollow of your hand, in boiled water and then strain them off and drink the water. You should do this once a day for seven days and this should quiet your bowels. It would be better for your comfort if you did this in the morning rather than at night. You are not to think of paying me. If you will think kindly of me that is payment enough. Embrace my dear Philip for me, whom I know only through letters. It seems indeed that nothing can be done for his feet, but is he not happier with his feet broken than many men who walk twenty miles on splendid feet but with their minds bleeding?

"Now I will write you about Saul, who has told me candidly of the great change God wrought in him and how this came to be. He was, as you know, scrupulously following the practices of the Jews, believing firmly, without the slightest quiver of doubt, that if he followed the customs and dictates of the fathers to the last detail, he could not fail to gain everlasting life in the bosom of Abraham.

"He believed that he had been called out of all the Children of Israel to defend the faith of his fathers from all change and apostasy and so threw himself with every fiber of his body into the persecution of the followers of Jesus. Hearing that the word of Jesus was being openly preached in the synagogues of Damascus, and being scandalized that not a finger was lifted against the Christians, even by the most pious of the Jews there, he got a blank warrant from the High Priests to arrest all who offended in the slightest degree against the Law and bring them back to Jerusalem for trial and correction.

"I am sure you know the roads to Damascus well. There are two of them—one following the wadi south of the Lake of Gennesaret and crossing from the fertile valley of the Jordan up into the highlands and so striking northeast to Damascus. The other one is pleasanter and passes west of the Lake of Gennesaret through Nazareth and Capernaum and then, crossing the Jordan, strikes boldly into the highlands direct for Damascus.

"This is the better road, as you will know, for though it was traveled of old, it has been rebuilt by the Romans, whose roads are among the wonders of the world.

"It was this road that Saul took, for besides being more scenic (have you not yourself told me of the little valleys scarlet with poppies in midsummer?) it would give him an opportunity to denounce Jesus in Nazareth, where he was raised after his family had returned from Egypt, as I have told you. Also Saul could denounce him again in the synagogue at Capernaum, where Jesus was well known and Peter and John and James and many of the others were also well known. Be sure that a man such as Saul would not miss these opportunities.

"He was happy to find that everybody in Nazareth agreed with his denunciations, fulfilling those words which Jesus himself had uttered that a prophet is never a prophet in his own country and among his own people. In Capernaum, however, he did not fare so well, for there he learned of that first miracle of Jesus of which I have written you, when he filled the nets of Peter, James, and John with mullet to the point of breaking.

"Nor were the fishermen at Capernaum afraid to testify to that miracle which was still well known among them, and Saul was mocked by several in the crowds which he addressed.

"'Rabbi,' one shouted at him, 'everything is correct about you. Not a doubt of that. I have even counted the tassels on your sleeves and they are the correct number and the correct length, I suppose, so we must respect you as the strictest observer of the Law, and one whom God must favor.'

"This pleased Saul and pointing to the man he said, 'Behold one who has listened to the voice of God.'

"But the man said, 'Jesus, when he lived among us, did not care how he dressed and often ate without washing his hands, and ate food from people whose hands had not been washed, which is, of course, to invite death at the hands of the Strangling Demon, as everybody knows. Yet, ignoring all these things to the point of scandalizing us, he was able to cause a great draught of fish to be taken up at the worst time of the day with the sun bright on the water by Cephas, who is called Peter and is the son of Jonah, and by John the son of Zebedee and James his brother. Everybody knows that. How could such a power be given to one who puts the admonitions of the Law aside?'

" 'He did this by the power of the devil and when he was crucified, that power deserted him, for the devil cannot save those condemned by the priests of God,' replied Saul.

" 'Rabbi,' said the man, 'all ate of those fish, which were freely shared among us. None became sick. Does the devil provide nourishing food? And furthermore the best of the fish were sent to the Temple and there accepted. Can the fruit of Satan be accepted in the Holy Place by priests of God? Would not the God of our fathers send fire from Heaven to destroy those who brought so foul an offering?'

" 'Who do you say the imposter Jesus got his powers from then?' demanded Saul.

"But the fisherman replied, 'Rabbi, I do not know. I tell you only what happened. I will add that there are fishing boats pulled up to the dock and the nets all cleaned are aboard. If, observing the Law to the last tittle, as you do, you would like to do what Jesus did, we will launch a boat for you.'

"Saul flew into a rage at this and had the man seized. But the Galileans made such a disturbance that the man was released and Saul left Capernaum, shaking the dust of the town from his feet.

"Saul is a tentmaker and also a maker of sails, for these two trades flourish on the same bench. He had with him a good tent for himself and another for his servants, and, moving off into the highlands on the other side of the Jordan, put up his tent there that night. He was up before dawn and went on, still in the mountains but approaching Damascus.

"As he traveled suddenly a great light flashed about him. He fell to the ground. At the same time he heard a voice saying, 'Saul. Saul. Why do you persecute me?'

" 'Who are you, sir?' he asked.

"The voice answered, 'I am Jesus, the one you are persecuting. Get up and go into the city where you will be told what to do.'

"The men who were traveling with him stood there speechless. They had heard the voice but could see no one. Saul got up from the ground, unable to see even though his eyes were open. They had to take him by the hand and lead him into Damascus. For three days he continued blind, during which time he neither ate nor drank.

"There was a disciple in Damascus named Ananias to whom the Lord had appeared in a vision. 'Ananias,' He said.

" 'Here I am, Lord,' came the answer.

"The Lord said to him, 'Go at once to Straight Street and at the house of Judas ask for a certain Saul of Tarsus. He is there praying.' (Saul saw in a vision a man named Ananias coming to him and placing his hands on him so that he might recover his sight.) But Ananias protested, 'Lord, I have heard from many sources about this man and all the harm he has done to your holy people in Jerusalem. He is here now with authorization from the chief priests to arrest any who invoke your name.'

[222]

"The Lord said to him, 'You must go. This is the instrument I have chosen to bring my name to the Gentiles; and their kings and to the people of Israel. I myself shall indicate to him how much he will have to suffer for my name.' With that Ananias left. When he entered the house he laid his hands on Saul and said, 'Saul, my brother, I have been sent by the Lord Jesus, who appeared to you on the way here, to help you recover your sight and be filled with the Holy Spirit.' Immediately something like scales fell from his eyes and he regained his sight. He got up and was baptized, and his strength returned to him after he had taken food.

"Saul stayed some time with the disciples in Damascus and began to proclaim in the synagogues that Jesus was the son of God. Many who heard him were greatly taken aback. They said, 'Isn't this the man who worked such havoc in Jerusalem among those who invoke his name? Did he not come here purposely to apprehend such people and bring them before the chief priests?' Saul for his part grew steadily more powerful and reduced the Jewish community of Damascus to silence with his proofs that this Jesus was the Messiah."

That is the end of the story as Luke gave it to me in his letter.

It was in this manner that the Nazarene threw a mountain at Saul, as Mary Magdalene had said, for the complete and utter reversal of all his beliefs; this about-turn from persecuting the followers of Christ to becoming the most zealous leader of his doctrines was as great a wonder as if a mountain had indeed been thrown at him. (I hope you will not criticize my manuscript in that I have introduced into it the exact words of Luke without rewriting them to make them conform to my own style. I will admit that the effect is awkward, and Luke has not the Roman talent for expression. But I have done this as a service to my reader and in the interests of authenticity, though purists will rightly condemn the practice.)

Now I will give you Saul's account but in my own language since he did not write it down for me. He agreed with all that Luke wrote, but added more. He said that the light which shone around him was so intense that just to call it a light is not a good description at all. He said it was as if not only the mountains around, but all the world and the heavens, had been converted into an intense beam of light which was focused on him, and with such impact that he was thrown to the ground and utterly lost his other senses as well as his sight. "The sun burned inside my skull," he said, "as if my skull were the heavens and the sun filled it." The darkness which followed this turning of the whole world to light was, Saul said, infinitely greater than the darkness of sleep, being the darkness of death or indeed the darkness of the unborn and the unconceived, and in fact the uncreated, which is the darkness of nothingness or what the Jews call the Outer Darkness if one can conceive such a thing.

No darkness, Saul told me, could ever match that into which he was plunged, and even when other men took his hand to lead him this way and that and so get him to Damascus, he had no sense of direction but felt as if he were entirely lost in a void without any recognizable features.

"Now, Theophilus," he said, "since I am both a sailmaker and a tentmaker, you will appreciate that my eyesight was of the finest and you may think that being deprived of sight gave me this feeling of utter blackness more intense than others, blinded, might experience. But since you have a good head for business, you will readily be able to understand why my blindness was so intense, in fact why I was blinded by the Lord in the first place, and not for instance paralyzed or made deaf, which He might have done just as easily."

"Blindness would make you dependent on other men," I replied, "and it is only when we are dependent on others that we are prepared to listen to them."

"So also will paralysis," said Saul. "Remember there are no accidents with God, no whims of fancy nor amusing coincidence. Everything has its reason. So what was the reason I was struck so blind that I would have been less blind if I had been born without eyes?"

"Saul," I replied, "since, as you say, I am a businessman, why do you not just tell me why you were struck blind and save time?" To speak the truth I could see nothing especially significant about his blindness and his cure.

"The reason was this," Saul replied. "God struck me blind to bring home forcibly to me how blind I had been all my life, though I thought I saw clearly. I had believed that exact obedience to the Law would, by the discipline it enforced on me, the many self-denials it demanded, the inevitable shaping of my character, make me acceptable to God and win me eternal joy with Him. So I spent hours of my time insuring that the way I dressed and arranged my hair and my beard and the number of times I washed my hands and the earnest and painstaking inquiries I made about all that I ate were all in accordance with the Law. So I knew the Law and had read the Law and had studied the Law and practiced the Law.

"But I was blind to the Law, Theophilus, for I knew only the letter, which is but the shell of the Law, and knew nothing of the spirit, which is the kernel. So I was as blind as a man who, shelling nuts, throws away the meat and tries to get his nourishment from the shell. There is no greater blindness than that. Thus, I was struck blind to show me my spiritual blindness; and when my sight was restored, it was done to mark the first real opening of my spiritual eyes so that I could see not the written words of men, but the loving, creating, all-encompassing spirit of the one God who made me and you and everything on earth, and whose son and Messiah was the same Jesus of Nazareth whose followers I was persecuting."

"Saul," I said, "remembering how harsh you were against the followers of Jesus and how you yourself took the principal part in the stoning of Stephen, how can you be so sure you are right now, when you were so sure you were right then?"

"Because," said Saul, "I was so convinced of my righteousness formerly that only God, and not man, could ever have convinced me that I was entirely wrong. Plainly then, it is God who has changed my heart."

Certainly, as you see, Saul, whether orthodox Jew or champion of Jesus, was never given to doubts. He was a man of great pride and of great temper, which are two faults which have brought about the downfall of many men. From the day we met I believed that that temper of his, and his pride, would one day cost him his head.

XXIX

WHEN SAUL WAS CONVERTED he took the name Paul. The reasons for this change of name were several. The first reason is quite obvious. When a man, after deep consideration, changes his name it is to mark a change in himself, in his behavior, in his beliefs, and in his method of thinking.

Such a change had come over Saul, now Paul.

The second reason was that Paul is a Roman name. His complete about-turn would now make him the bitter enemy of that section of the Jews, upholders of the law, who had been his closest friends and his strongest supporters. The new name reminded them, whatever their hostility, that he was a Roman by birth, and not to be lightly imprisoned or harmed.

The third reason was that he believed that the doctrines of Jesus were to be preached to the Gentiles and that the

Gentiles did not have to become Jews in order to receive them or become followers of the Nazarene. The Gentile name symbolized that Paul was the messenger sent to the non-Jews.

All this did not happen immediately, of course. Far from it. The quick-tempered, headstrong man who believed himself more Jew even than the High Priests went into the desert to live among the Arabs as Saul and it was many months later that he returned to preach in the synagogues of Damascus as Paul.

Meanwhile my own business had taken me to Alexandria to organize the assembling of the grain fleet, then to Rome to oversee its arrival and the thousand details of docking and inventory and storage which though entrusted to others are never satisfactorily performed unless done by oneself, and then to my neglected villa in Crete for a short rest before returning to Jerusalem to attempt to regain my spirits. Yes, I have to admit that in the midst of all my affairs, I would often be overcome by a great feeling of melancholy so intense as to make me want to cry out.

This melancholy was unexplainable. The fact remains that everything gave me less and less pleasure until finally nothing at all pleased me. Not even food. That, I know, is hard to believe, yet it is true. Cestus prepared the best dishes for me—lobsters in a sauce of wine and lark's eggs; delicious sow's udder in tuna sauce; even those delicate little birds called fig peckers, roasted and laid on a bed of young asparagus. I ate a mouthful or two and then the pleasure palled. As for women, enjoyment of them lasted for but a few moments and within the hour I could no longer stand their company and banished them from my bed and my house. Even prostitutes, trained in every artifice, failed to rouse me, so that I became increasingly a burden to myself and a sorrow to my household. My only relief was to plunge myself into my business, acquiring more ships and warehouses and docks.

But tell me this—does a man live to work? No. He lives to enjoy himself, and his work is only a necessary means of attaining enjoyment. But my enjoyment grew less and less and although I consulted astrologers and soothsayers, and even visited many famous oracles, none could offer me relief.

You may be sure that I visited Tutmoshe when I was in Alexandria but only to add to my melancholy and experience the sadness of watching him die. He had made up his mind to cut his life short now that the phoenix had returned ushering in the new era, and to be absorbed in Aten, the sun god. He died propped up in his garden, naked and bathed in the golden-red glow of the setting sun. I came, among other things, to ask his advice, but who will be so hardhearted as to present a dying man with their troubles? Yet I had forgotten that he could read all that was in my mind, for he said to me, "You cannot escape, Theophilus. You are hunted and will be taken. Why then do you run so hard?"

When he died, which occurred at the precise moment that the sun set, the sacred ibis stretched its wings and flew westward to accompany his soul to Aten, and that terrible asp, which he had called my sister, glided from its hill of rocks and, coiling itself at the feet of the corpse, guarded it through the night.

His death was a heavy blow to me. Why should one mourn a man almost two hundred years old who dies? Has he not had his fill of life? Is not mourning such a person ridiculous? Yet mourn him I did, for here is the truth of death—it is we ourselves who die, not another; and at each death we attend our own funeral.

You may be sure I arranged for an excellent funeral for Tutmoshe when the asp would permit us to touch the body, and he was mummified and put in a triple case which was stood facing eastward to catch the first glimpse of the rising Aten. Thousands attended his funeral. They were not merely the few surviving followers of Aten, but

Greeks and Jews and Egyptians who worshiped Ra and the many gods of Egypt as well as the gods of Rome. The people of Alexandria love gods. They cannot have enough of them, and they had soon converted Tutmoshe into a god and he had a cult of followers. I do not mean among the Jews. They have but one god, and this is a source of great hatred against them among the Egyptians and Greeks of Alexandria. Of that hatred I will tell you more later.

Tutmoshe was buried and was soon a god then, and by that childish reasoning of the Alexandrians, he was mixed up with the phoenix, so that very soon there were people in that credulous city who would take you to the tomb of Tutmoshe and tell you that that was where the phoenix had expired and given birth to itself once more.

You have perhaps forgotten about Tabitha. Well, so had I. But she was now free and Tutmoshe in his will had left her all his possessions including, to my annoyance, that orb of black stone from the Pretannic Islands which I had given him. I had hoped that in his will he would return it to me, but he did not; he gave it to Tabitha. He had given her a great deal more, including some of his magic, for she could now feed that terrible basilisk, the hooded serpent which came to her as a kitten and would coil in her lap.

Also I found her often talking to flowers and to birds, holding the blossoms between her palms and making little noises of endearment in some language which I did not understand. Birds of all kinds came readily to her and I suspected that Tutmoshe might have told her that secret of longevity which he himself had learned from a golden dung beetle. When I asked her whether this was so, she laughed at me and said, "Life knows no death and we are all doomed never to cease from living. This is a mystery but it is also the truth. We cannot die. We can only change. To postpone what is called dying is merely to postpone a change. It is to postpone rebirth."

Here she had something in common with the Nazarene,

who had preached that unless a man is born again he cannot attain the kingdom of Heaven.

It was plain that now she was as great a magician as she had been when I had unwittingly cast the spirits out of her. Since she was convinced that Tutmoshe had not died but had merely been born again or changed into another form, she was not sad except at the loss of his physical presence, which as I have told you was at first sight quite revolting.

I congratulated her on obtaining her freedom and her fortune at the same time and said that I assumed that she would now remain in Alexandria. "If you take my advice —and I am a man of more experience that yourself—you will be very careful about marrying," I said. "You may expect very many suitors now, but the more handsome they are, the greater their debts. Of that you may be sure, since you yourself are quite plain and unattractive, as I told you before, so they will be looking for your money, of which they will soon relieve you. Therefore do not be swept off your feet by thought of hours of delight in the bed of a handsome stranger. Rather, when you do marry, marry someone who is quite ugly and whom you must seek out yourself, rather than one who comes seeking you. In that way you will be sure that he is not attracted to you by the modest fortune which you have inherited as a result of my giving you to Tutmoshe."

I wished to remind her by that latter phrase that all her good fortune had come from me, for Tutmoshe himself, as you will remember, had scarcely been sufficiently grateful when I made him a present of Tabitha.

"Master," said Tabitha, "I am well aware that all of my good fortune has come from you. Yet I am bold enough to ask you for one more favor."

"What is it?" I inquired cautiously. Surely, with money of her own she could not want a new dress.

"Take all I have and let me come with you," that astonishing woman said. Nor would she have it any other way, and the tears she refused to shed over the death of Tut-moshe she shed now at the prospect that I would refuse her. Really there was nothing else to be done, and Caballus, who of course accompanied me on all my journeys, threatened another bout of sulking if I refused her again. Philip also said that I needed a permanent woman in my household to attend to my health and nurse me when sick. So at last I agreed but insisted that she keep for herself the villa of Tutmoshe and the money she inherited from him, as well as the small plot of land attached to the villa. A young Ethiopian was found as caretaker for all that property and so Tabitha accompanied me again on my voyages, and noted the depressions from which I suffered and sorrowed over them.

In honesty I must admit that in permitting her to join my household, I hoped in return that she would use those magical powers she had learned from Tutmoshe to alleviate or banish my depressions. But when I asked her to do so, she said, in tears, that I alone could cure myself. Yet I did not know how, and her advice, involving, as it did, less and less indulgence in pleasures, was, of course, pure rubbish.

XXX

CIRCA A.D. 37. I come now to a very important part of this testament to which I hope you will give the closest attention, and not stop to discuss points of style. I refer to the death of Tiberius. I was at my villa in Crete when the news was brought to me, and though at his behest I had nearly been hurled to my death off the cliffs at Capri, I wept that the father of our great nation was with us no more. One could sense that a great blow had been struck not only to Rome but to all the world with his death, and later I learned of the very many omens and other signs which had foretold his end. I will list some of these here, for they form a proper part of his memorial.

A day before his death, a multitude of ravens, which are birds that do not fly any great distance, flew to Rome, where they settled cawing on every public building. The raven, as all know, says only one word, which is *cras*—that is, "tomorrow"—plainly indicating that on the following day a great misfortune would befall the empire. Again a large eagle which had been perched for many days on the roof of the temple of Jupiter the Greatest and Best fell dead into the streets, and by another astonishing omen a further eagle fell out of the sky and lay dead at the feet of Claudius, the idiot nephew of Caligula, who had such a terrible stammer that even the unrelenting blows of his schoolmasters and tutors had been unable to loose his tongue. Moreover, he was so clumsy that he stumbled constantly on his pigeon-toed feet, so that he stammered both in his speech and in his gait. All Rome at one time knew the doggerel about him:

> *Claud the unsteady, since he was a nipper,*
> *Has provided for Rome its champion tripper.*
> *He stumbles afoot, he stumbles at ease*
> *He stumbles on stones, 'esses,' 'gees,' and on 'tees,'*
> *He has stumbling feet and a stumbling head*
> *But never yet stumbled into his wife's bed.*
> *Poor Clo Clo in trying to ply the man's art,*
> *Would fumble and stumble with the wrong part.*

That an eagle then should have fallen to death at the feet of Claudius, a certain sign that he would one day be emperor of Rome, was astounding and dismaying to all who knew it.

But to return to the omens which foretold the death of Tiberius. In the week before he died, a lion roared nightly in the Field of Mars and Caesar's ghost was seen three times in the Forum, holding out its hands towards that palace of Tiberius which he had not occupied for years, having lived so long at Capri.

A bolt of lightning struck the statue of Tiberius erected near the temple of Jupiter and tumbled it from its pedestal, and it was reported in many of the city's innumerable taverns that red wine turned to white and was without any strength. Also the Tiber flowed backwards for many hours; and during the night a hundred horsemen, each carrying an extinguished lamp, galloped through the city, sparks flying from the hooves of their mounts.

I know myself that in Crete there was an earthquake, which three times rocked the whole island and split four of the columns before my villa, which plunged me into gloom as being an omen of great misfortune to myself.

These are but some of the omens which warned of the death of the Emperor. Concerning the death itself, I have fullest details from my friends, Pallas and Narcissus, who, though attached to the house of the idiot Claudius (who lived close to poverty in a small villa on an obscure street of the Roman suburbs), nonetheless had very close contact with the slaves and freemen who surrounded Tiberius and were fully informed in the matter.

Thrasyllus, the magician of Tiberius, had died a little while before, his death being announced to him by a small lizard. Tiberius also had his private herald of death, as I will tell you. When Thrasyllus had gone, Tiberius decided he would return for a while to Rome, and set off to do so, even reaching the Tiber and venturing some distance up the river until indeed he was in sight of the walls of city. There, news was brought to him that a huge lizard which was his personal pet and came from the island of Comodus in the seas beyond India had died. This foul creature, which lived on rotted flesh, Tiberius used to feed himself. In any case it was discovered dead, and not only dead but crawling with flies and ants.

Tiberius was profoundly affected by this sign, interpreting it to mean that if he entered Rome he would be set on by the people in their hundreds of thousands and killed. So he put about and returned to Capri, but he never reached that terrible and yet beautiful island of his again. Indeed his dragon had prophesied correctly about his death as you shall see.

He decided to travel by land to Misenium on the Bay of Naples, where he could easily take ship back to Capri, but passing through a garrison town, got news that the soldiers there had organized a wild-animal hunt in an arena.

The details of these hunts are too well known to be repeated. A number of wild beasts are released, one at a time or in large numbers, in an arena or circus and various warriors or hunters fight and dispatch them. Lions and tigers provide the best sport but only if opposed by spearmen or swordsmen, for archers can too readily cripple them as they crouch to spring.

A wild boar on this occasion was released and Tiberius, to impress the soldiers, called for *pila* to throw at the beast. However he missed with every cast and instead of proving his youth, proved his age and his infirmity and also, sweating excessively, caught a cold.

He continued his journey, with a chill east wind blowing, and arriving at Misenium found the easterly had set up a heavy chop in the bay and so he could not sail for Capri. He stayed, however, at the villa of Lucius Licinius Lucullus, conqueror of Mithridates. Lucullus was, of course, long dead and his villa stood on a finger of cliff overlooking the sea. I would have liked to own it myself, but it is not wise to own so lovely a place and so I built my own villa at Crete away from envious eyes.

Emperors, particularly tyrants, may not be ill, for even the rumor of illness encourages their enemies. Tiberius then, when he had moved into the villa of Lucullus with all his train, which included both Macro, head of the Praetorians, and Caligula, gave a sumptuous banquet for the officials of the area. Now among the attendants on Tiberius was the physician Charicles, who was a Greek, but I think his mother had been a Persian. He, knowing that it was full moon begged leave to be excused to gather certain herbs which he alone could recognize and which must be picked at that time.

The Emperor excused him, but in taking leave of him, Charicles allowed his forefinger to rest on the Emperor's wrist during the handshake and noted that his pulse was erratic and feeble. Tiberius, who was no fool, understood that his pulse had been taken and, to show how strong he was, ordered that the banquet be renewed, nor would he leave the table until the sun was full up, when he went to bed. A little later he slipped into a coma and Macro and Caligula were jubilant, for Charicles said that Tiberius could not last more than two days. Messengers were secretly sent to the Senate and to the nearby legions to prepare their minds to accept Caligula as the successor and Macro as his right-hand man.

At last it appeared that Tiberius was not breathing and no pulse could be found. Caligula, jubilant, took the ring off his finger and servants, slipping into the death room, stole several jeweled cups and medallions, and, others following suit, the death chamber was soon stripped of everything but the blankets with which the Emperor was covered.

Then, to everybody's astonishment, the Emperor recovered. He groaned, opened his eyes, got out of bed and, staggering around the room, demanded where everybody was. He called for a dish of roast chicken and a cup of Chianti wine, and howled with fury to find that not only was his room stripped of all its ornaments but the signet ring had even been taken from his finger.

Immediately there was consternation. Caligula, who had but a moment before been rejoicing at his powers as the new emperor, fled and hid in one of the servant's cubicles under the bed. But Macro was up to the situation. He rushed into the room, picked the bony old Emperor up in his arms, put him back on the bed, face down, straddled him, and held blankets and pillows over his head until the great Tiberius was smothered. Yes, that was the end of that tremendous fighter who in his youth had been a splendid general. He was murdered in his own bed by a palace soldier.

When the deed was done Macro came out of the room, out of breath himself, and announced with sorrow that Tiberius was dead and, falling to his knees, hailed Caligula as the new emperor. Caligula, who pretended that he had gone to the servant's room to be alone with his grief, received the news with a doleful countenance, though actually he had never heard anything more joyous in his life. All about dropped on their knees and hailed him as emperor, but later Caligula, still fearful, went to the bedside of Tiberius and, opening the eyelids, put his finger in his eyes, and then stopped up his nostrils and his mouth to be absolutely sure that he was dead.

Those terrible German guards immediately transferred their loyalty to Caligula. They had, of course, not been on guard when their master was dying (when they could have saved his life at least for a little while) for their barbarous religion demands that they desert the dying lest they be seized by his ghost and so become mad.

So the great Tiberius, who had been stripped of his possessions as he lay dying, was finally stripped of his life.

When the news of his death reached Rome, the exultation throughout the city was as if our armies everywhere had achieved tremendous victories. I have the most detailed description from the letter writer Pimentus, who, as everybody knows, puts out the most accurate newsletter issued in that city. People, it was reported, bedecked with flowers and garlands of vines danced through the streets and temples, (it was mid-March when Tiberius died, and that year every crevice of the hills about was white with narcissus). They sacrificed so many birds and beasts in gratitude to Apollo, to Mars, and to Jupiter that the cost even of a rabbit went up to ten denarii. Wine flowed like a river. Taverns threw their doors open in defiance of licensing hours, and the Roman mob took over the city, ignoring the Praetorians, whose leader Macro was in any case at Misenium.

But the greatest rejoicing was among forty or fifty shop-keepers and officials, seized on one pretext or another, and imprisoned in that terrible dungeon at the end of the Forum—an underground place where every week half a dozen were strangled, and their bodies flung down the Stairs of Mourning to be insulted by the mob and then, impaled on hooks, dragged off to the Tiber. Well, all these prisoners, awaiting either the executioner's sword or his horrid noose, which he would tighten around their necks with a stick, believed their lives saved. They were to be executed on March 17 and Tiberius died on March 16 and they could well hope that the new emperor, Caligula, would pardon them all. But such was not the case.

Caligula at Misenium was not available for an appeal, and the governor of the prison, fearing that he might answer with his own life if he postponed the executions, had all fifty of the poor wretches strangled. When the prison guards began to bring the bodies, still warm with their blackened, protruding tongues and terror-stricken glazed eyes, to the Stairs of Mourning to be pitched down them as was the custom, the Roman mob was outraged. If they had made their anger known before, all these lives, many of them men and women, would have been saved.

"To the Tiber with Tiberius," they shouted. "He is a wasp who stings even when he is dead." Bands of ruffians swore that they would never allow the Emperor's body to be burned but would put the grappling hooks under his big jaw and drag him off to the river, which throughout his reign had not failed to receive its daily quota of corpses. Indeed it took all the prestige of Caligula and the cudgels of the Praetorians to prevent something of the sort happening.

Mobs collected around the temples and demanded that the priests lead them in prayers to Mother Earth, to Air and to Water and to Fire not to provide a resting place for the corpse of Tiberius. I do not think that such an outpouring of hatred against any man had ever before been seen in Rome. Believe me, it sickens my heart to write of it, for although I had myself been in danger of my life from Tiberius, yet I must say that in the provinces of Rome no man was more respected and with good reason. Only in the city was he hated. Elsewhere his firm rule had made of the Roman empire a haven for all men; and in Crete and Greece, Syria, Cilicia, Spain, and Gaul—indeed in every part, even including Judaea—his passing was mourned. Only Rome rejected him and flung down his statues.

In the end, however, authority prevailed. The body was brought into Rome under a strong escort of Praetorians, who broke down a barricade erected to prevent its entry into the city. It was consumed by fire on the Field of Mars, but no cage containing a white dove was placed on the pyre. This had been first done at the cremation of Augustus and the dove released to soar into the heavens, symbolizing the departure of the soul of the great Emperor. Since the Praetorians were fearful that many would be on hand with slingshots and stones to knock the dove out of the sky, that part of the ritual was dispensed with. Gaius Caligula gave the funeral oration, which was really a funeral oration for his own father Germanicus and for his mother Agrippina and his two brothers, all done to death by Tiberius.

"How noble a man is this," he said, "who to preserve Rome destroyed in great grief my own mother and father and my two brothers, who were starved to death, and every day went over the list of Senators and knights to see who was plotting against the state. How generous of the gods that they should have left a man of such virtue and patriotism with us so long, and should have resisted time and again their great desire to snatch him into their bosom. So let us burn his body now on the Field of Mars knowing full well that his work can never be undone." So he went on making skillful innuendoes against Tiberius, each one of which exalted him as the sole survivor of a martyred family.

"My love. My star. My chick." These were the terms with which Caligula, the sole surviving son of the great Germanicus, was greeted in the streets of Rome, for few but the inner circle, who had come in contact with him, knew his true nature. But with the death of Tiberius I was on the verge of discovering the true interpretation of that dream which had so disturbed my sleep in the inn at Emmaus—the dream of tumbling buildings and flood-waters breaking through mountain ranges to destroy me. For Tiberius, I soon found, had been the mountain which held the flood back from me and the solid earth on which my whole fortune had been erected.

And now Tiberius was gone, amidst general rejoicing in which I took no part.

BOOK IV

XXXI

CIRCA A.D. 36–37. You will perhaps be impatient with me that in my last book I dealt mostly with Peter and Saul who became Paul but made no mention of Pontius Pilate. Well, if you will try writing yourself sometime you will find that it is not possible to tell everything at once exactly as it happened, but you must tell one thing and follow it through and then you must come back and tell another thing. So now I will come back and tell you about Pontius Pilate.

He had, as I have certainly made plain, made the mistake of being always at war with those over whom he was called to rule. Such a policy can never succeed. I had been to him, as you know, with a proposal for the financing of his aqueduct, but he had found another means of financing it—namely, he had seized the funds of the Jewish Temple (funds which poured in from all parts of the world) and used them for this purpose. Over and above that he had displayed shields and standards of the legions of his command on the walls of the Antonia fortress so that they were visible from the Temple, and the militants among the Jews, who called themselves Zealots, had stormed the fortress and died in large numbers in their efforts to remove the standards whose exposure in plain sight of the Temple was for them blasphemous and sacrilegious. Their law is that no image of any kind must be allowed in the sacred city of Jerusalem, which name, you will be surprised to learn, in view of its history, means "Peace of God." They put up with a giant eagle on one wall of the Temple which Herod the Great had placed there in loyalty to Rome and to remind Jews that it was through the generosity of Rome that the Temple (one of the marvels of the world) had been rebuilt. But they resisted every other infringement of their laws against images.

Circa A.D. 35. Finally, to continue with the rough outline of Pilate's warfare against the Jews, he had made the mistake of slaughtering thousands of Samaritans who gathered on a mountain convinced by one of their magicians that he was going to produce for them the sacred vessels of the Jewish leader and lawgiver Moses. Really, you do not have to be bothered by these details. Nobody can ever understand the sensitivities of the Jew unless he is himself a Jew. If, however, you can say to yourself, "I am of a people whom the only god there ever was or ever will be chose to be his special concern, indeed made into his own children"; if you can say such a thing to yourself and believe it with every fiber of your being, then perhaps you can understand the Jewish superego. In any case, Pilate, after ten years as Procurator of Judaea (a record length of time during which to hold that office) had made himself so thoroughly detested by the Jews that they managed to convince Lucius Vitellius, who had but recently been appointed governor of Syria, that he, Pilate, had broken the laws of Rome.

Vitellius was only too glad to order Pilate to go to Rome and justify to Tiberius his actions in Judaea. (This Vitellius was that same flatterer who had given that enormous party in my honor and at my expense. It was his growing influence with Caligula and through him with Tiberius that had brought about his appointment as governor of Syria. I will perhaps have more to say about him later.)

Very well, Pilate could not refuse the order to go to Rome and justify himself to the Emperor, and he was the more defenseless because he had been appointed by Sejanus and Sejanus, as you know, was now dead. But he believed that he might still find a friend in Macro and set out in some trepidation. He had, of course, ample funds from ten years as procurator with which to bribe witnesses, senators, and judges, but you understand that nothing will bribe an emperor, whose one word can command anybody's wealth.

Alas for Pilate. He had hardly arrived in Rome before Macro ordered him seized and imprisoned. To be sure, Pilate immediately made Macro a very handsome present, not merely of money but also of those fine Arabian woolens which command such great prices in Rome. Perhaps this would have been sufficient, in time, to secure Pilate's release, for he had many friends in Rome though hated by the whole Jewish community, which, though banished, lived openly now on the western bank of the Tiber where there was indeed a Jewish Rome established.

But Pilate had delayed too long in reaching Rome. Tiberius might have acquitted him of any misdeed, but Tiberius died. Pilate's two friends Sejanus and Tiberius (if indeed Tiberius could be counted friend to any man) were then gone. The Jews had given large sums to Marco and to Caligula and they wanted Pilate's head. So Pilate was among those forty or fifty unfortunates who were slaughtered the very day after Tiberius had died.

So great was the tumult in the city on the news of the death of the Emperor that the execution of the Procurator of Judaea went by unnoticed, or known only to those who were closely interested. Indeed, had you asked the average Roman of the mob—the constant attendant at the baths or at the gladiatorial games or at the circus where he bet on the Green faction in the chariot races—if you asked such a person who was the Procurator of Judaea he could not tell you and he could not tell you either, except in very general terms, where Judaea lay. Do not be surprised at this. Reflect that such men knew nothing but the streets of Rome, and a little perhaps of the countries which they might have passed through and fought in when serving in the legions.

No person is more ignorant than a member of the Roman mob. His ability to resist learning and to fill his mind with superstitions is beyond all belief. You may have traveled to the ends of the earth—to the brick streets of Antioch with its multitude of beautifully tiled wells, to the palm-shaded streets of Cyrene, where the Great Sea is purple as wine in the autumn of the year, or to Ancyra in Gelatia, where there is a certain tree which, it is said, sings a hymn to the rising sun—you may have been to all these places, but a Roman will mock you as an ignoramus if you do not know the site of the "Golden Duck," or the "Ass and Corn Mill" or the "Twin Stars" or some other tavern in Rome. I spoke to one who had served with the Tenth Legion Fratensis in Britain and asked him what those isles were like, and whether the same flowers grew there as grew in Rome and the same trees, and he could not tell me for he had never noticed. He brought back only a memory of mud and in his mind the Pretannic Islands were but a vast mudpile lying across a stormy sea from Gaul.

Now to the degree that it was possible, Pilate had always been my friend. Of course, real friendship is out of the question between a businessman and those placed in high authority—business and government must come first and it is quite understood that one may have to sell out or betray a friend for the protection of business or in the interests of government. Those who cling to other views are children and unfit for public affairs. However, I had always been frank with Pilate and he with me, and I made the most careful inquiries as to the manner of his death and the disposal of his body and what had become of his wife Procula, with her frizzy hair, her heavy freckles, and plump, unattractive body.

There were a multitude of stories about the two of them; that is to say, about the manner in which they were killed. According to one story, Pilate had been permitted to open his veins, and, seated in a bath of hot water, bleed peacefully to death and Procula also. Another story said that he had been beheaded by a centurion of the Praetorians, having refused to take his own life. Another story said he had been strangled and his body flung down the Stairs of Mourning and dragged off on hooks to the Tiber. One would think that it would have been quite easy to have established the truth of the matter, but the utter frenzy into which Rome fell on the death of Tiberius obscured many important matters. All I could ascertain for sure was that Pilate was dead. You would think that friends and relatives would gain possession of the body and arrange for it to be properly burned, for certainly Pilate, although only of the equestrian order, was no small man.

But the turmoil of the city prevented that and I came to believe that his body and that of Procula had been pitched into the Tiber, to be stoned as they floated by by the crowds of youths who line the banks for such sport. I wondered, when his last moments came, whether Pilate thought back to the Nazarene whom he had been forced to condemn to death, but that was a foolish fancy, for Pilate had been the judge of not one but of a thousand men. Yet I recalled how hard he had tried to preserve the life of that Nazarene, who, doomed, had looked upon Pilate himself with pity.

Certainly we do well to remember in our days of wealth and power how slight is our hold on these things. Is there a greater contrast in all the world than that between Tiberius in his pride—commander of the greatest of all empires—and Tiberius in his old age pinned to his couch by a rude soldier and smothered with his own pillow with no one to help him? Or a greater contrast between Pilate ordering the slaughter of five thousand Samaritans gathered upon a hill, and then the stripped corpse of Pilate floating down the Tiber a target for the stones of laughing boys?

Philip has suggested at this point another contrast—that between the shivering Nazarene, with the mob jeer-ing about his bloody body as he died, and the thousands who now sought every word he uttered in his life. Certainly the Nazarene dead had more power than the Nazarene alive and had already converted many of his enemies to his doctrines. But so it was too with Caesar, who was widely hated while he lived by some of the best Romans and is now, not a hundred years later, worshiped daily by thousands. So I told Philip that his contrast was beside the point and unworthy. "After all," I said, "from what great height did this Jesus fall—from stonemason to crucifixion? Is that to be compared with the fall of Tiberius or even of Pilate?"

"Master," said Philip, "Jesus fell from Heaven to the gallows, and to the worst death it is possible for a man to die. Surely in all history, through all time, there can be no fall greater than that, nor a triumph greater than to come back from death to life, and not merely to mortal life but to eternal life."

Well, I had not meant to get into these theological discussions at this point. It is not that they do not concern me but that this is not the place for them, for I was telling you of the fall of Tiberius and the accession of Caligula.

Now when Caligula had given the funeral oration, and when the will of Tiberius (it had been witnessed by only a few freedmen and some illiterate fishermen who lived on the island of Capri and put their mark where they were told), when the will of Tiberius was read in the Senate, it contained a surprise even for Caligula. For it did not make him sole emperor. The authority was to be shared with Gemullus, who was the grandson of Tiberius; a person of so little importance that it has not been necessary to bring his name into my story until this time. He was not yet a man and had not even the right to wear the toga. The boy was sickly, susceptible to colds in the throat and the chest, largely because he was made to sleep in an unheated room even in winter to save expense. He was always biting his nails, which he had bitten down to the quick, and he had the same stammer as his great-uncle Claudius.

As soon as Caligula discovered that his nephew was his co-heir he determined to get rid of him. He first convinced the Senate that Tiberius had not been in his proper mind when he named the boy as co-heir, pointing out that no one not yet in his majority can rule as emperor. Then he spread stories about that the boy was plotting against him.

In the end he sent a message to the boy that he must die for the good of the state. The little fellow, who had been brought up to believe by his tutors that the good of the state must come before all else, expressed himself as perfectly willing to do so, and bared his neck for the centurion to strike off his head. But the centurion drew back from the deed, either out of pity or for fear lest he himself be later accused of the murder of one of royal blood. The boy then, in his duty to Rome as he saw it, offered to kill himself. But he had no training with the sword, and had to inquire where he should stab himself in order to be sure of dying. With tears in his eyes the centurion told him how to place the sword point at his heart and then fall upon it. Alas, the boy fell so awkwardly that the sword did not enter deeply, and the centurion himself had to thrust it in properly and work the blade about to ensure that the heart was pierced and, indeed, minced.

So died the first Roman to fall to Caligula—a miserable, lonely boy deserted by his tutors and freedmen who might have advised him that since he was co-emperor with Caligula, he had as much right to say that Caligula should die for the good of Rome as Caligula had to say that his own death was necessary. But the weak have no allies. Whatever philosophers say, the day will never come when strong men will go, at peril to themselves, to the help of the unprotected and the unfortunate. Had I followed such a policy myself, I would have spent my life chained to a galley bench, saying prayers to the heavy oar which was my master and which I had to serve with all my strength.

The second to go of any importance surprised no one. He was none other than Macro, whom Tiberius had used to get rid of Sejanus. He was a dull man, strong as a bull, brave, but stupid in that he could not see more than one move ahead. That was the way his life had gone. He was the man Tiberius had picked, on the recommendation of Caligula, to take the place of Sejanus. Since Caligula had been the immediate cause of his rise to fame, Macro kept close to him and, to gain his favor, lent him his wife Ennia whenever Caligula wanted a woman. Caligula promised Ennia that he would marry her, swearing that he loved her, and to oblige him, Macro divorced her. But Caligula did not marry Ennia and that did not even strike Macro as strange. He felt himself entirely safe and his future completely assured. Had he not personally murdered Tiberius so that Caligula could become emperor? Didn't Caligula then owe him a great debt in that he had both given him his wife and also made him emperor with the murder of Tiberius? (There was a rumor that Tiberius had several times thought of disinheriting Caligula and, whether these rumors were true or untrue, it was certainly better that Tiberius should be disposed of before, in his dotage, he changed his mind.)

So Macro, who was a great fool, thought his future assured. He did not know how dangerous it is to be in the power of a tyrant indebted to him. That is something which neither emperor nor tyrant can endure. Caligula, however, like a cat, loved to play with those whom he was going to kill.

He told Macro that in return for his many services he was going to give him a great reward—he was going to make him governor of Egypt. That meant that he had to resign his position as head of the Praetorians, which Macro did with joy. A big feast was given him, and he went off with all pomp and ceremony to board a royal galley at Ostia to be taken to Egypt as governor of that richest province of the Roman empire.

At Ostia, however, Macro was arrested by a plain centurion and brought back to Rome. What was the charge? It was one that set the whole of Rome laughing—the charge of corrupting the morals of Caligula by encouraging his wife to seduce the Emperor when he was but a young man, and taking him around the stews and brothels of Rome.

Really it was so ridiculous that everybody thought it a joke, for Caligula was known to be the most frequent and lavish patron of the Roman stews. He might have had half the noble-born women in Rome for his pleasure, but they perhaps would have been appalled at the unnatural practices he would have expected of them, which were but part of the trade of the prostitute. Caligula, in short, preferred whores and nobody could believe for a moment that he, who at the age of fourteen had been found scuffling in the bed of his sister Drusilla, had been led astray by Macro's wife.

When Macro himself got back to Rome, under escort, he was given an audience with Caligula, and it was Pallas who told me the story. Macro was brought in chains into the presence of Caligula, and Ennia also. They prostrated themselves before Caligula, and he gave each of them a sword, saying, "Here is a fine tool. Now both of you go and have intercourse with it." Everybody laughed at this witticism except the two condemned, who, fulfilling his harsh orders, had to kill themselves within the hour.

Other deaths which followed the accession of Caligula were not especially notable. One was that of his maternal grandaunt Antonia, who was the mother of his halfwit uncle Claudius, whose father had been Drusus, the brother of Tiberius. She brought about her own death by denouncing to his face Caligula's murder of Gemullus. Caligula told the old woman to go and cut her throat, which she was obliged to do, but not before she had first of all made all arrangements for her funeral in the old Roman manner and had written out for her halfwit son the eulogy he was to speak over her pyre, warning him not to stutter in any part.

Claudius did very well at the funeral. Caligula did not preside, of course, but watched it from the palace window, so Claudius alone represented the family. Everybody expected that he would be the next to go, but being a half-wit and a stutterer saved him. With Gemullus, Antonia, Macro, and Tiberius all out of the way, Caligula now ordered the death of his father-in-law. His father-in-law was the Senator Silanus, whose daughter, Junia, Caligula had married some years before. She had died a year or two previously in childbirth, and the child had also died. Silanus was a Senator in the old style—an upright man who alone had never been suspected even by Tiberius of any but the most honorable motives. Caligula sent him his good wishes and a request for his death and the old gentleman, without demur, put his affairs in order and slit his throat with his razor.

I do not pretend that these deaths all occurred in the order in which I have related them. That is not an important matter. Nor were the first months of the reign of Caligula entirely confined to murders. Not at all. He himself went to the islands of Pandataria and Pontia to collect the remains of his mother and his brothers, who had been starved to death under Tiberius and half-burned. These he brought back himself and gave them a full funeral on pyres at the Field of Mars and personally spoke their eulogy, weeping bitterly over them.

He distributed money in great quantities to all the people of Rome as soon as he was emperor, doubled the grain allowance for every citizen, and also doubled Tiberius' bequest of three gold pieces to every man serving with the legions. You must remember that Caligula had been brought up as a boy with the legions on the German front. He was there while his father Germanicus had put down the revolts among the soldiers and had recaptured the lost eagles of Varus and given a proper burial to those of Varus' command who had been massacred by the Germans in the Teutobergian Woods, as I have already related. The adoration which the army had for Germanicus was now transferred to Caligula—Little Boots, as he was still called, though emperor. The soldiers had a song about him to which they marched, which went:

> Born in a camp.
> Weaned on war.
> A noble heritage
> For a Roman emperor.

To say a word against Caligula in the presence of a solider was to risk being killed, and indeed in the first eight months of his reign his popularity with the army was matched by his popularity among the civilians, who in any case always followed the army lead and delighted in proclaiming themselves just as patriotic as the soldiers. The deaths Caligula ordered raised not a murmur against him among the soldiers or the Roman civilian mob. "Little Boots is clearing his camp," was a common phrase. One would have thought that the death of Macro would have at least stirred up the Praetorians, but Caligula had first of all made to each member of that body a handsome present of gold. In fact he had assembled the whole body and gone along the files handing each man his gold coins, joking with them and warning them not to spend all on Messalina or Portia or Lucy or some other famous whore. So the soldiers decided that Macro had certainly done something very wrong to their wonderful emperor, something very serious which must be kept secret, and so was hidden under the great joke of having seduced him away from virtue in his youth.

Also, Caligula appointed in Macro's place an old white-haired senior centurion, Cassius Chaerea, whose integrity and courage were respected even by the worst man in the army. This man had cut his way through the mutineers who surrounded Germanicus with Caligula on his back when the troops were rioting and when Germanicus feared for the life of his son. He had without a doubt saved the boy's life at that time. Also in the Varus massacre, he had managed to lead his men out of the terrible trap and save many of them. Again he had held an important bridge-head across the Rhine during one onslaught of the German hordes under Arminius. He was in fact reckoned the bravest man and the best soldier in Rome, so when he was appointed head of the Praetorians instead of Macro (who was something of a garrison soldier in all truth) the appointment was the most popular one that could be made.

"Little Boots is a soldier first and an emperor second," the men said. "Now we will all be paid our pensions and there will be a good war somewhere and plenty of booty for everybody."

XXXII

CALIGULA DID NOT PROVIDE his adoring army with a war right away. Indeed there was only one place with which he could go to war with any hope of success and that was the Pretannic Islands, for the Germans were very hard fighters and there was no profit to exchanging blows with them, and the Parthians were even worse, for they used the bow and arrow, which put the legions at a disadvantage. It was, of course, regarded as entirely unworthy for a Roman to use such a weapon and so none were trained with bows, and they did not even like to use slingshots. Let men pause a moment to praise them for this. What manliness is there in killing a foe at a distance of a hundred yards? Is it not in the sweaty, bloody, face-to-face encounter with sword and shield that men are proved worthy of their fathers? Must not those nations perish whose warriors are so cowardly as to fight from afar? Surely the gods will not allow them to prosper, for to kill from afar is murder and how can those who practice this earn the favor of the gods?

However, Caligula, in place of war, provided Rome with chariot races and gladiatorial games and wild-beast hunts in great abundance. Herds of elephants and of ostriches, of lions and of tigers, of rhinoceros and those strange beasts which the Greeks call river-horses, and of crocodiles and of every wild and fierce creature that might be found were brought to Rome to be hunted in the arenas there. Great dogs from that island called Hibernia (there is much gold there) were set on lions and on tigers, men wrestled with serpents and with crocodiles from the Nile, barehanded Nubians fought the giant ostriches which, with one unexpected kick, can disembowel a naked man, and with terrible blows of their beaks pluck out his eyes and peck a hole in his head.

I saw many of these shows myself, you may be sure. They are always exciting. It is comical indeed to see a giant bird pecking at a man as if he were a rabbit. And there is excitement in seeing an elephant pin a struggling, screaming man to the ground and crush him to death. You may hold it ignoble of me to say such things. But I wish to tell the truth and there is pleasure in cruelty; otherwise the arenas would not be crowded. It is no use lying about these things at all.

After such shows, however, to which I always took Caballus, for there is as much fighting among the spectators as there is in the arena, I often felt a sense of gloom and deep depression, which neither food nor wine could banish. What was the reason for it? Why should I feel so cast down in taking my honest pleasure in watching men fight men, and men fight beasts in the arena? Did not the gods themselves enjoy these things? Why should I, in the evening, after such a glorious day, feel dejected when but a few hours before I had exulted when the charioteer of the Leek Green team had with his lash cleverly blinded the horses of the Scarlet charioteers, so that screaming in pain, they rushed to the wall, destroying chariot and driver? Why should life, as the years advanced and my wealth increased, become emptier rather than fuller?

When in these depressions I cast around in my mind for some topic of relief and thought of Tutmoshe, he seemed far, far away from me—much farther away than the gulf which separates the dead from the living and which is bridged by memory. It seemed at such times that I had never been the friend of Tutmoshe or ever belonged to his world, and the peace which I had felt in his company by that little lake, with the sacred ibis standing guard, had been experienced by another and that person himself dead.

Everywhere I looked in such times of depression I saw only the great tyrant Death. Sejanus dead; Tiberius dead; Pilate dead; Germanicus dead; Tutmoshe dead. The dead were piled high around me, and I could not escape the thought that I would someday be added to that horrid pile. There was for me only one source of comfort when such thoughts overwhelmed me, and that lay in thinking instead of the Nazarene and the plum blossoms.

It is odd, you will have to admit, that though I had seen the Nazarene twice since he was put to death, this did not mean so much to me as the sight of those flowers on that withered twisted tree against the blue Roman sky. I think the reason was this—test it yourself to see whether it is spurious or not. Man is not comforted by magic. Man is comforted by what is natural and therefore unmagical. The blossoms on the tree were natural, not magical. And as I am natural and not magical they could speak directly to me about life and death in terms I could readily understand and which were soothing. What they seemed to say to me was that death does not triumph. Life will persist. There would be plum blossoms a thousand years after I died. There was comfort in that.

I spoke to Philip about the ability of nature and natural things to comfort man. He had read over and over again the account of the life of the Nazarene and all the letters on him I had had from Luke. He took a surprising view.

"Magic is surely what we do not understand and does not seem normal to us. Yet why should we hold ourselves the judge of everything which is normal and natural in the world? Are there not 'normalcies' and 'naturalnesses' which go beyond our understanding, and are 'miracles' only because we have not the mentality to grasp them?

"Jesus of Nazareth rose from the dead. There are too many witnesses to that for it to be put aside as Caiaphas would have it put aside merely as a lie. You cannot get seventy people to agree on the same lie. Yet we should not regard his resurrection as magic or a miracle. Perhaps it is a very natural thing in the terms of those who can understand it, but men cannot understand it. What his resurrection means is that all men are immortal. But since in the face of death they cannot understand that this is so, then they must resign their reason as too limited a tool and just believe in eternal life.

"Belief is the key, master. It is what makes this special kind of naturalness available to us. Jesus of Nazareth always tested people's belief before he did any marvel for them. That is very significant. It may even be that those who do not believe they are immortal, lacking that one ingredient of faith, will die for all time, as sterile seed, falling to the ground, does not rise again but merely rots. In such a case death is triumphant, but faith gives eternal life."

Really I was quite impressed with Philip's powers of analysis and argument. As you can see, they had greatly improved as a result of the years spent in my household. I asked him, however, on the matter of faith whether a man setting out on a voyage would experience fair winds if he believed the weather would be favorable to him. He said that in his opinion this would not follow as the weather was an impersonal matter and the power of faith could only be demonstrated and have any effect in personal areas. So I asked him whether his crushed feet would be made whole if he believed they would be made whole.

"Yes, indeed," he replied, "if that is not contrary to the will of God." That, of course, was the Greek in him. They are always hedging.

So I taunted him and said, "And suppose it is not the will of God that you should be immortal—of what avail is your faith then?"

"God cannot go against His own will," said Philip. "He cannot go against His own divine nature and having given us immortality (provided we believe in it) He cannot take it away."

"And how do you know that he gave us immortality?" I asked and I knew that I had him, for the Greek mind, with all its wiles, cannot prevail against Roman common sense.

"Did you not see Jesus risen from the dead yourself?" he replied. So, you see, he returned to magic to prove what he asserted is unmagical. That was also a fault with Luke, likewise a Greek.

Still Philip's talk diverted me from my gloom and I had many other discussions with him, and thought enough of what he had to say to try his theories out on Seneca. Seneca was himself trying his hand at writing now. His fame was increasing and he had many clients whose lawsuits he handled. One of his essays came to me and I wrote to him saying that I had read it and thought it polished but inconclusive. "Life," I wrote to him, "is something that must be lived before it is written about. You have tried to write about its values before living it. Thought must come after experience and not before, and what experience have you had, my dear Seneca, pleading other men's troubles in the luxury of the most civilized city in the world, never having to miss a meal or spend one night shivering under a bush?" (You must remember that Seneca himself had not been complimentary about my own writing; otherwise I should not have been so hard on him. He who thinks that literary criticism is always impartial knows nothing of human nature.)

My criticism of Seneca's essay (it dealt with anger, or so the title said) produced the most surprising result. He showed it for their amusement to several of his friends, and it got into the hands of Caligula—yes, Caligula. And Caligula, to my dismay, sent for me, saying that he himself had exactly the same opinion of the writings of Seneca. "They are mere prize essays, my dear Theophilus," he said. "Do come and talk to me about them."

I was, of course, in Rome. I had gone there after the death of Tiberius to see all my affairs were in order, for as I have said before you cannot leave these matters to stewards. Tiberius died in March. The summer sailing season was already beginning and in a few months the grain fleet, which I now owned almost entirely either through charters or through purchases or through the building of new ships, would begin its annual voyage.

Caligula had not taken up his residence in Capri, but in what was now being called the Palace in the center of Rome. It was hard by the temple of Capitoline Jupiter. Actually the temple of the divine Augustus lay between the Palace of Caligula and Capitoline Jupiter, and one day Caligula announced to the Senate that Jupiter had invited him to come and live in his temple. Responding to this invitation from the god, he had a bridge thrown across the roof of the temple of Augustus to connect the Palace with the temple of Jupiter. Then he pushed the walls of his own Palace outward until they reached the Forum and embraced the temple of Castor and Pollux, those two gods so beloved by seamen, for, shining unflinchingly in the sky, they many times lead ships safely to port. But all this happened a little after my unwilling visit to Caligula.

When I visited him work on the extension of his Palace was just commencing, and I found him directing the work personally, ordering pillars or balustrades removed, terraces torn up, waterways rerouted and so on. I thought, seeing him rushing from place to place, that I had certainly come at an inappropriate time to discuss literature, though I was there by appointment. I was about to withdraw when he caught sight of me and beckoned me to him. He led me through the atrium of his palace and into the interior garden in which there was a beautiful lake and many pieces of statuary. These had once been statues of various gods, but now the heads had been removed and replaced with the features of Caligula; and since it was scarcely two months since the death of Tiberius, it was plain that he had ordered these heads sculpted even before the Emperor had died.

We were not alone, but surrounded by a crowd of others who, however, did not press too closely around Caligula. Among these was Claudius, Caligula's mentally defective uncle, and attending on him Pallas. Apparently he had weak eyes, for he kept shielding them with his hands and I noted that he did this most often when called upon to answer a question posed by his imperial nephew. But later I discovered that there was another reason for this. Eventually, having criticized every feature of the peristyle, as it was called, as if he were not a Roman emperor but a master architect, Caligula with a wave of his hand made everybody withdraw from earshot and beckoned me to sit on a bench beside him close to the lake, which had a fountain in the middle. Now I thought we were going to talk about Seneca, but Caligula said not a word about him. Instead, his first words were so entirely unexpected that for a moment I could not make head or tail of them.

"You did not tell me he could walk on water," he said.

"Who, Caesar?" I exclaimed.

"The Nazarene Jesus, you fool," said Caligula. "Who else? But I am to do him one better. Do you know what Thrasyllus once said? Thrasyllus told Tiberius that I had no more chance of becoming an emperor of Rome than I had of riding a horse dryshod across the Gulf of Baiae.

Well, I am Emperor of Rome. Thrasyllus was never wrong and so very soon I will do exactly that, ride across the water from Baiae to Puteoli."

I thought him mad, and replied as one would to a child, "Of course, Caesar." He questioned me then a great deal about the Nazarene. He was quite fascinated by him. You will recall that this was the second time he had questioned me on this subject, and after the first occasion, I had sent him some extracts of the life of Jesus prepared for me by Luke. He asked me whether it was true that I had twice seen Jesus since his death by crucifixion and whether others had also seen him. Now there was no sense my trying to deceive him on these questions, for the story of the resurrection was common now. Peter, John, Philip, James, and the other disciples of the Nazarene had been preaching and writing about it throughout Judaea and even in Syria and Egypt. And, as you know, the story had reached as far as Ethiopia. So I said, Yes, it was true. This reply pleased him very much.

"You know, of course, that I am greater than he," he said as if confiding a secret. "I have been studying his life and also the life of the gods. It is plain to me that Jesus was only a demigod like Hercules. But I am entirely divine, the result of a mating not merely between a god and a mortal, as in his case, but between a god and a goddess. Yes. The whole world thinks that my father was Germanicus and my mother Agrippina, but that is not so. My father was the divine Augustus and my mother his sister Julia. I am entirely divine, but have not yet revealed my divinity. As Jesus, the demigod, forbade his Apostles to say anything about his true nature until he had risen from the dead, so I forbid you, Theophilus, to say anything about my divinity until I announce it myself."

He explained this curious modesty by confiding in me that at the present time he was in human form, though he was having exceeding difficulty in preventing his divinity from shining through. "As you can see, my Uncle

Claudius has to shield his eyes from me. In your case I am making an exceptional effort to remain human, but if you find I blind you at any time, do not be fearful of throwing your arms before your eyes. The gesture will be understood. I will soon undergo an apotheosis and then my divinity will be evident to all. The Nazarene, as you know, said plainly that unless a man is born again he cannot enter the kingdom of the gods, and that is exactly what will happen to me. I have been born once as a human being, though my parents are divine, and soon I must be born again as a god. It may be very painful."

I now knew that Rome was ruled by a madman, and that knowledge was confirmed beyond any doubt as Caligula went on drawing parallels between his own life and that of the gods, the demigods, and Jesus of Nazareth. A particular star, he insisted, was not only present at his birth, but followed him wherever he went and was visible to him as a burning globe by day as well as by night. He had lived for many years with shepherds on Mount Olympus and been attended at times by sylphs and centaurs. (This was before he was handed over to Germanicus and Agrippina as their infant son.) He had done everything the gods and demigods did, only better. At the age of two, he had quelled the revolt of the legions on the Rhine (history says Germanicus was responsible). He had copulated with all his sisters, but of them only Drusilla was divine. He had killed his human father by poison, though Piso, governor of Syria, was the one accused and Piso, rather than face trial, had committed suicide. Also he had cured a great many sick and blind people, just by touching them or even with a glance. Others, however, he had killed.

"I cannot keep the secret of my divinity hidden much longer," he repeated, "but I have revealed it to you since you are a favorite both of Jupiter, who saved your life on Capri, and of Jesus of Nazareth, who has shown himself to you. Do you recall, by the way, how at his own rebirth, when Jesus assumed his semidivine character, his father appeared over him in the form of a dove? Well, that was nothing to the appearance of the phoenix, witnessed by countless thousands, which marked the end of my human life and the inception of my divinity. For the phoenix appeared when I had adopted the toga and been summoned by Tiberius, on the instruction of the gods, to his presence at Capri. A dove, you know, is not to be compared in splendor with the phoenix."

When he let me go he said I could, in thanksgiving for the secrets he had given me, present his favorite horse, Incitatus, who already had a manger made of ivory, with a golden bucket. He dismissed me with a casual inquiry—his first show of sanity in the whole interview—as to whether the grain fleet would have reached Ostia as usual by the end of July, on which point I was able to assure him.

So my literary criticism of Seneca's essay brought me an interview with a madman and cost me a golden bucket for a horse. Really it requires a certain kind of madness to write. The reward is measured in jealousies, spites, loss of friendship, and even money penalties. But how else is one to preserve history for posterity?

XXXIII

THE NILE FLOOD was early that year and of the greatest extent. The waters even swirled through the streets of Alexandria which were, when they receded, covered with the fine fertile silt of the river. The extent of the flood was such that a tenth more ground was available for the planting of every kind of crop, with grain principal among them. It seemed then with the accession of Caligula that the gods were smiling on Rome at last. Dour, long-legged

Tiberius, with his reptile look and his love of blood, was gone and although Caligula had killed a few people here and there, everybody was in a mood to love him and to rejoice.

There are no people gayer than the Egyptians. They love bright colors, music, dancing, singing, big gatherings, and spontaneous demonstrations of affection. When they tell a touching story, they will burst into tears or, if it be a happy story, will be full of smiles and laughter which not even a Roman can resist. They are generous with everything, and they are industrious as well. Indeed, if, as the Jews say, they are the chosen people of the one god, then it seems to me that he made an error, for he would have done better to choose the Egyptians, who had a mighty empire, are magnificent builders and artists, great writers (though their style is involved and not plain as is Roman writing), and beloved by all but their traditional enemies.

In their happiness at the early and extensive flood and the prospect of a huge crop of all kinds, the Egyptians decided that the gods were showing their favor for Caligula. They have, of course, a multitude of gods. Almost everything in Egypt is sacred. I must say that I like that idea. If there is but one god as Peter and his disciples and indeed all the Jews insist, then no man can expect to get a hearing from him, viewing the millions upon millions of people there are in the world. How can that one god listen to one voice in all that multitude? How can he be mindful, say, of the young man in love going to his temple with a sacrifice of one white dove, when I have seen at the same temple princes and indeed kings making offerings of chests of treasure? No, I prefer many gods, for if one is busy, another may be found who will listen. The Egyptians have more gods than anybody and although they do not have as we have in Rome (and as also there is in Ephesus) an altar to the Unknown God, as soon as a new divinity is discovered, they raise an altar to him.

Well, in their gratitude for the generosity of the Nile flood, they sacrificed to the gods of the Nile, and it was not long before they were putting statues of Caligula in the temples of these gods, since he was plainly favored by them. These were not really likenesses. The Egyptians have not got the Greek ability to produce a likeness but draw like children. Even their pictures of palm trees are what a child might do. These were statues of others, relabeled with the name of Gaius Caligula. Soon flowers were hung in necklaces around the statutes or put in wreaths on the head, for the happy Egyptians love these decorations. Nor was it long before the statues themselves were worshiped as gods, so that Caligula, among the Egyptians of Alexandria, became a god even before he died, thus outstripping Tiberius, Augustus, and Julius. Really I had to smile when a young Egyptian told me that he had become a priest of the Soldiers Bootkin (Caligula). But he thought my smile one of pleasure and so no harm was done.

This transformation of Caligula into a god in Alexandria by the Egyptians (fulfilling Caligula's own prophecy to me) worked a terrible hardship upon the Jews.

There were a great many Jews in Alexandria, and they were among the richest of the Jewish communities anywhere in the Roman empire. They were largely engaged in banking, land speculation, speculation in commodities, and so forth. One must admire these intelligent and active people who can succeed in any kind of business. I did a great part of my business through the Alexandrian Jews; for instance, the renting of storehouses for grain awaiting transport, making arrangements for collection of the grain, its cartage, and its loading into amphorae (marked still with my own Theta though I had now sold the clay pits and factories where these were made). I could, at a pinch, command money from these Jews at but 8 percent whereas Roman moneylenders demanded 12 and that on the full amount of the loan until all was paid. These Jews of Alexandria also knew the interior of Africa far better than any

Roman and could lay their hands upon ivory, slaves, rhinoceros, or other beasts for the amphitheater and all at prices which permitted a profit to the middleman, for the Jews themselves preferred to trade in the wholesale rather than the retail market.

Well, I think I have said enough about the Jews of Alexandria to demonstrate that I respected them and held them in some kind of affection. They were far more free in their culture than the Jews of Judaea. You would scarcely find among them the skullcaps and long hair of the orthodox. They wore the toga and shoes when abroad, spoke excellent Greek and wrote in Greek too. Indeed there were not many of them who could speak Aramaic, so that they were Greeks in all but religion.

Their religion was their stumbling block. You know already that the religion of the Jews forbids the making of images in the form of animals or men since this might lead to the worship of these images, which, of course, is abhorrent to their god. When the richness of the Nile persuaded the grateful Egyptians to put the statue of Caligula in their temples, they approached the Jews asking that they should put the statue in their synagogues also. The Jews, they insisted, had benefited just as much from the generosity of the Nile and the favor the gods were thus showing to the Emperor as they themselves. But the Jews refused to do any such thing. This seemed to the Egyptians ungrateful. In any case they were not fond of the Jews, who were after all aliens among them, but mostly because of that curse of the Jews under which they insist they are the chosen people of god, making them superior to all the other people on earth.

Some of the Egyptians laughed about the refusal, but those who had been beaten in business dealings by Jews of more acumen, or those who envied the prosperity of the Jews (the result, as is all prosperity, of hard work and hard thinking) demanded of the Jews that they put statues of Caligula in their places of worship. When these demands were refused synagogues were burned down, and many Jews were beaten in the streets, their places of business destroyed, their goods flung over the streets, and their accounts thrown into the river. Really it would have been very much wiser of them if they had just put the statues in their synagogues. But they would not do so, though on previous occasions they worshiped golden idols in the form of a calf, and the Phoenician god Baal (whom they later turned into a devil, Beelzebub) and so on.

Now I was in Alexandria when these anti-Jewish riots started. It was natural that I should be there on my business and also I had a pleasant villa to live in, which was formerly owned by Tutmoshe and now belonged to Tabitha. I liked that villa very much, for it reminded me of Tutmoshe.

My Jewish business acquaintances in Alexandria came to me and asked that I do what I could to abate the fury of the mob against them. I called on the governor but he refused any aid. Who is to blame him? How long would he last as governor if he were to chastise a mob infuriated because (as they said) their emperor had been insulted by the Jews? I pleaded with my Jewish friends to bend a little and put a statue in the synagogues.

"You do not have to worship it," I said. "Just put it there and enjoy peace and prosperity and amity with your Egyptian neighbors." But their fearful god, they explained, forbade them to do that even to save their skins. What an unfortunate people they are to serve so jealous a deity. All that I could do for them then was provide a place of refuge for the families of those whose houses were burned down and a place where they could store whatever portion of their goods and furniture they could rescue. This I did at my warehouses, instructing the warehouse guards that they were to protect the possessions of the Jews as strictly as they guarded my amphorae of grain, of wine, and of that excellent honey from the Upper Kingdom.

This brought the mob surging around my warehouses

and two of my ships were burned. But that problem was readily solved, for it is one thing to attack the Jews and another thing to attack the storehouses of Rome. The governor acted quickly enough in the matter and so the grain and the possessions of the Jews were safe, as were those Jews who found shelter in my warehouses.

I soon learned that they were praying for me in their synagogues and with the grain fleets about to sail I was very pleased at that.

"Pray for a south wind," I said. "But if that is impossible, a wind from the east, and clear weather." Those who know nothing of the sea dismiss a voyage from Alexandria to Rome in a sentence. But I do not think there is any voyage in the world more dangerous than that which the grain fleet undertakes every year. The expense is huge, slaves must be used at the oars when the wind fails or is contrary, and they must be fed. Also marines must be paid to accompany each ship because of the danger of a slave revolt, not to mention attack by pirates. It is usual to lose one ship in ten. In bad years the loss is often two ships in ten or even three. In such years there is no profit from the grain export, but a huge loss in the undertaking. You will hear to this day arguments as to whether it is best to ship the grain in small vessels, which are handier in the rocks and reefs of the Aegean, or in large vessels, which are stouter and return a greater profit and cost less to handle, though they are unwieldy.

I will not go into details in this matter, for seamen will understand all its complications and a book of explanation will not be sufficient for those who do not know the sea. You will hear arguments as to whether it is best to ship the grain in amphorae or loose in the cargo holds. I incline more and more to shipment in amphorae because otherwise the spoilage of grain from sea water is very heavy and there is no ship whose decks and planks do not leak in heavy weather. Also when grain is wet it swells and there have been many cases of ships being burst apart by wet grain and going to the bottom, with every penny lost, not to mention the loss of expensive slaves and experienced seamen.

The voyage itself is one of twelve hundred miles by the shortest route, which can only be taken in the most favorable weather. If the wind is south or southeast, it is sometimes possible to sail directly north to Rhodes and then, following the Greek coast and islands, make the crossing over to the toe of Italy and so coast around to Rome from headland to headland. But often the wind is westerly, and then the best that may be done is to fetch Cyprus, where the wind backs around and, influenced, as it is said, by the mountains of Greece, comes more favorably from the north.

But the Greek coast is the curse of mariners. Not even the fishermen there know all the islands about for certain. Take them one day beyond their fishing grounds and they are lost. Those islands are like stars in the sky and abound with rocks and reefs. Also the winds are very unpredictable. At one place the sea may be as calm as a silver mirror. Around a headland half a mile away the sea will be whipped to a caldron by a wind sent by one of the spites.

There is no counting the ships which have sunk off the Greek coasts. The gods of Olympus war constantly with Neptune and the ships of mortals are counted nothing in this divine warfare. There is not a captain in the grain fleet who does not sacrifice to Neptune and to Castor and Pollux as soon as he nears the Greek coast, for though men safe ashore scoff at these gods, they will not do so amidst thundering seas on a thick night.

I have put all this in, though it is a digression in my story, to remedy that injustice which is always done by historians to mariners talking of sea voyages. Now I will return to my tale. Having offered as a matter of good business some shelter to the Jews in my warehouses in Alexandria, I left Egypt by sea and went again to my villa in Crete for, as the height of the summer approaches, Egypt stifles in heat and is filled with flies.

I made the voyage there in a light vessel with lateen sails manned by Syrians, for the Egyptians will not sail beyond the mouth of their river. The captain was one Belshabar, a witty fellow who came from Festula, a small place close to Damascus. We had our meals together, and to my surprise, at our first meal he made the magic Sign of the Cross and, breaking a loaf of bread, handed me a piece saying beneath his breath, "In his memory."

"What is this?" I cried. "Are you a follower of the Nazarene, Jesus?"

"Yes, indeed," said Belshabar.

"But you are not a Jew," I exclaimed.

"Saul of Tarsus, who is now Paul, says that is not needed, to become a Jew," said Belshabar.

"Well," I said, "as a seaman you have certainly chosen the right faith. For this Jesus, as you undoubtedly know, was very fond of sailors, three of the twelve who followed him being fishermen from the Sea of Galilee. When he was alive he exerted great influence over the weather, so I look forward to an easy voyage."

We did not, however, have an easy voyage. Two hundred miles from Crete we met a northerly which set us on our beam ends, and one of the rudders carried away. A forward hatch came loose and the angry seas, sweeping our decks, threatened to fill the ship when she would founder. The crew despaired and said this was the judgment of the gods because their captain had deserted the old gods to worship a Jewish criminal. They threatened to throw him overboard. Indeed they would have done so, but Caballus and one or two others including myself guarded him. Eventually enough sense was put back into the crew by blows to get them to secure the hatch forward and start bailing and after two days the wind moderated and we were able to continue our way.

But I was disappointed that a ship commanded by a believer in the Nazarene should have come so near foundering. "I am sure you prayed to Jesus during the storm," I said to Belshabar. "Why did he not help you? I know very well that he is a wonder worker."

"God is not the servant of man," said Belshabar. "We cannot say to Him, 'Do this,' and it is done. And perhaps I am not worthy of help, for I have lived a sinful life."

Later, however, he came to me and said, "We got on very well on one rudder, as you see. Perhaps he did not help me so I could find out that two rudders are not needed."

XXXIV

When I got to my villa in Crete, I found a great surprise waiting for me. Luke was there and he had with him John of Zebedee and also Miriam or Mary, the mother of the Nazarene, whom I had not met. They were living in a house in the little hamlet of Thekos, which is actually situated on my land, though I have permitted all the inhabitants to remain and not interfered in the slightest with their farming and fishing rights though they were farming land which was actually mine.

Still, what need had I of more money? Surely there is enough misery in the world without adding to it for the sake of wealth that I did not need. Also, it is not good business to make enemies of your neighbors, however mean.

I did not know that there were visitors on the island until my steward mentioned that they were in the village. He regarded it as part of his function (as indeed it was) to tell me all changes which had taken place during my many absences. So I sent a message to Luke and John begging them to come and visit me and bring the mother of

Jesus as well, for I was certainly anxious to meet one who, according to the Nazarenes, had been impregnated by the god of the Jews.

In the first instance only Luke came. This was our second or third meeting since he first attended to me at Herod's palace, but I have not thought it worthwhile to mention the others, as it was through his correspondence that Luke had the most effect on me. He was now a Nazarene himself or Christian as these people were called. He was always gentle and pleasant and happy to see me.

"You are well, Theophilus?" he asked as soon as we met and with real concern. "Something has aged you. You have many troubles?"

"I have just been through a sea voyage on which I was nearly drowned," I replied and told him of our adventure, mentioning that the captain of the vessel had been a Christian but that this had not saved us from the fury of the wind and the sea.

He ignored that. He inquired after my digestion, whether I slept well, whether I had drunk any unboiled water in Egypt (the Nile water, excellent for animals, will kill men) and whether my bowels were in regular order. It was very annoying. It was not these things that plagued me, but the recurring and increasing heaviness of my spirit. But it is a waste of breath to complain of this to a doctor, for he will immediately decide that something is the matter with your bile, or that you should not eat fig peckers on asparagus, or that you should take fewer hot baths. For doctors, man is just an engine that works and when it does not work, some part needs repair, like a broken catapult or a cart or a watermill. I was annoyed to have Luke asking these silly questions and I told him angrily that my illness had nothing to do with my digestion or my bowels and if he was going to tell me not to eat fig peckers again, he could save his breath, as I intended to serve them at every meal. (There is a variety which comes from the western end of Crete so delicious that the bones will dissolve in your mouth.)

"Why should I have no pleasure anymore?" I asked him angrily. "What have I done wrong to be so plagued by depression? Do you know that I do not even get any great pleasure in business? When I was in Alexandria, wanting to buy a particular craft for a hundred thousand sesterces, the owner put up the price to a hundred and fifty thousand, knowing who was the would-be purchaser. So I offered for sale three of my own vessels of like tonnage, for eighty thousand sesterces, which so panicked him that he sold the ship I wanted to me for ninety thousand. Yet I could take no joy in that victory. Indeed it bored me and depressed me, though the man is a villain and underpays his workmen more than is needed."

"Tell me more of this," said Luke.

So I told him of how even at the gladiatorial games and at the circus—yes, even in the excitement of chariot racing—an emptiness overcame me; a feeling that all this was meaningless, and it did not matter whether Scarlet, Blue, or Leek Green won, or whether Julius or Gaius Anagius or any other particular hero of the arena won or lost his bout.

True, Luke was a doctor, but he was sympathetic and I could talk to him about such troubles without being given some foul-tasting purge and charged a hundred sesterces, or some kind of an amulet (at high cost) to ward off a demon.

"You are under the spell of the Nazarene," said Luke. "He is calling you to come and be one of his followers. He called Peter and John and Saul the rabbi and they were not able to resist him. And he calls you. You will not be able to resist him either."

"But why should he be concerned with me?" I said. "I have nothing to do with him. I gave him a cup of wine before Pilate. That is all. Why me of all the men on earth?"

"He wants all men on earth," said Luke earnestly, "and he calls them all. But some do not listen. But you were listening to him even before you met him before Pilate."

"How could that be so?" I demanded.

"Theophilus," said Luke, "what prompted you to give him that cup of wine?" That is the way with these Greeks and lovers of philosophy. Instead of answering questions they ask them. But I was fond of Luke and so did not scorn his question.

"Pity," I said. "Pity to see such a fine young man, so helpless and in such danger."

"Theophilus," said Luke, "was that the first time you felt pity in your life? Did you never do such a thing before then?"

"Well, of course, I did," I replied. "My first bodyguard, a Thracian, who beat and robbed me when I was drunk— I sold him to a gladiators' school instead of having him crucified but," I added, not wishing him to think me, a Roman, guilty of womanly softness, "I got fifteen sesterces for him. Remember that."

"And . . . ?" said Luke.

"And what?" I demanded.

"And John the Hammer?" I do not know how he had found out about him.

"It is true I bought him from slavery in the galleys, and set him free," I said. "But you are to remember that I needed a good villain to police my warehouses at Ostia. We Romans make good bargains, otherwise we do not survive."

Luke smiled. "You do not deceive me any more than you deceived the Nazarene, who knew of you before you met him," he said. "Your secret thoughts were known to him then as they are known to him now. He knew before you met him that though you drive a hard bargain you will not cheat; that your nature is truthful and that you have mercy on your fellowmen. You try to play the Roman, Theophilus, and go to the gladiatorial games. Then you shelter the Jews of Alexandria in your warehouses and protect them—"

"It is a matter of business," I said. "They lend me money and they procure goods and slaves for me, and keep my accounts. I must insure their good will."

"You will lie about nobody but yourself," said Luke. "Because of your mercy to your fellowmen he is calling you and you will not be able to resist that call. Do you remember how before Pilate he said he was a king—the King of Truth? By that he did not mean just the king of speaking the truth, but the king of seeing the truth and understanding the truth in all things. . . ."

"All things such as what?" I asked.

"That the gladiatorial games are not a healthy exercise in courage, accustoming the Romans to the sight of blood and the use of arms, but an exercise in cruelty in which men are called upon to kill their brothers for the amusement of other men, who are also their brothers. And that the chariot races are not exercises in skill in handling horses in chariots but exercises in cruelty to animals that are creatures of God as man also is a creature of God. You find less and less enjoyment in these things, Theophilus, because more and more you come closer to the truth of them. And you complain about the lack of pleasure in your business because more and more you begin to suspect that the truth of your life is not that you should win a vaster and ever vaster fortune for yourself. That is not a sufficient use of your life. The real truth is what the Nazarene is driving you to find."

Of course I was not prepared to accept such womanish arguments and I was irritated to find Luke misinterpreting various actions of mine as un-Roman weakness. When he reminded me that I had taken Philip to Peter to have him cured, I asked him angrily whether a secretary who could run messages was not a better servant than one who could scarcely get about. "As for your view of the truth of gladiatorial games and chariot racing," I said, "it was that kind of thinking that brought Greece down. For had you had fewer philosophers and more men of mettle like Philip of Macedon and his son Alexander, Greece would not now be tributary to Rome."

I thought that would have hurt Luke and pricked him out of his unmanly view of things. But it did not.

"A mountain was thrown at Saul," he said. "I wonder what will be thrown at you."

Afterwards I met John, but he was so far gone in the madness of the Nazarene that I found him almost impossible to talk to. Luke understood him and so to my surprise did Philip—or at least he pretended to. But I did not. Tell me, do you understand this, which John (remember he had been the beloved Apostle of Jesus of Nazareth) said to me once? I asked him to tell me something of the birth of Jesus as he had heard of it from Mary, the mother of Jesus, of whom he now took care. I thought I might hear again about the miraculous star that led the magicians from Persia to the stable outside Bethlehem in which he was born. Not at all. This is what I heard, as well as I can remember it.

"In the beginning was the word, and the word was with God and the word was God. He was with God at the commencement. Through God all things came to be and nothing came into being without Him. All that came to be had life in Him, and that life was the light of men, a light that shines in the dark, a light that darkness could not overpower. . . ."

Luke wrote down what John said on that occasion and Philip too and the two versions agreed, so I have not scrambled it all up but recorded it accurately from Philip's notes. Now you will see that while it seems to make sense, or have some sense hidden in it, it is entirely obscure. John spoke in Greek and used *logos* for word and Philip has pointed out to me that *logos* means also order or plan or concept, Greek being a very weak language compared with Latin, which is explicit.

So it could be read as: "In the beginning was the plan."
Or, "In the beginning was the concept." Or, "In the beginning was the wisdom." And then any reasonable man will
ask, "What plan? What concept? What wisdom?" I much
preferred Luke's story of the star and the angels singing in
the sky and the shepherds. I could understand that. It was
reasonable. After all when a demigod is born (and I was
quite prepared to accept Jesus of Nazareth as a demigod,
if pressed) one expects some magic.

John went on, "The Word was made flesh, he lived
among us and we saw his glory, the glory that is his as the
only son of the Father, full of grace and of truth."

But what was the *logos* that was made flesh in the person
of Jesus of Nazareth? What plan or order or concept or
wisdom? I was no better off with John than I had been
when, seeking that interpretation of the dream I had had
at the inn at Emmaus, years before, I had gone to Tabitha
to seek its meaning from her python.

"Strife and struggle, pains and ills," one of her verbal
spirits had said.

> Seek the red door in the seven hills
> Through the red door you must go
> Beyond lies all you wish to know.

I had found no red doors in Rome nor even red curtains, that color being reserved to the army and the Scarlet
faction of the charioteers. I was driven to this conclusion.
The gods (and demigods) do not speak at all plainly to
men. A great deal of thought must be given to whatever
they say before any meaning may be perceived in it. Those
who are busy with their affairs have not then the time to
decipher the messages of the gods. We cannot, after all,
all be priests. Thus it is clear that the gods do not really
want us to know anything, and are perhaps jealous of men,
since they always hide their meaning so carefully.

I pointed this out to Luke, who had once worshiped
Zeus and Mercury and the other gods before he became

a Nazarene. There was no sense pointing it out to John, who had after all always worshiped one god and so could not understand a non-Jewish point of view.

Luke disagreed with me. "On the contrary, Theophilus," said Luke, "when God speaks to you, His voice will drown out every other sound in the world. His meaning will scatter and dissolve every other meaning in your mind. From that moment there will be only one voice and one meaning."

"Then he has certainly not spoken to me," I said.

"You must first listen," said Luke. "And He will not compel you to listen. He will try to gain your attention but He will never compel it. When you surrender your attention to Him, and you listen, then you will perceive the truth so clearly that nothing else but His truth will have any value for you."

That is what Luke said. I have put it down very carefully and I think you will agree with me that at times he did not make very much more sense than John.

Now I must tell you one further thing which happened to me while I was resting at Crete at this time. I repeatedly asked Luke to be taken to the mother of Jesus, but he repeatedly found ways of avoiding this encounter. I could, of course, understand this, for I was a pagan and Jewish women are very fearful of Gentiles and avoid being in their presence. Indeed they veil their faces in the presence of strangers, even their fellow Jews, so it was not entirely surprising that Luke was unwilling to bring me to the mother of Jesus.

One day, however, I had gone down by the shore at the foot of the cliffs on which my villa is situated. The tide was out and I came upon a woman carrying a basket of those small clams which are to be found in the sand and which are delicious either eaten fresh with sour wine for a sauce, or stewed, when they must be cooked with a little wild garlic. Now those clams are to be found only in one place in Crete, which is in the sand at the foot of the cliff and that is my land and so the clams were plainly mine. Therefore I was angry that I should be robbed by this woman and I called out to her to stop, intending to take them from her. She turned and I saw that she was quite old and also Jewish.

"You are stealing my clams," I said. "Give them to me," and I reached for the basket.

"Sir," she replied, "you are mistaken. They belong to my son." But she handed the basket to me.

"Those clams grow nowhere but here," I replied. "And I own this part of the beach for a mile on both sides of this point. How then can you say they belong to your son?"

She made no reply, but prepared to go. Now you cannot put clams of this kind, once they have been dug up, back into the ocean, for they will die. Nor will they keep. And Cestus, I knew, was preparing a broiled peacock with shrimp for my dinner that evening. Also the woman, as I have said, was old and the basket and her clothing, both well mended, showed that she was poor. Why then waste the clams? I thought. Certainly Roman justice demands that you do not reward the robber by letting him keep his spoils. But does Roman justice demand harshness to the poor? Also, remember I had been a slave, and I had stolen many things.

"Woman," I said, "I will give you the clams, and I understand your lie. After all, I have been a slave myself. Indeed I will carry them for you a little way."

When we had gone some little distance down the beach, she said, "Sir, let me have the basket now, for my son will meet me at that corner and he will carry it for me."

I did so, and watched her go. And when she got to the corner her son did indeed appear and take the basket from her. He turned to look at me and I knew him immediately. He was the Nazarene.

[279]

XXXV

THE FIRST SHIPS of the grain fleet set sail that year on the nones of the month of the divine Augustus. How I wished all Romans could see those mountains of golden grain, shining in the Egyptian sun; could see the hordes of slaves, black as ants, filling the amphorae and carrying them aboard the ships. How their hearts would swell with pride in the greatness of Rome at such a sight and how they would be stirred to see first one, then two, then five, then ten, and then twenty ships warped away from the loading docks and, unfolding their sails slowly, move with majesty across the azure sea to Rome, monarch of the world.

The air was blue with the smoke of sacrifices as the first ships set out, offerings to Neptune, to Castor, to Pollux, to Venus, and to every god or goddess connected with the sea, being made by priests in their ceremonial robes (not forgetting offerings to the Egyptian gods, Osiris chief among them.) The smoke followed the ships seaward, for there was a south wind at this first sailing, so that I reflected that the prayers of the Jews in the synagogues on my behalf had indeed been answered, and paid one of the priests of Jupiter to offer prayers for them in turn in gratitude.

The weather that year was the best in the memory even of veteran captains. The south wind held for five days and then moved westward, which drove the fleet towards Cyprus. However, sacrifices being offered on each vessel to Aeolus, god of the winds, the westerly wind died and for two days the sea fell into a flat calm in which the rowers could work as on a lake. Then Aeolus, whose home is said by some to be on the island of Lipari, north of Sicily, sent out an east wind from his cave, the rowing tiers were quickly dismantled, and the vessels, spreading their sails, sped to Ostia.

The first to arrive made the passage in but twelve days, to receive the garlands of flowers and the feast of roasted meats and of spiced wines, and to be made the heroes of that town which is the darling of all sailors. The grain barks are, of course, too big to go up the Tiber, so the cargo was off-loaded onto barges and taken up the river to Rome, where soon the rich Egyptian grain was filling the depleted granaries of the city, and the multitude of poor in Rome received, each one, his heaping dole of new grain with joy.

Certainly I felt godlike myself to be the man whose foresight and organization had resulted in this efficient early carrying of grain to the capital of the empire, for hardly a ship sailed that was not mine or under contract to me. Of grain barks, each carrying two hundred tons of grain in amphorae, I had two hundred, and of lesser vessels carrying from eighty to a hundred and forty tons of grain, some four hundred, so that my whole fleet could carry in one sailing eighty thousand tons of grain.

Soon the Roman granaries were bursting, but you are not to believe that the grain was received with joy on every side. To please one is certain to anger another. Farmers in Italy soon found they could not sell their own little surpluses of grain because of the abundance flowing from Alexandria. They rioted and set fire to two of the barges and tried to set fire to a granary, for which seven or eight were strangled and their bodies pitched into the Tiber. This is proper. It is a serious matter to set fire to Roman grain, but whereas on the first arrival of the grain, I had been the darling of the city, now stones were thrown at my litter as it went by, and once, despite the efforts of Caballus and his Germans, I was dragged out of the litter and beaten, and later horse manure and cow dung were flung at my house during the night. Worse still one morning the body of a man, strangled for his part in the grain riots, was put in my garden with around it a scrap of papyrus on which were written the words, "A Roman citizen choked by the grain of Theophilus."

It is false to pretend that I was unaffected by these happenings. You know how well I love my fellow citizens. To be hated by them was a heavy blow, nor could I be consoled by those who said these were but the scum of Rome, ready to riot at a word. That was not so. Some of the rioters certainly were members of that Roman mob which swelled year by year, unable to find work, their farms unproductive and attracted to the city by the free issue of grain, the free baths, and the games and circuses. But others were honest farmers, men whose reward for their years with the legion was the granting of a piece of land on which to grow their food and make a little profit. The man whose body was flung into my garden was just such a one—an old legionnaire pensioned off with a farm. It went to my heart that there was no market for the few sacks of grain he had brought into the city and his reward for all his work had been the strangler's noose about his neck.

Well, I found his widow and gave her some money, but can you restore a life with gold? I also asked those Senators who would listen to me to pass a law demanding that the grain of Roman farmers be bought before that of Egypt as Tiberius had also desired. But though some promised to do such a thing, they in fact did nothing. Others refused outright. "Unless we provide a market here in Rome for the grain of Egypt, there will be riots in Egypt, and they cost more to put down than riots in Rome," said one. Nor could I persuade him that Rome owed a duty to Romans.

"My dear Theophilus," he replied, "we give to our

dear fellow citizens free baths, free seats at the circus and at the gladiatorial games, and free bread. What more can they want? They can live without working. Is not that the object of every man; to spend his life in idleness and pleasure?"

But this Senator and many others never moved beyond the villas of his friends, the Palace, the temples, and the more exclusive baths and the Forum and theaters. He and many of his kind knew or cared nothing for the shacks tacked onto each other like moldering honeycombs in which half of Rome lived. I think I have said when last writing about Rome how I came to dislike the city and finally fled from it. Well, the same dislike and disgust overtook me again after the first triumph of the arrival of the grain fleet and the feasting which accompanied it. Then one day, when the last of the grain was off-loaded, I received sealed tablets from Caligula and when I opened them found written this message:

"My dear Theophilus, it is time for me to walk on water. Send all your ships to Puteoli. I impose sacred silence on you. Gaius Imperator."

Would you believe that I did not immediately understand the significance of that message? I thought that Caligula, in imitation of his famous father Germanicus, planned a campaign perhaps against Britain (he had been talking of such a campaign for months) and wished to embark the legions at Puteoli, for since Caesar's seizure of power, no legion might encamp within twenty miles of Rome. In any case, there was nothing I could do but obey the order of the Emperor and so all my vessels were sent to Puteoli, which is as fine a port as Ostia and has excellent loading jetties and lies deep in the Bay of Naples protected from every storm. Many wealthy men had country villas at Puteoli and would be able to view the embarkation of the legions.

But the sight they were to see was entirely different. As each vessel arrived, the masts and rigging were removed, the high stern castles demolished so that they were converted into huge flat barges, and then they were moored across the bay, two by two, their sterns together and their bows pointed outwards. Planks were then laid from deck to deck, and so a causeway of ships was constructed a hundred and fifty feet wide and three miles long from Puteoli to Baiae.

On this causeway, this mad emperor proposed to "walk on water" as the Nazarene had done but before the whole world and in his own way. On the planks laid from ship to ship was put a layer, two feet thick, of rocks, and then small stones were rammed on top of these, as in the building of a road. When this causeway of six thousand ships —yes, that is the number of vessels required to float it— when this causeway was finished, Caligula invited all of Rome and all of Naples to attend the dedication ceremonies and watch him put it to his divine use.

The people came in scores of thousands. After offerings had been made to the gods, they were allowed to go out on the causeway; and when a vast number were on it, Caligula had a cavalry charge sounded, and a troop of cavalry charged down the causeway, scattering people right and left so that they fell in scores into the water. Those who tried to climb back were beaten off with spear shafts and swords and oars and boathooks. Hundreds were drowned, many children among them. And this Caligula said was but part of the sacrifice needed both to dedicate the highway and to provide an offering to himself, for he now publicly announced his divinity. So human sacrifices were offered for the first time in her history to the gods of Rome—first among those gods, Caligula.

The day after this slaughter, while the bodies of those who had drowned still floated in little groups around the hulls of the ships, Caligula set out from the Baiae end of the causeway to make his triumphal crossing; to perform his "walking on water" to belittle and outshine the feat of the Nazarene.

You can imagine the hordes of people who gathered to witness this pageant. The shore was black with them, and every fishing or rowing boat that could be found was put to use to take sightseers out on the bay to points of vantage. Stands had been erected on the shore, which now looked like a huge amphitheater, and here the various royal hostages held in Rome to secure the goodwill of their countries—from Britain and from Germany, from Gaul and Spain and Parthia and from India—were assembled to watch the spectacle. Caligula, mounted on Incitatus, his favorite white horse, for whose use I had been permitted to supply a golden bucket, led the parade. He was dressed entirely in gold. He wore an oak-leaf crown of gold and a cloak and tunic of cloth of gold. His shoes were covered with gold and even the bit of Incitatus was made of the same metal.

This horse (which he had formally married by priests to a mare at the temple of Venus and which later was made a consul by the Emperor) was nervous about stepping onto the floating causeway and, when it did, promptly relieved its bowels. This undignified dumping of a load of horse plums on the sacred causeway brought shouts of laughter from the crowd who pressed about and Caligula was about to order his cavalry to cut them down when one, with more wit than the rest, rushed to the steaming manure, picked up a handful and cried, "It is sacred, fellow citizens. Let us preserve it." The others, to save their lives, scrambled to pick up every scrap of horseshit and Caligula had them eat it—yes, he made Roman citizens eat the excrement of a horse—before the parade started. Then he called them his sparrows, being reminded of the sparrows that everywhere pick manure off the streets of towns and cities.

For the first crossing of the causeway to Puteoli, Caligula, riding ahead, was accompanied by one hundred picked cavalry from Spain (these are the best horsemen) all dressed in red and white and each carrying a banner of the same colors streaming from the head of his lance. Then followed five thousand selected men from the Twenty-ninth legion, the beloved Legion of Rome, whose eagle, you will remember, his father Germanicus had recaptured.

Before starting his crossing he proclaimed his divinity, and he made it clear it was because he, a god, though in the form of a tiny boy, had been the foster son of Germanicus that the latter had been able to reclaim the eagles of the legions. In fact, he said, it was he who had really recaptured the eagles.

Now the Roman army is very well trained in the crossing of bridges and knows perfectly well that it is necessary to break step on such spans lest the resonance aroused by the marching feet weaken or break the structure. However, Caligula had given strict orders that the legions behind him, marching in companies of a hundred men, were not to break step but keep up their cadenced march. This produced a tremendous thundering from the empty hulls of the vessels on which the causeway floated. This thundering echoed back from the hills which surrounded the bay so that it seemed as if Jupiter himself (ancestor of the Claudians) were applauding the spectacle.

But this rhythm of blows from the feet of the men had its effect on the moored ships and on the causeway. Before the procession was halfway across, the ships started to roll. The seamen aboard, occupying cramped deck spaces at the bow and stern of each vessel, struggled to tighten up the moorings. The rolling continued and increased. There was no means at all of making the ships steady in the water. They rolled against each other, their motion increasing under the thunder of the feet and in several places the causeway split.

Caligula took no notice. He was ahead and safe. But the wave effect on the causeway produced by the pitching, rolling ships below flung the men about, staggering and lurching here and there, so the glorious legions could no longer march. The soldiers staggered and fell here and there and the whole march came to a halt and became an utter rout. Then everything settled down again, though now there were several bad breaks in the causeway. The trumpets were sounded, the drums produced their dry, harsh rattle and the march continued. But this time the centurions in charge of each company told the men to break step and so they crossed the rest of the way safely.

That was not the end of the day's display, however. As Caligula approached the Puteoli end of the causeway, he reined in Incitatus to allow all to catch up with him. Then the charge was sounded on the trumpets and the whole cavalry with the legions behind them flung themselves upon Puteoli as if attacking an enemy city. For two hours they looted and burned in the town, which Caligula finally announced he had captured. He had had a Stand of Victory erected for him already in the central forum of the city, and he now harangued the people. He shouted in his coarse, booming voice about his divinity and about a long grievance he had had against the god Neptune who, when he had gone to the island of Pandataria to collect the ashes of his mother (he was a bit mixed here, because he referred to his mother as Agrippina, though she was supposed to be the divine Julia), had raised a stormy sea. He had sworn revenge, he said, and had challenged Neptune to battle by building the causeway across his domain. But the coward god had not dared even to appear on the field. He would, he said, challenge Neptune again tomorrow. Then he announced that he was going to give two pieces of gold to every soldier and three pieces of silver to every civilian to celebrate his triumph, and for hours this distribution of largess, from the treasury at Rome, went on. But why do I write so much of Caligula? It is only to permit you to guess for yourself what had now happened to me.

I was entirely ruined. Yes. My whole fortune was gone in this madman's gesture. I had put all my capital into the ships and the ships were now barges floating Caligula's causeway. I had a wild hope that he might pay me for the damage done to them from the public treasury. But I soon learned that the treasury was utterly empty. Not only would I not be paid for the loss of my ships, but I would not even be paid for the delivery of the grain.

I have told you that I had already sold my public baths, my clay pits, my works for the manufacture of amphorae, and, scraping together every penny, had invested my whole fortune in the Egyptian grain fleet. Well, that fortune was gone. What remained of it was in those hulks of what had once been fine ships over which the lunatic Emperor paraded his horsemen and his legions out of sheer jealousy of the fame of Jesus of Nazareth.

Nor was Caligula done with me and his ruination.

The following day he made a return across the causeway from Puteoli to Baiae, this time in a chariot, followed by a host of other horsemen in chariots, and followed by his legions, who had now baggage carts on which they carried the furniture, the chests of clothing, the sacks of goods and of food and boxes of money which they had "won" in their conquest of Puteoli.

This time, however, Neptune showed more fight. A choppy sea arose, the causeway bucked and swayed, Caligula, in fright, whipped his horse and charged the rest of the way to the safety of the land, leaving his marching legions to get ashore as best they could. They were not past the middle of the causeway before it broke behind them. First one and then two of the hulls broke loose from their moorings. The planking across their decks splintered and soon there was a gap of a hundred yards in the road, all made by Neptune with but a mild chop. That night the little wind outside the bay that had produced this chop died, and Caligula had the damage repaired. With other shipowners, I went to him and begged him to now give us back our vessels when we would save what we could.

"Impossible," he said. "I have been challenged by that upstart Neptune and I will fight him. The causeway is to be rebuilt. It is to remain for two weeks to show that cowardly god that he is no longer ruler of the seas."

In the face of such madness, there was no argument which could prevail, so I remained silent. My silence angered him. "Admit it, Theophilus," he said, whirling around on me. "Admit it. Am I not greater than the Nazarene? He walked on a little lake, probably in shallow water too or on a sandbar he knew about. But I have taken my army twice across three miles of sea."

If only I had fallen on the ground and worshiped him or had thought to suddenly shield my eyes from him as his Uncle Claudius always did and moan that the light from him blinded me. Alas, I did not. I was enraged that all my ships had been destroyed. I could not say anything, but stood there dumbfounded.

"Seize him," he shouted to his Germans, and then when I was seized, he thrust his rage-distorted face into mine and shouted, covering me with spit, "Theophilus, Tiberius was going to teach you to fly like a bird. But I will teach you to walk on blood—your own blood—and on your own guts."

XXXVI

I WAS IMMEDIATELY TAKEN in chains to Rome and there imprisoned in that jail at the end of the Forum. The jail is on two levels. One level is only halfway sunk in the ground and there you can see out of a barred window. Below that is the second level, where prisoners are strangled. There is no light there except from torches and what light can pass through a grating in the ceiling which is actually the floor of the place in which I was imprisoned.

Several were strangled in the two weeks I was kept in this place. We could count on three or four a day—men and women. Most of them screamed while they could, and then the sound of screaming was replaced by the drumming of their feet on the floor as the noose tightened. The victim was seated on a stool placed before an upright pole with one end firmly cemented into the ground. The noose was slipped over the victim's head and over the pole and a stick inserted in the noose and then twisted. This tightened the noose and strangled the victim.

Women, however, are sometimes just strangled by the executioner's hands for they like to show their strength by doing this. There were two of them, big fellows and quite good-natured. They said they often had intercourse with the women before strangling them. "Why waste a good thing?" was the way they put it.

I expected, of course, that some charge would be laid against me by Caligula, and thought of asking Seneca to defend me at my trial, though since Caligula so disliked Seneca he would be able to do nothing for me. The charge, when I heard of it, was that of belittling the dignity of the Emperor-god by remaining silent when he asked me whether I did not think him greater than the Nazarene.

My friend Pallas secretly advised me to get together every penny I could and make an offering of it to the Emperor. If I signed over everything I possessed this might save my life, he said.

I resisted doing this for two weeks. But those daily stranglings which we could hear taking place in the room below us finally broke down my nerve. I called a notary and made an offering of all my assets to the Emperor, but first of all I set free all my slaves so that they would not fall into his hands. I thought then I might be tried and hoped to be set free. I was certainly tried, and by Caligula himself, for he had not done away with the right of Roman citizens to be heard by the Emperor on capital charges.

He was eating grapes and roast chicken at my trial but he could not remain sitting in the seat of justice, but kept rising, darting here and there to talk to this Senator or that, or even going out into the columned portico outside the Palace. He was always unable to sit still for more than a minute. At times he raised his hand for silence and cocked his head to one side and said, "Yes, Jove. Yes, I know that," as if conversing with the god Jupiter.

"Ah my dear Theophilus," he said when I was brought in for trial, "where have you been? We have missed you. We had an excellent feast last night and another the night before and everybody was saying, 'But where is that witty fellow Theophilus, who is so quick with his tongue?' "

"As you know, Caesar," I replied, "I have been in prison at your pleasure awaiting this appearance before you."

"And what is the charge?" asked Caligula, mumbling the words through a mouthful of chicken.

"I do not know, Caesar," I replied.

"You rogue," he yelled, suddenly quite furious, "when I asked you who was greater—a Jewish traitor who was condemned to death by crucifixion or the divine Emperor of Rome, you did not reply. Do you hear that, Senators? He could not choose between a Jewish rebel and the Roman Emperor. And I myself am the principal witness against him."

"Death," yelled the Senators. "Crucify him. Flay him to death." They outdid each other in their zeal to make an end of me and gratify Caligula. He held up his hand for silence; but one or two, in their desire to demonstrate their loyalty to the Emperor, did not stop right away and he shouted in that bellowing voice of his, "Silence! The next one among you who says a word after I hold up my hand for silence will be hung up with a hook through his mouth, like a fish, until he dies." Yes. That is the way a Roman Emperor spoke to Roman Senators while trying a citizen of Rome for life. I know it is scarcely believable, but it is true.

"What have you to say for yourself, Theophilus?" asked Caligula. He leaned forward, cocking his head to one side, his left ear turned in my direction as if most anxious to hear whatever I had to offer. I believed myself a dead man anyway. My only desire now was to be permitted to die without torture. Since Caligula was the principal witness against me, there was no question of acquittal and I had certainly done Seneca a favor in not asking him to defend me.

"Caesar," I replied, "I am not a man of ready speech. Even with my life at stake I am not able to bring forward any arguments that might save me. I can only say that I did not intend to give the impression that I was unable to choose between a condemned Jew and a Roman emperor. Far from that. I am a citizen of Rome. I earned that citizenship myself. Why should I then, after such pains, belittle a Roman emperor? I was amazed that the choice should be put before me—of choosing between that almost unknown Jew and a Roman emperor. That is why I could say nothing. That is all I can say. Not disrespect but amazement produced my silence."

It was not much of a defense, but it shook Caligula. To gain time he belched and he was offered a cup of rose water with which to cleanse his palate. He took a swig, rolled it around in his copious cheeks and then squirted it out into a vessel held not by a slave but by one of the knights—one of the Equestrian Order.

"Senators," he said, "an offense against Gaius Caesar would be nothing at all, and as you all know many offenses have been offered him in the past. Were not his two brothers starved to death and his mother also and his father poisoned, or rather his foster father for my true father, as you all know, was not Germanicus but the divine Augustus.

"However, an offense against the emperor of Rome, who has revealed himself to you now as a god, living among you in the flesh, is sacrilege and the penalty for sacrilege is death by torture. . . ."

He was drowned out again by the horrible chorus of frightened old men demanding my end by disemboweling, by the lopping off of my limbs, by crucifixion, and by flogging.

He silenced them, and this time the silence was immediate. "Man is cruel," said Caligula. "But the gods are merciful. And I am a god. Therefore I will be merciful. Theophilus, you not only offended against the Emperor of Rome and therefore the people of Rome, but also against a god. But since, in way of atonement—though for such an offense no atonement is possible—you have deeded to me all your possessions and have in so doing relieved the Roman republic of any obligation to pay you for bringing the yearly harvest of Egyptian grain to Rome, you are mercifully sentenced to death at a time to be decided by yourself. In short, you are sentenced to the arena, and there you will live as long as you can defend yourself against your opponent."

Would you believe that my heart actually leaped with joy at these words which have thrown so many into despair? That was because I had expected to be strangled before sunset, or more likely flogged to death. The actor Menon had been flogged to death while I was in jail because, meeting Caligula in the temple of Jupiter Palatine, he had hesitated in answering which was the greater of the two gods—Jupiter or Caligula. Furthermore, when it seemed that Menon was dying too fast, Caligula had told his Germans to revive the man with water and then give him but one lash every five seconds. "Let him know that he is dying," he said. "Never hurry a pleasure which I am enjoying."

At this time I was, I think, fifty years of age. I do not know, of course, what was my age, for I had not known my mother nor my father, nor could I find out the month or day of my birth. This had often vexed me, for it deprived me of all the warnings which might be had from astrologers. My hair was frosted with gray and so was my beard, and that was testimony enough to my years. But I had been twenty-five years away from the galley oars and had grown soft. What would I have given now for the condition I was in then! As I was led away I reflected that my big belly and my spindly legs and fat arms would be the death of me. Yet, as I have said, the thought that I was not to be killed that very day elated me.

Now I was to learn again that everything that has befallen man, however, unfortunate it seems at the time, may be put to good use and prove a blessing. Not for nothing have people said of me that I could pick a coin out of a dunghill with my teeth. For I soon found that it was the best of training, in the circumstances in which

I now found myself, to have been a slave. Without that previous experience, I would have died of grief. Again, the slave has no anger. Whatever is done to him, whatever his reaction, he hides it and endures it. That habit of slavery I could put on again like a cloak when I was handed over to Petrus, the lanista or trainer, at the gladiatorial school at Menta, outside Rome. It saved me time and again.

Ever since the revolt of the gladiators under Spartacus, the gladiatorial schools were situated far from cities and heavily guarded. Wooden weapons were issued to the gladiators under training or when exercising and they received real weapons only a little time before appearing in the arena. This was not only because of the fear of an uprising, but because the gladiators might otherwise kill themselves. The very night I was chained in my cell at the school of Petrus, another, condemned to the arena for cheating in the collection of taxes (an offense so common that it was expected of every tax collector) managed to kill himself by wrapping his chain around his neck and begging those on either side of him to pull his hands apart.

I must pause to tell you that gladiatorial games, on which Augustus had frowned, had become very popular under Tiberius, and Caligula was even fonder of them than he. And since the encounters were always to the death, there was a growing shortage of gladiators. So it was that men like the tax collector were sent to the arena, so I was not the only man of advanced years and soft flesh handed over to Petrus. There were many others and also a great number of boys whose parents had met with some misfortune or who, unable to support or control them, had sent them to the arena. Do not waste your pity on these boys. They were worse than tigers. My greatest hope was that I would not be pitted against one of these terrible youths. Some of them did not know fear at all. They were as hard as the rocks of Greece, and one of them, Balius, took delight in cruelty and never failed after a fight to go around to where his slaughtered comrades lay piled up (some of them still breathing, I might add) and, turning them this way and that, see how they had received their death wound.

I have said it was good training for me to have been a slave because I could dissimulate and control anger. Also despite the black despair which overtook me when I was first chained, soon I was quite used to my chains. It seemed indeed but a few days and not twenty-five years since I had been released from them on purchasing my freedom. Those who had not before been chained fell into a melancholy from which they could be removed only by the rod and the whip. But my melancholy did not last long because I used the slave's art of excluding every thought from my mind. I did not remember my villa at Crete, my household, and my servants. I dismissed all thoughts of Philip, of Caballus, and of Tabitha, who were the closest to me, from my mind. Since I had fallen into such deep disfavor with Caligula there was nothing they could or would do for me. Certainly it would have been very foolish on their parts to attempt to see me or to send me a message. Far better for them, now free, to forget about my existence as I attempted to forget about theirs. Like the successful slave then I lived from moment to moment without a past and without a future but with only a present.

My training was arduous. I will not dwell upon it in detail. I do not require Philip to tell me that the training of a gladiator is hardly worthy of literature. In any case it is the same as the training of the soldier but very much more refined. Three qualities are aimed at—endurance, agility, skill. That is all. To this must be added courage, which comes from all three of these and is most readily achieved by deciding that one is dead already, so no further harm may befall you.

This concept of having already died, I fixed firmly in

my mind. On the other hand, I did all I could to increase my other three faculties. You know, of course, that a gladiatorial school has in its center a huge exercise area, covered with sand. It is surrounded by a high wall and the distance around the exercise ground of the school in which I was held was a little over a mile. Around this we were required to run five laps every morning and five laps every afternoon. Tottering, blind, breathless; it did not matter. The ten laps had to be run and several died, just in this exercise, of exhaustion. Again the slave's training helped me. I did not think of ten laps as others did. Not at all. I thought only of each step as I took it. Soon I could do my ten laps at a good speed. We were not chained at exercise. But when I could do my laps well, I asked Petrus to let me carry a piece of chain while running them, which he did. When I could manage with this, I added to it another piece for the weight and then I added to it again. Soon I could run the laps carrying ten pounds of chains draped about me.

Also I used my chains for exercise. At night I lifted my arms, bearing the weight of their chains, from the floor overhead as many times as I could, seeking each night to accomplish this feat one time more. On the "cornmill" I used the same method. This, as everyone knows, is an upright drum with an iron rod twenty feet long through it at the top and another of equal length through it at the bottom about a foot above the ground but at right angles to the one on the top. With the drum turning you are made to run into the radius of these bars and jump over the bottom one and duck the top one which will crack your skull if you fail to duck in time.

This exercise is at first slow, but it is quickened each day by making the drum revolve faster and faster. The running exercise having killed several older men, more were eliminated by cracks on the skull by the upper bar of the cornmill. But I ask your forgiveness for these unseemly and trivial details. I want only to tell you that whatever had to be done, I did that and added something to it, not out of zeal but to prolong my chances of living a little longer in the arena.

Also I watched the others train, very carefully—all kinds of fighters, heavy-armed Thracians, light-armed Samnites, Gauls with war axes, Germans with axes and hammers or hammer and spear, netmen with their nets and tridents, Scythians with their small bucklers and curved swords, and boxers with their heavy-spiked knuckle-dusters.

Nor did I ever lose my temper or brag about my skill though the youth Balius spat in my food many times and contrived, when he was wearing the lead-soled training sandals, to stamp on my bare feet to break a toe or two. He had taken a dislike to me because it was soon known that I had once been very rich, and he had been sold to the arena to relieve the poverty of his shiftless parents.

"The rich always have sauce to their food," he would say before he spat into my bowl. But I said nothing. Petrus, however, knew all things about the gladiators, whom he called his children. And so when I had been four months in training, he said to me, "You will fight in a week with the net and trident, since you were once a seaman. It is the Emperor's orders."

"And whom will I fight?" I asked.

"Balius," said Petrus, and he gave me a grin very much like that reptilian smile I remember so well having seen on the face of Tiberius.

XXXVII

WHEN GLADIATORS HAVE BEEN MATCHED, they are put in special cells and guarded day and night lest they attempt to kill themselves. Since they are chained at all times except when exercising, and in any case have no arms, you may well ask how they could commit suicide. Well, a number of methods are known. The most popular is to stuff a ball of rags down the throat with the fingers as far as it will go. If you have first expelled all the air from your lungs, it will not come out again but at each desperate effort to breathe, be sucked farther down and soon death results.

Another method, if there is room or opportunity, is to run head down against a wall, when the skull is often crushed. This was a favorite method among the African blacks. Again, it is sometimes possible (though this has to be long planned) to work a sharp edge on the manacles around the wrist and then by rubbing the wrist fiercely all night against this edge, to cut the veins and bleed to death. In short, the ingenuity of man in escaping the arena is equal to almost every circumstance, making the close watch on matched gladiators necessary as I have said. The pair who are to meet each other are also kept apart lest one secretly manage to injure the other or drug his food so as to get the advantage of him.

So in being matched against Balius I was at last relieved of his adding daily his spittle to my food. Also the quality of my food was improved, pork and chicken being added to the lentils and bread which was my usual fare. It was permitted as well to exercise with a real trident instead of a wooden one. It was, of course, a joke of Caligula's that I should fight as a netman, for these are usually young men, very lithe, who can quickly throw and rearrange their nets, and must rely on speed for their safety, for they wear no armor. (Netmen are popular among spectators, for since they have no helmet to hide their features, the spectators can savor all the grimaces the netman makes as he dies, should he be defeated. The reticularii then were big drawing cards at the games.)

The secutor, against whom the netman must fight, is armed with straight sword and rounded shield, off which the net will slip, and his helmet is devoid of crest, again so that the net will slip from it. All this is well known. But the secutor, who was often called the executor (for that is usually his function), is often the older man since he has the advantage. In my case the positions were reversed, I, the older, being the netman and Balius, the younger, the executor.

The pairs who are to fight are allowed to be visited by their friends on the eve of the day they are to appear in the arena, and the more famous are even permitted to go to the villas of rich men to be wined and feasted and provided with whatever entertainment they desire. Many Roman ladies vie to be the bedmates of these men, whom they often call Hercules and Apollo and such names and beg them to fight as hard upon the bed as they will the next day in the arena. I had expected no wine and no visitors but was surprised by both. My first visitor was Seneca.

"I have come to say farewell, Theophilus," he said. "Do not be unhappy. Reflect that death is our common end, and you have this consolation, that yours will be quick, rather than the lingering death of illness or of madness, or death by hunger or torture, which awaits so many. Indeed, if you take a balanced view of this matter, you are a lucky man and should rejoice at your plight."

"I feel unworthy of such good fortune, my dear Seneca," I replied. "Will you not change places with me?"

He smiled thinly. "My time will come too, Theophilus," he said. "I trust I will accept it with humor and dignity. Our life is only a story without beginning and without end. It happens. Nothing more. To make sense out of that happening is the proper object of every man. You have risen from slavery to riches to be reduced again to slavery. But you have enjoyed many things that others were denied. And since this is the last time we will meet, I would beg a favor of you."

"I haven't a penny," I said. "Caligula took all."

"You should know me better than to think I came to you for money. My favor is simple. Answer me this question truthfully. In all your life, now about to end, tell me what most moving memory remains with you now."

"A twisted, gnarled plum tree blooming on the Appian Way among all those tombs," I said.

Seneca stared at me. "Is it possible, Theophilus, that I have known you all this time, yet have not known you?"

"It is entirely possible, my dear Seneca," I said. "For philosophers do not know men. They only know ideas and concepts and tricks of argument."

"I accept your rebuke," said Seneca quietly. "It is perhaps just, though I will think more about it. But I have one more question to ask you. In all your life what do you most regret at this moment?"

"That is readily answered," I replied. "What I most regret is that tomorrow it is a boy gladiator called Balius I have to meet and not the god-Emperor Caligula. For it would be marvelous to prove or disprove the divinity of Caligula in the arena."

"You endanger me with such unseemly words," said Seneca. "And you do not answer truthfully but out of emotion. The truth does not lie in our feelings but in our thoughts. Compose yourself and answer me truthfully."

[301]

"How wrong you are, my dear Seneca, to say that the truth does not lie in feeling," I said. "Let me for once turn the tables on a philosopher and ask the questions myself. Is hate a truth and love a truth and anger a truth and envy a truth? Or are all these falsities and are only mathematics and logic truth? And if so, should man live by mathematics and logic and reasoning, or by the love of his fellows or his hatred of others? For, my dear Seneca, if man is to live entirely by your reasoning and debating, putting all feeling aside as false, then it is better that he were not born. For in my view, in such circumstances, he does not live at all, and a donkey has a more enjoyable life, and I indeed wasted my money, when many years ago, I sent you a barrel of pickled herrings."

I do not pretend that I spoke this with the grace with which I write it. Although I am not a boastful man, I am sure that you will see some good phrasing in my testament up to this point. No, my tongue has ever been clumsy, but Seneca understood me well and said softly, "It has taken the prospect of immediate death to make a philosopher of you, Theophilus. You have given me much to think about, and you can reflect yourself that death has produced more improvement in you than life. Farewell." Off he went, to continue to live in his own curious world of thought and reason and logic and debate —to live, then, among the cold shadows of the mind. Life is surely wasted on such creatures. Has Seneca ever wept?

When he had gone I reflected on that last question he had put to me—what did I most regret in my life. And immediately before me was the face of the Nazarene and that was what I regretted—that I had ever met him. I remembered that he had said that he would always be my friend and that he would never leave me. Well, I certainly wished he had never made me that promise and that we had never met, for it was because of him that I was facing my end in the arena. Had I not known him and had I not then been curious about him, Caligula would have had no reason for asking me which of the two were greater, he or the Nazarene Jesus.

A strange friend he had proved indeed, I reflected, to have put me twice in peril of my life and cost me all my fortune. Peter, John, and Luke said he did nothing without a divine reason, not always clear to men. But is it not right to ask what kind of friend it is who twice imperils his friend's life, and then destroys him? Certainly on reflection, he was very close, Jesus of Nazareth, to the mad god of the Jews. Well, I thought, I was still sorry he had been killed and I hoped (despite what happened to Stephen) that when I was killed myself he would entertain the thought of raising me from the dead.

I could not hate him for all my misfortunes, all of them plainly his fault. A condemned man cannot really hate anyone. He looks anxiously around for friends, not enemies, and I was sincere and not mocking when I asked him to raise me from the dead. You say that is madness? My friend, wait until you are dying and then see if that is madness. At that moment, such a prayer will seem to you the only sense in the world. My prayer to the Nazarene was sincere.

My next visitor was a great surprise and a great hurt—none other than Philip, dragging himself down the corridor to my cell on his crutches. The guards made him leave the crutches outside (a determined man can kill himself with a crutch, even in the presence of a guard). So poor Philip had to use the wall for support and then he entered the cell and threw himself at my feet sobbing.

"Master, master," he cried, "what wrong did you ever do anyone that this should happen to you? You have been the kindest man in all the world." Of course, on such occasions, one expects a few lies, and I was glad to hear Philip, whom I had beaten often enough for crossing me or criticizing my manuscript, speaking so warmly of me. Lying at funerals is often a virtue. I lifted him up and consoled him, and scolded him for coming lest he incur the displeasure of Caligula. "Get away from Rome as soon as you can," I said. "Go either to Judaea or to Crete and if to Judaea go by sea. Assassins abound now on the roads, but one is safe enough on a ship. Is all well with you? Where are you living now?"

"Master, Tabitha and I, Caballus and his wife, and a few others all live in one place in the Jewish quarter on the west bank of the Tiber. And we are well taken care of by our brothers."

"Your brothers?" I exclaimed.

"Yes, master. I must confess it to you, even if you are angry. We are all now followers of the Nazarene. I have been secretly a follower of his ever since you took me to Peter in Jerusalem to cure my feet."

This was a surprise indeed, and I was annoyed. I was not annoyed that Philip had become a Nazarene, nor Tabitha. I was annoyed that it was I, who was not a Nazarene, who had been brought to this plight by Jesus, while Philip and the others who were Nazarenes were better off than they had ever been.

"If you are a Nazarene," I exclaimed, "and I am not, why has he done this to me? Why does he not leave me alone and visit his misfortunes on you who follow him?"

Well, Philip had no reply to that, other than to continue weeping and he begged me not to speak bitterly of Jesus. "He has His reasons," he said. "You will understand them sometime. Since He is God, He can do nothing foolishly."

"Philip," I said, "do not lie to me. Do you really believe the Nazarene is a god?"

"Master," he replied, "not a god but the God—the one and only God."

"Then you really believe that in Jerusalem with Pilate, I saw the one and only god with my own eyes, his beard all bloody and his nose torn in half, standing as firmly before me as you now."

"Yes, master, you saw Him made flesh in the form of a man."

"He did not blind me," I said, mocking and remembering Caligula, who also said he was a god.

"Master, do you not see that that is why He took the form of a man, for man himself may not look upon the face of God. As a man He died, master, for every man on earth and raised Himself from the dead, to show us that if we believe in Him we will all be raised from the dead and live eternally with Him. Can you believe that?"

"Philip," I said, "I wish I could. How happy it would make me. To think that half an hour after I enter the arena tomorrow I would be dead and born again to eternal life—what a relief that would be for me. I would very much like to believe it. But I have seen too many dead, with their eyes crawling with worms."

"But you saw Jesus yourself twice after He was crucified," said Philip.

"Three times," I replied, remembering the figure who had joined his mother on the beach at Crete.

"Master, you are a very hardheaded man," said Philip. He was still sobbing.

"Philip," I replied, "I do not like to be fooled."

Prostitutes are supplied to those gladiators who wish them on the eve of their arena appearance, the payment being made by the owner of the gladiatorial school, though, of course, the lanista receives from each of them a portion of her fee as one of the sinecures of his office. The guard now brought several to me to make my choice, but though I want to make it quite plain that I still retained my full sexual powers and indeed they had been stimulated by my training, I had decided not to weaken myself by copulation. So I sent them away and one viewing Philip said peevishly, "He prefers lame Greeks who cannot run from him." Who could blame her? Unless she gave services, she would not be paid and living, despite the grain, was hard in Rome. I assure you had I had a penny in the world I would have given it to her cheerfully.

When they had gone, Tabitha came. She was as scrawny as ever. I have not told you that she had a prominent thin nose and no chin? Well, it was so.

"Master," she said, "if you had wanted one of those other women I would have stayed away and not intruded on your privacy. But I have loved you from the day you set me free from the spirits and although I am ugly and have no attraction for men, yet if I could bear your son, I would love him all my life and give him everything I have and he would be a great comfort to me."

So I put aside my resolve concerning copulation and it was Tabitha who stayed with me, and the guard was a good fellow and turned his face to the wall and did not ask for shares. It was no surprise to me that she was a virgin.

"If you bear me a son," I said, "call him Tree, and if a daughter, Blossom." For that vision I had had on the Appian Way was still with me, even at such a time.

XXXVIII

YOU KNOW THE SCENE at gladiatorial games well, but perhaps you have not viewed it from the position of the gladiator, and I may be excused for composing a few paragraphs on that subject.

The games in which I was doomed to take part were held in the amphitheater of Statilius Taurus, located near the second bend of the Tiber, and on the east bank. The games, as you know, start at first light so that not an hour of daylight is wasted since most programs are very big. The gladiators were roused well before dawn, and I said farewell to Tabitha by the lurid flicker of torches and then ate a good meal of lentils and drank a cup of warm wine.

The mind of man is certainly curious.

At that, my last meal on earth, I was sharply reminded of the meal of soldiers' lentils I had had with Pilate after the earthquake which had followed the execution of Jesus of Nazareth. It was the indigestion which resulted from that meal which had brought Luke to me, and I wondered whether he was still on Crete with John and the mother of the Jew who was believed by so many now to be god made man.

Thinking of him and his two disciples whom I had met on the road to Joppa, I took a piece of pasta and tore it apart and gave one half to my guard, who was eating opposite to me, chained to me as is always the case. "In memory of him," I said. And I also gave him some of my wine and said again, "In memory of him."

"In memory of whom?" he asked.

"Jesus of Nazareth," I replied.

"A friend?" asked the guard.

"So he told me," I answered.

The guard laughed. "I did not see him here last night," he said. "It is at such times a man discovers his real friends."

I was then taken to the baths to wash. Gladiators pay very great attention to washing before combat. It is a belief among them (I do not know where such a belief came from) that if they go unwashed into the arena, where they are a sort of sacrifice to the gods, and are killed, they will certainly be subject to the worst tortures of Hades, being bent on the iron wheel or hung on a spider's thread over those cliffs which are a thousand feet high, swaying and spinning in a terrible wind and forever waiting their appalling fall into an ocean of fire below.

Even the Germans washed before the games though these, being war captives, looked forward to the arena as did the first and second swords, that is to say, the best swords in the gladiatorial school.

These who had twenty or thirty victories to their credit, should they lose, are not likely to die, for a wave of handkerchiefs from the crowd saves them from the death thrust. But for the tyros, such as I, defeat means death. A man who loses his first fight is rarely spared.

After the baths, the Greeks who were to fight oiled themselves and dressed their hair carefully, which is their custom. The Scythians made magic signs over all their weapons, and the Romans were permitted to offer incense to Mars. There was a great sale in these last moments of magic symbols and medals of many kinds, and again the owner of the school was compelled by custom to pay for these and the lanista or trainer took his percentage.

The sellers, allowed in for an hour, pressed their wares with vigor, claiming that this particular feather would make the wearer invisible at certain moments, or this bag of dust would quickly stanch bleeding. I was offered something which I recognized immediately—a little section of hollow cane, stopped at each end with wax and containing the scrapings of an Egyptian mummy's fingernails. I recognized it, for you will remember that I once dealt in these things myself. The price asked was fifty denarii. I was outraged, for I had sold them myself for five.

"Keep this up, my friend," I told the man who offered me one, "and you may soon own not one but five villas in Crete." He scurried away from me, afraid of my "evil eye," for to be scorned by a man about to die is the worst of luck. Another talisman offered to gladiators was a small cross on a piece of string to be worn around the neck. On one side of it there was a crude drawing of a fish and on the other side the abbreviation Fil.D.Sal.Hom.

"It is the best of them all," whispered the seller. "It comes from the Jews. You know how strong their magic is. Wear this and even if you fall, you will rise again." That is how widespread the belief in the Nazarene was already.

Crosses, symbolic of his death, were being sold to gladiators and soldiers and he was scarcely dead eight years.

"What is the fish for?" I asked.

"The Jew whom this cross symbolizes was a friend of Neptune," said the huckster. "He could calm storms at sea. Buy it. It will save you."

I bought it because of the fish. You well know how I have always loved the sea. Also I was to fight with the net and trident. To have ignored the cross with a fish on it—so queer a thing to find carved on such a shape—would certainly have been to invite bad luck. Balius bought two of the little capsules of mummy nail filings. His guard told me this, as I would, of course, be interested in what magical powers my opponent intended to invoke. But since I knew the nail filings were not truly magical, I was relieved by the news. However, my guard told Balius what I had bought, so he could not complain that he had been put at a disadvantage, and he also bought one of the crosses.

Washed then, and armored, though still armed only with wooden weapons, our sacrifices made to our gods and our magic talismen obtained, we were ready when the first rays of the sun struck the floor of the arena for the trumpet blasts which announced the beginning of the games. As soon as their echo had died away in the surrounding hills, the gates were opened and we marched out in procession, the crowd on its feet and roaring.

Five hundred pairs were scheduled to fight that day, so a thousand of us streamed through the door into the arena in that procession, each in his particular armor and led by the horse fighters—that is to say, those who would fight with lance or sword on horseback and those who would fight in the British style from chariots. Once around the arena we went and then, lining up in ten lines of one hundred, stood at attention before the platform of stone on which Caligula sat with his idiot uncle and his court.

"We who are about to die salute you, Caesar!" we shouted. That was the traditional greeting given to the

Emperor, and it was the custom since the time of Julius for the Emperor to rise and, as supreme pontiff of the Romans, give a blessing to doomed men. But the god Caligula was talking with his sister Drusilla, who was also his mistress, and did not rise but with a wave of his hand either blessed us or dismissed us. He had his white horse Incitatus on the platform beside him, for whom you will recall I had once provided a golden water bucket, and the horse took more notice of us than Caligula. There was a growl from among the gladiators at being thus ignored, but that was soon quelled by the guards, who carried horsewhips.

Of course, a thousand of us could readily have overcome the guards, whips or not, but there was no way out of the arena. The walls were too high to be scaled, and in any case were faced with tiers of well-oiled rollers, which turned as soon as they were touched, so they could not be climbed. Also there was always a regiment of troops on duty so even if we did escape from the arena they would soon cut us down one by one.

However, as we were about to march off, Caligula turned and, holding up his hand, stopped us. He had a tremendous voice, as I have said elsewhere, which he considered one of his divine qualities. "Where is Theophilus? Bring him forward," he shouted. I was hustled to the front—standing even before the First Sword in his scarlet cloak with gold edging and his helmet studded with pearls and amethysts and itself either of gold or gilt.

"Ho there, Theophilus," said Caligula. "Do you not now repent the indignity you offered to my divinity?"

For answer I threw up my arm as if to shield my eyes, though the imperial platform was on the northern side of the stadium and the sun still in the east. Caligula was pleased.

"Ah," he said, "now you see the divine rays. But it is too late. They cannot save you."

"Caesar," I replied, "it is not divine rays from you

which caused me to shield my eyes, but the beauty of your horse, which alas far outshines your own." The air was entirely still and not a sound was made while Caesar spoke. So there was a big shout of laughter, for Caligula's divinity was indeed a joke among the Romans.

Caligula was furious. "Let him fight first—and now," he bellowed. "Let him fight before the mock battle."

You know, of course, that it is usual for the gladiators, once they have entered the ring, passed around in procession, and saluted Caesar, to return to fight battles with wooden weapons for the amusement of the spectators, before real weapons are issued to them. This puts the spectators in a mood of anticipation and allows them to better judge on whom to bet, though often a man, to put his opponents off guard, will fight badly in this sham battle and find an astonishing skill when he has steel in his hand.

To be ordered to fight before these mock encounters was without precedent. The crowd did not like it and murmured its discontent.

"Silence," shouted Caligula above the tumult. He had lost all dignity and was really furious. "Silence! I wish you all had but one neck, so I could chop your head off." The soldiers started to move about with naked swords and that quietened the crowd.

This was not the first time that I had been in the Taurus arena. I had been there many times as a spectator, but usually came in the afternoon when the better swordsmen were at work, the poorer always starting the games in the morning. But as I was led away to be armed for my bout my eyes involuntarily turned to the door through which the dead or dying were dragged on grappling hooks. And then I saw something about it which either was new or I had not noticed before and it made my heart pound with terror. For the door was painted bright red.

The mysterious words of the pythoness returned to me with terrifying impact:

The pigmy warrior brings pains and ills,
Seek the red door in the seven hills;
Through the red door you must go,
Beyond lies all you wish to know.

I knew then that for all my training to save myself, I must die.

XXXIX

I DO NOT RECALL being armed for combat. I do not re-member exchanging my trident of wood for one whose tines were of steel, with, at the end of each, flesh-tearing barbs. Certainly I arranged my net, for it may only be thrown well if allowed to hang in folds from the center. It is almost the same net that fishermen use for catching bait. But it is smaller and the lead weights around the edges are heavier. But I do not remember arranging it. I remember my heart pounding like a ship caulker's mal-let, not in my chest, but almost in my belly, and becoming almost deaf through some insensitivity of the ears. I re-member too the spreading of my nostrils as I stepped into the arena, as you have seen animals' nostrils twitch and dilate when danger is near, and the weakness of my limbs so that I was surprised that I was able to remain upright, let alone stride into the arena.

I did stride in. You know, of course, that at the last moment many gladiators refuse to fight. At such a time, whips are useless on them for they would sooner be flogged to death than face the butcher. So one of the guards, as each gladiator steps from the arming room, follows him to the very door of the arena with a red-hot iron to force him out should he at the last moment lose all control and courage. The iron was not needed on me or on Balius. Balius went ahead, grinning at me as he passed.

"You will trip over your own guts in a moment, old man," he said.

I am glad he said that. It restored my courage. Not in full measure, but a little of it. "Look to your sword, Balius," I said. "The mummy scrapings won't help you. I have sold them by the shipload."

Then he was gone, and when he was twenty yards ahead with his two guards, I followed between mine. We marched before the imperial box and this time Caligula was watching us and not toying with his sister or his horse.

"Let the games commence," he shouted in that huge boom of his. The trumpeters sounded their fanfares, the guards retreated, and Balius and I faced each other in that huge cockpit of sand, the guards standing by the walls.

Having had to follow Balius into the arena, I was at this disadvantage—I faced the sun, which he had behind him. He had burnished his shield so that if I should maneuver him so that he had the sun in his eyes, he could use the glitter of his shield to dazzle me. But for all his assurance, he was nervous. I kicked off my sandals, which I had managed to unlatch as I entered the arena, and he started at the movement and withdrew a step. I feinted with the trident and loosed the net on my left shoulder and he started again. Yes, he was nervous indeed.

Then he flung himself at me, using his shield as a battering wall and in stepping backwards to avoid the charge I made the biggest mistake the netman ever makes—I trod on the net, dangling too low behind me, stumbled, and fell. But the net which had tripped me also saved me. Down came his sword, but the blow glanced off the shaft of the trident, which had fallen across my front, and struck the net which, of course, it could not penetrate. He was off balance when the blow was delivered, for he thought that with one stroke he could put an end to me. I struck him in the face with my right hand—a broad, open-palmed slap—and he lost balance and fell.

We were on our feet in the same instant, and the roar of the crowd sounded like surf on rocks. I did not intend to give Balius time to recover, however. I thrust immediately with the trident at his feet, and drew blood. He hopped back and I thrust again and again, for he was unbalanced, and then I made a cast of the net—not over him, which would have been useless at this point, but at his feet, hoping to wrap it around his ankles and jerk him to the ground. He had had his training on the cornmill too and jumped readily over the net and thrust with his shield once more, this time with the edge, which caught me on the top of my head. I could feel the warm blood trickling down through my hair.

It was strange to find Balius using the shield so much for attack. That is a reckless manner of fighting, exposing the body, though he was armored about the chest and wore one greave on his right leg. We fell apart again and this time it was I who rushed him. I dropped the net and charged him with the trident and caught him under the shield on the breastplate and made him stagger, and struck again at his feet and then when he came back with his shield, as I expected, caught the rim between the tines of the trident and wrenched it aside. Down he went, for the shield was strapped to his arm. As he hit the ground, I kicked his sword arm on the wrist.

There is a place there (and also above the elbow) where if you strike a man a sharp blow, his fingers will unclench. Balius' sword flew from his hand, but in the elation of the moment I had forgotten his shield. The tines of the trident no longer gripped it and he swung the rim against my unarmed legs, slicing them to the bone in the front, and was on his feet and had regained his sword in a moment.

Now I was separated from my net and Balius knew enough to keep me from it. I feinted towards it time and again and time and again he blocked me and counter-attacked. But the net put him at a disadvantage also. He had to keep it behind him and so he was rooted to one place, which he must constantly circle and defend.

There are two ways to catch fish, you understand. You may throw a net around them or you may drive them into it, and the latter is often the better way. So I circled about Balius, who scarcely dared charge lest, moving too far from the net, he lose his prize. I drew him around so that he now faced into the sun and also into the small amount of wind which had now arisen and was coming, as is often the case in Rome, from the east.

As I suspected, he now used his shield to dazzle me with the reflection of the sun's rays. But it is not that easy to focus a shield on a dodging man. I feinted to the right, he countered, I feinted at his feet and he jumped and as he came down I swung the trident, gripped in both hands, like a flail at him. He did what I wanted him to do. He stepped back onto the edge of the net. One more feint at his feet and he jumped again, but this time I followed through with the feint, hooked the net with the barbs on my trident and jerked it towards me. Down he went, backwards, and it was nothing at all to fling the net over him and leaping astride his body to pin him with the trident to the ground.

My fish was trapped. I put the tines of the trident at his throat and Balius, loosening his useless sword, managed to thrust one finger through the net in an appeal for life.

I glanced up at Caligula, having trapped my fish right before him. There was a flutter of handkerchiefs among the people in the amphitheater, signaling that they wished Balius to be spared. But Caligula did not. He was gesticulating rapidly with his thumb to his chest, meaning that I was to kill him.

Exhilarated and triumphant I prepared to drive the trident home. The tines pressed against his neck and it was a strong, young man's neck, like the neck of the Nazarene. The face was a young man's face but it was not like the Nazarene's. It was dark with fear and utter hopelessness. Some drops of blood had fallen on his breastplate from my head and as I prepared to put my weight on the trident and so dispatch him, the cross that he wore around his neck lay before me. In a moment my exhilaration and triumph were gone. Caligula was still gesticulating with his thumb, but I stepped off the frightened boy and removed the trident. A deathly silence settled over the whole amphitheater. It was broken by Caligula's brazen shout.

"Guards," he cried, "seize and kill the netman. He has disobeyed the orders of his emperor."

One of the Praetorians, a naked sword in his right hand, touched the cross dangling on my chest. "All who wear this become mad," he said. "Farewell, fool," and plunged the sword into my belly.

XL

FOR WHAT FOLLOWS IMMEDIATELY I have to rely on the testimony of others; that is to say, on the testimony of Tabitha and of Philip, of John the Hammer, and of Caballus. For many weeks I lived halfway between this earth and the next—in limbo, as we Romans say; on the edge of something but in nothing. In a world filled with pain, whose pangs were scarcely dulled by the use of henbane, I caught but glimpses of reality, or perhaps as I have come to think, I saw some of the reality behind what we call real.

After the sword thrust of the guard in my belly I went

immediately to hell. It is a place of intense pain, of utter darkness and of absolute abandonment. Thought is impossible in hell. No philosophy can comfort you there. The pain, the darkness, the abandonment are all-powerful and drive out hope and prayer so that the mind cannot even think of these sources of comfort. In hell my belly was opened and a brazier of burning coals was poured into it with every breath I took. And this continued for an eternity, which measured in time was, according to Philip, three days. From this experience I arrived at this truth—eternity can be contained in time. Yes, as a road crossing another at right angles may itself be one thousand miles long, but is only twenty feet long where it crosses the other, so the road of eternity crosses and recrosses time and can be contained in a second of time or in a part of a second.

I will not describe hell for you any further. Pray that you yourself never go there. For when you get there, you cannot pray. Hell devours hope. I will tell you instead how I was pulled back from hell, by the efforts of my friends.

As soon as I fell to the ground with the sword in my belly, the cleaners of the arena arrived with their grapnels, which they flung over my body, and then dragged me off to the death pit, while others scuffed sand over the blood, which otherwise not only makes a slippery footing for those who follow, but attracts flies in hordes. The grapnels hooked in my calf and my buttocks, and so did no vital damage to me. As soon as I reached the death pit, Caballus was ready for me and John the Hammer also. You were surprised that Caballus did not come to see me on the evening before combat, since we had had so much beer together and I had taken the iron collar off his neck and got a wife for him?

I was not surprised at all. After all, a man must look to himself and what loyalty does a slave owe to a master who has fallen into disrepute with the Emperor? None at all.

But Caballus had kept away from me for other reasons.

The death pit at the arena is put in charge of Germans, who are less corruptible than other gladiators. It is their duty to see that no bodies are stolen. Caligula had started the practice of using these bodies, cut into joints, to feed the wild animals that would provide games later. This served two purposes, giving them an appetite for human flesh (so they attacked with more gusto in the arena), and also being a great economy, for lions and tigers eat a great deal of meat in one day.

It was also the duty of the guards to dispatch gladiators who were not dead when they reached the death pit, however hard they pleaded to be allowed to live and promised to fight better on the morrow.

Caballus, instead of wasting his time dining with me, had spent the evening drinking with his fellow Germans and had obtained from them a promise, sworn on that tree-spirit which they regard as sacred, to turn my body over to him, and not to do me further hurt, should I be alive. John the Hammer bribed the other guards to permit a closed litter to be brought close to the death pit. He had also bribed the grapnel men not to stick their hooks through my throat in dragging me off, and really they managed very nicely by getting only the buttock and the calf. But then, they have their skill, as have all men. There was some luck in this too for who should be in charge of the Germans but Minades, the Thracian who had been my bodyguard before Caballus and whose life I had spared when he had beaten me? He remembered that favor and helped arrange all.

So, with the sword thrust in my belly, I was put immediately in a litter with a physician and taken to a dwelling on the west bank of the Tiber, where the Jews were permitted to live. This house, however, belonged to Christians and was the same place in which Philip and Tabitha had been living with a Christian community. The physician was not a Christian but a Greek who had served with the Eighteenth legion in Parthia for twelve years. He knew a great deal about wounds and how to deal with them. For two days he made me lie on my back and did nothing but keep me clean, examining my stool and sniffing and tasting my urine to see whether it contained blood. He was greatly relieved when he found that it did not. Also he kept sniffing my wound but after a while he did not need to sniff for the stench from it pervaded the whole house.

He then said that the gut had been severed or nearly severed by the sword thrust, and the wound was putrefying. He would have to open it and cleanse it, find the broken parts of the gut and join them. He said I would probably die and the operation was hardly worth performing. However, he would try, but he would have to receive a greater fee and must not be held responsible if I succumbed. John the Hammer gave him what he needed. (You are aware, of course, that he had been in charge of policing my warehouses at Ostia. He had warned me when I hired him that he would never be able to resist stealing and I had told him that it was better to be robbed by one man than by hordes. He had then stolen about a million sesterces' worth of goods from me, or perhaps more, and now used some of this money generously to save my life.)

Most of the Christians were opposed to the operation. They said that I should be baptized and they would continue their unceasing prayers for me. If I died, the baptism would assure me of peace in Heaven and if I lived, it would be the result of their prayers. John the Hammer, however, said that the operation should be performed and they should continue their prayers, since if God wished to save me, He would save me even in spite of the operation. This seemed sensible to all, so I was first baptized at the insistence of Tabitha.

She told me when I asked her why she did this that I was a Christian whether I knew it or not, and baptism (it is a lustration ceremony using water) only made official what was already the case. I asked her how could someone who sacrificed to Jupiter be a Christian, and she replied that the children of God were those who did the work of God, irrespective to whom they sacrificed in their ignorance. Well, there is no arguing with women, and in any case I was made a Christian by lustration on the head, for the surgeon said he would not allow water to flow over the wound, which would chill it and cause further putrefaction.

A small dog had now to be killed, not as a propitiatory sacrifice but because some of the leg bones would be needed. It had to be a healthy dog and a small one, but one was obtained and dispatched by the surgeon and the legs, cleaned of all meat, put to boil in a pot of water. Philip says I should not give all these details as they are not a seemly part of my story, but if my spirit plunged into hell was recalled to my body by the use of the bones of a dog as well as the prayers and love of my friends, then it seems right to say so.

The surgeon also boiled his knife with the dog bone, which bone he then cut into small lengths so that each, cleaned of its marrow and thus hollow, was like a short tube. When this had been done, he opened the sword wound sufficiently to pull out the intestine, which he let fall into a pot of water which had itself been boiled to drive out by the heat all the evil spirits which might reside in it.

He found four places where the sword of the guard had cut into the intestine, and of these two had been partially sealed by the gut wrapping itself around the broken areas like a bandage. Two, however, were festering and to get rid of the festered area he cut the festering sections out, and joined the other two ends, inserting a piece of the dog bone as a connector. With a touch of a hot iron he sealed off those veins which were bleeding from his cutting, and, smelling here and there in the wound he had made, he put the iron to any place where putrefaction lingered and washed out the body cavity in which the gut is contained with wine. So you are not to be surprised that I felt while in hell, braziers of burning coals being put into my belly. When he had finished all, and he had washed the intestine lying in the bowl of boiled water, he put it back and sewed up the opening with thread made from the intestine of the dog killed for the purpose.

"He is still alive—give me the rest of my fee," the surgeon said when this was done and this John the Hammer did, for he had agreed to give the surgeon a further hundred sesterces if I survived his probing. Then something occurred which frightened everybody. A bird flew into the room and, careless of the people about, approached the bed on which I was lying. It fluttered over me as if thinking to perch and then, in a moment, darted off.

Now birds are bad omens and it was thought by the Christians that this one was a messenger sent to announce that I was to die. But Philip said that if it was indeed a messenger, then the fact that it had flown away without landing on my couch (as at first it seemed to want to do) meant that death was postponed and I would live.

Philip was right. From the time of the operation I grew better and returned from hell to limbo—a boundless and therefore shapeless place halfway between the two. At times I was thrust back into the darkness and pain and loneliness of hell. At times I heard the voices of my friends around me and was aware of their presence.

My eyes, it is said, were often open, but I saw only dimly, for the eye is but a window and unless the soul is there to look through, nothing is seen.

I had many visions and all of them terrifying. Colors of a shade never seen on earth swam about me as living things—emerald green and deep orange being the chief and also a brown red of which I was most afraid. Choirs of voices broke out into shattering chants to be answered by other choirs of voices so tiny that they were less than the chirpings of insects. Each part had its counterpart, the colors being opposed to another and the choirs of voices being also opposed. But both terrified me.

I did not see the Nazarene, nor any human or godlike persons, unless the gods are colors and voices and have no shapes. This ordeal was more frightening than being in hell, but far less painful. Yet is not fear a kind of pain and also a pain for which there is no poultice or bandage? I do not mean the normal fears of men—of hurts or of loss of fortunes or of another's anger. The fears I experienced were of a deeper character. I fancied myself utterly alone in the void of space, without a light or a star about me, falling, falling, falling, without end and with my terror mounting with each second.

Again I fancied myself as small as an ant crawling about in mountains a thousand miles high with cliffs over which waterfalls a hundred miles in length plunged roaring like thunder. The fear was of solitude—desertion by all other creatures. During this time Philip, who never left my bedside, said I "spoke in tongues," and he wrote down all he could of what I said. But having heard some of the Christians later speaking in tongues, throwing themselves wildly about and mouthing all kinds of gibberish in Aramaic, Latin, Greek, and even fragments of Celtic, I found this so disgusting that I ordered Philip to destroy all I had said without even looking at it. (Paul also disliked this "gift of tongues" and said it would be better if people did something else, like praying or caring for the sick or working in the communal fields. I agreed with him.)

At last I left this terrifying place and clearly saw those around me. There was a pot by the side of my bed, of brown earthenware, and I looked at it with the greatest affection, it was so quiet and ordinary and assuring. Also I smelled roast lamb.

"Bring me some of the lamb to eat," I said to Tabitha, who instead burst into tears because she said she knew from those words that I would live. But I did not get roast lamb but only a little of the gravy, which I sucked down into me as if it were liquid life in itself.

The surgeon would permit me to eat only the kind of food that is given infants, and this without a doubt retarded my recovery, for how is a man to grow strong on what will scarcely feed an infant? Most doctors have little sense, but he insisted that I must eat nothing but pap until I passed the dog bone in my stool, which would be the sign that the gut had healed. No man ever examined his stool with more care than I, for I was so hungry I could have eaten the sheets off the bed. At last the bone appeared and roast lamb was served (may the gods bless the Jews that they cook it so well) and thereafter my recovery went rapidly and Tabitha informed me that she was pregnant and I was now a Christian.

Now I had wanted to be a Christian, as I have told you, in order to be able to work miracles and preserve the grain fleet, into which I had put my whole investment, from storms. But since that was impossible at the time (necessitating that I first become a Jew) I had given up the idea and was not entirely pleased to find that I had now been Christianized in any case. I tried to see whether I had received the power of other Christians and, calling Philip, made the Sign of the Cross over his feet and said, "In the name of Jesus of Nazareth, I command you to walk." But he was still as crippled as ever. So Christianity had given me no increase of my powers and I might just as well have remained a pagan.

Yet I had received this benefit—that my former slaves, now Christians, and their "brethren" as they called each other, had united to get my body, and had summoned a surgeon and had paid all the expenses and kept me in their house (at great risk should Caligula learn of it) and prayed for me unceasingly.

I asked myself who of the cult of Apollo or Jupiter the Greatest and Best, or Mercury, or of Osiris or Mithras would have done so much for me? Those who worshiped these gods generally felt, quite sensibly, that a man's misfortunes are visited on him by the gods and they will anger the god and so share in his misfortunes if they help him. But the god whom the Christians and the Jews worshiped had commanded them to love each other as themselves, even at grave risk to themselves. For the first time the thought came to me that perhaps the Jews and Christians were not mad. Perhaps they were sane; the only sane people on earth, the rest of the world being full of madmen.

Is it possible that that which is held insane is in fact sanity, and that which is held sensible—looking to your own interests first, avenging wrongs, plotting the downfall of enemies—madness?

XLI

ROME, WHILE I WAS RECOVERING, was as full of spies as it had been in the last days of Tiberius, and the terror was far worse than it had been then. Caligula, both Christians and Jews agreed, was possessed by a devil. Some thought he was the antichrist of whom the Nazarene had prophesied during his life. He had said that one opposed to his doctrines would appear and would rule the world and shortly afterward the world would be destroyed by fire and by flood. Even Peter and John thought the end would be soon and awaited the second coming of Jesus, which he had promised, but Saul, now called Paul, was not so sure. He said the end might not come for thousands of years and in any case people should live the doctrines of the Nazarene and not worry about it. They should build houses and plant crops and so on.

Paul was more of a practical man than Peter and John, and I got along easier with him, though he had a very bad temper. His trouble was that having been a man of great authority as a Pharisee, he never got over the habit of laying down the law as to what was right and what was wrong, and getting very angry with those who disagreed with him.

He even scolded Peter publicly because Peter (himself a Jew) was very troubled at times about sitting down to eat with Gentiles as Paul did openly. Yet Paul introduced a great deal of Jewish usage into Christianity, making the women subservient to their husbands, for instance, which they certainly were not under Roman rule. I did not like this but Paul didn't really like women. I think he was afraid of them, though they were always kind to him. He set himself such standards of chastity that I think every woman was a temptation to him. He realized that marriage increased chastity, satisfying desire, yet he would not marry himself, nor take a mistress, but remained as far as everyone knew, strictly a virgin.

"You would suffer less if you would slip once in a while," I said.

He turned on me angrily saying, "I have had a thorn in my side since birth which I have begged God time and again to remove, and yet it remains and I must suffer it." I think he was talking about women, or perhaps about his temper.

In any case, to return to my story, Rome, as I have said, being full of spies, it was very dangerous for me to remain there once I could be moved. So all was arranged to move me to Alexandria and I was got out of Rome in a carriage into which a bed of straw was placed. My little household accompanied me. Yes, though they were no longer my slaves, they were bound to me by affection. They were all Christians except Caballus and his wife. He would have become a Christian except that he did not like some of the doctrines. The idea of, having been struck on one cheek, offering the other for a further blow was outrageous in his view. Also the doctrine that one should not seek vengeance on one's enemies, or get drunk, or eat too much just for the delight of eating, he thought abominable. He told me that as soon as I was well, I could un-Christianize myself and we would go and get drunk together and sing a lot of good songs. But when I did not seem entirely anxious to do this he said sulkily, "You would never make a German. I watched you in the arena. When you had that young cockerel under the net, you could have put the trident through him and washed your face in his blood, but you let him off. Why did you do that?"

I told him it was because for a moment the young gladiator had reminded me of the Nazarene. This made him gloomy and he said I was a victim of witchcraft. "If I could get you to Germany there is a Druidess who would free you. In any case you should talk to Tabitha. She was a witch once and she might remember something."

Tabitha was now my wife. We were married in a Christian rite, which was really the Jewish rite, only being Gentiles we used rings as the Romans do, putting them on the fourth finger of the hand, that being the finger, as all know, which leads directly to the heart. Tabitha in due time gave birth to a son. I wanted to call him Neptune, the sea having been mother to me, but she opposed this and, she finally bursting into tears, I agreed that he should be called John after John of Zebedee, who as she pointed out, had been a fisherman.

But I am ahead of my story. I went by carriage to Ostia and from there took a vessel to Alexandria. The hulks of my own lovely ships were still to be seen wrecked on the shore of the Bay of Baiae. You remember that after Caligula had made a highway of them with which to cross the water and so better the feat of the Nazarene, he had demanded that they remain in place for two weeks further to show his defiance of Neptune. But Neptune was not that readily defied. A storm arose and the whole causeway was wrecked and the ships, mastless, driven ashore to fill with sand and rot. The next year there was a shortage of grain in Rome because of the lack of shipping, and grain was diverted by land to Rome from the provinces. The shortage then became acute in Jerusalem, in Antioch, and other great cities. So Neptune had his revenge.

You will see from my mention of Neptune and other gods that I was not really a Christian, for Christians refuse to believe in these deities. But I could not drop the old gods immediately, and I am not sure that I can ever drop them. It is very hard to turn your back suddenly and completely on gods to whom you have sacrificed all your life, and I have always looked with suspicion on those who did. If people can, under the emotion of a sermon or their wonder at a miracle, throw great Jupiter aside and accept Jehovah and Jesus, then, under the stress of another emotion and another wonder, it is possible that they will throw Jehovah and Jesus aside and reembrace Jupiter and Osiris. There are very many well-attested miracles performed at the shrines of these gods. Also I have seen many miracles performed by non-Christian priests. Miracles alone are not a good reason for worshiping one god or another.

While I was waiting for my wound to heal, in Rome and then in Alexandria, I was compelled for pure distraction to listen while Philip or Tabitha read to me. There was nothing else to do, so they read to me for hours and mostly from that life of Jesus which Luke had compiled for me—and also these letters Luke wrote me concerning the actions of the Apostles.

In listening far more intently than I had before to Luke's account of the life of Jesus, many things he said had a deep effect on me. Let me give you one example. He had said that all men were to love God and after

God, they were to love their neighbors as much as they loved themselves. Pressed then by the Jews, who as I have told you loved to split hairs, as to who was a neighbor, Jesus had picked a Samaritan as an example— and the Samaritans are sworn enemies of the Jews.

Neighbors then included enemies. Now, if you love your enemy have you an enemy? Of course not. So it seemed to me as Philip had pointed out before that the teaching of Jesus might really do away with strife among men and, if adopted by all the people on earth, would bring peace between individuals and nations, since nations are built of individuals. Thus there would be no more wars, no more slavery, and those who had food would feed the hungry and those who had clothes would clothe those who had not.

This was the hardest point for me to accept. Surely I do not need to remind you that I am a businessman, and I could see the ruin of all business if food and clothing, housing and other needs were supplied to everybody free of charge.

I argued this point many a time with Philip. It is still not settled between us. What I have to say is this. It is one thing to be told to love your enemies. It is another thing to be able to do it. If you had seen Paul or Peter in a temper, you would quickly realize that even they did not always love their enemies. So a man may wish to become a Christian and he may feel that the doctrines of Christianity provide a true solution for the problems of the world, but despite all this, he may well remain un-Christian and pagan in his attitude most of his life.

Well, Jesus of Nazareth it seems to me will have to accept that if he is sensible. It is true that love is better than hate, and help is better than hurt, but you cannot, at a word, love people you hate, and help people who have set fire to your house.

During such arguments as these, Philip was often close to tears. Once, hoping to convince me, he pointed out

[328]

that in what had happened to me, I had fulfilled a prophecy which Jesus had made concerning himself. "You died, you were three days in hell, and you have been raised from the dead; which is to say, born again," he said.

"That is only a wily Greek way of looking at it," I replied. "The fact is that I never died at all. I was three days unconscious and I was cured by a surgeon using the bones of a dog—and also by the prayers of Tabitha and the others," I added, since Tabitha was listening to the conversation.

But you cannot argue with these Greeks.

"Master," he said, "I talk of your spirit. Your soul was dying even before you entered the arena. Life had no pleasure for you at all—no sense and no direction. You descended then into hell at the will of the Nazarene for a terrible baptism, and you were born again as his child and a child of the true God."

Well, that was one way of looking at it, and certainly the parallel was remarkable. Also I reflected that Luke had said that God had thrown a mountain at Saul, and had wondered what he would throw at me. Well, what he had thrown was hell, into which I had been plunged, but also, Philip said, love, for it was the love of my friends which had brought me back to life.

Yet there remains this question. If the Nazarene was the son of God, and if there is but one God, as all his followers maintained, why should he be interested in me, Theophilus? Of all the millions of people upon earth—kings, princes, emperors—who am I that he should hunt me down to make me his own?

Compared with all the treasure poured into the Temple of Jerusalem, and all the beasts sacrificed there daily, what was my offering of a cup of wine? Again I ask who, after all, am I, Theophilus, that God should be so concerned about me?

That is the great mystery.

But there are many other things. . . .

EPILOGUE

THE REST OF THE MANUSCRIPT of Theophilus is missing, leaving some tantalizing questions unanswered. However, reasonable answers to such questions can be arrived at by reflection, bearing in mind the character of Theophilus as he reveals it and the nature of his times.

The first question might be whether he was ever tempted, when restored to complete health, to get into business again, for, Christian or quasi-Christian, he was certainly a businessman, and there was nothing in the Christian or Jewish faiths (despite Theophilus' misunderstanding) to prohibit the use of a business talent. He had, it will be remembered, sheltered the Jews during their persecution in Alexandria. They were not likely to forget this kindness. They knew Theophilus as an honest man and a competent one, and it is highly likely that they offered him sufficient credit to reenter the shipping business.

There is an indication that he did engage in some business activity, for he opens his account with a description of his villa at Crete, where he is writing seemingly as an old man. So he got together enough money to repurchase his estates on that island. It is almost certain that he lay low, however, until the assassination of Caligula in A.D. 41, for he was supposed to have been killed at the Emperor's orders.

Caligula was succeeded by his uncle, Claudius, brother of Germanicus. Claudius had lived through the terror of Tiberius and of Caligula and it seems he had merely pretended to be halfwitted to preserve his life. As Emperor he encouraged trade and order, undertook the further conquest of Britain, and restored some reverence for the old gods. He was very much in the hands of his freedmen, notably Pallas and Narcissus, who were friends—to the degree that pagans had friends—of Theophilus.

So very probably Theophilus reentered the shipping trade with the backing of the Alexandrian Jews in the time of Claudius. He would now have a purpose in the amassing of wealth—to share it with his Christian brethren—and probably he did so. Many of the early Christians literally followed the doctrine of Christ and gave up everything. There are hints in the letters of Paul that there were among them, however, what we would call "bums," who used the preaching and the profession of Christianity as a means of getting free lodging and food.

Paul points out in one of his letters that wherever he stayed, he always earned his keep, presumably with his trade of tentmaking. There were other sincere, pious people who sold their little businesses or farms to live the communal life of the early Christians and these had to be supported in one way or another. Contributions from those who still had possessions were the greatest source of support and Theophilus would have been a pretty good provider of funds. Nor, practical man that he was, would he beggar himself, regaining, as we know, his own villa on Crete.

The Acts of the Apostles, written for him by Luke, tell the story of Peter but mostly of Paul up until about A.D. 63. Theophilus was, then, alive at that time. He writes, he says, as an old man and thinks of Peter with tears. So he wrote after the martyrdom of Peter, which traditionally took place in Rome about A.D. 67 in the reign of Nero. Whether he himself was martyred, going twice through "the red door," is unknown. It would be nice to think, after all the hardships of his life, physical and spiritual, that he died quietly in the garden of his villa overlooking the sea that he loved, and probably still unsure in that practical mind of his about the divinity of Jesus of Nazareth.

A few facts of history may help to round out the manuscript.

Caligula, having proclaimed himself a god while still alive, went to the extreme of demanding that a statue of himself be erected and worshiped in the Temple of Jerusalem. So sacrilegious a project, if given effect, would have brought the whole Jewish people in arms against him. Publius Petronius, legate of Rome in Syria, and Agrippa I stalled on the demand until Caligula was assassinated. Philo Judaeus, eminent leader among the Jews in Alexandria, led an historic mission to Caligula to beg him to rescind the order and had to present his petition as Caligula darted from place to place overseeing architectural improvements in one of his many building plans. He got no firm commitment on the matter from the Emperor.

Herod Antipas, who was the Herod who imprisoned John the Baptist and who sent Christ to Pilate for judgment, was dethroned by Caligula and exiled to the Pyrenees, where presumably he died, still in exile. His domain was given by Caligula to Herod Agrippa I. He was the Agrippa who ordered the arrest of Peter and, when Peter miraculously escaped from prison, had the sixteen soldiers guarding him beheaded. According to the Acts of the Apostles, he was later hailed as a god and died "eaten away with worms."

Of the Apostles themselves, perhaps because of the persecution of the early Christians which really got under way with Nero (though Claudius had them expelled from Rome), what is known is largely known by tradition handed down orally from one person to another.

Peter and Andrew are traditionally held to have been crucified—Peter upside-down as he did not hold himself worthy to be crucified in the same position as his Master, and Andrew on a curious form of cross in the shape of the letter X. There is a later tradition that Andrew was bound

[333]

to his cross, not nailed, and surviving on it for three days preached to the people who gathered around him during that time.

James of Zebedee was beheaded about A.D. 43 or A.D. 44 by order of Agrippa (Acts of the Apostles). James, the relative of Jesus, was stoned to death in 62 by the order of the then High Priest, Annas. Thomas (Doubting Thomas) preached the gospel of Christianity in Southern India and died there a martyr. Of Matthew, the Evangelist, who is thought to be the Levi who collected taxes and was called by Christ, it is unsure whether he died a natural death or was martyred. John of Zebedee died a natural death at Ephesus in about the year A.D. 100. He was the last of the Apostles to die and his death caused a deep shock through the Christian community, for there was a story that John would still be living when Christ came again. Accordingly some held that he was not dead but asleep and begged others to pass quietly by the tomb where John was resting.

There is nothing in literature or tradition to tell of the death of the Apostle Philip, whom Theophilus identifies with Philip the Deacon who at the bidding of an angel converted the eunuch of Queen Candace of Abyssinia to Christianity, thereby founding what was to become the Coptic Church. If Apostle and Deacon are the same, then it would seem that Philip settled in Caesarea, where he lived with four daughters, all unmarried, who had the gift of prophecy. He was very close to John.

Bartholomew, according to tradition, was skinned alive.

Of Thaddeus we have scarcely a line beyond his listing among the twelve Apostles and Simon the Canaanan is almost equally unknown. The tradition that he was martyred is not an early one. Judas Iscariot hanged himself in despair. Luke escaped martyrdom, it seems, and died at the age of eighty-four or thereabouts in the province of Boeotia, Greece.

Why were so many of the early Christians martyred?—

[334]

some thirty or more of the popes in an unbroken succession were put to death. The major factor was not that they were Christians, for the Romans practiced freedom of worship to a remarkable degree, but the emperors began to insist that they were gods and demanded that dead emperors should be worshiped. Not to offer a pinch of incense before the statue of Augustus or Caesar was reckoned as treasonable as avowed communism is reckoned in the United States today. The identity of religion with patriotism (the situation still exists in the north of Ireland) produced the Christian martyrs and without a doubt many Jewish martyrs as well. In the case of the Christians there was the added attraction that martyrdom meant instant entry to paradise. It appears that quite a number welcomed martyrdom, insisted on advertising their Christianity and defying Roman worship. Indeed with such a conviction what sensible man wouldn't?

Yet there was, of course, very much more to the devotion of the Christians than that. With Christianity there appeared in the world, available to all men, a doctrine of compassion, of universal brotherhood, of love for others, which flourished in a slave society and, by the purity of its selflessness, found converts among the highest Roman officials.

The vigorous continuance of Christianity, despite its many perversions and distortions by sectarian thinkers, reminds one forcefully of the words of the Pharisee Gamaliel cautioning against the persecution of Peter, Paul, and others.

"If this plan or this undertaking is of men," Gamaliel said, "it will fail; but if it is of God you will not be able to overthrow them. You might even be opposing God."

Two thousand years later "the plan" has not yet failed.